FROM THE BLOCK

A NOVEL
BY

Steven Schindler

The Elevated Press

Published by
The Elevated Press
P.O. Box 65218
Los Angeles, CA 90065
USA
www.theelevatedpress.com

Library of Congress Control Number:
00-134669

ISBN 0-9662408-7-1

Printed in the U.S.A.
Book cover layout by
Suddenly Chadwick! Design Services
Sherman Oaks, CA
Book cover design and photography
by The Elevated Press

Also by the author:
"Sewer Balls"
ISBN 0-9662408-6-3

This book is dedicated
to the memory of
Thomas Fleming,
Gerard Murphy,
and all the other children,
from all the other blocks,
who left this world
too soon.

●   ●   ●

I'd like to thank
my wife, for teaching me
the meaning of the words
dedication and *discipline,*
and my parents,
for always being there,
even when I wasn't.

ONE

New Year's Eve is amateur night. People who don't hang out in bars nightly should just stay home and get drunk on New Year's Eve and leave the rest of us alone. I have no idea who these people are, except for Mikey Lenihan and Patty Dunn, hunkered down at the end of the bar at their usual corner stools, totally oblivious to the fact that the place is actually jammed with people. Usually "Third Base" is a drinking bar, open at eight in the morning with a few hard cores who bring a cup of coffee and a *Daily News* and have a shot of Jameson's for dessert before heading off to work. It continues with a steady stream of people who come through the hollow wood front door, warped at the bottom from decades of beer, vomit, and ammonia-soaked mops slopping up against it. And some nights, for some inexplicable reason, the place can get packed to the rafters.

"Who ordered the five Old Fashioneds?" Shouts an overwhelmed Noel of Sligo into the mostly anonymous crowd of revelers taking advantage of the free corned beef and cabbage, party hats, and plastic "glass" of champagne at midnight. The hats aren't really "hats" but colored tissue paper "crowns" that could easily double as toilet paper and probably will for some of the more sloppy, falling down New Year's drunks. The champagne is the cheapest carbonated rotgut wine that makes a Thunderbird spritzer taste like Dom Perignon. But who cares? Everybody downwind of this former coal and ice store on the ground floor of a prewar apartment building at 116 Fort Independence Street knows that there isn't a more delicious layout of corned beef and cabbage in the city. Not even at the Irish Consul on Fifth Avenue.

"Who the fuck ordered five fuckin' 'Old Fashioneds?'"

Noel must be in a really bad mood. Admittedly, he can curse like a stevedore, but normally never in front of women, children, or clergy.

"I beg your pardon, dear. Please excuse my foul mouth.

1

I'm sorry, I just needed to catch your attention," Noel says, genuinely embarrassed as he hands the drinks to a chunky Puerto Rican lady in her fifties with a wall of hair sticking straight up and red fingernails that could definitely use a touch up job.

"Oh, that's OK Noel, you look busy tonight. You've got to give me your recipe for the corned beef and cabbage. It comes out so stringy when I do it."

"Certainly, darling, come by any time when my hair's not on fire like it is this fine evening."

Funny but Noel's hair does look like it's on fire. It's carrot red and he must put some kind of gook in it to slick it back so perfectly. He's got the Rock of Gibraltor for a jaw and a mouth overflowing with crooked teeth. Noel's first night tending bar here was almost his last. Having just arrived off the boat from Sligo in Ireland, his introduction to the bar that would become his livelihood for the next twenty odd years was, as Noel recalls it, "mighty fucking dismal."

Twenty-four years ago, October 4th, 1955, was one of the darkest days in Bronx sports history. It was the day the Yankees finally lost to the Brooklyn Dodgers in the World Series. And not only that, it was the first World Series to be broadcast on television in color. And as Noel O'Hagan of Sligo has told the story, he arrived from Ireland on that fateful day to begin his life as a Bronx bartender at Third Base a local bar on the rise in the Irish neighborhood of Kingsbridge in the Northwest Bronx. Since Third Base didn't have a color TV, as did Grecco's down on Bailey Avenue, it was practically empty; but a few locals headed over to watch the game on the old Philco set sitting on a shelf in the corner. Nobody seemed to mind that a coat hanger wrapped with tin foil stuck out of the back of the set, and the fuzzy picture tended to roll every five seconds. As long as you could hear Mel Allen, and just barely watch Yogi and the Mick pummel the Dodgers into the Yankee Stadium clay, as they did for what seemed like every October for the past decade, it didn't matter. Actually, the Yanks had beaten the Brooklyn bums for five World Championships, without a single

2

win for the Dodgers. But this year something was wrong. It went to seven games and Mickey Mantle was injured and hardly playing. Noel had never seen a baseball game in his life and surmised that it was something like cricket or hurling. He was the lone bartender, and as the TV's already tenuous picture started to fade even more, he was helplessly immersed into the ugly side of what is referred to in most other parts of the country as that "shitty New York temperament." Shouts of "Fix the goddamned TV, you stupid fucking donkey! You off-the-boat moron! Use the fine tuner! You potato-headed fucking mick! We're missing the game!" were being hurled at him.

The Yanks were losing it, and so were the dozen or so patrons too lazy to walk down to Grecco's to watch it on a brand new RCA color set. Noel immediately understood the importance of not just baseball, but what these denizens of the Bronx were made of. He received no tips that night and in fact several people broke their glasses in disgust on the barroom floor, prompting him to make a pact with himself that although he'd be a polite and courteous barkeeper, he'd never stand for that kind of abuse again. He also discovered the reason the bar was called Third Base was that it was the last stop before home. But to the regulars, it was home. It was their family. And everybody knows how fucked up families are.

Things are really starting to cook here at the bar tonight. I had to work today, and I haven't called anybody to see what they're up to. Just like any night, the guys'll probably just show up around eleven or twelve, check out who's at the bar, and take it from there. No plans. No expectations. Just take it as it comes. Not that incredible things don't sometimes happen. But things seem so much sweeter when you don't expect it.

"Hey, Mikey, hey, Patty," I say to the guys squeezing through the unfamiliar faces, finally reaching them. They're both forced even further into the corner of the bar than usual, right under the TV, next to the cigarette machine and the door to the ladies' room, which, like the men's room, has a stench emanating from a door that won't quite close. I can only assume that since some women haven't resorted to peeing between the parked cars on Fort Independence Street that it's not quite the assault on the senses that the little boy's room is.

"Hiya, Jerry, how are ya?" Patty asks in his usual lilting voice. He's one of the many guys from the neighborhood whose parents came over on the boat from Ireland, when they were in their teens or twenties, and never lost the thick Irish brogue. The kids all seem to have a trace of the old country in their manner of speech, and the more Irish whiskey they drink, the thicker it gets.

"Hey," grunts Mikey, barely audible and moving his eyes in my direction, but not his head.

"You guys see Stubby or anybody tonight?" I inquire.

Naturally, Patty's the one to respond.

"No, Jerry. And we've been here since when, Mikey?" Patty says to his stern stool buddy Mikey.

"Fucking noon."

"Since fucking noon, Jerry, and we have not seen the honorable lad Stubby or any of his playmates all day, have we, Mikey?"

"No, and not Grumpy, Sneezy, Dopey, or Shitty either."

"There you go, Jerry. Not a one. By the way, have you noticed the unusual presence of delightful young females in the establishment this evening? A lad such as yourself may just find some pleasant new acquaintances this holiday evening, and perhaps a chance at a romantic interlude ."

"Yeah, just watch out for those two baggers," Mikey mumbles. In this case, making reference to a joke from fifth grade is about as close to "cuddly" Mikey ever gets. (The joke is that you need two bags to screw the girl...one to cover her face and one to cover the guy's in case hers breaks.)

"Hello, Jerry, what can I get you?" Noel says, finally making it to our end of the bar.

"Just a Bud nip."

"That's right lad, pace yourself," Noel says as he makes one sweeping move with his right hand pulling the small bottle of

4

beer out of the ice in the sink, popping off the cap from a bottle opener under the bar, grabbing a coaster with his left hand, flipping it right next to Patty's, and putting the beer on top.

"Happy New Year, son," he says as the knocks the bar, meaning it's on the house.

Noel likes me a lot better now that I have a steady job, such as it is. Once I graduated from hanging out in parks and "kid" bars and moved up the ladder to this place, I went a year or two hanging out here without drinking or leaving a tip. I didn't know it at the time, but it was only thanks to the grace and manners of Noel that I was allowed to remain a patron in good standing; but he was mighty pissed at me just the same. Once I was semi-gainfully employed and started paying for a beer or two, buying a round or two, and leaving a buck or two tip, he certainly noticed, and actually acknowledged my presence.

"Back atcha, Noel."

There really are some good looking girls in here tonight. Mostly Irish and Italian, but definitely several cute Puerto Ricans and Blacks, too. The neighborhood has been getting more integrated lately. But where in New York hasn't been? As far as I can tell, they work and play just as hard as the rest of us, although I seem to sometimes be in the minority in that opinion with some of the old-timers around here.

"Yeah, I noticed the chicks tonight, Patty."

"You must be a fucking criminology major at college right?" Mikey barks at me.

"How's that?"

"You know, with a fucking marvelous grasp of the obvious like that, you must be a criminology major."

"What are you on the fuckin' rag for, Mikey? Can't you even pretend to be civil even on fucking News Year's fuckin' Eve?"

That brought a smile to Mikey's face as he picked up his Jameson and finished it off.

"You're right kid. Have a shot on me."

Mikey's one of those guys who's only happy when he

gets other people pissed off. And he's good at it, too. And the more he drinks, the more he likes to get people enraged. And when he's really stewed to the gills, and his friends won't even listen to his idiotic rants, raves, and moronic challenges, he'll try pulling his act on total strangers. We call him "the dentist" because he keeps drilling and drilling and drilling until he gets way under you skin and you can't take him anymore. That's why his nose is a little crooked. Only friends take shit like that. Not strangers. I've seen Patty save his life on more than one occasion.

"And how is college, Jerry?" Patty says in all seriousness. "Are you doing well? Getting good grades? When will you be graduating?"

Shit. Now he sounds like my parents. This is a constant source of anxiety for my parents, and yes, for me. I'm basically finished with school, having completed all my classes. But until I finish three final papers for three courses, I'm not graduating.

"Well, technically, I'm finished with school. But I have to write some papers before I can get my diploma."

"Yeah, I had the same dilemma," Mikey chimes in.

"You never even finished high school," says Patty.

"So what. Technically I'm finished with school, but because I didn't hand in various papers, I never got my diploma from college. I've got you on a technicality, Jerry. We're in the exact same boat. That's why I'm here every night of the week drinking my life away. I got fucked on a technicality. Just like you."

"He's right Jerry," Patty says with a knowing nod.

That's why Mikey's such a pain in the ass. Sometimes he's too right.

Someday I might just go to Times Square for New Year's Eve. I don't think there are any real New Yorkers who go to that. Every cop I know who works it, calls it a "controlled riot." People come up to the cops to report robberies and assaults and the cops

6

just laugh at them. Dumb tourists.

"Are you and Mikey staying here all night tonight, Patty?"

"I don't know, what do you think, Mikey?" Patty confers with Mikey.

"Nah, I've got a limo coming at half past twelve filled with Viet Namese hookers, free blow, and all the hotdogs you can eat, and we're going to Studio De La Disco. Wanna come?"

"Yes, Jerry, we'll be here until the morning sun is bright enough to illuminate the sidewalk pizzas to guide us home."

"Patty, you are wasting your time at the Sanitation Department. You should be an Irish poet, doing one-man shows at some SoHo artist loft," I tell Patty, only half kidding. "I think I'm going back to my building to check on Stubby and the guys. I'll be back before midnight. After all, I wouldn't want to miss Mikey turning into a fuckin' rat when the clock strikes twelve. Noel, I'll be back," I say as I put my bottle on top of a ten dollar bill and my coaster, signifying my return. I push my way through the corned beef and cabbage reeking revelers towards the door, and as I enter the no-man's-land between the two door exits separated by a small four foot foyer, two of the most gorgeous Latinas I have ever laid my eyes on wearing real party hats I might add enter the space just as I do.

"You're not leaving are you?" The one with the jet black wavy hair cascading down her back asks.

"Oh, uh, I'll be back," I mutter.

"We'll be looking for you!" She sings with come-hither eyes, her equally enticing friend giggling as they push their way into the bar.

I exit and begin my walk down the long hill, thinking to myself what a jerk I am. Why didn't I say something like: "I changed my mind." or "Not anymore." I know why I didn't say those lines...because when it comes to beautiful women, I'm like every other guy around here: a total ignoramus.

It's not all that cold tonight. Maybe in the thirties. That's great for New Year's. I mean there are St. Patrick's Day parades that take place on colder days. I feel particularly comfortable because I'm able to wear my trusty old jean jacket with a sweater and a down vest underneath. I always feel a little more comfortable with my jean jacket. Especially these days, when it seems everybody's wearing such goofy shit like wide lapeled white blazers with shocking pink shirts and skinny black ties. Once "Saturday Night Fever" hit, it was like a guido explosion. "Guido" is the term we use for stereotypical Italian life-style and "look" which has dominated the New York scene since...probably the 1920s, but really took off in the fifties. We had a brief respite in the late sixties and into the early seventies when it was cool to look like a hippy. But here in the late seventies, it's as if the Beatles, Woodstock, and the Grateful Dead never existed. I mean it's freaking New Year's Eve 1978 going into the last year of the seventies, and you look around in some of these clubs, and you'd think we went from doo wop straight to disco.

Believe me, I've got nothing against Italians, especially since I'm half Italian on my father's side, but come on! This whole disco thing takes the absolute worst of Italian culture and shoves it down everybody's throat. Sure, Italians like to dress nice; so how does that translate into polyester floral shirts and white bell-bottoms with black vinyl belts? "Guido" doesn't just mean Italians only. There are Irish guidos; Polish guidos; Puerto Rican guidos; Albanian; Russian; Jewish; even Black guidos. They drive Monte Carlos, wear pinky rings, get perms, put stuff in their hair, and in the summer they wear those "wife-beater shirts" (white undershirt tank tops) and listen to nothing but disco.

"What the..." I say out loud to no one, as I round the downhill bend which my building, the same building Stubby lives in, is just around, as three cop cars zoom past me without their sirens on, but going at least seventy miles an hour. And a split second later, I can hear sirens coming from the other direction, getting closer. I pick up my pace to a jog and can now see and hear a definite situation from a little over a block away. Assorted sirens and cop cars screeching to a halt, with fat cops pulling out billy clubs running into

8

my building. Shit!

I break into a full-blown run down the hill just as a cop holds up his billy club horizontally right in front of me at throat level.

"Hold it right there," the chunky Fiftieth Precinct Irish cop shouts at me. The Fiftieth used to be where they sent cops just before they retired so they could take it easy during their last year of street duty. But the past couple of years, they've gotten more than they've bargained for. With the influx of drugs and drug dealers, there's just as much action here as almost any other part of the city.

"I live here!"

"That's your problem."

I hate wiseass cops.

"What's going on?"

"Some of your neighbors decided to celebrate New Year's with some dangerous noise makers, SHIT!"

The cop and I are both scared shitless when we hear some kind of enormous crashing sound coming from the courtyard of my building and turn to see a mass of bodies tumbling through the plate glass doors, down the five steps onto the front courtyard of the building.

"Motherfuckers don't make a fucking move or I'll fucking blow your brains out," the cop who was talking to me screams at the top of this lungs. Now, the slowly moving five or six bodies that just had the ride of their lives through the front door of my building (which, by the way, has been there for about two years since they decided to upgrade the front of the building by tearing out all the shrubbery, covering everything with concrete, and replacing a beautiful ornate cast iron double door that was probably handcrafted in Europe in the 1890s, with an aluminum door that hasn't closed right since day one) begin to stir.

I can see two cops separating themselves from the pile of bodies as I hop up the three stairs from the sidewalk onto the courtyard. There are screams and curses from both men and women in

9

the cavernous tiled lobby of my building with guttural sounds of agony, pain, and threats, from probably a dozen people just beyond the main entrance to the lobby.

"Mr. Lynch..." I whisper.

Holy shit. Among the half dozen or so men who are now coming to their feet after crashing through the plate glass door and tumbling down the stairs is Bobby Lynch's father. And now I can see Bobby Lynch coming to his knees with the help of a cop. Two other cops come over, one Black and one Puerto Rican, each with a billy club in one hand, and they begin to lift two Puerto Rican men in their thirties to their feet.

Mr. Lynch and Bobby are too shaken to even notice me at this point.

Another big crash in the lobby has everyone jerking their heads to see what's next.

"Fuck you, you spic motherfuckers! I'll fucking kill you, you spic bastard."

Oh, no. Fucking Billy Maloney. Shit. This asshole has to always fuck things up on somebody else's block. If there was ever a more explosive, violent, moron on the face of the earth, he must've been riding with Attilla the Hun. He got kicked out of seventh grade in Visitation for throwing a desk out a classroom window onto Monsignor McNulty's Bonneville. I was surprised he made it as far as seventh grade without landing in prison or getting killed.

I could now see Billy holding his side as if he was injured. The cop holding onto his neck yells for two ambulances.

Billy comes into my building a lot these days. There's a drug dealer on the top floor. In my own fucking building. And because of shitheads like Maloney, he stays in business. I'll tell you this, if Mr. McHugh were still alive, there wouldn't be a drug dealer in the building. That tough old drunken mick would've crashed through his front door and beat his brains out with his sawed-off baseball bat. But those good old days are long gone.

"You fucking spics think you can do whatever the fuck you want and get away with it! Well, not anymore, not anymore, not

10

anyfuckingmore, you motherfuckers!" Maloney yells, totally out of control, and being led past the group of cops with Mr. Lynch and Bobby towards the awaiting ambulance.

"That mother fucker is crazy! He's fucking crazy!" A Puerto Rican man yells as he is being led down the stairs in handcuffs. I guess he got to know Maloney pretty quickly. Some people don't find out what a lunatic he is for months, or weeks, or days. He must've found out in a minute or two, passing in the hall. He's the guy who just moved into the Monahan's old apartment. The Monahan's were there for about ten years, and Mrs. Monahan grew up in the building her whole life. This was where she moved after she got married. But now that they have kids, they decided to move to Jersey. Poor kids.

I've never even seen the new Puerto Rican guy. I don't even know if he's got a family or what, and he must've moved in six months ago. Leave it to Maloney to find him.

"Prisco, Prisco, Prisco, call me, call me!" A young Puerto Rican woman with a baby in her arms sobs after the man being led away. And right behind her is another Puerto Rican man holding a bloody towel to his face as he is being led through the courtyard to the other ambulance.

A scuffle breaks out in the center of the courtyard.

"You assholes, what are you doing?" Mr. Lynch shouts to the cop putting cuffs on him and his son, Bobby.

Mr. Lynch in cuffs? Being arrested? Mr. Lynch who's an usher at church and a member of the Sanitation Department Emerald Society, not to mention the Holy Name Society? I've never, ever heard him curse. He once banned me from hanging out with Bobby, who's two years younger than I am, because I said the word "lousy." I mean I was in third grade, but "lousy?"

And out of nowhere, a blinding flash. Then another and another and another and another. A photographer is sticking his camera lens in Mr. Lynch's face snapping pictures like a Japanese tourist in Times Square.

"Get that damn thing out of my face, goddammit," Mr.

11

Lynch screams at the photographer. "Get that guy out of here!"

"If you don't want to be in put in a zoo, don't act like an animal," the photographer snaps back at him.

He's got *New York Daily News* written all over his camera bag. Great. *The News* is read by everybody in the neighborhood and just about everyone in the city. Poor Mr. Lynch is going to be plastered all over the paper on New Year's Day. What a damn shame. You'd think the prick photographer could let him suffer in private.

One by one the perpetrators, or perps as we call them, were led to the ambulances or squad cars, with flash bulbs blasting away, as a couple of guys with greasy hair and cheap Alexander's Department Store suits were escorting witnesses back to their apartments for just the facts m'am.

"Jerry!"

Stubby. Shouting from his fifth floor apartment.

"Want me to buzz you in?" He yells, making reference to the fact that there are no more front doors.

"Yeah, I forgot my keys."

Stubby and I are the only two kids left in the building from the old days. His parents moved out three years ago leaving him with the one hundred and five dollars a month three bedroom apartment. My parents are still living here, but I have no idea what's going to happen when my dad retires this year. I figure they'll split the year between here and Hollywood, Florida where Uncle Vito bought a large house when he retired.

The lobby looks like a war zone. There are splotches of blood on the tiny black and white tiled floor, shattered mirror glass all over the place, and bloodstained white towels scattered around.

I don't have to go far since our apartment is right next to the lobby elevator. A quick turn of the four locks on the door and a fast "anybody home?" means all is quiet on the Pellicano front. But the elevator is occupied. Two cops are in there examining various stains, marks, and I guess, evidence.

"This elevator's out of service; get some exercise," a pissed-off cop yells at me, due to the fact that he's working on New Year's and hates his miserable life.

These aren't just five short flights. These old prewar behemoths have huge stairways. I'm pooped by the time I get to the fifth floor and bang on Stubby's heavily secured steel door.

"Who's there?"

"Police, open up."

The door whips open, blowing a gust of pot aroma into the hall.

"Don't even fuck around like that, shithead."

"Well what are you asking 'who's there' for? You knew it was me."

"I always ask 'who's there.' I should stop after twenty seven years just because it's you?"

Stubby didn't get his nickname from being short and fat, but from his last name, Stubenz. Stubby may not sound like the kind of nickname a kid would want to hang onto, but it beat "Stupid Stubenz" which really rolls off the tongue of a fifth grader. Plus the fact that his real name is Francis makes the moniker even that much more preferable. No, Stubby isn't stubby in stature. He's more like Smokey The Bear. Big-boned, big-waisted, long-legged, thick-necked, fat-fingered, and thunder-thighs are all accurate descriptions. And top it all off with a shock of fuzzy black locks that reach the top of his ever-present army fatigue shirt and you get the picture. But he's no clod. If he had maybe a couple less inches on the waist, and traded them in for a couple in height, he probably would've been a starter on the All Hallows High School varsity team, and who knows what that would've led to. Instead, he graduated Bronx Community College and got a job with the city like almost every person on the planet that I know or am related to. He's a track worker with the Transit Authority, which means he does everything from retrieving body parts to putting down rat poison. I still think he has the talent to go after his real dream of being an FM radio deejay.

This apartment sure doesn't look like it did when Mr. and Mrs. Stubenz ruled the roost. Stubby's idea of interior decorating is scamming someone with a car to drive around Riverdale on Tuesday nights to see what people with money are putting out on the sidewalk for garbage pick up early the next morning. And he wonders why he can't get rid of roaches. It's not that he doesn't have money. He makes an OK buck as a track worker for Transit. But if we don't call him "Stubby," we call him "two slices and a Coke" because that's about the extent of his living expenses. He's probably going to buy this building in a few years from that slumlord Geller. I think I prefer Geller.

Sitting on the red velvet sofa with gold trim and white wooden legs, trying to get the last seed out of a tiny pile of pot from the inside crease of an opened "Live At The Fillmore East" Allman Brothers album is Terry Byrne. He's Stubby's buddy from Inwood who works with him in the hole (the subway tunnels). I didn't know somebody could smoke pot every hour on the hour, seven days a week, and still have a pulse, but Terry is living proof. He's the only guy I know that makes me look fat and healthy, and I've been mistaken for an anemic junkie on more than one occasion. His thin, sandy hair is tied into a long ponytail, and it's been said that he has a look not unlike Neil Young's. And I think that's the only reason he has a very good track record hooking up with the barefoot hippy chicks at concerts. That, and the fact that he's a walking drugstore.

On the other side of the room, sitting in a barber's chair reading a book that looks like it came out of the stuffing from the sofa that Terry's sitting on is, Merrill Sepos. Stubby and Merrill were three years ahead of me at Visitation Grammar School; the local Catholic school that believe it or not, up until five years ago was absolutely free to attend. Which is why every classroom had sixty five kids and nuns with brass yardsticks to keep us all in line. Actually, Merrill is only two years older than I am, but he skipped a grade. Merrill is soft. With his round features and thin eyes, if someone told you he was Somoan or part Korean, you'd believe

14

them. But he's much too large to be part Chinese. And he has a natural Afro. Not like the permed Afros that everybody from Irish to Italians are getting, but a real pick worthy natural 'fro. Merrill isn't working right now. He graduated from City College, summa cum laude with a degree in philosophy, but still lives with his father in an apartment above Third Base.

Merrill started hanging out with Stubby and the rest of us during high school when most of his friends from up the hill started beating up hippies, Jews, and anybody else who had more on the ball than they did. Sometimes he's so smart he's scary. Sometimes he's so weird it's even scarier. And sometimes he's balls to the walls hilarious.

"What the hell happened in the lobby?"

Terry and Merrill, being too intensely preoccupied in their respective endeavors, ignore me. Stubby is over by the stereo, which is balanced on a board across two wooden milk crates, which are impossible to find these days.

"Hey, where's the *Live At The Fillmore East* album cover?"

"I'll be finished in a minute, Stub," Terry says, careful that the sound waves from his voice won't disturb any microfibers of marijuana.

"Have you heard this *Talking Heads* album, Jerry? I just got it over at Cousins for $2.49. You gotta hear this *Psycho Killer.* "

"Why the fuck are Mr. Lynch and Bobby in a paddy wagon, blood all over the lobby, the last mirror that wasn't broken shattered, and Maloney and some Puerto Rican guy on the way to Montefiore Hospital?"

"Oh, yeah," Stubby says as he puts *The Talking Heads* on his new Zenith stereo with round "surround sound" speakers.

"Well, from what I could pick up from Mrs. O'Sullivan, Maloney was in the elevator with one of his buddies, going up to the sixth floor to cop no doubt, and the two new Puerto Rican guys in the building, who I guess are cousins, got in on the second floor.

15

They exchanged dirty looks and when the Puerto Rican guy said 'Happy New Year' to Maloney, Mr. Charm School reciprocated by saying, 'Same to you,' and flicked his lit cigarette right into the guy's face. So the fight starts, a knife comes out, punches thrown, people stuck, mirror smashed, cops called. The end."

"Well, what about Mr. Lynch?"

"From what I can tell, Bobby was probably the one with Maloney in the elevator. Mr. Lynch must've stumbled onto it and got caught up in the colorful cultural exchange program."

"Why'd they bust him?"

"I heard it was 'incite to riot.'"

"Are you serious?" Merrill says finally looking up from the dusty pages of what I can now see is *The Stranger* by Camus. And his perturbed, pensive expression flashes to uproarious laughter.

"Mr. Lynch! Incite to riot. He was my sponsor when I was confirmed. That's so in-fucking-credible. Haahhahahahaha!"

And just as quickly, he reverts back to studying, with furrowed brow, his existentialist tome.

"This is fucked, Stubby," I say to Stubby as he reads the liner notes on the *Talking Heads* album.

"This is our home. Where we live. And right in the lobby there's a bloody near race riot on New Year's Eve. This is totally fucked."

"It was Maloney, Jerry. If it wasn't a Puerto Rican in the elevator, it could've been a fucking Klingon and Maloney would've started something. And too bad it wasn't a Klingon. He would've fuckin' smoked him. For good."

"This sucks." I said out loud, but it was as if I was saying it in an empty room.

"You guys going to Third Base tonight?"

Just then I can hear pots and pans being banged together from an apartment window a few floors down.

Terry looks up from his botany project. "What time is it?"

I look at my watch, and see it's 12:01 a.m. We missed it.

16

"It's 12:01. We missed New Year's, guys," breaking the news to them.

"Well, let's just smoke the rest of this and then head out," Terry says, not fazed by the news.

The others agree with their indifferent silence.

"I'll just get a head start and walk up there now," I tell them, knowing they won't try to talk me out of it.

They didn't.

"See ya up there."

Well, 1979 is sure starting off with a bang. As I grab the smoothly worn hardwood bannister, I notice that the round brass ornament that was on the landing post is missing. It was the last one in the entire building. As I hit the turnaround on the fourth floor landing, I can see freshly drawn graffiti reading *Latin Eagles* on the hall wall right next to the apartment where Tina Robustelli and her strange family lived for the five years, after her father left their house for a pack of cigarettes and never returned, until they moved to Jersey in 1972. In retrospect, we were so cruel to Tina and her family. We thought we were being clever and funny with our not-so-innocent practical jokes. What is it that drives kids into a *Lord Of The Flies* frenzy? I just hope Tina has found happiness in Jersey. That is, if such a thing is possible.

As I round the corner on the third floor, I can see at the bottom of the stairs a female sitting on the bottom step, head in hands. I can just barely hear her whimpering. I stop dead in my tracks wondering if I should go use the other stairs; but in that moment, she snaps her head around to look at who is approaching her as if she's scared to death.

Holy shit. It's Mary Markowski. Sweet, beautiful Mary. Mary Markowski, the object of every boy's desire the summer after graduating from grammar school. She was one of those girls no one really noticed until the eighth grade boat ride when we all went for a dip at the Bear Mountain pool, and the girls debuted in their modest two-piece bathing suits. We had all fantasized what might be hidden under those Catholic schoolgirl jumpers, but had

17

no idea how incredible Mary Markowski, Tina Robustelli, and Lois Peckerino actually were. I'm happy to report that I did in fact get close to tasting the fruit of Mary Markowski, even if it only consisted of wrestling on the damp centerfield grass of a baseball diamond in Van Cortlandt Park for several warm summer evenings the month after graduating high school. Mary defended herself like Sugar Ray Robinson, allowing me to touch only the most neutral body parts. I don't know why people always refer to those *wild* Catholic schoolgirls. Oh yeah, there's one in every graduating class, but 99.9% of those Catholic schoolgirls would just as soon knock you out with a left hook as let you get under their bloomer elastic band.

Mary Markowski was just one of those girls. Beautifully thick, long, wavy blond hair. A "Barbie" doll turned-up nose and oriental blue eyes. And after several rounds of heavy petting in every imaginable location from a broken glass and garbage-filled alley to an empty subway car ride home on a Saturday night, Mary never once strayed from protecting her most sought-after assets. Oh, I tried. And tried and tried and tried. The Mary Markowski I knew, knew how to say "N-O."

"Mary?"

"Jeremiah?"

No one ever calls me Jeremiah. I hate when people call me Jeremiah. A couple of hot summer nights, I actually got into one of those wild, windmill-swinging slap matches we call "fights" over it. But I never minded when Mary called me that.

I could see that she's been crying hard. For a while. Her baby-blue eyes made her look like an alien against the dark red streaks cutting across the whites of her eyes. And her black mascara running down her cheeks made her look like one of those sad female clowns that always scared the living be-Jesus out of me when I was a kid at the circus. Why the hell do they make SAD clowns anyway? What kind of sick psychology is behind that? *"Let's see, I've got all this clown makeup....should I make a funny face to make the kids laugh? Nah, let's see how SAD I*

*can make myself look! Yeah, I'll look like I'm always crying!
What fun!"* ...sick bastards...

"Mary, what are you doing here? Are you alright?"

"Jeremiah, it's so good to see you. Oh, Jeremiah..." her
voice trailed off as she got up from sitting, and walked very slowly
up the stairs to greet me. She isn't wearing a jacket, but a tight-
fitting, low-cut black and white horizontally striped blouse with more
than a little bit of cleavage revealed. I don't remember her breasts
being that large, but when she pulled me close to give me a weak
hug, I immediately had to remind myself that I was dealing with an
old friend in a time of need. But, my, oh my, how she has devel-
oped into a gorgeous woman!

"Are you sure you're OK, Mary?" I ask while she still has
her head against my shoulder, with her face towards me, and I got
a good strong whiff of her perfume. OK, Jerry stop it right there.....

"Yes, I'm OK, I'm OK."

Mary is fucked up. Stoned on pot, or maybe downers or
qualudes.

"What are you doing here, Mary?"

"Oh, I was visiting a, uh, friend, and uh, we got into an
argument, and, uh, I need a lift home."

"I don't have a car, but I can get you a cab, no problem.
Who's your friend?"

"Oh, he lives on the sixth floor."

I get it. Fuck me. Ronnie Donnelly. The drug dealer on
the sixth floor. Shit.

Then a loud shout echoes through the whole building
amplified by the tiled floors and walls, "Maaarrrryyyyy. Come
Back. I'm sorry."

Mary pushes me away and has a look on her face like
she just remembered something. Not necessarily something
good, but something urgent. For a moment she looked as though
she was hearing voices. Her bloodshot eyes darting back and forth,
and her head twitching like a poodle listening to a silent dog whistle.
She closed her eyes and took a deep breath, like a child getting

19

ready to go underwater. When she opened her eyes again, she looked straight at me. In a sudden wave of clarity, she grabbed my hands. Hers were cold and clammy.

"Jeremiah, you're a very sweet person. Someday I'm going to call you, and we'll talk about old times, OK?"

"Uh, sure," I say, once again establishing myself as a world-class moron when talking to women.

And out of the clear blue, she slowly pulls me slowly towards her and places a tender, absolutely not platonic, kiss on the lips. I remember that kiss. How many times I tasted those lips, smelled her Prell-soaked hair, caressed her long neck as white as a new baseball with a mole on the left side, and desperately tried to contain myself and not even think about doing what I really wanted to do. How I lusted for her soft, slender body. How I made an embarrassing mess of my sheets several times a month by fantasizing about her nude body next to mine on the bottom bunk. If she had ever allowed me to sneak her away to some private place where I could rip off her clothes and make mad passionate love to her for hours, days, weeks, and months...I don't know what would have happened. I'd probably be married to her, with two or three kids, working at the same deli job I had when we were going out in high school, living in this same building with no way out.

But this kiss wasn't like that. I didn't feel lust at all. Just pity.

"Yeah, call me, Mary. But please, Mary, take care of yourself, OK?"

"OK."

She turned away and used the railing to help her climb the steps back to Ronnie Donnelly's apartment and drug emporium on the sixth floor.

Ronnie Donnelly is from St. John's Parish about ten blocks away. A neighborhood that's always been a little tougher than this one. St. John's Grammar School was a lot bigger than Visitation. In fact, if you got kicked out of Visi, you'd wind up in St. John's.

Back in high school we played basketball every day; rain

or shine, sweltering or freezing. And every once in a while Ronnie Donnelly would come by for some game. Kevin Flynn, who was one of our gang but got kicked out of Visi in the sixth grade and went to St. John's, would bring some guys from his class to play ball with us. Kevin was great in basketball. We called him "Chonk" because that was the sound his jump shot would make when it hit the back of the rim and ricocheted straight down for a basket. And one day Chonk brought Ronnie Donnelly around. Tall, slender and quick as a purse snatcher, Ronnie was better than everybody on both teams and the three or four guys sitting on the sideline waiting to get into the next game, except for the two best guys in the neighborhood, Pete McCardle who started on the Manhattan Prep varsity team, and Lenny Levine, a five-foot six-inch dynamo who was the sixth man on the varsity at Clinton. But Donnelly gave even them a run for their money.

In those years, we never drank beer out in the open in broad daylight. That was reserved for the cover of darkness. But Ronnie not only drank during the game, he had a pint of Southern Comfort he kept on the sideline. And after each twenty one point game, he'd pull out a pack of Marlboro's and light up a joint. I mean, we weren't angels, but right there? Across the street from the Church? I mean Mickey Bowen lives in the building right across the street. What if his mother looked out the window and saw it? Yeah, I smoked pot once in a while in high school. Maybe at a concert where you were with twenty thousand other kids in total darkness, and even if you weren't smoking, you'd get a contact high from the secondhand grass wafting by. But there was no doubt about it; Ronnie Donnelly scared me. To death. In fact, his best friend died at a Jefferson Airplane concert in Central Park in 1973 while they were hanging out doing drugs together. I never got the whole story.

I just hope Mary knows what she's doing.

As I headed back up the long hill, I could hear the party going on in Third Base a block away. I tried to look in the front window to see what I was walking into, but couldn't due to the extreme condensation on the inside of the window. But as I peered in, a finger on the inside began writing in the moisture: C-O-M-E-O-N-I-N-! Which wasn't easy because, don't forget, the person had to write backwards. I peeked through the two "O"s to see who the author of the provocative invitation was, and much to my pleasant surprise, it was the stunning Latina I saw when I was leaving just over an hour ago. Maybe '79 is my year!

I pushed open the doors and was hit with a strong smell of overheated bodies. The entire place was one undulating mass of drunks dancing to the blaring Seeburg jukebox that usually cranks with Frank Sinatra, The Clancy Brothers, or old Stones. I didn't even know it, but the jukebox actually had disco on it. The sounds of The Village People had every able-bodied patron bouncing together in a mad unified frenzy to the homoerotic sounds of "Macho Man." As if that wasn't a memorable enough sight, as I scanned the wild crowd, just soaking in the wonder of such a joyously improbable sight after what I had just witnessed, I see over in the corner, next to the TV in the corner by the door next to the ladies room next to the cigarette machine, Mikey Lenihan and Patty Dunn standing on their stools with blow ticklers in their mouths, totally topless. No shirts on. Just bare-naked soft, flabby guts happily gyrating to Macho Man with their cheesy red tissue crowns on their heads, and not a care in the world.

But back to the business at hand...there she is! My guess is she's Puerto Rican or possibly Cuban; but whatever she is, I've never seen a more exotic beauty in this bar before, although she does look slightly familiar. She's wearing those designer jeans you have to be poured into and a flowered silk blouse with frills that go right up her neck, actually touching her chin. I can clearly see she has the kind of look one would normally only see on magazine racks in this neighborhood. And although this package is tightly wrapped, there isn't one tiny bit of skin showing. Even the sleeves of her blouse are frilled right down to her long delicate hands tipped with long ruby red nails. She's ignoring me, hiding behind the little white umbrella in her pink drink. I just need a sign. A subtle invitation. One little out-of-the-ordinary move, like an eyelash flutter, the slightest upturn of the corner of her mouth hinting at a smile, or the really, really, slow blink. It's not quite a blink, but more of a slow motion blink where the female moves her eyes in your direction only for the duration of the slo-mo eyelid closing and by the time it's finished, maybe two seconds have gone by. But for a guy, those two seconds set off a tidal wave of reactions that starts off somewhere at the base of the skull and explodes down the spinal cord surging through every vein, nerve-ending, and neuron in the body, culminating with a distinct sensation that your jeans are a size too small in the groin.

I'm still waiting, trying not to look too obvious as I notice that Mikey is now riding piggyback on Patty's shoulders, both still shirtless, much to the enjoyment of the throng now forming a circle around them and clapping to the pulsating bass drum of *Macho Man.*

Aha! There it is! It wasn't the slow motion eye close, but the more traditional eye contact with eyelash flutter! Whoops. There it goes. Jeans...too tight.

Now I'm not exactly a bumbling idiot when it comes to meeting attractive women for the first time. But then again, Frank Sinatra I ain't. I've gotten my cue, however, and I am going to follow-through on this one. But I'm no fool. There are no guarantees. I could push my way through the crowd, weasel my way into the conversation she is having with two friends, and be totally ignored as if the eye contact eyelash flutter maneuver never happened. Or worse yet, wind up buying several rounds of drinks for the threesome, based purely on the eye contact eyelash flutter maneuver, and THEN get the old "on your bike" as the Irish like to say. As the hormones soar through every cell of my being, I start to make my way across the bar. And just as I pass the entrance...

SLAM!

The front door swings open revealing a sight that will forever be imbedded into the memory-banks of every person in the bar regardless of their state of inebriation. Stubby, Merrill, and Terry come storming in not only shirtless, but stripped down to their loosely fitting, tattletale grey BVD briefs, waving their clothes in the air as they join in the *Macho Man* chorus. This is one of those nights when the zeitgeist is upon us, and it is good.

Oh, there have been nights when everyone in the bar seems to have a bug up their ass, and before the night is through some jerk, (usually Mikey Lenihan) says something stupid and a few minutes later Noel's out from behind the bar mopping up blood and picking up teeth. Fortunately, this is one of those nights where everyone is riding a wave of pleasure; dancing, singing, drinking, and having friendly conversations with strangers you would ordinarily be thinking insults about in a crowded subway car.

The sight of three almost nude men, two of which are quite unsightly beyond their years, thanks to years of beer and "two slices and a Coke," and the other one making Johnny Winter look tanned and toned, is cause for unanimous celebration. Mikey and Patty, still piggyback are dancing around the three gay caballeros with their huevos dancing pretty much in plain view. But it's New Year's! Screw it!

"Noel! Noel!" I scream at the top of my lungs across the bar.

"Yes, lad?"

"Gimme two double JDs on the rocks."

In a flash, Noel pours me the four plus shots of Jack Daniels in two tumblers, never taking his eye off the maniacs on the dance floor.

"Isn't it grand, lad?" Noel says, giving me my drinks. Before he deposits my money in the cash register, I've already downed one double. I want to get in on the action. This kind of bizarre partying doesn't happen every day. The bourbon hits my stomach, shocking my innards. Whew! I love Jack. In a matter of seconds, I can feel the effects of the smokey elixir spread through my brain cells. I close my eyes and count five Mississippis. Eyes open, I clutch my second tumbler and about as quick as you can down four ounces of water, the next bourbon bomb is coursing through my system.

"This is with me, son," Noel says as he pours himself a Jameson, and me another JD double.

"Bless you, Noel!"

"Here's to your health!" Noel says as he flicks the shot down his throat. And still reeling from my second glass, this next glass doesn't go down quite so smoothly. Hold on. Don't gag. Down boy.

"Noel, a two-cent plain, please."

There. That does it. Suddenly my head is light. Buzzed. Not spinning, but leaning in circles. I'm going to enjoy this! I'm not so screwed up that I'm getting naked, that's for sure. But I jump right into the middle of the action, and am greeted with much fanfare from the guys. We're dancing, singing, bouncing off the walls and each other.

Now my head is spinning.

Oh, shit. Across the bar I can barely make her out through this Jack Daniels haze, but she's leaving. Putting on their overcoats a group of three girls led by miss eyelash flutter have had enough. Oh, well, like Stubby says, "Chicks come and go but the boys go on forever."

And looking around at the spectacle that I'm right in the bull's-eye of, I'm afraid he might be right.

TWO

Oh, my God, I'm choking! But on what? There's something in my throat. Open your eyes, stupid. YOW! Why does my head feel like it's going to explode? What am I doing on the floor of my bathroom? How did I get here? What the hell is that just coming into focus right next to my face?

I didn't really want to know the answer to any of those questions but the answers were slowly becoming oh, too, apparent. I was choking on that thing at the back of the roof of my mouth. The answer to "What the hell is that?" is something we call a "sidewalk pizza" when we spot it on the sidewalk: A large round pile of multicolored puke. I don't know how I wound up lying on my bathroom floor, but considering all the other places I may have collapsed in a drunken stupor, this is probably the best. If I had dropped on my bed, I'd be cleaning vomit from my bedding rather than the tiled bathroom floor. And the reason my head feels like it's going to explode can be answered in two letters: J.D.

I mustn't blink. It's too loud. Thank goodness my parents aren't here to see this. They had the good sense to spend the holidays down in Florida with Uncle Vito. In fact, if my father was home, and I came home in this condition, I probably would've had many black and blue marks to complete my look of total Bowery bum debauchery. He may be pushing sixty-five, but I hate to admit he can still kick my ass from the city line to the South Ferry and back.

I can only guess that since neither Stubby, Merrill, Terry nor myself even have cars, we must have somehow stumbled our way back to our respective hovels in one piece.

I've never felt this bad in my life. And I'm never drinking...oh, no.....just the thought of that brown liquid... here I go again... Oh God, time to drive the porcelain bus.

(pause for barfing)

OK, OK, believe it or not, I feel a little bit better now. I've

26

got to clean this place up.

And once I do that, I'll just take a nap. That's all. Oh, my head! God help me! Why did I drink so much? OK, just clean everything up, get these vomit-soiled clothes into the hamper, and some sleep would be great. Yeah, sleep... perchance to dream... of that girl in the bar...

"What the hell happened?" A crazed voice yells.

"What, what, what, what's going on?" I scream, trying to shield my eyes from the blinding light of day.

Seeing my father hovering over me as I slept like a rock scared the life out of me.

"I thought you weren't coming back until tomorrow?"

I knew by the way my father was going into a slow Edgar Kennedy burn that I just said something beyond stupid.

"Get your ass up! Why aren't you at work? It's Monday January, 2nd, 1979 you moron! You knew we were coming back this morning!"

Monday? I just closed my eyes and my head sunk into the pillow. I hoped I could just keep going and get sucked into the soft down and keep going all the way to China. I must've experienced a double blackout. Not only did I black out on New Year's Eve, but apparently I slept entirely through Sunday, New Year's Day.

"What the hell happened?" Dad again says in a firmer and louder voice, but not yet crossing the threshold of outright screaming.

"Oh, I guess I had too much to dream, I mean drink."

"Yeah, and the Pope's Catholic, what the hell's all this about a race riot in the lobby? It was on page three of yesterday's *Daily News*."

My brain still feels like it's being held in place by pins. The race riot? Oh, yeah.

"Oh, it wasn't anything really. One of the neighborhood jerks started a fight, that's all."

"That's all? Mr. Lynch got arrested. Bobby Lynch got stabbed, and two other people wind up in Montefiore and you say 'that's all?'"

Peeking around the corner of the doorway, my Mother appears with a silent scowl.

"You made a total mess in the bathroom, you know."

"I know, Mom, I'm sorry. I'll clean it up."

"It's already cleaned up. Come in the kitchen, there's coffee and juice. How do you want your eggs?"

"No eggs, please. Just cereal."

"And a banana?"

"Yeah, potassium, great. I'll be right in."

My father sits on the end of the bed. He seems to have taken an emotional fork in the road. I could've sworn he was going to take a right turn onto Accusation Avenue then a left onto the Major Insult Highway and exit at Rage Road. But instead he's pulled over at the side of the road, put on his flashers, sitting quietly at the wheel.

"Jerry, this is it."

"Dad it was New Year's so I got drunk, give me a break! I know I drink once in a while..."

"Jerry, that's not what I mean. This building. This neighborhood. This city. Your mother and I just can't take it anymore."

"What are you talking about, Dad?"

"Well, I know we've talked about what we were going to do after I retired this month..."

"This month? I knew it was this year...but this month?"

"Yeah, this month. Your mother and I had a long talk with Uncle Vito, and you know, now that Marge is gone, and he's all alone in that big house in Florida..."

"Yeah, go on."

"Well Jerry, your mother and I decided to take Uncle Vito up on his offer. We're going to pay to have the house in Florida

28

turned into a two-family house, and we're moving there. Then we're going to split the mortgage and everything."

"Good for you! That's great. Who needs these winters?"

"No, Jerry, for good. Year-round."

"Year-round?"

"Year-round."

"When?"

"Right away. Before the end of the month."

"The end of the month? What am I gonna do?"

"Jerry, do you really want me to lay it out for you."

"I can't believe this. This is the sanest conversation we've ever had my entire life. And you're exactly right Dad. You don't have to say it. I'm twenty-three years old, and I'm three papers away from graduating college because I'm a lazy asshole..."

"Watch your language..."

"And you are right, Dad. It's time to shi....I mean fish or cut bait."

"Jerry, shit or get off the pot," Dad says as he gets up from the edge of my bed, looking at me exactly the way he did when he told me that the reason all those toys that were hidden in the closet and then magically appeared under the tree on Christmas, was because there was no Santa Claus. And I feel just as stupid as I did on that Christmas morning nearly twenty years ago.

I thought I had months to get my act together. I could live here for nothing while I finished off my incompletes at school. And when Mom and Dad retired, they'd spend the winter in Florida with Uncle Vito and I'd have the apartment to myself for half the year. I'd even pay the rent while they were away. Or at least part of it.

But all that was down the garbage chute now. I make $2.37 an hour at the library, working maybe fifteen hours a week. That's barely enough for subway fare, beer, and an occasional concert. And one of the reasons I never do drugs. Who could afford it? Stubby and Terry make a great living working for Transit. They get four weeks vacation and take enough sick days off to recover from brain surgery every six months. And I don't think either of them has worked a full eight hours unless it's a major holiday, which puts them into some ridiculous pay rate that's more than what the average brain surgeon gets an hour. My only hope is if the library lets me work more hours and kicks in a few more dimes to my hourly wage. That is until I get it together.

"Here's your breakfast; Sugar Pops and a banana," my Mom says as she carries in a tin TV table with Superman imprinted on the tray.

"Do you know what the medical term is for a hangover induced headache?"

"No, but I have a feeling I'm going to find out," I say as I plunge my spoon into the yellow balls of sugar, making a crunching sound loud enough to remind me of my post Jack condition.

"It's called 'severe membrane outrage.' You could look it up."

There's no need for me to look it up. She wasn't a nurse at the Transit Authority for twenty-five years for nothing. My mother doesn't speak unless there's a truth that needs to be heard.

"Your father and I thought long and hard about this, Jerry. We've both worked hard to raise you and your sister and make sure you both went to college. Peggy got married and moved to North Carolina all within a month of graduating from college. Your sister did it, and you can, too. But our job is done. We're moving to Florida. We know you'll get your act together soon."

"Yeah, like I'm going to marry some rich Harvard graduate from Scarsdale who's going to take over her father's cheap beach chair manufacturing company like a certain female sibling of mine."

"That's not fair, Jerry. You've had every chance that Peggy's had. We supported you in everything you did. It's time to...shit or get off the pot," Mom says forcefully.

She looked more surprised than I think I did after saying that and left the room. I could feel my brain pulsating with each

30

heartbeat as the blood surged in its "severe membrane outrage" and each time I chomped a Sugar Pop, the crunches were like land-mines exploding. I held up my milk-filled spoon and noticed that I couldn't keep my hand steady enough to prevent the liquid from spilling. As I looked around the room I could see the scattered bits of my life. On the top shelf, a dusty Little League trophy for second place sits as it has been for as long as I can remember. But now that I think about it, it's probably a symbol of my greatest accomplishment in life. The other shelves, closets, and drawers are overflowing with my failures. My clarinet from high school, for one. Sure I had enough musical talent to get into the music program, but never practised enough to get past playing our marching theme "Promotion", by heart, and had to lie about needing an after-school job in order to be allowed to quit in senior year.

And next to that are my dried oil paints and brushes, my broken photographic enlarger, my juggling clubs, my Super 8 camera, my Voightlander 35mm camera, what's left of my coin collection, my ice hockey equipment, my ink drawing pens, my charcoals, my sketch pads, my Hermes typewriter, my dried hunks of sculpting clay, my guitar with no strings, and a secondhand "sound on sound" reel to reel tape recorder that I was going to use to make demos when I had a rock band; all one giant dust covered trophy for my life's accomplishments up to this point.

I could hear the phone ringing in the other room, and my father shouts that it's for me. I manage to sit upright and feel the blood drain from my head and into the rest of my body. I make the long journey into the adjoining room.

"Dugout. Yogi here," I say into the mouthpiece.

"Jerry! Me, Terry, and Merrill took the day off. Wanna get high and go to the zoo? It'll be empty."

"No thanks, I've got to go into work today."

"Hey you sound like shit."

"Yeah, I feel worse. I'm not going to be hanging out for a while, I got some stuff I have to take care of."

"Aw, you just got the humbles. Go feel sorry for yourself for a few hours, and we'll catch you later. Later."

The humbles. That's what Stubby calls it. It's after a bender when you swear you'll never have another drink, or joint, or line, and promise yourself you'll turn your life around, starting today, and all your getting high buddies are a bunch of losers, and you don't deserve the love of the people who really care about you. The humbles. Maybe that's all I got. Maybe there is a Santa Claus.

That face! What a jerk I was on New Year's Eve. Just when I was ready to use my best line on a new girl, "Excuse me, but may I be so bold as to engage you in a polite conversation?"; Stubby, Merrill, and Terry came prancing into the bar, almost nude, and I quickly drank myself into what I thought at the time was an orgasmic, dumb bliss. Yeah, it seemed like a good idea at the time. But that face!

I'm certain she saw me at my unabashedly neighborhood local worst. That's precisely the reason none of the intelligent, attractive, sensible girls from the neighborhood hang out at Third Base. They know damn well that when the guys are there, they play the same dirty little boy games they've played their whole lives. *Our* whole lives.

The smart girls from the block figured it out in about eighth grade. If a guy is hanging out with the same kids, he pretty much experienced every aspect of growing up; from asking each other if they ever saw what a girl's "pee pee" looks like, to bragging about the first time they whacked off, to relating in tantalizing details the first time one actually managed to trick a girl into letting you dig down deep where no boy had ever gone before. Yeah, "trick" a girl. Like that was even a remote possibility.

The neighborhood girls discovered at their first freshman dance in high school that boys from *other* neighborhoods actually fell all over themselves just to get their attention. Even the girls from the neighborhood who weren't the cutest, or the most shapely, or with the best skin, suddenly came to the eye-opening revelation that would guide them through the rest of their lives; Boys from other neighborhoods went nuts over them. Or at least paid attention to them. Local girls who were constantly teased, or worse yet, ignored, while the boys went through their street rituals from stickball, to moons-up, to king-queen, to curb-ball, to skelzy, to pitching pennies, to poker, to cigarettes, to dirty magazines, to fights, to looking for kids from other neighborhoods to beat up, and continuing right up into hanging out in the local gin mills where the rituals change slightly, but the boys don't.

So I'm certain that the somehow vaguely familiar Latin beauty, whom I was so close to surrendering my heart to on New Year's Eve, was from another N.Y. neighborhood, escaping the local boys from her block, only to find different boys doing the same silly things they do in the bars in her own neighborhood. Just as the desirable women that I used to tease and ignore as kids, now venture to Throggs Neck, Mount Vernon, Yonkers, and New Rochelle only discover a lot of the same knuckleheads they were trying to get away from in the first place. And then there's Beverly Brester.

Throughout all eight years of grade school, she may as well have been invisible. Not the smartest, not the dumbest. Not outstanding or inadequate at anything to merit ridicule or attention. No huge breasts, no horrible pimples, no unusual desire to have boys attempting to take her under the railroad bridge. None of us guys even looked at her. Even when she went to Mount Saint Ursula High School, and we started to notice her skin was so white, you could almost see her intricate blue veins just below the milky white contours of her smooth face. It was becoming evident that she didn't have a huge chest, but you were never quite sure if she was wearing a bra the way her breasts bounced so freely, yet seemed to point straight up. And her long, pale, thin legs now were toned and went on forever. It wasn't until Beverly Brester appeared on the cover of Cosmopolitan Magazine as Beverly *Lorraine* that anyone from the neighborhood noticed they hadn't seen her in a while. And a few jerks even thought "she didn't look so hot compared to last month's cover anyway." Yes, Beverly Brester gave up on the neighborhood boys early on. In fact, the gossip columns she appears in say that she isn't from the neighborhood at all but grew up on Park Avenue. Now she rides in limousines and is photographed with movie stars, rock stars, and even Yankees. I don't think she'd be caught dead in this neighborhood ever again.

"Are you going to work today, Jerry?" Mom yells from the next room.

Oh, shit. Work. Today's Tuesday...open until 9 P.M.

"I'll call."

Well, my big boss, Mr. Healy, was in a good mood on the phone at least. He said he was extremely disappointed that I wasn't in on time, but it just so happens that Douglas, my immediate boss, called in sick and he could really use me from four until closing. So, onto the iron horse, and downtown I go. I just hope I don't throw up on the train. There's no lower, more disgusting or humiliating place to vomit. Believe me, I know.

Next to my job in the neighborhood deli during high school, with Stubby as my boss, my present job at the George M. Cohan Music Library is my best ever. Better than packing false teeth (even though it was fun taking pockets of false teeth home to spit out during fake fights), better than washing dishes at The Minetta Tavern down in The Village, better than driving a cab during the worst blizzard of the century, and better than being a cabana boy at the White Hall luxury apartment building in Riverdale where I listed Willie Mays among my "clients." This job is so much better than all those jobs, not merely because I haven't been fired from it, as I was from all the others, but because I've learned more about music in my ten months working there than I've learned in my entire life. And that includes Mrs. Schmelzer's music class in grade school, three years playing third clarinet in the Cardinal Hayes marching band, singing and playing rhythm guitar in several pathetic garage bands, and getting As and Bs in several college level music courses including two advanced courses in electronic music at Manhattan City College.

I have three major responsibilities at my library job. First is to respond to a music request via intercom from a librarian several floors above to find a recording among the 250,000 on the shelves of the archives. After pushing the proper button (yellow: please stand by; green: selection now playing; or red: selection has ended), playback the selections on a turntable or tape recorder for a music researcher upstairs. Secondly is to go upstairs to the research/listening area to wipe the headsets clean with Windex. And thirdly, to alphabetize and file away the several hundred Library of Congress cards that come into the music library every week.

I'm great at finding and playing back records. I'm a superb cleaner of headsets. And I suck at filing. This, I'm afraid, will be the tragic flaw that will precipitate my firing from this job, just as each of my other short-lived jobs had a tragic flaw that was ultimately revealed.

But the reason I've learned more about music these past ten months, is not solely the act of playing back the world's greatest recorded music from Edison cylinders to stereophonic quarter- inch reel to reel tapes, but the virtual tutorship of my musical mentor and immediate boss, Douglas.

Douglas Wagner is a musical genius. We have this game where I could play virtually any classical piece from the 17th Century on, and he would tell me the composer. So far, according to his notations dating back to the library pages since 1970, he has been correct 359 times out of 416. But even more impressive is the fact that if you stick to the classical giants such as Bach, Haydn, Beethoven, Brahms, and Mozart, he will tell you the composer, and the piece it's from. And if you stick to Mozart, he will tell you its Kirschel number, the title of the piece, the movement, the orchestra, the conductor, and the freaking label of the record. Douglas is also a Beatle freak. Which segues into why Douglas drives his 1967 VW Beetle an hour and twenty minutes from a northern New Jersey converted chicken coop to work each day. Douglas is on Thorazine daily. That's because Douglas took another drug on pretty much a daily basis in the late 1960s: LSD.

I'm a little worried that Douglas is out sick today. I hope it's not due to the same reason I missed my shift this morning. Douglas isn't supposed to drink anymore. And he's especially not supposed to take any drug, except his Thorazine. And that includes marijuana, which is the only drug Douglas seems to miss from his earlier wild years. Wild years that included experimentation with everything that the sixties could offer a Yale student on full scholarship. Douglas' connection to sixties pop culture began the first time he heard *Eleanor Rigby* on AM radio. It was, he says, the first time he heard a pop song utilizing high art to express the theme of death. As a typical Yale student of the mid-1960s Douglas was a self described intellectual elitist. While a deejay at the Yale classical radio station, he refused to read the advertisement "Winston tastes good, like a cigarette should" as written. No, not because of his anti-tobacco stance, but because of the poor English. He would read, "Winston tastes good, AS a cigarette should" and damn those Madison Avenue infidels!

But somehow *Eleanor Rigby* eventually led to the hard stuff, culminating with *Revolution #9* several years later, and an LSD trip one day on Cape Cod that resulted in a mental breakdown from which he would never fully recover.

I hate being a "strap hanger." That's what those phony newscasters on the radio and television call the several million of us who have to depend on the subway as our main means of transportation each and everyday of our lives. Oh, I'll bet Mr. and Mrs. million dollars a year, hundred dollar haircut, limousine riding, teleprompter reading news bimbos hop on the subway once every few months for a stop or two, going from a three martini lunch at The Plaza back to the studio so that they can say they're in touch with the "real" people. Oh, yeah, that's real. Let's see them stand on an el platform at 7:30 on an icy February morning, watching train after train pass you by because they couldn't squeeze one more frozen miserable soul on there if they used pig grease and a battering ram. And when one does stop, you're so fucking cold that you actually LIKE being crammed into a mass of quivering overcoated flesh with alternating whiffs of Hai Karate, morning breath

36

from strangers, and putrid body odors that somehow manage to ooze through the seams of layers and layers of cheap S.Klein winter wear. And imagine that same scenario on a ninety-nine degree July afternoon with the smells from bodies too numerous and intermingled with polyester, bodily secretions, and pollution to even begin to categorize them.

There aren't "straps" in subway cars anymore. It refers to a time when there actually were leather loops hanging from the ceiling of the old-time subway cars for people to hang on to. There were also ceiling fans to circulate the air, cushioned cane seats, and windows that opened on the bottom and the top. And on hot days, the conductors would leave the doors open at the ends of each car, providing an efficient cross-ventilation system. In the winter, every station had a pot bellied stove stoked with red-hot burning coals inside a waiting room where people would warm their bones until the train arrived at the station, and the conductor would actually wait an extra moment or two for everyone to get aboard. And my mother tells us stories about how she and her girlfriends would travel all the way from the Bronx to the South Ferry at all times of day or night and never be bothered.

The straps we hang onto now are aluminum. The ceiling fans, cushioned seats, and pot bellied stoves are long gone. And so are the days when a woman could ride the subway alone at one in the morning and not be hassled. But we're still called strap hangers because as far as the people who fill those luxury towers in Manhattan, and gardened estates of the suburbs serviced by limousines and the Metro North Commuter train line are concerned we'll always barely be hanging onto a strap.

I can't even read on the train today my head is pounding so much from the aftereffects of copious amounts of sour mash whiskey, the humbles, and several miles of train tracks. It's after three in the afternoon, so the cars aren't too full, and it's mostly kids getting off from school. As usual, I just stand at the end of the car and zone out. It's a quick twenty five minutes to my station at 66th Street/ Lincoln Center.

As I approach the bulletproof token booth next to the stairway exit, I can hear an agitated token booth attendant through the distorted booth speaker.

"I said let's see the subway pass!"

In front of the exit gate where students with subway passes are allowed to enter for free is a Black kid over six-foot tall, and maybe weighing a hundred pounds soaking wet. He doesn't have any schoolbooks, and he's waving his arms in the air shouting.

"Yeah, and what if I don't show you my fucking subway pass," the teenager yells, obviously taunting the attendant.

The attendant inside the bulletproof fortress is an Italian or maybe Puerto Rican man in his thirties resembling the Yankee cigar-chomping Cuban pitcher, Luis Tiant.

"I said don't go through that gate unless you show me your subway pass!"

Standing next to the increasingly steamed token booth jockey is a small Asian man, probably a couple of months from retirement. The smaller man is tugging at the larger man's shirtsleeve, and his mutterings come across the distorted speaker as garbled pleas.

"Yeah, and if I go through the gate, what the fuck are you gonna do about it?"

A crowd consisting mostly of high school kids, probably his classmates, and a few strap hangers has stopped to take in the subterranean drama.

"I said don't go through the gate unless you show me your pass!"

"Oh, yeah?" The brazen teenager says as he walks to the gate without showing his pass, goes through the portal entering the subway station, stands in his position, and throws both arms in the air as if he has just scored a knockout in a championship boxing match. He walks back to the gate and exits to his earlier position just outside the entrance.

"OK, now what the fuck are you going to do about it?"

I could barely hear the words exploding out of the token booth because the attendant was already too far away from the cheap microphone for his expletives to be distorted by the speaker. He was tearing ass for the door, with the Asian man now trying in vain to stop him. As the heavy steel token booth door swung open, I could hear the mantra: "Whatthefuckamigonnadoaboutit whatthefuckamigonnadoaboutit whatthefuckamigonnadoaboutit..." over and over and over until it quickly changed to: "Hereswhatimgonnado hereswhatimgonnado..." as the Asian man tried holding him back by his belt.

The teenager's eyes widened to the point of being comically bugeyed, but his skinny legs were frozen in place. His previous stance of bravado had quickly transformed into one of bracing one's self for an oncoming disaster; Much like the look one gets while crossing the street, noticing far too late that a car may or may not hit its brakes in time.

"Hereswhatimgonnafuckingdo. Here's what I'm going to fucking do you motherfucker!" The token guy screams as he grabs the teenager who, in a last second of desperation, tries to swat the rushing bull of a man away as if he were an annoying bee. The token guy with the Asian man now hugging his left ankle envelopes the teenager with a bear hug, lifts him off his feet, and body slams him onto the station floor with the flourish of Captain Lou Albano. And once the teen hit the ground, the out-of-control man began pummeling the teen wherever he could, despite the now pathetic cries from the high schooler.

"Here's what I'm fucking gonna do you motherfucker!'

It was obvious to everyone from the teen on the ground to the Asian hanging onto his coworker's ankle that this poor kid was bearing the brunt of all the other kids who have told this token booth maniac to go fuck himself for the umpteenth time. How many "fuck yous" can a person take before he snaps?

I could hear the sounds of billy clubs clanging against flashlights and handcuffs clomping down the stairs that lead down from the street as two Transit cops appeared on the scene. They immediately pounced on the crazed token booth guy, dragging him off the kid. Three more cops were right behind them, and they began to quickly calm the assailant and victim down and start canvassing bystanders who could tell them what happened. It was easy to see. Just two New Yorkers who couldn't take it anymore. Me? I'm already late for work.

Coming in to work at four is tough. It's the busiest part of the day with grade school girls carrying tiny violin cases or the very demanding music PhDs with their thick glasses and expanding briefcases bursting with papers and the odd number of actual show biz celebrities. The most regular celebrity, and certainly my favorite, is Tiny Tim. If you didn't know it was Tiny Tim, you would think it was just another eccentric long-haired, poorly dressed New Yorker with suspect hygiene coming into the library to keep warm, loaded down with his Gristedes, and A&P shopping bags overflowing with books, papers, crumpled brown bags and wax papered sandwiches. They all line up to hear any piece of music recorded on the planet since the very first wooden needle scratched across a wax cylinder at the turn of the century. There are about 250,000 items catalogued in our stacks. But in the warehouse next door, there are about 400,000 other selections that have yet to be catalogued. And every day it just grows and grows and grows. There's probably more bad music, poetry, plays, and speeches recorded this century than have been performed during the entire history of civilization. And it all has to be catalogued, put into alphabetical order, numbered, and put on a shelf until the end of this civilization as we know it.

"Am I glad to see you," says Greg, third in command next to Mr. Healy and Douglas. "It's been insane all day long, and the third turntable isn't tracking properly and Douglas didn't fix it and if I don't put on the last movement of this Mozart piano concerto soon, I think Mr. Healy is going to come down here and fire us all."

buzz buzz buzz buzz buzz buzz buzz buzz

When listeners are having problems, they can press buzzers which sound off from a single speaker, making it impossible to tell which of the ten listeners is having a problem until you run by

40

every station to see which one has a red light flashing. Greg, who on a light day is just a buzzer away from running out of the building screaming, is literally trembling with nervousness.

"I got it, Greg. You take those five, and I'll handle this end."

"Oh you're a doll, Jerry."

Like Douglas, Greg is also gay. The difference between them is that I never would've thought in a million years that Douglas was gay if he didn't nonchalantly mention it in idle conversation while discussing John Lennon's relationship with Brian Epstein, who was also gay. Greg on the other hand may as well have a red neon sign on his forehead.

"And I'm going to crucify Douglas. He wasn't the only one staying up all night at the baths. And I showed up for work dammit!"

I didn't used to know what the "baths" were. But after working with Douglas and Greg for ten months, I know a lot of things that I never dreamed existed. Like what a "glory hole" is and other things that I would never even admit to knowing about when hanging out at Third Base.

"Is Douglas sick?" I asked Greg while almost putting act three of the Mikado on first.

"Yes Douglas is sick," and breaking into his best Paul Robeson and sings "I'm sick and tired of Douglas, being sick..."

And believe me, ten months ago I wouldn't have known he was doing a Paul Robeson parody at all.

"I hope he's OK."

"Oh, he'll be fine," Greg sighs.

"Maybe he just needs to get laid."

Greg looked at me, stunned.

"Yeah, you're right, Jerry."

You can learn a lot in ten months.

Once the cacophony of buzzers died down and Greg could sit with his third cup of coffee since I arrived and take in with great pleasure Frank Loesser's *Standing on The Corner* playing on turntable five, I decided to discuss with him my dilemma of suddenly having to pay rent. I wanted to talk to Douglas about it, and never would have talked to Greg, but since he and I are alone....what the heck.

"Can I ask you something about work, Greg?"

"Well, well, well, I never thought I'd hear a question like that coming from you! OK, are you quitting or do you need a raise?"

"Um, well, I ah, need a raise."

"Haaah! Good luck! Remember the *New York Post* headline 'Ford To City: Drop Dead!'? New York Public Library System to Jerry: Drop Dead! Just like they told me. You know how long I've been here? Seven years! Oh, my God, I hate it when I get going on this. Seven years! After The School for Performing Arts, Julliard, The Actor's Studio, and five summers on the Cape doing summer theatre. Did you know I was musical director for the revival of *No, No, Nanette* starring Ruby Keeler and Don Ameche?"

"Um, no."

"Well I was. Eight weeks of rehearsals and twelve weeks on the road. Ruby Keeler and Don Ameche. They're both wonderful, you know. And here I am seven years. Oh God, it's this fucking coffee. From now on one pot an hour. That's it, I swear."

Greg walks over to the coffee machine, dumps his cup into the pot, and walks towards the men's room. Seven years in this place? I thought ten months was long. Greg returns with an empty coffeepot.

"You don't even want to know what my salary is. I'm at the second highest grade already. A wage freeze Mr. Healy says, we might have cutbacks, Mr. Healy says. We could be shortening library hours, Mr. Healy says. Did you know I have an agent?"

"Um, no."

"Well, I do. But he does me no good here. He's supposed to find me work in the legitimate theatre. Legitimate theatre. Not this everybody get naked and grunt and jump up and down and throw-dog-shit-at-the-audience crap you see all over the *New York*

42

Times Arts and Leisure section every Sunday. Have you seen that experimental, open theatre mumbo jumbo garbage they call theatre?"

"Uh, yeah. I took an acting class with Roberta Richards. We did all that pretend you're a vegetable in a salad bowl stuff."

"Roberta Richards? THE Roberta Richards, co-founder of the Post-Modern Theatre with Joseph Jeanblanc?"

"Yeah, that's her."

"That miserable bitch is one of the people responsible for destroying the New York theatre. Before her and her ilk invaded this city from Bard or Barnard or Vassar or Sarah Lawrence or where ever the fuck bored little rich girls are sent off to, you had to have dedication, and commitment, and TALENT to make it in New York. Not big tits and hairy armpits and an ability to improvise total gibberish! I hate to get this way. I just hate it."

"She's been very nice to me."

"Oh really. I thought you had a penis."

"Oh, come on Greg. She's a very nice person. She even turned me on to some auditions."

"That's all. Done. Enough. What did you want to ask me?"

"Well, maybe I'll just ask Douglas."

Greg is actually hyperventilating. He's looking at me with one eye almost closed, and I believe he's grinding his teeth. He's one of those guys who can lower one eyebrow and raise the other in a huge arch. I could never do that, although I've tried. A lot of actors are really good at that.

"Well, what do you think the chances are of getting the maximum hours and maybe a raise?"

"Zero. Is that all?"

"Um, yeah."

"I didn't take my break this afternoon so I'm leaving fifteen minutes early, which is let's see, oh, NOW. So I'll just grab my things..."

He starts to put on his long overcoat, black leather gloves, and long red scarf as he talks.

"...and go home to my lovely apartment and take a nice hot bath."

buzz buzz buzz buzz buzz buzz buzz buzz

"Oh, that must be for you. Bye," he sings as he flings his long scarf across his shoulders and makes a dramatic exit, stage left.

buzz buzz buzz buzz buzz buzz buzz buzz

I guess I pushed the wrong button. Whoa, that's not a researcher's buzzer, that's the intercom from the librarian upstairs, who on this day just happens to be Mr. Healy. He's not just a librarian or supervisor or manager or director, but the freaking curator of the entire music library. He used to be a trombonist in the New York Philharmonic Symphony Orchestra, which is probably why he tolerates me. My late uncle Hans was a percussionist and archivist for the Philharmonic for many years starting in the late 1920s. When he died in the early 1960s, he was 88 years old and still volunteered as their archivist.

"Audio Center," I pronounce professionally into the ancient intercom mouthpiece that looks like a prop from a 1930s gangster movie.

Mr. Healy is on the other end. I can hear him talking to a researcher.

"I'm sorry, dear, I only have two hands and each one can only do one thing at a time, so if you'll please be patient. Jerry? Jerry?"

"Yes, Mr. Healy?"

"Is Greg there?"

"No, Mr. Healy, he's gone for the day."

"Godfrey Daniel. Listen, Jerry, can you do me a favor?"

"Sure, Mr. Healy, I don't have to turn any LPs over for another ten minutes."

"Splendid. Go to the Theatre Archives, and ask to see Ms. Fairchild's assistant and tell her you are there on my orders, and request the transcription recording of the D'Oyly Carte's 1939 BBC matinee performance of Iolanthe. Not the evening version, the matinee, got it?"

"Sure, Mr. Healy."

"OK, madam, it's on the way, so if you'll just be..." SLAM goes Mr. Healy's end of the intercom as he hangs up on me and has to deal with what he refers to as "the great unwashed beast"; the general public.

The Theatre Archives is in an adjacent building. Since I'm stuck in the basement of our building, I rarely get an opportunity to enjoy this part of the library. They have grand floor to ceiling windows that look out onto the lovely Lincoln Center plaza, resplendent with its fountain, and picturesque landscaping and a constant parade of artsy fartsy New Yorkers and hick tourists who think the Metropolitan Opera House is where Minnie Pearl performs when she's on the road.

Being a theatre and film major, or should I say "experimental" film and theatre major, in college, I have spent some time in this area. It's the second best place to look for chicks. The best is, of course, the Dance Department. I can spot a dancer from the other end of a subway platform during rush hour: Hair tied tightly in a bun, slightly bowlegged, back arched, head high, long neck, shoulders back, feet pointing in opposite directions, and small breasts always standing at attention. All neatly wrapped in black Danskin leotards, no matter what the season. There is nothing sexier than a dancer, but try and have a relationship with one. Unless you're a dead-ringer for Mikhail Baryshnokov, or Mishy as they all tend to call him, forget about it. Sure you'll be able to buy them a couple of vegetarian dinners at a dingy East Village Indian restaurant, but that's it. They always disappear into an ocean of rehearsals, performances, seminars, classes, auditions, and workshops never to surface again.

I still get a kick out of being able to go behind the counters and into doorways where "the great unwashed beast" is prohibited from entering. *Library Staff ONLY Beyond This*

Point! NO Admittance Except Authorized Personnel! Low Life Library Cardholders KEEP OUT!

As I turn the corner of the reception counter, I can see the glass door leading to Mrs. Fairchild's office, and sitting in front of that door is something that stopped me dead in my tracks. Maybe I should quit right here and now. Not even grab my coat but run, don't walk, to the subway station and NOT pay my fare, risking another beating from an enraged token booth clerk. Hop on the number one train never again to return to my $2.37 an hour part-time job. This I can't believe. It's her.

I knew she looked familiar! The gorgeous Latina from New Year's at Third Base. She works right here at the library. Great. Boy, did I screw this up. I don't even know her name and she already knows that: A) I hang out with a bunch of guys who like to get wasted and dance pretty much in the buff, and B) I'd rather hang out with them than talk to a beautiful woman who gave me the famous eye-flutter come-on.

"Excuse me." I barely get the words out of my cotton mouth reminding me that I'm still hung over and probably look like shit.

She looks up from a drawer of Library of Congress cards and cocks her head like a puppy that has just heard something in the distance.

"I know you," she says with a mysteriously sexy smile.

"Aren't you? New Year's? Drunk friends in underwear? No, I don't believe I've had the pleasure," I say.

"Oh, stop it. I can't believe you work here? Why haven't I ever seen you before?"

"Well, I'm usually stuck in the basement of the music library playing Edison Cylinders for Tiny Tim."

"Does he go there, too? Oh, he's so funny!"

"Well, look at this. We hang in the same bar. Work at the same place. And we're both personal friends of Tiny Tim. Now if that's not fate, I don't know what is. By the way, I feel like a real jerk about the other night."

"Don't worry. It was getting a little weird in there. I knew it was time to leave. Did you have fun?"

"I hope so. I mean I don't know. I mean, well, actually no. What, may I ask brought a nice girl like you to Third Base, of all places on planet earth, on New Year's Eve?"

"The girl I was with, that's my cousin, Iomara. We were supposed to go to a party in Riverdale together, but her car wouldn't start and we couldn't get a cab."

"So instead of a lavish affair in a Riverdale mansion you would up slumming it with us?"

"Don't put it like that! We actually had a good time! Until it got a little out of control."

"You made a smart move leaving when you did. It got really crazy."

"How crazy?"

"I wish I could tell you."

buzz buzz buzz buzz

"Excuse me," she says politely.

That same antique intercom.

"Yes, Mr. Healy, he's here. I'll tell him," She says with that same sexy smile spreading across her face as she hangs up. "I think I got you into trouble," she playfully tells me.

I'm getting the feeling my job is done here. Mission accomplished. For some reason I have a sneaky suspicion that she actually wants to pursue this a little further with me. Go figure.

"Yipes. Mr. Healy needs the D'Oyly, er, C'Arte's performance of Iolanthe from the BBC, 19....?"

"1939. Matinee or evening?"

"Matinee."

"I'll be right back."

She rises from behind the counter, revealing those dangerous designer disco jeans. Those jeans represent everything I hate about the disco and the seventies. They took something as basic as workman's dungarees and transformed them into just another trendy bourgeois symbol of crass commercialism. And on her, they look unbelievable!

She returns with the oversized records and hands them to me with a piece of paper. Now I'm nervous. I'm not used to women coming on to me. It makes me all paranoid. I guess it's my Catholic upbringing that the only good girls are proper girls. And good girls don't come on to guys. She wants me to write down my phone number. I just know it. She's coming on too strong.

"You have to sign this release."

"Oh. Yeah."

"Bye."

"Yeah. Bye."

So much for coming on too strong. Fearing the wrath of Mr. Healy exacerbated by a woman demanding her 1939 Gilbert and Sullivan, matinee not evening, I rush through the stacks and stairwells only to realize that not only did I not get her phone number, I didn't even get her name!

It's never fun going to the third floor where the Music Research Library's main office's and public listening areas are. That's where all the things I don't like about my job are: the big boss, greasy headsets, and Library of Congress cards that need to be filed. And it's obvious that before I sidle up to Mr. Healy to ask for more hours and a raise, I better start making sure those headsets smeared with stuff I don't even want to think about get squeaky clean more than once every other day, and that stack of cards to be filed that's now higher than the telephone gets lower and lower until each one is properly filed.

"Here you go, Mr. Healy," I report dutifully to the curator, hoping he doesn't call me on my tardiness.

"Madam, here you are," Mr. Healy announces to an elderly woman who looks like she may have performed in this very matinee. She's wearing a hat, or should I say a bonnet, with a babushka holding it in place, and white cloth gloves. She looks quite displeased that her request took so long to fulfill and removes a large magnifying glass from a forty year old overnight bag that she uses as a purse. With the intensity of Sherlock Holmes examining a fingerprint on a wine glass, she examines the label of the radio transcription.

"This is NOT what I requested. This is the matinee performance. I specifically requested the evening performance."

Mr. Healy has that same look on his face that Oliver Hardy gets when he looks into the camera just before he clobbers Laurel.

"Madam, I distinctly made a point of clarifying whether or not you wanted the matinee or evening performance, and you wanted the matinee. Now, I'm sorry, but if you want the matinee you will just have to wait until another time because we're quite understaffed right now."

"Oh dear. I have to catch a bus back to Nyack in two hours."

Here's my chance to be a hero and take care of some unfinished business.

"Mr. Healy, I could run downstairs to check on the music, then head over to the theatre section again to get the correct record."

"Oh, could you young man?" The lady says in an accent befitting one of Groucho's female foils.

"OK, Jerry, but chop-chop."

Not bothering with the elevator, I scan my turntables, flip a couple of records over, and head back to my new reason for living. I stop just beyond the entrance to her desk to catch my breath and compose myself.

"Me again. Turns out they need the evening performance, not the matinee."

She looks at me somewhat suspiciously.

"Are you sure?"

"Absotively, posilutely."

Still not one hundred percent sure of my motive, she relents and returns with the record.

"Thanks. By the way, my name is Jerry," I tell her, as I hold my hand out for a courteous shake of the hand.

"I'm Berta, nice to meet you Jerry. Again."

"Well, OK. Did you say *Bertha*?" I said almost unable to get the word Bertha out. When I hear the name Bertha, the first thing that pops into my mind is the *Daily News* cartoonist Bill Gallo's creation, Basement Bertha who normally rags on the Yanks and Mets when they are slumping badly. Basement Bertha is a fat, unkempt creature who wears a torn housecoat and has her stockings rolled halfway up her chubby legs. Not the image of the fabulous beauty I see before me.

"No. It's spelled B-E-R-T-A. It's a very common Cuban name. It's pronounced *BARE-ta*. With a little roll of the *r*," she says demonstrating the roll of her tongue a few times, which has me reeling.

"Oh. I see. That's pretty," I say softly.

This is where most guys totally screw things up. My hormones are rushing through my system so fiercely, I could easily blurt something really stupid out like, "Marry me PLEASE!" instead I manage to mumble,

"Uh, do you think I could give you a call sometime?"

"You know my extension."

"Um, yeah. OK, well, I'll call you. See ya."

"Jerry."

"Yeah?"

"Aren't you forgetting something?"

Oh shit. What am I forgetting? A kiss? Her home number? Her last name? Her birthday? Her favorite color? What she wants to name our first child? Oh. The record! She hands it to me with that suspicious smile.

"Thanks again."

"Bye."

The rest of the evening was spent turning over records, listening to almost the complete works of The Maguire Sisters, cleaning headsets, filing a few cards, and wondering when I should call Berta. That question would linger unanswered through the streets of New York and right into the tunnel of the number one local. Tonight I'll just get a good night's sleep, alcohol-free, think about Berta, and go into work a few minutes early tomorrow to plan my strategy for the day, which will, of course, include a call to Berta. Shouldn't someone named Berta look more like the lady with the babushka who insisted on the evening NOT the matinee?

But just out of curiosity, Third Base is on the way home if I go up 238th instead of Bailey Place... what the heck. As I peek into the front window of Third Base I can see Stubby, Merrill, Terry, Patty, and Mikey sitting at the bar in deep conversation with Noel. Oh well, just one beer won't hurt.

THREE

Oh my aching head. I knew I shouldn't have started with those guys, but Noel and Mikey were on such a roll. What were they arguing about? Oh yeah, whether the 1927 Yankees would beat the 1977 Yankees. When did I get home? Must've been three in the morning. Great.

As I look through my appointment book, I see that I won't be calling Berta today at all. I don't work today. And while foraging for food in the kitchen, I notice on the counter some notes, written by my Dad: *Movers Jan. 15th, fly Jan. 16, furniture arrives Feb. 1. Ask Jerry re: car.*

It's happening. They'll be gone by the end of the month. The only thing I don't understand is the "car" part. Dad's 1969 Oldsmobile Cutlass Supreme is his pride and joy. It's garaged about a half-mile away and he uses it maybe twice a week, which is about the same number of times he washes it a week. I can't imagine him going to Florida without it, but who knows?

It looks like I've got to make things happen fast. I've got to complete my three classes at Manhattan City College so I can graduate. Increase my hours at the library, get a raise, pay the rent, and start to live my life as an adult, as soon as I figure out what that means.

I never thought I'd utter this sentiment, but unfortunately, Manhattan City College does not have Irish Christian brothers. The memories I have of being threatened, screamed at, belittled, and sucker-punched will stay with me for a lifetime. But in retrospect, it probably did as much good, as it does make excellent fodder for cold sweat nightmares that place me back in high school after receiving a letter from Monsignor McCormick informing me that my transcripts have all been lost and I have to return as a freshman for four more years. (NOOOOOOO!!!!!!!)

The freedoms in college were at first overwhelming. "What? This instructor doesn't take attendance? Every third class should be enough." Well after a year or so of solid Cs and Ds, somehow

I wised up and actually took school seriously. So what if I only enrolled in classes I wanted to take after my requirements were fulfilled? I'm not sure if a major in Experimental Film and Theatre will ever get me a job, but I went from solid Cs to all As during the next, well, several years, and brought my grade point average up to honors level. That is, IF I ever complete these three incompletes!

Advanced Television Production III; Avante Garde Music II; and *Advanced Acting III* are what stand between me and my diploma. I did well in class. Probably got an "A" in all three. That is, if I hand in a term paper for each. I must admit, my instructors have been immensely accommodating; way more than an Irish Christian brother would be. But it will be six weeks this week, and my deadline is two weeks. Then my incompletes becomes Fs and no diploma.

In the special program I'm part of called the City University of New York Baccalaureate Program, I am allowed to create my own major, hence the wacky Experimental Film and Theatre. It's just another benefit of having the student radicals, who spent the sixties throwing bottles at administration buildings, now controlling the universities. Students like me, who have no idea why they are going to college in the first place, get to make-up worthless majors.

Karl Mark is my sponsor. Everyone assumes he's British because he talks with a slight English accent. It's the kind of accent a Brit would have after living over here for several decades. He's a small wiry man about forty, with thick, untamable salt and pepper hair that reaches down to his shoulders. With his John Lennon glasses and oriental eyes, he resembles a sort of rumpled version of what John Lennon would look like if he actually did manage to combine his DNA with Yoko's. The puzzling thing is that Karl Mark hails not from merry old England, but merry old Toledo, Ohio. Karl does not like being my sponsor. I believe I am the only CUNY BA student under his sponsorship that is not a female. I'm the token.

Karl, as he makes all his students call him, has no idea who

I am. It usually takes me several declarative sentences to a receptionist to joggle enough memory of my existence for him to acknowledge that, yes, he will take my call. In my four plus years at Manhattan City College, I've actually met with Karl Mark on three occasions, each one shorter than the previous. Usually I just drop off my papers, and that's it. But I've never had to deal with three incompletes before. So another visit is in order.

It's one of those rare winter days where you actually wish winter would last the year through. The air is crisp enough to make you aware that you have skin exposed, but not cold enough to be uncomfortable. The sky is that deep blue they paint the bottom of swimming pools, and the puffy clouds are so brightly white they seem to be a source of light, not merely a reflection. No need for gloves, but it sure feels good sticking your hands in your jacket pocket.

It's blinding coming out of the 72nd Street subway station at Broadway. On days like these, I love making the crosstown walk along 72nd Street past the Dakota where John and Yoko live, through Central Park, across 5th Avenue and over to Manhattan City College on East 68th Street. Each time I pass the Dakota, I, of course, look for Lennon. Friends tell me that if you stand outside the 72nd entrance to the Dakota for four or five hours, you are guaranteed to see him. And he nearly always stops to give an autograph. Someday I'll do it.

The 72nd Street station is one of the few old-time aboveground subway entrances left. It's on an island in the middle of the intersection at 72nd and Broadway where Broadway crosses 7th Avenue. It's one of those huge Manhattan intersections where cars, taxis, trucks, bicycle messengers, hot dog vendors, pyschos, and pedestrians battle each other in all directions as they attempt to take advantage of the slightest opening between objects, moving or otherwise. On the outside, the subway station has been unchanged for close to a hundred years. Whereas most subway entrances are merely stairwells descending into darkness,

72nd Street has a kiosk entrance, complete with old fashioned thick wooden turnstiles, ceiling fans, and windows that actually open. From a distance there's something quaint about this turn-of-the-century anomaly sitting in the middle of one of the city's most chaotic intersections. I can imagine this scene seventy-five years ago, and probably the only difference would be that there would be lots of horse shit mixed into the equation.

Manhattan City College has no campus. It's a twelve story office building in midtown. Not one tree, not one blade of grass. No quad, no student union building, no dorms, no football field, no field house, no alumni garden, no parking lot, no plaza, no fountain, no big statues of dead people. It's a city school for city kids. Brown baggers. Strap hangers.

There's no one sitting at the receptionist's desk that guards the doors to the theatre and film faculty offices. It's a tiny reception area with unframed posters from Joseph Papp's Public Theatre barely hanging on by a pushpin. I can hear voices, but it looks deserted. Professor Mark's, I mean Karl's, door is closed, but from what I can surmise, that is the source of the noise. Yup, I hear a man, and woman in lively conversation through the thick oak door. Well, mostly man.

KNOCK KNOCK

"Hold on," Karl says from behind the door.

The door opens just enough for a young woman's head to poke through. I remember her being the "star" of the theatre department a couple of years ago. She had a walk-on on some moronic soap, and you'd think she won an Oscar.

"Do you have an appointment with Karl?"

"No, I tried calling but there was no answer."

"Hmmm. Just a minute," she says as she sticks her head back into the office and closes the door.

The door creaks open again.

"And you are....?"

"Jerry Pellicano. Karl is my CUNY BA sponsor."

"Hold on," as the door shuts again for about five seconds and reopens.

"OK, he can see you."

Karl's office is small, but the piles of books, papers, files, magazines and 16mm film cannisters give it an uncomfortably claustrophobic feeling. Although Karl is between smokes, he has three overflowing ashtrays balanced on different piles and the room reeks of stale tobacco. Books are placed haphazardly on shelves, a filing cabinet drawer is open, and I notice at least three bottles of liquor. He moves one of the two chairs from behind his desk, and places it on the other side.

"Yes, what can I do for you?"

"Well, I have three incompletes...."

"And why is that....what's your name again?

"Jerry."

"And why is that, Jerry?"

"Well, I completed the courses, but as a CUNY BA requirement I have to turn in term papers for each, and due to some personal problems, I haven't turned them in yet, and the deadline is two weeks away. And I wanted to know if I could get an extension."

"Certainly not."

"Oh. No?"

"Jerry, were you in any of my classes?"

"Yes, Intro to Cinema."

"Good. So then you are well aware that although I don't take attendance or give quizzes, I have no tolerance for tardiness when it comes to final papers. Sorry, old chap, but a director must meet his delivery date. He can't tell the studio he's having personal problems and hope to get an extension. He must have discipline. Order...."

Just after he says "order" a pile of tin 16mm film cannisters falls off the corner of his desk crashing to the floor sounding like a box of pots and pans fell off the kitchen counter.

"Is everything OK?" The receptionist asks, poking her

56

head in to see what all the commotion is.

"Yes, yes, that's it. See you in two weeks then. Good day."

"Yea. Good day, old chap."

Two weeks is a long time. *I can help my parents pack, increase my hours at the library, and finish these papers in two weeks* was my mantra all the way home on the subway. And I made it a point not to walk past Third Base. As I turned the corner to hop up the steps into the courtyard of my building, I can see a guy standing close to the wall. I can't believe this. He's pissing on the wall in the courtyard at the main entrance of my building.

"Hey!" I loudly yell from the sidewalk into the courtyard. My voice echoes up the six stories and back down again, giving it an unearthly, authoritative quality.

I can see the guy shake it a couple of times, slowly zip up his pants, and casually glance over his shoulder to see who's making such a racket. This guy is what is commonly referred to as a "puke." Barely past high school age, with long stringy hair, a chipped front tooth, terrible skin, and stoned out of his mind.

I'm not the type of person to confront people, but my somewhat streetwise upbringing tells me to be assertive in this situation.

"What the fuck are you doing?"

The puke glares at me with a look that reveals utter contempt at the sheer audacity of my question.

"Taking a piss."

"Don't piss here. This ain't no fuckin' slum."

"That's what you think," he says as he walks slowly past me. "When you gotta go, you gotta go."

What could I possibly say to someone like that? And I know exactly where he's just come from: Ronnie Donnelly's. More and more stoners, junkies, and pukes are parading through the building each day. And something's going to have to be done about it.

Oh, there have always been stoners, junkies, and pukes walking the halls, but I knew them. They lived here. This is different.

"We're leaving the living room furniture," my mother says as she stands over the kitchen sink, washing the wine glasses that have sat on the top shelf of the cabinet for the past thirty years, and never been used once. "There's probably roaches in everything."

"Oh, great. Leave me with the roach-infested furniture."

"Just in case, Jeremiah. Why take a chance. If we take Bronx cockroaches to Florida, they'll overtake the entire state. And Uncle Vito will kill us both."

"OK, I'll take the roach-infested furniture. What about the car?"

"Didn't your father talk to you about it?"

"No. What about it? Is he giving me the car, too? Are there roaches in it?"

"No, we're taking the car. But we were going to ask you to bring it down after we get settled."

"Oh. Sure," I flatly say, not wanting to reveal the excitement I was anticipating by having a car all to myself for a month or two.

"Jeremiah, you know how your father feels about that car. Swear to me you'll be careful."

"I swear, I'll be as careful as humanly possible," knowing full well of the giant loophole I was creating by stating it just that way.

"By the way, call Stubby."

Since Stubby is a couple of years older than I am, we weren't that close when we were really young. A year of separation was enormous. But sometime around the age of fifteen or sixteen, when kids started to separate more into "life-style" cliques rather than pure "age" cliques, we began hanging out every day. Some kids began to gravitate towards a more violent outlook on life; you know, kick ass on anyone who was a little bit different, say Jewish, or Puerto Rican, or Black, or maybe you just didn't like the

58

look on their face. But Stubby, Merrill, me, and later on, Terry, were more into music, reading Tolkien, Kerouac, and Steppenwolf, and smoking a little bit of weed, which led to really heated discussions about important stuff like, "do you think there are more light bulbs or records on the planet?"

"Dugout here, Yogi speaking," Stubby says, answering the phone.

"Get the Goose ready," I snap back at him.

"Hey, Jerry, did you hear who they found dead?"

"No, who?"

"Charlie the Chinaman."

"Shit. No. Charlie the Chinaman?"

Sweet, old Charlie the Chinaman's Hand Laundry is under the el just north of 238th Street on Broadway, as it has been for the past, I don't know, fifty years or so, but since there are no other stores on that side of the street, and the store next to his is just a boarded up storefront that McNichol's bar uses as a storage room, there's no reason to pass by his Chinese Hand Laundry unless you're one of his customers. No one in my family has ever brought a garment there. It was drilled in my head at an early age that bringing a garment to a Chinese Hand Laundry was an outrageous extravagance that no one in our household would ever partake in. And if I dared mention that a I had walked a friend there, and told a colorful Charlie the Chinaman anecdote over the dinner table, the tale was ignored, and my mother would demand to know which of my friend's mothers could possibly be so lazy and wasteful as to bring a shirt into a Chinese laundry to be washed and ironed. "That's just pure laziness!" She would say, shaking her head as she scraped the last of the chicken a la king onto our white toasted bread.

"Found dead? What happened?" I asked Stubby.

"You're not gonna believe it."

"What?"

"He committed suicide."

"Get out of here!"

59

"This is going to freak you out. They found him hanging from a pipe in the cellar of the store. He even still had on that white paper hat he always wore. It's really fucked."

It was hard to put the image of that out of my mind. Saying somebody's dead is one thing. And mentioning the word suicide, of course, conjures up many other images. But grisly details like this stick in my brain like the flash frames of a slasher movie. Sweet God almighty, Charlie the Chinaman committing suicide?

"How do they know it was a suicide?"

"Well, I guess there were still a few bucks in the cash register, and due to the circumstances, it's case closed, I guess."

"How do you know?"

"A cop from the 50th was in Third Base.

"This sucks."

"Listen, Jerry, I gotta go. I'm at the end of a two-hour lunch, and I have to go back to work and punch out."

"Yeah, see ya later at Third Base, Stub."

Charlie the Chinaman was one of those people who were just as much a part of the neighborhood as the el, or the cobblestones on Review Place, or the shamrock that was painted in the middle of West 238th and Bailey every St. Patrick's Day eve. Things that were always there, and you just took it for granted that they would always be there.

His storefront hasn't changed in the half century that it's been sitting there. The front plate glass window always had a frosted look to it because after five or so years, the dust on a window doesn't really change all that much. Everything in the store was painted green, probably by the landlord the day before Charlie took the place over. The red letters painted on the front window were flaking away, but you could still read them: CHINESE HAND LAUNDRY.

The ceiling was pressed tin, and there was a ceiling fan dangling from it that rotated ever so slowly on only the hottest days of the summer. There was a skylight above the counter, and the bare electric twenty five watt light bulb hanging by a cord from the ceiling was not turned on until it was totally dark outside and the free sunlight was long gone.

But the store was clean. You would always see Charlie sweeping the floor of the store, or the sidewalk, or even the street. He wasn't one of those shopkeepers who just swept the dirt into the gutter. He picked up the dirt on the sidewalk with two pieces of cardboard that he would scrape together on the ground gathering up every last bit of grit.

Charlie was a small Chinese man whom I thought of as ancient even when I was a tiny kid. Some of the bigger kids would taunt him, calling him Charlie the Chink, but I never once saw Charlie grab one of them and smack the shit out of them like I saw old man Reilly from McNichol's bar do on more than one occasion.

Charlie would keep injured sparrows, robins, blue jays, woodpeckers, or even pigeons, in his back room. I remember Charlie yelled at us one time because we were throwing rocks at pigeons in an empty lot by his store. I mean everybody hated pigeons, didn't they? But when Charlie invited us back to look at the birds he was nursing back to health in a jerry-rigged animal nursery, I immediately learned then and there an awareness of how important it is to be kind to all God's creatures, great and small.

He didn't mind it that we called him Charlie the Chinaman. His first name wasn't even Charlie. I think all little kids called Chinese men Charlie, thanks to Charlie Chan, which used to be on every Saturday morning along with The Dead End Kids, which I much preferred to the more comedy oriented Bowery Boys.

One time I saw an envelope on the counter with his name on it. His real name was Ying Long Wang, which actually had more comedic possibilities if we had known that actually was his name. I remember hearing a long time ago from Vito the shoemaker that Charlie had a wife and a son, but they both died many years ago.

61

Maybe that was why Charlie was nice to us kids. If you were a jerk, or did something really stupid like running into his store and yelling "muka hiya ding ding," which was supposed to mean "kiss my ass" in Chinese, he might pick up his iron, scream some Chinese and take a few steps towards you. If you were polite, he would let you put a bake sale sign in his window, or give you some string for free to fix a kite tail, or buy a raffle ticket for a quarter, or take in an injured bird or squirrel you managed to pick up from somewhere.

But the one memory of Charlie I'll never forget was one very special Christmas Eve a long, long time ago. A week or so before Christmas, Sister Fidelis gave us a lecture about helping the poor children of China in conjunction with the handing out of a Maryknoll Missionary magazine and passing around a cardboard box for the poor pagan babies. So a few of us decided why not help the Chinese right on our block. So me, Whitey Shelley, Jocko Finneran, and Bobby Bailey decided to each chip in a few bucks, take the subway all the way down to Chinatown, and buy Charlie the Chinaman a Christmas present. We decided on a "happy coat," which I think is actually kind of a Japanese smoking jacket. It's a silk, or perhaps in our case, rayon, three-quarter length robe with bright primary colors. The one we picked out had a "neato" design (as I remember Jocko calling it) on the back. We had no idea that we had picked the ancient symbol of the positive and negative life-force essential to balance and harmony, the yin-yang. And to go along with it we had enough money left over to buy him a small dark brown Buddha that was hard as a rock. The shopkeeper even personalized it on the bottom for free by inscribing "Merry Christmas Charlie." He didn't tell us why, but he thought it was hilarious that we would write such a thing on a Buddha statue.

Most people didn't know it, but Charlie lived in the back of his store. He tried to keep it a secret, but like all nosey kids who peek into skylights, we knew all about it. It was a white Christmas Eve. We must have been in the seventh grade, because Jocko and Bobby were the altar boys at midnight Mass. By eighth grade we were too cool to don the lame altar boy outfits and ring those bells on cue. It was decided that we'd meet outside the sanctuary after Mass and deliver our gifts to Charlie. Why we insisted on delivering them at one in the morning I can't recall, but I'm sure we had a reason that made sense to four seventh graders.

We trudged through the virgin snow, so dry and crisp it crunched under our galoshes rather than sloshed. As we stood in front of Charlie's store, the idea of presenting our gifts so late into the night didn't seem like such a good idea anymore. Nevertheless, we started banging on the glass front door with the weathered shade pulled all the way down, rattling not only the door but both plate glass windows on either side of the door and the bell attached to it on the inside of the store. We didn't see a light come on, but suddenly the door swung violently open, revealing Charlie in a tattered terry-cloth robe holding his iron high above his head in a striking position ready to do battle with whoever was intruding upon his sanctuary. But we stopped him dead in his tracks before he could even get out a Chinese curse with a cheerful "Merry Christmas" in unison. I can imagine the sight of the four of us, dressed in our winter church-going best standing there with a gift wrapped box being held by all four of us.

Charlie turned his stance from attack to appreciation faster than you could say "And Happy New Year!" Which we did. I could see in his eyes that what we had done was something more than any of us had anticipated. For whatever reason, Charlie was quickly moved to tears. They streamed down his face as he apologized for his iron-swinging defense and melted into the sweet man who fed the animals with an eyedropper as he petted them on the head and sang mysterious Chinese rhymes.

He invited us into the back of the store, where his feathered patients slept through the commotion, and boiled some hot water on an old-fashioned countertop gas stove that had a black pipe attached to the wall. He made us green tea. It was the first time I saw tea being made without tea bags. He opened his gift box, careful not to tear the paper or damage the bow. I stared at

63

his face, not the gift, as he opened it, and watched his face go from delight to sheer ecstacy. He laughed, and cried, and laughed, and whimpered. To tell you the truth, we didn't know what the hell was going on. But in his thick Chinese accent, he told us how he once had a little boy who died, and if he had lived, he knows he would have been as thoughtful and generous as we were that night. And he told us how the spirit of his son lives through the four of us coming together as we did in love and generosity. Just as the yin yang symbolizes the coming together of separate things to form one greater thing.

He stepped behind a curtain for a few moments and returned wearing the happy coat, placing the statue next to a bird cage. He told us it was the best Christmas he had had since his wife and son went away. When he said good-bye, he hugged each one of us. And sure enough, there were silent tears in each of our eyes.

We didn't really know why we did what we did that Christmas Eve, but it was a Christmas I'm sure none of us will ever forget. There wasn't a time when I stopped in to see Charlie when he didn't pull out that old happy coat, which he preserved in a cellophane wrapper, and the little rock-hard brown Buddha we gave him. He never forgot that Christmas eve all those years ago. And neither have I.

I haven't talked to the guys from that special Christmas Eve in years. It just seems that the closer people are, the further apart they drift after a betrayal, real or imagined. Everything seemed to change at puberty. Certain guys went gaga over girls quicker than others. It was strange to see best friends totally abandon one another just to become jesters of the courtyard ruled by the newly crowned chewing gum clicking queens from the block. Admittedly, I was one of those months behind the others who were in relentless pursuit of Tina Robustelli, Carrie Vitelli, Donna Murphy, Dee Dee Lannon, and the other girls in the neighborhood who suddenly abandoned their training bras for the real thing, and whispered to each other about cramps, bloating, and getting their periods. Those of us whose testosterone was yet to be released from our glands and sent soaring through our cells called those in blind hot pursuit of these hormone-enriched females "the poopy group." We were totally dumfounded that they could totally abandon dirtbomb fights, slingshot hunts for rats, and rowboat rides into the swamps of Van Cortlandt Park for these creatures who couldn't throw, make armpit farts, or know how to make a Schaeffer shortie for the 4th of July. (Bend a tin can back and forth until a crease eventually tears the can in half. Take the top of the can and bend the sides in slightly so it fits snugly inside the bottom of the can. Push both sides together creating a short can, usually a Schaeffer beer can, insert a firecracker in the opening. Place the can on a smooth flat surface upside down. Light the fuse, stand back and watch the top portion of the can shoot several stories into the air.)

Needless to say, in due time, we all understood. We were all to become members of one poopy group or another, but in the process of leaving behind little boy games, we left behind friends too. Rivalries and rites of violent passage intensified once girls became part of the gang. Only the strong survived the new social order, and the weak were cast off, banished, and humiliated for their lack of size or maturity, pimples, or sexual attraction to the new leaders of the pack: The girls.

And somewhere along the road to us busy bees trying to pollenize little flowers, me, Jocko, Michael, and Bobby lost touch with each other. And not having one of the participants from that special Christmas Eve to reminisce with, it seems like a dream that comes and goes, becoming a little more faded with each passing Christmas.

The body is long gone. All that remains is the yellow crime scene tape stretched across the front of the store. I just had to take a walk down there to see for myself. There's a cop sitting in a patrol car eating what looks like a hard roll and sipping a cup of coffee from a Greek diner paper coffee cup. How did the Greeks corner the paper coffee cup market in NY? You'd think that the Italians would have monopolized that one. You know, every coffee cup in the city with the red, green, and white Italian flag and a drawing of the Roman Coliseum. But for some reason, it's a blue coffee cup with Greek ruins that dominates. Go figure.

"Excuse me officer, I used to know the owner of the Hand Laundry. Any developments?"

Obviously pissed to be disturbed from his gourmet snack, he begins talking before he's finished chewing his most recent mouthful completely. "No developments. A hanger. Case closed."

"No foul play?"

"Nah. No signs of forced entry. No signs of robbery. No signs of nothing."

"Thanks, officer."

"No problem. Hey, you know if this guy had any relatives? We can't track down anyone."

"Only relatives I knew of were a wife and son who died like twenty years ago."

"That's a shame. We found a secret stash of dough. Looks like the old man didn't trust the banks. Too bad, it would've made a nice nest egg for somebody."

"Oh, shit, that reminds me, were there any animals or birds in there?"

"Come to think of it, there's a pigeon still in there. The guys have been feeding it bread crumbs. We don't know what the hell to do with it."

"I'll take it."

"You sure?"

"Yeah, I'll take it."

As soon as the front door opened, I heard that same bell ring announcing our entrance. I thought of that line at the end of *It's A Wonderful Life,* "Every time a bell does ring, another angel gets a wing." I thought of Charlie getting his wings. But once we took a step onto the creaking hardwood floor, I got a whiff of the unmistakable smell of death. Everything was just as I remembered it. The old-fashioned gas cook-top was replaced with a small microwave oven, but everything else looked exactly the same. In a small cage was a pigeon that cooed as soon as I crouched down to get a good look at it.

"Do you think I can take the cage, too?"

"Sure. Don't worry about it."

As I picked up the cage and turned to leave the small back room where Charlie spent his life, I noticed next to the door something that made me realize our special Christmas eve so long ago was not a dream at all. There, hanging from a nail, looking faded and worn, was a happy coat. Not the one we gave him but a similar one. The emotion of the moment swept over me, making the sadness of what I was in the middle of too real. Too overwhelming. But I'd be damned if I was going to let it show in front of a cop. I bit my lip and thought about Yogi Berra nude. That always brought me back to reality.

"Could you possibly tell me what he was wearing when he was found? When we were kids, we gave him a robe for Christmas. Was he wearing a robe with a yin-yang on the back?"

"I don't know what a yin-yang, is but he wasn't wearing no robe?"

"Thanks officer. God bless you."

God bless you? I don't think I've ever said that in my life to anyone, except after a sneeze.

"Yeah. Look, here's my card. I don't know why I'm doing this, but call me at the station and I'll let you know if there's any news. Or ask for Lieutenant Paolicelli. He's in charge of the investigation...."

Just then, a police officer looking much too young to have lieutenant stripes on his uniform, and an Afro too large to pass inspection, enters the room. If he wasn't wearing a police uniform, but was wearing a Met tee shirt and a pair of jeans, I would think he was just another guy from the neighborhood. Most likely a guy I'd hang out with.

"Speak of the devil, here he is. Lieutenant this guy says he knew the deceased," the first cop says.

The lieutenant gives me the once-over and pauses for a second, as if processing the data.

"Did you know him well?" The lieutenant asks, still giving me the hairy eyeball.

"Well, I knew him well when I was a kid. But I still stopped by once in a while just to say hi, and see how the bird clinic was doing," I say holding up my new pet pigeon.

"Thanks. Did you get his number, Billy?" The lieutenant asks the first cop.

"Yes, sir."

"OK, we'll call you if we have any questions, and you can call me if you'd like. Here's my card."

"Thanks."

"OK, see ya," the lieutenant says as if we were buddies saying good-bye after a night at The Base.

Now I just have to convince my parents that it's OK to have a sick pigeon in the house while they're packing for Florida. Think I'll name him Charlie.

FOUR

Writing with a typewriter is such a hassle. By the time I wait for the liquid "White-Out" to dry, I've already lost my train of thought. That correction tape is a little quicker, but it's harder to use. Why is it that a typewriter never hits the paper in exactly the same place twice?

Even though I have to hand my papers in to Professor Mark, I must first hand them in to my class instructors for them to grade. Professor Mark, I mean Karl....I'll bet you that's not his real first name....I mean who in Toledo is going to name his kid Karl Mark? It's probably Dick.... So Karl just has to process them so I can officially be credited. Writing them shouldn't be hard. It's just getting started. OK, no hanging out in the bar or anywhere else until they're done. And I'm starting now. As soon as I figure out what the hell I'm going to write about. One thing I learned in college is how to write an acceptable term paper. It's done in thirds. The first third consists of letting the reader know what you are going to tell them. The next third is telling them. The final third is explaining what you just told them. But most importantly, tell them what you already know they want to hear.

Advanced Television Production III will be easy. Start off with Philo T. Farnsworth, mention "Playhouse 90" and Edward R. Murrow, and finish off with Naim June Paik and make a subtle reference to the fact that my instructor, Amy Gold, can certainly be included among the small format video pioneers with their Sony Porta-Pacs. *Avante Garde Music II* begins with a caveman banging a drum with a bone, segues into Stockhausen, makes a left turn at Harry Partch, mentions Raymond Scott, Frank Zappa, and The Beatles' Revolution #9, and refers to my in-class performance which consisted of banging on a drum with a bone. *Advanced Acting III* pays tribute to Lee Strasberg, but quickly makes reference to the fact that the class instructor, the almost famous off-off-off Broadway and SoHo loft writer, director, actor, and performance artist Roberta Richards has transformed stage actors from "fleshy marionettes to organic ghosts of truth" as she loves to say. I will not reveal how most of my stunning class improvisations were in fact based on Curly's "Three Stooges" routines.

Six typewritten pages each, double spaced should take nine hours max. All I need is paper, liquid paper, coffee, baloney (the meat kind), bread, and Coke (the soda kind). Starting....shit....now.

Monsignor Malloy would have laughed out loud, ran down the aisle with a textbook in-hand, and whacked me over the head with it, if I attempted to hand in the bullshit I just spent ten hours spewing onto my Hermes. *Ms. Richards' standard introduction to every class, workshop, or staged performance, requesting that audience members refrain from having sexual fantasies about the performers and those sitting around them should be a prerequisite for all high art mediums.* What a fucking joke! Since the first humanoid got a laugh by throwing his own excrement against a wall, to the line of mimes from the subway station at 86th Street right up the stairs to the entrance of The Metropolitan Museum of Art, the reason people get into show biz is to get laid. Look at me everybody? Aren't I grand? It starts out by singing "Twinkle Twinkle Little Star" at three-and-a-half, and finishes up with an eighty-two year old actor having a coronary with a twenty-two year old newlywed riding him bareback. And the more the performance group denies this sexual obsession, the more action there is at the wrap party.

But Monsignor Malloy isn't an instructor at Manhattan City College. Roberta Richards is. So I write to please Roberta Richards. Just as in high school I gave an excellent oral presentation on "Conservatism in Modern American Politics" despite the fact I was secretly a Nixon-hating, commie pinko who protested the war in Vietnam. Monsignor Malloy treated me like the son he never had for weeks because I quoted Lord Falkland in my opening line: "When it is not necessary to change, it is necessary not to change." But when a class discussion turned to the war in Vietnam a month later, and I repeated some of the things I heard Jerry Rubin and Abbie Hoffman say on Public Television's Channel 13, I became a dangerous subversive. He even went as far as to bring up John Lennon! I couldn't believe my ears. He mentioned that "that commie Beatle Lennon was posing nude with a Jap girlfriend" and if he was standing on the corner of 57th Street and Fifth Avenue nobody "would even give a rat's ass." That next August, for the first and only time in my life I slept overnight outside Madison Square Garden to get tickets for John Lennon's "One to One" concert.

I wound up getting a C from Monsignor Malloy. I didn't want to make the same mistake with Roberta Richards or my other instructors. Now that I think about it, it wasn't that hard to finally complete these three papers. It's like a huge weight has been lifted off my shoulders. Why was it I couldn't sit down and do them? I know in high school it was usually the threat of physical harm from a teacher, my father, and my mother, in that order. I've tried a million times to face the blank page and pay tribute to my professors only to come up empty paged and head off to the closest distraction.

Cooo coooo coooo coooo

"Oh Charlie, you must be hungry."

I forgot he was even there. I also forgot that the sun has started to creep through the closed slats of the venetian blinds. A pull of the cord and the room is bathed in the golden glow of the morning. Even the graffiti on the side of the el train looks appealing glowing so brightly from the early sunlight. The dropshadows that the more talented vandals utilize have the desired effect of giving "Taki 183" across the length of the car a 3-D effect. Don't get me wrong; I hate graffiti. I think they should be punished if caught. But instead of going through the juvenile court system, the perps should be brought before a panel of art judges. And the graffiti should be judged the same way an art museum panel decides whether a piece should be included in an exhibit. Is it original or just crass commercialism? Is it effective in communicating its message in an innovative fashion? Have they taken into consideration the placement of the work on the train? What about execu-

71

tion, colors, and themes? Points should be given for NOT covering windows. The worst offenders should be punished the most severely. Maybe like in "Clockwork Orange" they should be forced to listen to hours and hours of Debbie Boone and watch back to back to back episodes of "Three's Company." The more gifted graffiti painters (I refuse to use the word artist) perhaps could sweep up at The Guggenheim. Once they see a Jasper Johns or Jackson Pollock piece hanging on the sacred walls of the museum that would make a great roller derby rink, they would realize they could be making millions spraying large canvasses instead of jumping barbed wire fences at three in the morning at the 240th Street subway yard.

"Oops, Charlie. No more bread. I'll be right back."

It's the first time in ages that I've been up at the crack of dawn and not stumbling through the front door.

"Are you coming or going?" Mom asks as she pops her head out of the bedroom.

"What do you mean?"

"Well, this is the first time in a long time that you're up at the crack of dawn and not stumbling through the front door."

She doesn't miss much.

"Nah, I've been up all night finishing my term papers, and I'm getting some bread for Charlie."

"Is that bird still here? Oh Jerry, please!"

"As soon as he's well, Mom."

"Did you say you finished your papers?"

"Yeah."

"Well, hallelujah! Thank heaven! Good for you, Jerry. Now you can graduate, get a job, get married, have kids, and support your father and me."

"First things first, Mom. I'm getting bread for Charlie."

"Jerry, congratulations. Do what you need to do."

"Yeah. Thanks."

With a wink and a smile, like only the Irish can do, she went back inside the bedroom where my father was still snoring loud enough to knock the paint chips off the ceiling. How she can sleep in that room, I'll never know.

Charlie's happy to have his bread. He seems much more lively today. Maybe I can let him go soon. I darken the room by closing the blinds and the curtains and climb into bed for a well deserved sleep. Charlie's cooing doesn't bother me at all. In fact I find it comforting. Maybe that's how Mom manages to sleep.

Amy Gold is a nut. My two other instructors were more than happy to have me drop off the papers in their box at school. But not Professor Gold. She insists on me dropping it off at her SoHo "video workspace." Words are very important to some people. It's not a "television studio," it's a "video workspace." I've heard about her "video workspace" called "RadicalVideoVision." It's part of the underground video movement. At Manhattan City College, the equipment we used for television production consisted of black and white cameras about the size of a shoe box mounted on stationary tripods connected to video recorders that utilize reel to reel half-inch video tape recorders. The recorders are about the size of a medium-sized suitcase, and weigh as much as that same suitcase filled with bricks. But the new video equipment is portable. With a portable recorder about the size of a small suitcase filled with only a few bricks and a camera, you can now go on-location. And since the portable equipment in relatively inexpensive, you can also put together a small television studio, er, "video workspace." So now there is a video underground based mostly down in The Village and SoHo.

SoHo is a royal pain to get to. Unlike midtown, there aren't many subway lines crisscrossing every few blocks. It seems everything is a long walk from the Canal Street or Houston Street stations. It's another one of those blindingly bright winter days, but not the comfortable kind. It's bitterly cold and windy. The wind finds every tiny opening on your outer wear as though it's seeking the warmth of your skin. Since I was headed for the trendiest part of New York, I didn't want to look uncool with a hat and gloves,

73

so I'm a cool fool, freezing my ears off.

Like everything else in SoHo, RadicalVideoVision is in a loft that was once a garment industry sweatshop during the early part of the century. There is a hand-painted sign hanging over the nondescript steel grey front door that reads "RadicalVideoVision." There is a distinct smell of urine as I push the buzzer.

"Who's there?" A female voice says on the intercom.

"Jerry Pellicano. I have to drop something off for Amy Gold."

Nothing. No buzzer to let me in. I must've stood there for three minutes freezing. I pushed the buzzer again.

"Where are you?" The irritated female voice asks.

"The buzzer didn't work."

"Fuck," she says.

From behind the heavy door, I could hear another heavy door slam, and footsteps descending some stairs.

The door swings open and behind it is Amy herself, clothed in a thick man's robe.

"This fucking buzzer never works when you need it to," she says as she turns and rushes back up the stairs.

I can't help but notice that there is a hole worn right at the seat of her robe, revealing the bare skin of her ass underneath. I never thought of her as being attractive in class. Her hair was always flat, blunt cut at the bottom of the ears, and appeared greasy. She never wears a bit of makeup, and dressed like an American version of what a communist Chinese student might wear. But in reality she's not fat, has an attractive but plain face in an eastern European kind of way, and is probably only about thirty years old.

I follow her up to the third floor of the ancient industrial revolution building with my breath still visible in the cold stairwell. The door to RadicalVideoVision is a behind an old iron gate, like the kind you would see in an old elevator. There is a door behind it that is half chicken wire reinforced industrial glass that seems to have condensation on it. As Amy pushes the iron gate aside and opens the door, I'm hit with a blast of scented damp warm air.

It's almost like walking into a sauna, and I can hear the unmistakable sound of steam radiators hissing. The front reception area is lit only by candles, and incense sticks are burning. Amy whips around, and her robe separates just enough to reveal her pendulous breasts and nipples still erect from the chilly stairwell.

"Jerry it is, right?"

"Right."

"You have terrible timing, but actually it couldn't be more perfect. We are right in the middle of shooting a performance video, and I could use a director. We were taking turns, but it's not working out. The energy in the workspace is so intense, no one wants to be isolated in the booth. Could you do it for us?"

"Just switch shots on the switcher, right?"

"That's it. But it must be motivated. Let me see your hands."

She grabs both my hands, still red with cold, and examines them as if she is reading my palms and checking to see if they're clean enough for dinner.

"You have sensitive hands. You can do this, right?"

"Sure, I've switched in class."

"OK. Let me show you the booth."

Behind a cheap hollow core door that no one has bothered to paint or put a doorknob in the prefabricated hole is a video control room that looks like an explosion in a wire factory. The room is a tangled mess of cables hanging from the ceiling and strewn across the floor.

"Watch your step. Don't step on the cables," Amy implores as we tiptoe to the control board where three video tape machines sit on a counter precariously perched on two saw horses. Above the machines is a sagging board with small black and white monitors that looks like it may snap at any minute. It's at this point that I immediately think of Roberta Richards' introduction to every acting workshop: "Please refrain from having sexual fantasies about the performers and those sitting around you."

On each monitor is a different angle of four nude women

75

drinking hot beverages underneath the bright lights of a stark stage.

"This is very important," Amy says as she leans over the equipment counter, revealing even more of her naked upper body.

"We're in the middle of a dance performance, but I'm not happy with it. We're going to start over. I'll be on camera one. This tape deck will be an 'iso' of my camera. This deck will be an 'iso' of camera two, this deck will be the switcher 'out' record-deck. Tell me what that means."

Trying to block out of my mind the fact that I can see both of her breasts quite clearly, and she has enormous nipples as erect as pencil erasers, I answer, "OK, the 'isos' mean that everything that cameras one and two shoot will be recorded on their respective decks in their entirety, camera three has no 'iso,' and whatever cameras I switch on the switcher will be recorded on the master record deck."

"Good. I knew this would work out. I'll cue you."

Amy rushed out of the booth, and as she pushed open the door, she dropped her robe so it landed right in the doorway. I watched on the monitors as my nude instructor approached the nude women on break and began demonstrating various jumps, jerks, flops, waves, gyrations, and every un natural movement a nude body could make. And when Amy finished a series of movements, the four naked ladies would repeat them with the added dimension of doing it practically on top of each other in a kind of non-sexual orgy. Non-sexual for *them* maybe.

Apparently, there is a microphone in the room because I can hear everything that is going on in the studio.

"Charge, charge, charge. Retreat," Amy almost sings as she punctuates each word with the sudden thrust of a limb.

"Jerry, are you ready?"

Shit. There must be an intercom to the studio.

"Jerry, use the intercom. It's right there on the counter."

76

For the life of me, I can't find it. The entire room is a total disaster area of buttons, cables, switches, bare wires, and gaffer's tape. I see Amy leaving the studio on one of the monitors, and seconds later she enters the control room as naked as a newborn baby.

"I've been meaning to label everything in here," she says as she tries to make sense out of the electronic mishmash before her. I try not to look at her, but out of the corner of my eye, I catch a glimpse of her nude body and discover that not only is she not fat, she is quite slender and toned. She has hair under her armpits, not in a gross Italian *guy* kind of way, but in a delicate silk from an ear of corn way.

PLEASE REFRAIN FROM HAVING SEXUAL FANTASIES ABOUT THE PERFORMERS AND THOSE SITTING AROUND YOU is flashing in my brain like a Times Square cigarette billboard. I've got to think of Yogi Berra nude immediately.

"Here it is," Amy says as she pulls a black wire as though reeling in a blue fish, revealing a cheap Radio Shack microphone at the end.

"Just switch this on, and talk into it. Loudly."

She rushes into the studio and takes her position behind camera one.

"Can you hear me, Jerry?"

"Yes," I announce into the dented microphone.

"Good. Places."

The four nude women go center stage and lie on the floor in a fetal position in a kind of weird Busby Berkley formation. Suddenly a tape recorder in the studio counts down, three, two, one, and the music starts. It sounds like someone banging on some garbage cans, with sharp accents of a tenor saxophone and piano. And with each stab of music, the dancers react. First slowly and sensuously, then fast and violently. Before I know it, they are jumping around so much that they are sweating profusely. I'm pushing the buttons on the switcher slowly, each time capturing a different angle on the dancers or a close up. The three cameras are just as unpredictable in their movements as the dancers they are covering. Then suddenly camera one is no longer zooming, panning, or tilting. It's locked off. And then crawling on the floor like a snake, the nude body of Amy Gold slivers into the midst of the nude ensemble. Then the other two cameras are similarly locked, followed by the other two camera women joining in the nude performance. All I can do is switch between the three static cameras, mesmerized by what is displayed on the glowing black and white monitors in front of me. Seven nude women in an undulating pile of moist flesh in rhythm to the discordant sounds of the avante garde jazz playing on a cheap tape recorder.

As I pushed the buttons in a rhythm that somewhat followed the performance, I became mesmerized by the figures on the small monochrome television monitors. And then it hit me. I am not having sexual fantasies about the performers. It's not sexual at all. The lusty desires I had while Amy stood next to me, flashing her breasts as she bent over the equipment, were gone. The nude female forms don't remind me of an erotic lesbian orgy, but do resemble reeds in marsh blowing in the wind. And the next moment the forms take on the shape of pizza dough being mixed in those giant industrial bakery mixers. I'm not thinking about the sensual pleasure I could have if I rubbed myself down with some petuli oil and jumped into the middle of the pile, but trying to switch the cameras in a way that best captures the human tableau of the moment. When I squint my eyes, I swear that they now resemble sand dunes changing in the wind. Am I high, or what?

The music ends and they all collapse to the floor as though they were shot dead. They lay there motionless for a whole minute, then Amy jumps to her feet.

"Cut. Beautiful! Fabulous! Splendid! Did you get it all, Jerry?"

I fumble for the intercom microphone. "Got it all."

"Let's go look, come on everyone."

All seven of them pile into the control room, each wearing a robe of some kind. Although they've been sweating, the odor is not repulsive like a men's locker room. It's more like that smell when you first walk into the lion house at the zoo. It hits you hard at first, but then there's some kind of organic comfort you feel once you get used to it, and it's not unpleasant at all.

"Roll it back, Jerry, and let's see what we've got."

I managed to rewind the tape without screwing anything up, and started to playback the performance. There was total silence as it began. Then there were scattered "aaahhhs" and "mmmmms" and "nice" and "excellent" and other exclamations of satisfaction.

"Oh, this is the best take. Definitely the best take," Amy says as she lights a cigarette in the already stifling control room.

"What number take is this?" I ask, wondering how many times they could possibly go through this.

"This is take thirteen. Lucky thirteen. This is it. Fabulous, Jerry, fabulous!"

"Thanks. I enjoyed it."

"OK people, that's a wrap for today. Tomorrow at seven p.m. for the series of new pieces. Thank you."

The six almost nude women exit the booth leaving Amy and me alone.

"Jerry, I like what you did. Very in tune to what we were doing. Listen, I have a proposition," Amy said, punctuated by a long drag on a menthol cigarette. Then, while in deep thought, she opened her mouth slightly, and as the smoke slowly billowed out, she inhaled it straight up her nose, sucking it deep into her lungs. "How would you like to help us out? I can't pay much, but we could use you. I'm sure you've noticed this place is a mess. Spaghetti city. You can take care of the studio, dress cables, do some minor carpentry or whatever to stabilize the place, clean up, get the equipment in order, and help me out with my videos. In return you'll have access to the equipment, including the new three-quarter" gear Sony is going to lend me, and I'll pay you $2 an hour off the books, how's that?"

I couldn't believe my ears. I felt like I had just won the

lottery. A paying job with a group of women whose idea of "art" is to romp around in the nude and have me videotape them.

"When do you want me to start?"

"As far as I'm concerned, you already have. Talk to Sandra when she arrives. She's my Associate Director, and work out your schedule with her."

She put the cigarette in her mouth so it barely hung on to her wet lower lip and stuck her hand straight out for me to shake. As she did that her robe once again came apart just enough see one of her breasts glistening with sweat.

"Thank you."

"No, thank YOU."

Nobody at Third Base is going to believe this one.

I'm finished with college. Done. Not incomplete, but totally complete. My papers are handed in, and I'm going to get a diploma. Oh, it took longer than four years, and the degree I'm getting and thirty-five cents will get me on the subway, but I did it. And all it took was removing myself from hanging out for approximately forty-eight hours. Now it's time to celebrate.

With the holidays over, the first signs of spring, like dog shit on the sidewalk starting to defrost, are still far off. People are starting to get cabin fever staring at the close walls of their roach-infested apartments, and the bars are getting busy by three in the afternoon. That's when a lot of the cops and firemen finish their shifts, and other city workers sneak out before quitting time. The crowd at three p.m. is much older than the late night crowd. Guys in their fifties, sixties, and seventies, who are still working, stop in for a little numbing before facing whatever awaits them at home. Over there sitting where Mikey Lenihan usually sits is his Uncle Eugene. Uncle Eugene is one of the neighborhood originals. It's amazing how his stories sound just like the stories we tell. Even when something happens on the block or in the bar that blows

80

everyone's mind, like a stabbing, or a woman gives guys blow jobs in the bathroom, Uncle Eugene can tell you how it already happened in the late forties or early fifties.

"Hey, Uncle Eugene, how are ya?" Everyone calls him that.

"Hey, Jerry, how's it hanging?" That's his standard greeting.

"Have you seen Mikey yet?"

"Not yet, but I'm sure he'll show up soon. He likes watching the television news here."

I know Mikey will be here soon. If he wasn't here soon, I think they'd go knock his door down to see if he was dead in his tub or something. Noel's down at the other end of the bar deep in conversation with Mr. Boyle and King. King is Mr. Boyle's German Shepherd. King is as docile a dog as you'd ever see. The bar could be on fire and King would sit curled around Mr. Boyle's workboots. Any stranger can walk over to King and pet him on the head, and he won't even open his eyes. One thing though: don't EVER say the word "gasman" around King or he will ferociously attack anything that moves. Mr. Boyle trained him to do that when he suspected that the gasman, who goes from apartment to apartment during the day, was checking more than the gas meter when his wife let him into the apartment.

"Hey, Noel, how are you laddy?"

"Oh, Jerry, hello, haven't seen you in a while."

"Yeah, I've been busy with some school stuff."

"Oh, I know how dreadful that college work can be."

I flashed for a moment on my morning interlude with seven naked women. "Oh, it's not so bad sometimes."

"What'll you have?"

"Just a nip."

Noel reached into the ice-filled sink below and pulled me out a small bottle of beer we call a nip.

"Oh, Stubby called, and said if I saw you to tell you to stick around for him."

"Thanks, Noel."

Great. If Stubby's stopping by, I'm sure Terry and Merrill will probably be with him. And right on cue, here they are. Stubby and Terry still in their dirty work clothes, and Merrill, still in his dirty regular clothes.

"Hey, guys, long time no see."

"Yeah. I haven't seen you in days," Stubby says as he reaches out to give me a soul handshake.

"Hey, Stubby, how's it hanging?" Uncle Eugene shouts from his corner stool.

Stubby immediately reaches down just above his boot and grabs a big chunk of leg with both hands.

"I got it tucked into my sock. I'd say that's hanging pretty low."

Eugene is cracking up, and I can hear the forty years of smoking Luckys rattling around in his lungs. He has a short coughing fit and walks over to Stubby. Stubby tries to give him a soul handshake, but Eugene briefly wrestles with his outstretched hand to give a normal handshake.

"I'm going home guys, take care."

"Stick around Eugene, we're just getting started here," Stubby says, holding up my beer bottle.

"No, no, I've learned my lesson."

"Aw, you always miss all the fun, Uncle Eugene," says Stubby, feigning extreme disappointment.

"Let me tell you guys something I learned a long time ago. Anything that happens after ten p.m. is bullshit. I don't care if there's broads hanging off the chandeliers with their tits hanging out. It's all bullshit," Uncle Eugene says as he puts on his heavy red plaid wool coat and matching billed hat with flaps that cover his ears.

"Uncle Eugene, don't get all philosophical on me huh?" Stubby says apparently taking Eugene's words to heart.

"It's all bullshit," Uncle Eugene says as he exits. And not a second later, in walks Mikey Lenihan.

"Mikey, tell your Uncle Eugene not to bring my head down when he's leaving the bar?" Stubby shouts to Mikey before he has both feet inside the doorway.

"He brings my head down when he's coming into the bar," Mikey deadpans to Stubby as he heads straight for the stool just vacated by Uncle Eugene.

Terry and Merrill never seem to change their supporting roles with Stubby. Terry reeks of pot and his thumb and index finger are stained from smoking joints that are too small. Merrill has already pulled a dog-eared copy of *The Stranger* out of his pocket and is sitting there reading it.

"Hey, Noel, three nips."

"Sure, Stubby."

Stubby's dirty old work clothes and thick long hair make him look wild. But he's got a look on his face that tells me he's got something on his mind. Perhaps Uncle Eugene got under his skin.

"Stub, you're not gonna believe what happened to me today," I say, ready to go into every naked detail of my day. But that doesn't get Stubby's attention.

"What's going on, Stubby?"

Stubby slowly turns his head to me and looks deep into my eyes. "Charlie the Chinaman."

"I didn't tell you, Stubby; I went down there after you called me, and a cop showed me around the crime scene."

"Oh fuck, really? Didn't it weird you out?"

"Yeah, at first. It brought back a rush of memories. I've got one of his birds."

"A black pigeon?"

"Yeah, why?"

"I brought that in to him a few weeks ago," Stubby says sadly.

"Are you shitting me? Did he seem depressed. I mean, you know...did he seem like he was going to kill himself."

"Fuck no. That's just it. He was talking about fucking retiring soon and getting a place in Greenwood Lake."

"Should you tell the cops?"

"What's the use? Listen, Jerry," Stubby said softly as he looked over to Terry who was busy being mesmerized by The Mike Douglas Show, and Merrill equally immersed in Camus. "Charlie kind of made reference to the fact that he had a stash of money hidden somewhere. It's freaking me out. What if it's still in there, or something else."

"You're not going to believe this Stubby, but the cop told me that they found a shitload of money hidden in the store."

"Jerry, you know what that means. If he blabbed to me about it, he may have blabbed to someone else. And someone else could've gone in there and iced Charlie for the secret stash."

"Stubby, this is too weird man."

"Don't say anything to anybody. There could be more to this than the cops even want to deal with. How's the bird?"

"Fine. I named him Charlie."

"Nice. May he rest in peace," Stubby says as he holds up his nip in a toast.

"Amen."

The workers came, drank, bitched about their foremen, sergeants, captains, supervisors, co-workers, wives, girlfriends, in fact anyone who wasn't currently standing within earshot of their tragic soliloquy. The only ones safe from criticism were those lucky enough to be standing at the bar at that very moment. Even those who were taking a leak were subject to ridicule. It seemed the only subject that brought total joy was the 1978 Yankees. That is until the topic turned to the upcoming 1979 Yankees and all the fears and shortcomings that lie ahead there. Can Reggie repeat? Is Guidry done? Can Munson's knees hold up? Will Billy Martin be back? Oh, so many things to fret and worry about.

It's one of those weeknights for drinking. The Knick game on TV keeps most of the crowd's attention with occasional outbursts of joy or outrage. It's hard to differentiate between the two.

I don't think I'm going to tell Stubby about my new nudist boss while we're here. I'm afraid that my story will spread like wildfire, and next thing I know I'll have a Third Base field trip/beer party scheduled during one of my shifts. Especially if Terry hears it. For somebody who hardly ever talks when he's stoned, which is all the time, he can't keep his mouth shut when you want him to.

The hours rolled by and the small bottles of beer couldn't hide the fact that I've probably had enough brew to fill a kitchen-sized garbage can. I've been staring at the Knick game for the past hour and couldn't even tell you what the score is or even who they're playing. I should be happy. But Charlie the Chinaman was probably murdered and nobody cares. My parents are leaving for Florida. I'm lucky if I'll be taking home sixty dollars a week working two jobs. I haven't eaten anything all day, and I feel like throwing up.

Suddenly two hands start massaging my shoulders.

"Jerry, are you OK?" The voice connected to the hands asks.

It's Merrill. Sometimes I forget that Merrill is even in the same room. He'll drink, or get high, depending on what everyone else is doing, but then always seems to disappear into his own quiet world, listening intently to whatever is going on with a look on his face as though he is filing every topic away in alphabetical order inside his head.

"Merrill, don't do that too much, I might start to like it."

"You look bummed."

"I'm just tired. And hungry. And drunk. And bummed."

"Charlie the Chinaman?"

"Well, yeah."

"He was a wise man. Ever hear of *The Book of Tao*?"

"Dow, like Tony Dow on 'Leave It To Beaver'?"

"No, T.A.O. dow."

"No, should I?"

85

"I don't know. There's a part on the yin-yang? You've heard of that?"

"Yeah, like *yin-yang you're my thing*....Exile? Stones? Just kidding, yeah, I've seen it."

"It says "Loss sometimes benefits; benefits can be a loss.""

"Tell that to Charlie. You're into all that spiritual stuff huh, Merrill?"

"We'll talk about it some other time. Take care, Jerry. See you Stubby, Terry."

Merrill turned, put on his long Salvation Army black overcoat, and walked out of the bar. He didn't turn to the left, in the direction of his apartment building but went to the right where he paused in front of the bar window and looked right at me. He turned to the side, and pretended to walk down a flight of stairs, disappearing. He is one mysterious dude.

Surprisingly, I'm not too hungover. Maybe it was breakfast at the Shortstop Diner at three in the morning. Nothing like a plate full of grease and fat to absorb a few gallons of beer. Don't ask me why I still weigh the same I did in my freshman year of high school. As they have been for the past several days, my parents are out doing something "moving" related. Everything is nearly packed and in neat piles throughout the apartment.

Douglas will be back at work, and so will Berta. Douglas can advise me on my raise, increased hours, and on Berta. Douglas loves to advise everyone on everything. He uses the I Ching. He takes three pennies, shakes them up, drops them onto the desk, writes down how many come up tails or heads, and then looks in his I Ching book to see what action should or should not be taken. I think flipping one coin would be easier, but that's the way he lives his life. And I mean his entire life.

As I lock the front door, I see some new graffiti on the wall next to the elevator. Those damn Latin Eagles. More customers at Ronnie Donnelly's drug emporium I guess.

FIVE

I could hear Gershwin's *Rhapsody In Blue* from the elevator. Ten months ago I wouldn't have been able to name that tune, but thanks to Douglas, and the fact that I spend five to six hours a day listening to music, I can tell the difference between a symphony and a piano concerto. I'm familiar with Haydn and hi-dee-hos from Cab Calloway. I also know that you can tell how old a jazz record is by listening to the bass. If it has a bass tuba instead of a string bass, it's probably pre-1927, which is when the electronic microphone was introduced in recording studios.

"Hi, Greg," I say cheerfully, hoping he's forgotten about his hissy fit the other day.

"Morning," he responds icily, not looking up from his *Backstage Magazine.*

"Is Douglas in?"

Greg says nothing, but points to Douglas' studio at the rear of the cavernous room we work in.

"Thanks."

Thanks to my worn-in Converse All-Star sneakers, I'm able to walk silently back to the entrance of Douglas' studio where he spends most of his time. As the Head Archivist in the library, it is his job to prioritize which recorded works should be transferred to audio tape. It's a massive job that he knows won't even be completed in his lifetime, but each day he makes another small dent in the monumental project.

The door to his studio is slightly ajar, and Douglas is hunched over his workbench with his back to me. If I had to guess, I would say he is sobbing. Just another day on the job I guess. I knock softly on the door.

"Douglas?"

"Jerry, come in and close the door," Douglas instructs me while trying to control his sobbing.

Douglas turns to me, revealing that, yes, he is indeed sobbing. He's wearing a plastic lab apron and he is holding what appears to be a very old oversized 78 rpm record.

"Excuse me. Something quite horrific just happened."

Knowing that Douglas is on Thorazine daily and on occasion has been known to go on a bender, and even on good day is subject to emotional breakdowns over the most trivial of matters, I'm ready to be surprised.

"Do you want me to come back later?"

"No. Stay. *Der Rosenklavier* may be Strauss's best work. What I hold in my hand may be the rarest recording of *Der Rosenklavier* in the country, if not the world." The words are shooting out of Douglas' mouth. "While washing the record, as I do every record before transferring them to tape, it slipped out of my hand. I was lucky enough to catch is before it hit the floor and broke, but as it slipped down, a tiny nail head sticking out of the edge of the counter scratched the entire side of the record" Douglas looked at me, his eyes still red and teary. "Help me, please."

"OK, what do you want me to do?"

"Tell me not to panic."

"OK, don't panic, put the record on the counter."

He did so, and sighed as though he had just defused a nuclear bomb.

"Don't tell a soul, Jerry. Not even Greg, promise me, Jerry. Promise me."

Douglas looks brilliant. Smart brilliant. His grey hair is worn straight back, and his grey beard is meticulously groomed. He looks like he's in great shape for a man of about fifty. His vocabulary is sometimes intimidating to me, like an English Lit. Professor. He usually wears jeans and a work shirt, but I think he irons them with lots of starch, and his creases are so sharp you could cut yourself on them. If a function requires tie and jacket, he adds a hippie flower power tie, and a plaid wool blazer with patches on the elbows. Douglas still considers himself a hippie.

"I promise, Douglas. What are you going to do?"

"I don't know. I just don't know."

"I'll come back later, Douglas."

"No, I'm OK," he says as he pulls himself together. "You wanted to see me?"

"Well, are you sure?"

"I'm sure, go on."

"I need more hours, and more money, Douglas. I'm going to talk to Mr. Healy today, and I was wondering if you had any advice."

"Get out."

"Get out?"

"Don't get trapped in here like Greg and me."

Trapped? What's with these guys? As freakin' city workers, they've got the cushiest jobs in the city, listening to music all day, and they think they're trapped? I pray to God that I could work for the New York City Public Library and not work on the tracks with Stubby and Terry picking up dead rats off the third rail.

"I need this job, Douglas. Any advice?"

"If you must...promise Mr. Healy that you will alphabetize the cards more frequently."

"Is my filing that bad?"

"Yes."

"Promise you'll be on time, work any shift, mention you're uncle again, and that you'd love to attend one of his operas."

"His operas?"

"Yes, he sings in The Stuyvesant Town Opera Society."

"OK, I'll do it. Thanks, Douglas."

"Jerry, listen to me. Don't get trapped here."

I thought to myself, I should be so lucky.

"Thanks."

"Jerry?"

"It's our little secret, right?" Douglas says as he points to the damaged 78rpm record on the counter.

"Right. Our little secret." I said as I exited his studio and quietly closed the door.

So many hidden little secrets boiling just under the skin ready to erupt like an ugly white head on the tip of your nose. Everyone sees it coming and no one says a word. You can't hide it. You can't put a bandaid on it. You know how stupid that looks. You just watch it slowly boil to the surface in the mirror like everyone else does. Unless, of course, you pop it as soon as it appears in its early stages. But everyone notices that, too. Then it comes back uglier, leaving scars that are impossible to hide. Ever see those guys standing on a corner who you can smell from a block away, ranting and raving at the top of their lungs? Their hair is greasy and matted, clothes caked with dirt, grease, grime, and human excrement to the point of making any colored fabric a shiny black. They flail their arms, spitting out chants such as "Fuck you, you motherfucking cunt bastard cocksucker faggot son of a bitch asshole" They string together every awful word their mind can think of for all the world to hear. I call them "blood boilers." It's as though their blood is actually boiling. It probably started out as a whitehead on the tip of their nose.

Greg sits at his desk reading the score of *Most Happy Fella* as it plays for listener number three on the monitors. I'm not going to even bother asking him if he has any advice for my talk with Mr. Healy. He's lost in Frank Loesser and I'm not going to be the one to bring him back to reality.

"Greg, I'm going to see Mr. Healy," I announce just before I walk through the doorway leading to the elevators.

"Don't forget to drop your uncle's name," he says without looking up from the music book.

"Thanks, I'll try that."

Mr. Healy usually doesn't have to mix with the "great unwashed beast," as he calls the library going public. Right now, Joyce Washington, a college sophomore at Columbia who is interning for us, is handling that. Not being a paid employee, she doesn't have to file or clean the ear wax out of headsets like I do.

She's a very articulate young black woman with perfect posture from Washington, D.C., who could probably run this place if she wanted to. She's expert at playing the cello, and my bet is she will get her wish of playing with the New York Philharmonic. Mr. Healy loves her, and I'm sure he wishes that she was the one about to go into his office to ask for more hours.

"Is Mr. Healy in his office?" I ask Joyce, barely above a whisper.

"Oh, hi, Jerry, yes. He's in a bad mood," she mouthes to me.

Great. Screw it. I knock on Mr. Healy's door anyway.

"Enter."

Mr. Healy's office is a microcosm of the library itself. Everything government issue, neatly organized, void of any character or individuality except for a framed poster advertising a 1967 production of The Stuyvesant Town Opera Society's production of *Don Giovane*. He's on the phone in what sounds like an argument of some kind, but he's staring at me as he talks into the mouthpiece, which makes me very uncomfortable.

"I'm sorry, madame, but what you are asking me is out of the question. I'm already stretched beyond reason, and I will fight this if I must go to the mayor's office to do it. Good day, madame. Now Jerry, how can I help you?" He says as he gently places the phone back on the handset. What Mr. Healy says never seems to match the expression on his face. I've seen him cut people to shreds with his words while keeping a straight face.

"Yes, uh, Mr. Healy, do you have a few minutes?"

He looks at his watch, and his finger runs down an appointment calendar on his desk.

"Yes, I have some time, now what's on your mind, Jerry?"

"Gee, uh, that's a nice poster." I am such a moron. What a stupid way to start this off. How obvious!

"Oh, that was so long ago. Do you like opera, Jerry?"

I thought to myself, maybe it wasn't so dumb.

"Uh, well, my Uncle Hans taught me about opera at a young age." I may as well take a home run swing here.

"Oh yes. Your uncle was such a brilliant man. Even at the end, when he was close to ninety and confined to a wheelchair, when it came to knowing the Philharmonic archives he still knew where all the bodies were buried, er, so to speak. Forgive me."

Hey, he just apologized to me. Cool.

"Mr. Healy, I know that things aren't exactly in the expansion mode here at the library, but I was wondering if I could possibly request several things."

"Jerry, you couldn't ask at a worse time. The city is choking us with these cutbacks. It's a disgrace. A city is only as great as its library system. When only the rich have access to education and the fine arts, our entire society is doomed. Have you completed your studies at Manhattan City College, Jerry?"

"Yes, I have." Whew. I timed that just right.

"Manhattan City College is a fine institution. Many great people went through the city's university system, which has always been free. This city is being taken over by Wall Street, and it's an injustice to the working people."

I'm wondering where the "great unwashed beast" fits into all this.

"Mr. Healy, my personal situation has changed. I'm finished with college, and my parents are moving to Florida. So I'm at a point where I need a raise and close to full-time hours in order to support myself."

"I don't know, Jerry. I just don't know. I'll have to study this carefully and crunch some numbers. What kind of numbers are we talking here, Jerry?"

"Well, I'd like as close to three dollars an hour as possible..."

"...Jerry, that's staff money you're talking."

"Is that a possibility?"

"I don't know, Jerry. You want to be staff?"

93

Mr. Healy walks over to one of his large wooden filing cabinets and pulls out a drawer.

"This drawer is filled with people who want to work here. Many have library sciences master degrees. Some have music PhDs. from Ivy league universities. I just don't know, Jerry."

...So much for us schmucks from Manhattan City College...

"Well, Mr. Healy, I want you to know I'm ready to commit myself to doing whatever needs to be done in order to increase my hours, and perhaps my hourly wage. And, uh, do you think I could attend one of your operas sometime?"

Mr. Healy looked at me coldly. I guess that wasn't as smooth a transition as I had hoped it would be.

"I will look into your circumstances, and I will inform you of any upcoming productions. Good day."

I fucked that up.

"Good day."

Now it's time for my other library business at hand; Berta. Just a short detour won't be noticed by anyone. I can see her if I stand at the edge of the corner in the hall through the glass doors. She's busy filing those damn Library of Congress cards. How can anyone stand it?

"Excuse me, I need some help finding something," I say from behind the counter, pretending to be a researcher.

Berta looks a little bit startled.

"Yes," she says as if I am just another researcher, "How can I help you?"

"Well, I was wondering if you could meet me after work today?"

Berta's eyes couldn't have opened any wider if she was doing a yoga eye opening exercise. In fact, I think her ears are wiggling a little. And whoops. Peeking her head from just around the corner from where Berta is standing is Doctor Roberts, the curator of the Theatre Library.

"We're busy here, and I suggest you get busy as well.

You work for Mr. Healy, don't you?"

Suddenly, in the pit of my stomach I got the same feeling I had when Sister Julia caught me rubbing up against Tina Robustelli on the cookie line. I felt as though everyone in the class could see that little uncontrollable boner that came and went throughout the day during seventh and eighth grades. I might as well have been standing there nude, although I'm sure no one really noticed the tiny bulge in front of my pants. And I'm pretty much in the same situation right now. Minus the boner part.

"Yes, er, ah, I'll ah, just go back to what I was doing."

Doctor Roberts just stared at me, willing me back to my work area with her intense, narrowed eyes. Exactly what Sister Julia would have done.

"Well, welcome back," Greg says dropping his music book, putting on his overcoat and scarf in a single flamboyant motion. "I'm at lunch."

The turntables were spinning, and *Standing On A Corner* was blasting on the speakers, which I turned off immediately, plunging the room into a deep welcomed silence.

The in-house phone range.

"Audio."

"You almost got me in big trouble," Berta whispers.

"Sorry, Berta. Really, I'm terribly embarrassed."

"OK. But always call first. So what time?"

"What time what?"

"What time do you want me to meet you. And where?"

Oops. I can't help it. That uncontrollable eighth grade urge is back.

"Oh, around seven? How about at the main desk?

"I get off at six," Berta said as if she had no intention of waiting around for the likes of me, paused for a beat, sighed and continued, "but I'll be there at seven. Bye."

"Bye."

I guess guys don't change much from eighth grade, as I fantasize about rubbing up against Berta on the cookie line. And in the distance I hear a strange noise. It's faint, but it sounds like a burst of quick scrapes that slows until it finally stops. I trace the weird effect to Douglas' lab. The door is shut, but I can hear it. Repeatedly. So I knock.

"Who's there?" Douglas says from behind the closed door.

"It's Jerry."

The door slowly opens, and Douglas peeks around making sure I'm alone.

"Come in."

On his counter, he has set up his reel to reel audiotape editing system, which is really just an aluminum block with some slits in it, and a razor blade. There are several white grease pencils next to it, and tiny bits of audiotape on the floor, each one marked with a white "X."

"Could you hear me working up front?"

"Yes, but only because there's nothing on the speakers."

"Drat."

"Are you doing what I think you're doing?"

"Yes. I've transferred the opera to tape, and I'm removing every scratch by hand."

"Is it working?"

Douglas finally manages a trace of a smile on his face and gently taps his ear three times. "Listen."

He rewinds a few feet of tape by hand and presses the play button. Several seconds of *Der Rosenklavier* plays, with the usual slight hiss of an ancient 78, but no clicking noise from the scratch. It's perfect.

"That's beautiful, Douglas. How long will it take you to do the whole record?"

"Oh, maybe a couple of weeks. No big deal. But no one is to know. Ever," Douglas says with that trace of a smile long gone.

"You can count on me, Douglas."

"I've got work to do, excuse me."

"OK, see you later."

I sneaked out of there like I was leaving Frankenstein's secret laboratory and had just seen the monster. Maybe I did.

No matter how many times I go on a first date, I can't get used to it. It's a combination of opening night singing solo in a school play, and going up to bat in Little League with the bases loaded and two outs, down by three runs. I mean I've been chasing girls since before kindergarten. Ever since the very first time I finally cornered Mary Jane Martinson next to the dumbwaiter in the cellar, and had absolutely no idea why I was chasing her in the first place, going face to face with a potential wife is a terrifying experience. And they are all potential wives.

Even during the sloppiest drunken sexfest, deep in the back of your mind there was a glimmer of a ghost of a chance that the obesely overweight girl with the purple hair and bicycle chain around her neck could actually be "the one." Mind you, the thought occurred during the last snort of a fifth of Amaretto, and by the time the clock struck noon, was merely a disturbing unidentifiable memory as you tried to put the pieces together of how you wound up on the floor totally naked with a chubby purple haired stranger, and had bicycle chain marks all over the lower part of your body; but the spark was there, however briefly.

Berta is without a doubt the most beautiful female I ever had a date with. I've always been attracted to all kinds of colors, shapes, and sizes of girls and women, but it's always a sexual attraction that grabs me first. But even if a woman is drop-dead gorgeous, I could never have a relationship with someone who wrinkles her nose when she laughs and prefers dinner at The Plaza rather than egg creams and pretzels at Dave's Luncheonette on Canal Street; likes disco and hates The Ramones; wants to live in Scarsdale, not on Saint Mark's Place; shops in malls, not in army-navy surplus stores; would rather watch Saturday Night Live than hang out in a gin mill; only rides in taxicabs and won't ride the IRT.

"Hi, Jerry, sorry I'm late," Berta says as she bursts through

97

the front doors next to the main desk at the library. "I got off work a little early and met some friends for cocktails."

"Oh, no problem. Where'd you meet them?"

"At The Plaza. I love it there. Come on, let's get a cab and get out of here!"

Yeah, I know...but Berta is gorgeous!

"Great. Let's go."

Fortunately for my wallet, we didn't head back to The Plaza. But a nice family owned restaurant in the Village called The Minetta Tavern. The cab fare was killer, but I'll manage.

Dinner is always a great first date. Not only are you forced to communicate verbally the whole time, but you get to see what a person is really made of. Especially in an Italian restaurant. Even though it's my heritage, I insist that if you're a New Yorker and don't know your way around an Italian menu, you may as well be from a cave in Utah. Growing up in New York and not being accustomed to Italian food, or Irish bars, or Greek diners, or Black blues clubs, or Puerto Rican music, or Jewish delis or Polish Dairies or German brat houses, or Chinese dim-sum restaurants, or Indian vegetarian dishes or punk bars, or art museums, or street poets, or the Bronx Zoo, or The Circle Line, or the monuments in Yankee Stadium, or Rockaway Playland, means you haven't opened your eyes. You haven't taken advantage of all that is around you. You're not mining the streets of New York. It's all there. The streets are paved with it. You haven't been *living* in New York. I mean it would be like living in the Rocky Mountains and never seeing a mountain view. Or living next to the ocean and never going to the beach. Or living in the desert and never seeing the sand.

"What's this calamari?" Berta says as she looks up from her menu.

I'm devastated. That's like asking "Where's the Empire State Building?" or "What's the Staten Island Ferry?" or "Who's Frank Sinatra?." But to tell you the truth, all I see are those dark brown eyes, that thick black hair cascading down onto her large round breasts. Those lips made an even deeper shade of red by the house wine.

"You don't know what calamari is?" I ask delicately, hoping I don't reveal my utter disappointment.

"Of course, I know what calamari is! What is this calamari Siciliano like? I've never had it."

One step closer to a potential wife.

"I'm not sure to tell you the truth. I'll ask the waitress. Do you come to the Village much?"

"Not really, usually just around streetfest time."

"Like San Gennaro? Isn't that the one where they dress the Saint in a robe of dollar bills?'"

"That's my favorite," Berta says, her eyes twinkling from the candlelight in the red glass jar.

"You could pass for Italian."

"What do you mean, pass? Does that mean I've failed?"

"No! That's not what I mean. You look Italian, that's all I meant to say."

"I hear that all the time. I'm Spanish, but I was born in Cuba. Are you Italian on both sides?"

"No, Italian and Irish. So be careful because I'm a hot blooded drunk."

"I hope not. I hate drunks. All they do in my neighborhood is get drunk in the bar and gamble. Guys *and* girls, that's not for me," Berta says as she picks up a glass of red wine and drinks a substantial amount, while looking deep into my eyes with a coquettish grin. "But I do like a little wine once in a while."

The waitress arrived and Berta ordered perfectly, knowing her way around the menu and wine list, and more importantly, she did not order the most expensive thing on the menu as some first dates do.

Her long slender fingers are tipped with candy apple red fingernail polish that matched the red and white checked table-

99

cloth. And it's obvious by the way she rubs her fingernail along the rim of her wine glass and lowers her head to smile at me that she is in a deep flirtation mode. "Do you play any instruments?" She asks out of the blue, after taking her first bite of artichoke hearts.

"Yeah, a little guitar. I really just strum while I sing."

"You sing, too? I knew it. You look like you would be in a band."

"Why's that?"

"Well, your hair is long, and you're, I don't know, smallish, wiry kind of, thin in the face..."

"...I sound like a long-haired Barney Fife."

"No, I like long hair like yours. All the guys in my neighborhood look like Sal Mineo. You remind me of Jackson Browne."

"Jackson Browne? I've heard Barney Fife before, but never Jackson Browne."

"You do. It's your eyes. So soft and, I don't know, sensitive."

Here we go. The juices are flowing. Hormones, released. The needle is going into the red. The dashboard idiot lights are going full tilt: high temperature, check engine, check oil, fasten seat belt. When a woman compliments a guy on his eyes, she might as well be holding up a placard that reads: *YES. I'M INTERESTED IN YOU SEXUALLY. NO PROMISES, BUT YOU HAVE A SHOT.* It's the international symbol for saying that there's something about you that she digs. It's time to think of Yogi nude again.

"Well, I can stumble my way through a few Beatles, Kinks, and Stones, but no Jackson Browne."

"Maybe you can learn some."

"For you, I'll pretend to be Jackson Browne. Y'know... be a *pretender*."

Did I just say that? What am I doing?

"I like the sound of that," she whispers, slowly wiping the marinara sauce from the corner of her mouth, followed by her tongue licking her lips in an overtly sexual manner. "What was your major in school?"

100

"Funny you should ask. After weeks of coming up with fabulously important excuses, I sat my butt down, completed three incompletes, and this coming June will be receiving in the mail a diploma from The City University of New York Baccalaureate Program at Manhattan City College. That, along with exact change, will get me onto any bus in the city of New York. My major, believe it or not, is experimental theatre and film."

"Really? An actor? That's so exciting! Have you been in any plays?"

"Well, yeah, if you call spending an entire semester jumping up and down half naked pretending to be doing Macbeth."

"That's that modern theatre stuff, right?"

"Yeah, it's modern alright. As modern as aluminum baseball bats."

"Huh?"

"So the ball goes farther. That doesn't make the game better. I mean why try and make Shakespeare better? But modern dance, now that is better. I've pretty much been offered a job at this underground video center in SoHo called Radical Video Vision. I directed a nude dance video there."

"You made a porno video?"

"Not porno! Really. It's kind of like performance art. Do you know what that is?"

"Not a clue."

"OK, let me think for a minute on this...it's when you shine a spotlight on performers who think everything they say or do has some artistic value to it, no matter how stupid it is."

"Only the one you did had nude dancers."

"Exactly."

"Men?"

"No women. Even the women who were working the cameras jumped into the pile."

"Are you serious?"

"Serious as a heart attack."

"Do you think it's art?"

101

"Before I saw it, I would've said no, but now, yes, I think it actually is."

"I'd like to see it. Maybe you and I can make a video sometime. You know, one that's art."

Suddenly what could only be described as footsy was taking place under the table. She was rubbing her bare foot against my inner leg, and sipping her wine with a sexy Mona Lisa smile that had my jeans feeling too tight in the crotch, and boy is it getting hot in here.

I could be out of my league here. Thinking of Yogi nude metamorphises into thinking of Berta nude. This could be trouble. Then again, it could be the answer to twenty years of sexual fantasies.

"What was your major in college?" I ask, going in the exact opposite direction that my body chemistry is telling me to go.

"Library Sciences."

"Whoa! Lucky you, working right where you want to be."

"Luck has nothing to do with it. I know exactly where I'm going and how I'm getting there."

"I wish I could say the same."

"What's stopping you?"

"I don't know what I want."

"Now that's a problem we'll have to work on," Berta says holding up her empty wine glass, waiting for me to fill it.

"I can't imagine anything being called *work* when it comes to you and I," as I pour the wine into her glass.

"That's you and *me*," she says correcting my poor English. I hate it when my mother does that, but tonight, Berta can get away with whatever she wants.

"You and me it is," I say as we gently touch our glasses together.

The glasses kept getting filled and refilled. A new bottle of red wine replaced the old one, and something told me I was about to spend every last cent in my wallet escorting Berta back to Queens in a taxicab. But she wouldn't have it. She'd spend her own money

102

for a cab home. And go alone. She even flagged it down herself, totally aceing out a yuppie across the street on Houston Street.

As the cab screeched to a halt she grabbed my hand.

"Thanks for a lovely evening, Jerry. What's your full first name?"

"Jeremiah."

"Do you mind if I call you Jeremiah?"

"Not at all," I lied convincingly.

"Good night, Jeremiah," she said as she pulled me close to her, kissing me forcefully on the lips, actually starting to suck on my tongue. She gently pushed me away, knowing full well that she knew that I knew what she was communicating to me in no uncertain terms. "Call me tomorrow."

Since all of my blood had rushed to my lower extremities, I think I must have been pale white, but I managed to put a few semi-coherent words together. "Uh, yes. I will. Goodnight."

SCREEEEEECH

I was startled out of my puppy love hypnotic spell by a long black limousine that jammed on the brakes just past us. Now it's backing up towards us. As it pulled directly alongside of us, the nearly black rear window hummed as the electric motor lowered it, revealing a beautiful blonde dressed to kill; sequined black tube top barely concealing her breasts, eyes with so much black mascara and eyeliner, her face layered with pale makeup, her lipstick a deep shade of blackish red, in what looks to be an attempt to hide behind a mask.

"Hello, Jeremiah, what brings you all the way down here?"

Shit. Mary. Mary Markowski. My high school heartthrob. She doesn't look as strung out as she did on New Year's Eve when she was crying on the steps in the building, but to me she didn't look right. She was glassy eyed.

"Mary?"

"Yes, Mary. I thought that was you. I haven't seen you since New Year's. But that's our little secret, isn't it, Jerry?"

Sitting next to her is a fat bald guy smoking a fat cigar

which he is rolling around his wet lips, flashing a ridiculous diamond and gold pinky ring.

"Yeah, right."

"Say hi to Third Base for me, bye."

And with a patch of rubber, she was gone in her long black limousine.

Berta looked at me with one hand on her hip like a house-wife who caught her husband sneaking in the fire escape window at five in the morning.

"What the hell was that?"

"Oh, we went out the summer after high school."

"You'll have to do better than that, Jerry. How in the world do you know a hooker?"

"A hooker?

Could it be? No way! Mary Markowski? The same Mary Markowski who protected her breasts like Bruce Lee fending off a squadron of ninjas?

"Of course? Are you blind?"

"Not blind enough."

"And what's this 'our little secret' on New Year's? Was that why you disappeared that night?"

"You know we hadn't been properly introduced at that point, Berta."

The expression on her face quickly transformed from intense mock anger to sexy temptress as she stuck a candy apple red-tipped finger into my chest and pushed hard enough to hit bone. "Well, don't forget, we've been properly introduced now," she said as she moved her face closer and closer until just when I expected a tender kiss good-bye, she bit me playfully but hard on my lower lip.

She pivoted on one foot, quickly jumped into the cab, and sped off into the direction of the Mid-Town tunnel, blowing me a kiss from the back window. I don't know why but I've never been this scared and nervous while standing in the street with a boner before.

104

"Jerry! Telephone!" My Mom yells from the other side of the apartment, waking me from my red wine induced deep sleep.

"Be right there!" I wondered who would be calling me at seven-thirty 7:30 in the morning.

"Hello, Jerry here."

"Hi, Jerry, this is Sandra from Radical VideoVision. Sorry to call you so early but I've got so much to do, and we have a shoot this morning on top of everything else, and we never got to talk the other day about whether or not you thought you would take Amy up on her offer of a job as a technical assistant here at the studio and I really need to know because I'm already making out next week's schedule, and we've got five shoots planned, a workshop starting, and a video festival that starts in two weeks, and I have to know if you are going to be available to come in on a semi-regular basis starting yesterday. So what do you think?"

"I had a hard time following all that. I'm still waking up here."

"No rush, no rush. Can you call me by ten though because I've got some performers coming over and I need to load up the truck with some things...."

"...Sandra, yes, I will call you back before ten."

"Thanksbye," she said cramming the two words into a single syllable as she hung up.

By ten o'clock? Shit. I could go to work an hour early at nine and force Mr. Healy into giving me an answer regarding my work situation at the library.

"Jerry, can you come in here please?" My Mom yells from the kitchen.

Mom and Dad are sitting at the formica kitchen table surrounded by piles of boxes almost reaching the ceiling. I haven't been in the kitchen much the past few days and didn't realize how far along their packing has progressed. It looks as though they are just about done.

"Well, well, well, looks like Florida is just a hop, skip and a jump away for you two lovebirds."

"Jerry, the truck is coming this afternoon," my mother says, breaking the news to me gently.

"What? This afternoon? Why didn't anyone tell me?"

BANG

Nothing gets your attention like a Dad banging his fist on a formica table.

"Dammit, Jerry, we've been leaving notes on this table for days. 'We're almost ready Jerry. We could use your help, Jerry. When you have some time, Jerry.' We're out of time, Jerry, and you didn't help us one damn bit. You're mother and I are very....pissed off."

I couldn't talk. I felt like such an asshole. Such a selfish little prick.

"What it *is,* Jerry," my mother says in her usual cut to the chase way, "we needed your help with little things, Jerry, but that's done. What we need now is to know that you're going to be OK. Are you?"

Parents. I just pray to God that one day, I'll have half the understanding, compassion, and love to give my shithead twenty-three year old kid.

"I'll be fine. I've got a request in at the library for a raise and more hours, and I've got a job offer at this SoHo artsy fartsy video studio."

"I knew it! Pornography! That's what they learn from these radical colleges," my father rants as he hits the table again with slightly less force.

"It's legit, Dad. I swear. They're accredited by the college, they're....in the yellow pages."

"OK, but if I ever find out you're involved in pornography..."

"Stop it, Alby, Jerry would never be involved in that sort of thing would you, Jerry?"

"No, Ma."

My father prepares to get up from the chair by holding his knees and pushes off with that familiar grunt that older men with joint problems make.

"Hnnnnh. Jerry, this is very important," Dad says as he picks up a manila envelope that he had stashed in a drawer for several years, knowing one day he'd get to use it. "In this envelope is all the crucial, important papers..."

Oh, no. Here comes that awful moment all grown children dread. When parents start revealing all the secret information they've been hiding under underwear and socks for decades. The confidential documents about wills, and cemetery plots, and insurance polices, and who gets what, and who's getting buried where, and there's still room on top of grandma and grandpa for one more...I can't take it.

"....very valuable paperwork for the car. Here's the registration, all my maintenance records, triple A..."

"The car?"

"Yeah, you're going to have it for a month or so, and when the weather's a little better and we're a little settled you'll bring it down to us. You'll need all this stuff."

"Thanks, Dad. I won't screw this up. I swear."

"You're a good son, Jerry. But don't mess up that car."

I love being in the library before it's opened to the public. The silence envelopes you. No complaining customers at the checkout desk refusing to pay their thirty-five cent fines. The workers look calm and relaxed sitting behind their counters and desks quietly going through index cards and *The Library Science Journal*. This is the library most workers imagined when they were majoring in English and Music and Art History and Library Sciences in college. Not the library of a rainy Friday afternoon when the hordes of street people come in for several hours of sanctuary, requesting every *Opera News* since 1940.

Mr. Healy is the first in every day. He looks so peaceful at his desk sipping tea from his cup and saucer as he reads his *New York Times*.

"Excuse me, Mr. Healy?"

"Come in Jerry, come in. I've got some good news for you," he says putting down his teacup and motioning towards the chair in front of his neatly arranged desk.

"Thank you."

"I've looked into your request, and although it's not exactly what you hoped for, it is more than I thought I'd be able to arrange. Here it is," Mr. Healy says with the pomp and circumstance of the mayor about to read a proclamation in city hall as he holds up a single typed sheet of paper. "I'm authorizing an extension of your hours from ten to twenty hours a week to twenty to 30 hours a week. In addition, effective immediately, your hourly wage will be increased from two dollars and thirty seven cents an hour to two dollars and forty two cents an hour." He looks up from the sheet and adjusts his glasses pushing them up his nose with his middle finger. "I must tell you, Jerry, I had to bend quite a few rules to be able to institute this. I've pretty much told everyone else in the department that there is a wage freeze. I hope you'll respect the confidentiality of this arrangement and understand the effort that I've put into this."

All I could think about was the lousy nickel raise. In my head I'm trying to calculate how much this translates into. Probably five more hours a week; that's like ten bucks, and oh yeah, twenty-five cents a day, so let's see eleven bucks a week. Shit.

"I really appreciate it, Mr. Healy. I'll take this as a vote of confidence in my job performance."

"Well there is one thing, Jerry. I read your employee evaluation, and there are two areas you must work on. Punctuality and filing the Library of Congress cards."

"Yes, Mr. Healy, no problem."

"Fine, Jerry," Mr. Healy says rising from his chair and extending his hand for me to complete the deal with a handshake. "I'm sorry I couldn't consider making you staff at this time, but if you continue to show progress, I'm sure that is something that can be addressed in the future."

"Thanks, Mr. Healy," I say, numb from the realization that my handshake has sealed my nickel an hour raise.

"I wouldn't have done this if I didn't think you had some promise as a staff employee. But I've gone out on a limb for you here, and this shall never leave this room, but I feel I owe you special consideration out of respect for your Uncle Hans."

"Thanks again Mr. Healy," I say backing out of the room. Uncle Hans dedicated his entire life to the library, and the best his survivors can get out of it is a nickel an hour raise.

As I stood outside the door to my apartment, I could only imagine the sadness I would feel when I saw the emptiness of the only home I had ever known. It was the first and only apartment my parents had. Of course, they had hoped to move to a nicer, bigger place someday, but that day never came. First the girl came, then the boy, and as the bills mounted, a nicer, larger, more comfortable apartment would have meant less of the things they had vowed they would provide for their children. So they slept on the pullout sofa in the living room so that the boy and the girl could each have their own bedrooms. There were vacations, even though they were only to Rockaway bungalows. There were always plenty of toys and blankets and pillows and clothes and food because the rent was so low. Oh, the plumbing was bad and the hot water and winter heat infrequent and irregular, but the scrimping and saving and sacrifices paid off. They raised two college graduates in this tiny two-bedroom pre-war apartment. And now they were living the dream of every Bronxite: retiring to Florida.

As I opened the door and looked into what I had only known as a cramped apartment overcrowded with decades of memories and furnishings that somehow were never quite worn out enough to be replaced, the sadness I expected to overwhelm me never materialized. Suddenly the tiny two-bedroom apartment looked light and airy. With the piles of boxes gone, and only a pull out sofa and an overstuffed easy chair in the living room, the place actually looks comfortably large. My bedroom still has my dresser and my bed, but all the things that my sister left behind when she moved out are also on the way to Florida. What I always thought was a cramped roach-infested dump has suddenly become a funky bachelor pad with unlimited possibilities. Taped to the refrigerator door is a note that reads: "Dear Jeremiah, We decided to leave you the refrigerator and the kitchen table. Even though you're now on your own, remember...if these walls could talk, just imagine what they'd say if they ever saw you doing anything we didn't approve of. God bless you, and see you soon! With Love, Mom and Dad."

BANG BANG BANG BANG.

Someone at the door. My first visitor.

"Who is it?"

"The welcoming committee," Stubby's voice echoes through the hallway.

I swing the door open to see Stubby, Merrill, and Terry, each holding large brown bags brimming with beer, booze, pretzels, and Lord knows what else.

"It's party time!!!" Stubby announces, leading the way into my apartment, switching on his radio, which begins blasting the chorus of *Brown Sugar.*

"Finally, another house we can fuck up besides mine," Stubby says as he begins unloading the items from his large brown paper bag into the refrigerator; two six-packs of beer, a bottle of vodka goes into the freezer, a half gallon of orange juice, assorted candy bars and four packages of Sno Balls.

Terry and Merrill drop their bags off next to the fridge, head for the sofa, and take their familiar poses. Merrill pulls out a banged-up, dog-eared book which today is something called *The Sufis.* Terry pulls out a small white sack, that at one time held some roll-your-own tobacco, and begins rolling a joint.

"Shit," Terry announces. "I'm out of weed. Stubby, kick in some bread and I'll go cop some."

Such words have never been uttered within these walls. This is where my parents brought home their baby buntings. Countless parties were hosted here for christenings, communions, confirmations, graduations, birthdays, anniversaries, and even an ordination party when my cousin became a priest. I wouldn't dream of ever keeping an illicit substance in this home when my parents were living here. Discovering a half-smoked joint would have catapulted them into a rage worthy of inclusion in *Reefer Madness*. It just wasn't worth taking the chance.

"Terry, keep it down, huh," I inexplicably instructed him for no reason. "Uh, the neighbors may hear you!"

"Sorry," Terry complied, also without reason.

"Here's ten bucks, get a lid." Stubby says unrolling a ten dollar bill that was more than likely previously used to snort something.

"Where are you going to get it?" I ask Terry, still reluctant to even mention drugs in my parents home.

"Where do you think? On the sixth floor," Terry replies stating the obvious.

"No, you're not!" I shout above the closing "yeahs" of *Brown Sugar*.

"What?" Terry says incredulously, looking at me as though I had gone insane.

Merrill looks up from his book, and Stubby slowly turns to me with a perplexed expression on his face.

I snap off the radio.

"Don't fucking go up there! Don't support that motherfucker. He's fucking up this entire building,"

"Who the fuck are you?" Terry says, not raising his voice to the level I already have.

"Jerry, we've been buying from Ronnie for months. What's the difference?" Stubby says, trying to console me with a hand on my shoulder.

"Have you seen the skells that have been coming in here to buy shit from him? There's graffiti and people pissing in the stairwells, and who knows what the hell else these pukes are doing?"

"Jerry, you think this is the first time there were pukes in this building? Come on," Stubby says.

"Yeah, but they were pukes we knew. They were pukes who knew better than to rip off people that they knew. These assholes buying from Ronnie don't give a shit about this building. You know how many burglaries there have been the past six months? Probably a dozen."

"I don't give a fuck, I'm going to get some weed," Terry uncharacteristically declares with a definite air of rage in his voice.

"Well, don't fucking come back then."

"Who'd want to, you faggot?" Terry says as he walks through the front door and slams it shut.

Faggot. Yeah, I'm a faggot. That's the word assholes like Terry like to use to get my goat. It's a euphemism for somebody who went to college.

"Fuck him," I say to Stubby and Merrill who are both staring at me in disbelief.

"Are you OK?" Stubby asks.

"I'm fine. I just don't want anyone supporting that scumbag Ronnie Donnelly."

"Jerry, everybody buys from him. He only deals weed."

"Bullshit. To *you guys* he only deals weed. You see the junkies riding the elevator, don't you?"

"Oh, big fucking deal," Stubby says, obviously fed up with me.

Merrill closes his book, places it on his lap, and begins stroking his chin. "I think Jerry's right, Stubby. There's been some bad karma in this building. I get a bad vibe when I walk into the lobby."

"I've lived here my whole life! Nothing's changed!

It's always been a shit hole!" Stubby yells at Merrill.

I don't think Merrill is used to being yelled at by Stubby, which is why Merrill is usually reading and not talking

"That's precisely why you don't see it, Stubby," Merrill says, calmly. "It's like a room that gradually begins to smell because dirty laundry is slowly piling up. You don't notice the offending odor as it increases in small increments; but when someone else enters the room, it overwhelms them."

"You trying to tell me I got b.o., or what?" Stubby says as he begins sniffing his armpits.

"No, that you are blind to the gradual deterioration all around you because you are immersed in it."

"You guys are really bringing my head down. I'm going to Third Base. I'll catch you guys later, alright?" Stubby says as he puts on his huge green army surplus overcoat and heads for the door.

"What about your stuff in the refrigerator?" I yell just before he closes the door behind him.

Stubby scrunches his face so that his dark bushy eyebrows nearly meet his lower lip. "Waddyuh think, I'm never coming back again or something? Just don't let Merrill finish it off," he says with mock concern.

I'm trying to recall a time when Merrill and I were alone together. I mean, ever. Even though Merrill is almost always around, I don't think he and I have called each other or made arrangements to do something without Stubby. Since he's a few years older than I, and we didn't hang out together every day growing up as kids in the neighborhood, we don't have that free and easy familiarity with each other. For instance, even though Stubby is pissed at me, I know we'll both get over it. But since Terry is really Stubby's close buddy, the fact that he's pissed off just might have longer lasting consequences. But it is interesting that Merrill has sided with me on this issue.

"Do you want a beer, Merrill?"

"Yes. I do want a beer. That would be just great."

As I look through the brown bag that Terry shoved in the refrigerator, I notice that it's the same beer that Stubby brought; Ballantine India Pale Ale. I grab two of Terry's green bottles.

"Terry and Stubby brought the same kind of beers," I tell Merrill as I hand him the bottle and an opener.

"Oh, I know. It's just that it'll taste better knowing that Terry paid for it," Merrill says with a devilish grin.

Merrill has the best Afro in the neighborhood. Even better than the Black guys. He has a perfectly round eastern European face with Roy Rogers eyes. Although he never changes the Afro, he is constantly experimenting with different arrangements of facial hair. Pork chops, fu man chu, the Amish look, goatees, full beards, David Niven mustache. My favorite was when he shaved a perfect circle in his full beard underneath his chin. He then drew with a permanent black marker one of those stupid happy faces. And when he threw his head way back, revealing the happy face, you never knew what the reaction would be. Unfortunately, when Merrill was high on mushrooms, he kept showing it to a biker chick in a bar in The Village, and her biker boyfriend punched Merrill right in his happy face. He let the beard grow over it as soon as the cut from the guy's skull ring healed. He's perfectly clean shaven now.

"Terry can be weird," I say to Merrill, not wanting to reveal my true feelings, which are that Terry can be a real pain in the ass when he's not stoned out of his mind.

"Terry is weird. Usually. When he's not high on weed, he's very nervous."

"That's exactly why I haven't smoked in years. It makes me nervous," I say as I open my bottle of ale and look under the cap.

"What did you get?" Merrill asks referring to the puzzle under the bottle cap, which is the primary reason we buy Ballantine India Pale Ale.

"It's too easy," I say as I hand the cap to Merrill.

"It's not that fucking easy," Merrill says laughing.

The puzzle consisted of a "1/2" next to a drawing of

an egg; and underneath the letters "GR," the number "8," and a crude drawing of a knight's helmet.

Merrill is perplexed as he begins to slowly mouthe the clues. "Halfffff, eggg, grate, helmet, half, egg, grate, hat, no, have, egg, grate, hat, wait no, I've got it, I've got it, I've fucking got it, have, a, great, night!" He jumps from his chair runs around the room waving his arms high in the air in victory, jumping for joy. Then suddenly stops.

"I take it you're not as thrilled with my accomplishment."

"Merrill, we've had that one a dozen times already."

"I know, I know, I'm just enjoying the moment that's all. Are you?" Merrill says as he sits back in my father's favorite easy chair, out of breath from his impromptu celebration.

"Am I....what?"

"Enjoying the moment? Are you here, now, enjoying the moment? This moment? Now?"

"Uh, yeah, yeah, yeah. Right, be here now and all that shit. Yeah, sure."

"Why don't I believe you?" Merrill says, looking at me dead serious.

"I solved the pale ale puzzle before you did, why wouldn't I be fucking ecstatic?" I say trying to communicate the fact that I'm not in the mood for his philosophical inquisition.

"OK, you're right. You did solve the puzzle. Way before I did. Are you pissed at me, also?"

"Who says I'm pissed at anybody?"

"Well no one *said* it. But some things don't have to be *said* to be obvious."

"Trapped like a rat," I say holding up my beer. "Here's to the unspoken misery of mankind. The bloated nothingness of existence."

"Ernest Holmes?"

"Huh?"

"Are you quoting Ernest Holmes with your 'bloated nothingness' reference?"

"No, I never heard of him."

"He's a philosopher who founded a religion called 'Science of Mind.'"

"You know I remember in high school in senior year I had a fanatic religion teacher named Father Heck. That always killed me. He should have been named Father Hell, but I guess that would've been too obvious. So Father Heck gave us an assignment, which was to write a paper on what we thought heaven was. So I wrote this paper about how our bodies were like radios, and our souls were like radio waves, and when we passed away it was as if the radio was broken; but the waves went out into the universe and became one with all the other radio waves in the universe, which was God. I didn't research it at all. And when he handed me back the paper he wrote across the top 'Teilhard strikes again!' I had no idea what he was referring to, and when I looked into it he was inferring that I had ripped off my theory from something Teilhard de Chardin had theorized."

"That's amazing," Merrill said with his head half cocked like a puppy listening to a whistle. "Teilhard is high on the list of Roman Catholic mystic philosophers. Maybe the only one a conservative priest at a Catholic high school would be familiar with."

"You've read him?"

"Oh, yeah. I read a lot. Reading about religion and philosophy is like a puzzle. It's like every book reveals clues about the meaning of it all, and you have to put them all together."

"Why don't you read mysteries?"

"The same reason I don't do jigsaw puzzles; what's the point? There's no payoff. It's just a mind game. A distraction. If there's no true meaning, no gain, it's worthless. It's our job to find things in life that we don't understand, and bring them together to form something greater than each of those things individually."

Merrill's words were sinking deep into a part of my

116

brain I don't know much about. It could be the part of the brain where drugs and alcohol do their job of numbing so well. The place where questions you don't want to ask are hidden. The place where our bloated nothingness grows like a cancer.

"Did you know Charlie the Chinaman?"

I wasn't quite sure why I asked Merrill the question. Maybe it was the way this conversation reminded me in some way of the things Charlie said. Things I didn't understand, but for some reason I remembered the words and stored them in my brain for a later use. What is it that makes us remember things we don't understand at the moment but file away anyway? Maybe for the same reason my Dad stashed that manila envelope away.

"A little, yes I did," Merrill says with a gentle smile trying to form. "So sad. So tragic."

"Did Stubby tell you anything about the circumstances?"

"Did Stubby tell me anything about the circumstances? Let's see. Well, yeah. He was kind of freaked out about re-membering that Charlie said something, or not said, but hinted that he had this stash hidden in the store because he didn't trust anyone. It was very puzzling. Cryptic. It blew our minds."

"You and Stubby?"

"Me, Stubby, and Terry."

I had a strange sense come over me. I'm not at all high, and haven't smoked dope in years, but I'm experiencing that feeling you get when the pot sneaks up on you and something that you looked at a million times suddenly looks strangely different.

"Did you tell anybody about it?"

"Tell anybody about it? Are you grilling me?"

"No, I'm not grilling you, but there could be more to the death of Charlie the Chinaman."

"Are you stoned?"

"No, I'm not stoned."

"No, I don't think we actually *told* anyone."

"What does that mean?"

"Well, you know Terry when he's high?"

"Unfortunately, yes. What about it?"

"Don't get pissed."

"What about it?"

"We wanted some weed so we went to the sixth floor..."

"...Who went?"

"...me and Terry. And Donnelly had some good shit, and there were some other people scoring there, if I remember correctly..."

"...yeah?"

"...I think Charlie the Chinaman may have come up in conversation when I was in the bathroom."

"You think? Why think? Did he mention Charlie or not?"

"Perhaps."

"Perhaps?"

"Well, I think maybe he did, but..."

"But what?"

"Well, I was having a bad shit, OK? I didn't hear every word because I was having a bad shit. I thought I heard Terry mention Charlie the Chinaman, but I don't know what exactly was said. This is freaking me out. Can we talk about something else?"

"Shit. This could be important."

"Why?"

"Swear not to say anything to anyone?"

"Cross my heart and hope to die."

"If one of the scumbags at Donnelly's knew about the stash, then maybe somebody could have killed Charlie for it."

"The cops said it was a suicide."

"I was there. I talked to one of the cops. They don't want to deal with a murder. A Chinaman with no family is found hanging from a strap? Who cares? The less paperwork the better."

I walk over to Merrill, still sitting in my Dad's favorite chair, and lean over, putting both my hands on the arms of the chair. "Somebody could have killed Charlie to get the stash."

"I wish you didn't tell me all that. That's a heavy trip you've just laid on my head."

"Yeah, well, Charlie's head trip was heavier. So heavy, it broke his neck from his spinal cord."

PPPPSSSSSSSHHHHHHHHHHTTTTTTT

Merrill jumped straight up in the air and I swear I think the top of his Afro may have touched the ceiling as he shouted "What the fuck is that what the fuck is that what the fuck is that?"

"It's the damn valve on the steam radiator. It pops off every once in a while."

I picked up a dish towel and twisted the rocket-shaped valve back onto the radiator, careful not to get burned by the steam. Once the valve was screwed back in, I stared at Merrill so that there was no misunderstanding about my seriousness. "Don't say a word to anyone."

"I cross my heart. And hope to die," Merrill whispered as he made the sign of the cross over his heart and then kissed his fingers.

"Are you hungry?"

Merrill looked troubled. It's easy to see his mind is pondering something other than the pretzel rods and Taystee cakes stashed in the kitchen.

"I'm not hungry," he decides. "I think I should be going."

"Are you sure? The guys may be coming back."

"No. They aren't. I think I'll go to the Base. They'll probably wind up there. Mind if I take some beer for the road?"

"No, take a lot."

"I'm not going to tell anyone. Ever. I swear," Merrill says looking at me eyeball to eyeball, making sure I understand the gravity of his declaration.

"Thanks, Merrill."

Merrill went into the kitchen and took two of the three six packs of beer, the bag of pretzel rods, and an apple my parents left behind him in a brown bag.

I took another beer and sat in my father's favorite chair and popped the top off. Damn. That same stupid puzzle under the bottle cap. Again.

KNOCK KNOCK KNOCK

Merrill must've forgot something.

"It's me, Merrill."

I open the door to see Merrill standing there silently pointing to the wall next to my door in the hall. I take a step through the doorway to see in very large black letters "Latin Eagles" scrawled on the wall just inches from my door.

"Sorry," Merrill says dejectedly. "Want me to help you clean it?"

"Nah, I'll do it myself."

"See ya."

"Yeah, see ya."

Nothing a little elbow grease and a couple of pints of turpentine couldn't cure.

SEVEN

My schedule is set. Work at the library from 9 a.m. until 2 p.m. Monday through Friday and work at Radical Video Vision from 3 p.m. until 7 p.m. Thursday and Friday, and 10am to 6pm on Saturdays. It's certainly doable, and I should be able to pay the bills. And I just know one of them will turn into something good. I could get a staff position at the library, which would mean security, better money, and benefits. Or I could get Sandra's job at Radical Video, teaching video workshops and running the place. And with Berta looking like she's hot to trot, my life looks like it's actually starting.

The clickety-clack of the railroad tracks actually makes a good background for thinking. As long as you're able to filter out the other noises, smells, and sights of a morning rush hour commute on the number one train.

"Morning, Greg."

"Well, look who's on time for a change. I understand we'll be seeing a little bit more of you." Greg says between bites of a bagel as he pores over *Backstage*.

"Don't get any ideas, Greg," Douglas says as he writes something with his fountain pen on a small pad on his desk. "The library has strict rules about provocative dress."

Greg desperately grabs the telephone. "Operator, quick, send the emergency psychiatric team. Douglas is attempting humor."

"Oh. Ha," Douglas says, totally deadpan as he hands me the note he had been writing.

"Well, it's a pleasure to be here," I say as I read the note Douglas handed me: *1) file cards, 2) clean headsets, 3) call Berta.*

"Did she call?"

"Well, that didn't take long," Greg says with his mouth mostly full. "You could've waited until you were here more than a minute before you started attending to your personal affairs."

"She called at 8:55a.m. You can call her at her desk," Douglas says conveying a sense of being a tolerant boss. "I'll be in my workshop for a while, er, transferring."

I'll bet Douglas is still working on taking the scratches out of *Der Rosenklavier*. Sharing a secret with him gives me a comforting sense of power, and a special bond.

"There are many piles of cards to file and headsets to clean upstairs," Greg says, now working on a danish. "So little miss theatre department will just have to wait."

"No problem," I tell Greg as I head up the back stairway that will put me a little bit closer to the theatre department.

"That's very obvious, Jerry," Greg shouts after me just as I'm halfway up the steps.

I've never seen Berta looking disheveled or unkempt. There she sits with a cart filled with books and papers next to her as she goes through each one methodically, making notes, putting them in an appropriate pile, and switching little cards from one pile to another.

"Good morning." I say, stopping in front of her desk.

"Good morning, Jerry," she says, not even looking up from her job at-hand. "But I'm extremely busy. If you called a few minutes ago, I might have been able to chat. I'll call you later." Finally she looks up at me. "Sorry," she says accompanied by a weak smile and a not so subtle hint for me to get lost.

I rush back to my work area, and the worst part of my day: a pile of greasy headsets just waiting for me and my bottle of Windex. I wonder if they'd be this greasy if short hairstyles were in vogue.

"Jerry, come into my office for a moment," Mr. Healy says, peeking his head around the corner, and not waiting for a reply. I gladly drop a really gross headset with a few long hairs still stuck to it. Probably Tiny Tim's, I thought to myself.

"Yes, Mr. Healy," I say, standing just inside his doorway.

"Everything is in order. All the paperwork is being processed. I believe it's just a matter of sixty days." Mr. Healy rattles

122

off as he thumbs through some papers.

"What is, Mr. Healy?"

"What is what? Ah, here it is!" He says discovering the file he was searching for.

"What's a matter of sixty days?"

"Oh," he says, realizing I'm still in the office. "Your staff position will be processed in sixty days."

"That's fantastic Mr. Healy!"

"Well, let's just say that it helps to be connected, right Jerry?"

"Thanks. This couldn't have come at a better time for me."

"Well, frankly it could have come at a much better time for us, but we did what we felt we had to do. You're Uncle would have liked it this way, Jerry. But I hope you understand that there's a certain level of commitment we're talking about here. Between you and me, Jerry."

"I totally understand."

"OK. Run along, er, I mean, good day."

"Yes, thanks again."

I must have filed away more Library of Congress cards in one day, than I have in the previous ten months combined. I was on such a roll, I even forgot to return Berta's call. And now that it's quitting time, I definitely don't have time to call her, since I've got to get down to SoHo for my first full day in the workaday world as a studio technician, whatever the hell that means, at RadicalVideoVision.

Sandra and Amy were at the studio for all of five minutes before they left, leaving me with a corkboard of index cards prioritizing my projects. Just unraveling the cables in the control room should take two full days. But with one visit to a Canal Street store where I picked up some colored tape, marking pens, and plastic tie-wraps, I was on the way to dressing cable the likes of which were never seen before in this place. And within three hours, the control room looked almost organized; a far cry from the disastrously tangled mess of electronics barely kept together with gaffer's tape. They even entrusted me with a key. I can come and go as I please. That's what amazes me more than anything else. Why would they trust me? They don't really know me. I know one thing for certain; I wouldn't trust me.

I've been here less than four hours and this place already looks almost presentable. Just sweeping the floors, mopping up, dusting the most obvious dusty flat surfaces, putting things into neat piles, and untangling wires and cables, makes Radical Video look like it's not a junkyard office anymore. And this is one of the more successful of the "underground" video establishments that have sprung up around here.

Up until a couple of years ago, the only people making documentaries were filmmakers. And generally speaking, documentary filmmaking is exorbitantly expensive. In order to make a good documentary, especially in the cinema verite' style, the shooting ratio of shot footage to footage actually used in the film is astronomical; sometimes over a hundred feet of film for every foot used. But with the advent of small format videotape, the tape is relatively cheap and unlike film, there is no expensive film processing. The real problem has been that the technical quality of the half-inch reel to reel videotape is so poor. But that's all changing with the introduction of the three-quarter inch formatted video U-matic system. Instead of reel to reel videotape, the tape is encased in a large cassette, much like an audio cassette, but about the size of large rectangular slice of Sicilian pizza.

What this means is that filmmakers can now afford to shoot documentaries on videotape and shoot as much footage as they need to create their video verite' masterpieces. And all over The Village and SoHo video "resource centers" and workshops have sprung up to teach people the wonders of video production. And if they're smart, they don't have to invest a dime of their own money.

I know for a fact that the folks here at Radical Video charge

124

three hundred bucks a head to a studio filled with eager students, just for teaching video basics on a weekend! And that's on the dusty old equipment they barely keep running around here. And an eight-week course, fully accredited towards a masters degree, can cost over a thousand bucks a head. And with TV stations quickly converting from film to the three-quarter inch video format over the past couple of years, there is actually a job market for people with video skills. Hence, the need for training no matter how shoddy the school or inept the instructors.

"We're back," Sandra announces, pushing a dolly that must've been left behind when the original sweatshop owner left this building in the late forties. It's piled high with flimsy cardboard boxes filled with assorted tapes, cables, microphones, and lighting equipment.

"How did it go?" I ask as I help her unload.

"Well, don't say anything, but Amy forgot to bring the good microphone that she keeps in her desk, so we had to use the crappy mikes."

"What were you shooting?"

"We're doing a documentary on the effect of gentrification of The Bowery."

"You mean, how people moving into decrepid storefronts and abandoned lofts and cleaning them up is displacing the bums who've been squatting there."

"They're not bums. They're homeless. And, yes, well, sort of what you said."

"Oh."

"Hey! Jerry!"

"What?"

"This place looks great! It looks...nice. What did you do?"

"Well, I used a few secret procedures I learned from an old German who owned a deli where I worked. I took a mop and a bucket, filled the bucket with hot water and some ammonia, and swabbed the decks."

"Where did you get a bucket and a mop?"

"In the storage closet in the hall."

A scratching sound could be heard on the front door.

"Someone help me please!"

I opened the door to see Amy standing there holding a camera as if holding a baby. Instead of swaddling clothes, it was wrapped in cables.

"I don't have the strength to move another muscle. I have to take a hot shower. I must smell like vomit and BD whatever it is."

"BD twenty-twenty," I said. "We call it bad dog. It's a fortified wine."

"What does that mean?" Amy asks genuinely curious.

"They add a little extra alcohol and some insecticide to give it a little kick."

"Smell this, Jerry," Amy says, holding out a baggy stained sleeve from an oversized sweater.

"Uh, I'd rather not."

"Smell it."

Since I was under orders, I took a whiff it.

"Yeah, it smells kinda like bum puke."

"I knew it. Ruined. This sweater cost $150! I'm tossing it."

And Amy did. Right in front of me, she tore the thing off, revealing once again her naked upper torso. I've already seen more of Amy's tits than my last three girlfriends combined.

"I'll be in the shower for a while," Amy says, leaving a trail of clothing towards the bathroom at the rear of the studio.

The front door pushes open, and a tiny bespectacled young man with a pencil thin mustache, that looks as though it could have been drawn on, wearing a long black wool overcoat, a red beret and black gloves appears.

"Oh, hi, Charles!" Sandra says as she kisses him on the cheek.

"Hi. Is Amy here?" He says pretty much ignoring Sandra,

126

and definitely ignoring me.

"No she's in the back taking a shower. Can I get you something?" Sandra says, totally kissing up to this guy, whoever he is.

"Oh, this is Jerry, Charles. He's our new studio tech assistant."

"Hi," Charles says with the least amount of effort possible. "And yes, have you finished the proposals?"

"Yes, they're done. All three of them. Ford Foundation, N.E.A., and the Corporation for Public Broadcasting," Sandra says as she rushes over to her desk and starts frantically searching for some files on its cluttered top.

"The deadline is this week, Sandra," Charles says to her.

I have a feeling that he's said this more than once this week.

"And we need this funding if we're going to survive another quarter."

"Yes, Charles, they're all done. I know they're here....yes! Got them!" She pushes her hair back from in front of her face and proudly presents them to Charles.

Charles lifts up his glasses and holds the page about four inches from his face. "Which ball did you use for these? I thought I told you to use the 'times new roman' ball on the IBM typewriter?"

"Shit, I forgot to switch the balls?" Sandra apologizes.

"Well, OK, I guess this will do. I'll read them and let you know if everything is OK," Charles says as he exits as suddenly as he appeared.

Sandra lets out a sigh of relief at his exit. I can see that a visit from Charles is not exactly a highlight of the day.

"Who's that?"

"Charles Bradley. He *is* Radical Video"

"Who is he?"

"He represents a group of investors that controls this place. They own the building across the street too."

"The loft building? The one with the West-East Restaurant

on the bottom floor," I say knowing full well that the restaurant across the street is one of the trendiest, and of course, expensive, eateries in all of SoHo. "They own that whole building?"

"Yes. Now will you help me unload here."

I helped Sandra unload the boxes of gear, and neatly stored everything in new cardboard boxes I bought down on Canal Street. Afterwards I marked all the boxes so you could identify what was in each one without opening it. What a concept!

Amy emerged from the rear of the studio in her bathrobe, this time tied tightly around her waist. I could see she was beginning to notice my handiwork as she got closer.

"Jerry, I like what you've done here," she says as she vigorously rubs her hair with a towel, which by the way most definitely is already loosening the belt on her robe.

"This is the easy part. Once I get down a couple of layers into the Paleozoic period, I think I can make some real progress here. I was thinking of putting a black curtain across the front of the studio here so there's some separation between it and the office. And I'm going to put some shelves up along that wall, and then reinforce the shelves and editing console in the control room."

"Do we have the petty cash for that, Sandra?" Amy says as she begins toweling off her neck, shoulders, and yes, under her arms, showing more and more breast.

"I'll have to check. We went over budget last month when we bought those new light fixtures that are sitting in the back."

"Where did you buy them?" I ask, getting ready to demonstrate how a lifetime of looking for bargains can finally impress someone other than my Uncle John, who prided himself in paying less than cost on everything from apples to automobiles.

Sandra gives me a suspicious eye, as though I'm trying to outdo her, which I guess I am. "We bought them at Macy's."

"Well, at least you can return them. I'll bet I can get them at half the cost down in the lighting district on The Bowery. Same with all your office supplies, electronics, and even bathroom stuff."

"That's wonderful, Jerry," Amy says walking past me, and just as she gets right in front of me, towels herself under her armpits giving me a bird's-eye view of her breasts, erect nipples and all. Like she doesn't realize what she's doing. "We can use someone with your sensibilities to help us get to the next level. Show Jerry where those fixtures are so he can get on that, would you Sandra?"

"Yeah. Come with me Jerry," Sandra drones as we head to the back storage area. "I tried to do something with this place when I started here, too. I wanted to make my own videos, which is why you're probably here. But after I wrote a grant proposal for them, and got them $50,000 for it, I've been spending the vast majority of my time tracking down grant money and writing proposals."

"I guess you're good at it. How much have you gotten for them?"

"Don't ask. It'll make you sick. Here's the stuff," she says pointing to piles of unopened boxes of ceiling fans, light fixtures, and much to my surprise, brand new three-quarter inch video equipment.

"You've got new three-quarter inch gear here?"

"It just came in last week. It's on loan from Sony. Another one of my proposals, if you know what I mean."

"It's just sitting here?"

"Well, nobody knows how to put it together."

"Think I should take a crack at it?"

"Absolutely."

"I'll do it," I say, thrilled at the thought of putting together the latest in video equipment. "Hey, Sandra," I say just as she shuffles away. "Is that West-East Restaurant any good?"

"Oh, yeah, like I could afford eating there?"

"Yeah. Just wondering."

Once Sandra leaves, I tear into the virgin boxes revealing state of the art video equipment neatly packaged with connectors, cables, and operating manuals. And right behind the wall of gear and lighting fixtures are cardboard boxes filled with videotapes. And on those boxes are labels reading things like "Nude Nuances, takes 1 through 5," "Naked Selves half-hour jam," "Pure Passions vol. 12." Eureka, I have definitely found it!

It's freezing. It must be below zero with the wind chill. And the empty late night subway train sucks in the cold air as it zooms through the tunnel. Once we hit the elevated portion at Dyckman Street, the hard plastic seats feel frozen. Since I've become busy all of a sudden, I'm trying harder to cut down on my attendance at Third Base. But on a night like this, I need a stop-off point to break up the long, bitterly cold walk home.

As always, I discreetly take a peek in the frosted front window to see if it's worth my while going in. If it's just Mr. Boyle and Noel drinking boilermakers watching *Mannix* reruns I'll just brave the chill for the next three blocks and head home. But I can see a larger than normal weeknight crowd with the jukebox turned on. And, of course, Stubby, Merrill and Terry at the middle of the bar in their usual positions, with Mikey Lenihan and Patty Dunn at the end of the bar.

I push the outer door, and upon opening the inside bar door, I'm immediately enveloped in the almost too warm radiator steam heat.

"Hello, lads," I say, patting Terry on the back, trying to make amends.

"What are you drinking," Stubby says, with no hard feelings from the previous night's agitations.

"A nip," I tell him, and turn to Terry. "I'm sorry about last night, Terry."

"Yeah, me too," Terry says good-naturedly. "But if I had a knife, I swear I would've stabbed you, I was so pissed off."

"Well, that's about as sweet an apology I've ever had," I say, making an effort to not reciprocate his passive aggressive hostility, and we touch bottles in a toast. Noel makes his way over towards us as he wipes down the bar.

"Hello, boys. Have you heard the one about the termite who walks into the bar and says, 'where's the bar tender?'"

There's total silence among the three of us, until Merrill bursts into uncontrollable hysterics. Stubby, Terry, Noel, and I begin laughing, not at the joke, but at Merrill's reaction as tears begin rolling down his cheeks.

"I don't get it," Terry says as Merrill's chortles die down to mere laughing whimpers.

Noel starts again, "A termite walks into the bar, and says, where's the bar tender?"

Terry is blank.

Noel tries again, "Not where's the bartender. But where is the bar tender?"

"Ohhhhh. Now I get it. I still don't think it's funny," Terry says as he finishes off his nip.

"Did you hear..." Noel starts, but is interrupted by Stubby.

"Not another one Noel, Merrill might explode."

"No, no, did you hear that Mr. Boyle was mugged. Right in front of your building, Jerry. And the fuck of it is, he didn't have but three dollars on him, and the fucker stepped on his face so fucking hard you can see the outline of the bastard's fucking heel on his face."

"That sucks," Stubby says. "Can he identify the perp?"

"No, sucker-punched him. Thinks he was young and white though," Noel says as he continues wiping the length of the bar.

"I'll bet it's another one of Donnelly's customers," I say to no one in particular.

Silence. They know I'm right.

"Hey, where've you been?" Stubby says quickly changing the subject.

"I'm a double dipper. I work half the day at the library and I've got this new job at this underground video studio."

"You mean you're working down the subway just like me?"

"No, like counterculture, hippie underground TV."

"No shit. Like videoing concerts and stuff?"

"Well, yeah, but more like documentaries and artsy theatre performances," I say and as the words leave my mouth, I realize what's coming next.

"Hey, you do any of that nude theatre stuff like 'Oh...Caldonia'?"

"Calcutta. Well, actually, ah, yeah," I reluctantly admit, knowing full well what this will eventually lead to.

"Hey, everybody, Jerry's making porno," Stubby announces to the entire bar.

"Thanks, Stubby," I say as the first wave of comments come flying from all directions: "I'll give you twenty bucks to be a fluffer," and "Hey Jerry, you're half-Irish! What the hell is somebody with a little Irish dick doing in a porno movie," and "Let me know when you're holding auditions."

"Well, you're finally in the biz, you ought to be proud," Stubby says, happy to be breaking my balls in the truest neighborhood fashion we've all come to expect. If you're getting your balls broken by the guys in the bar, you know you're in good standing. If nobody ever breaks your chops, watch out.

"It's not porno, but I did direct a nude dance piece."

"I'll bet she was a piece," Mikey Lenihan shouts from the other end of the bar.

Lowering my voice a little, I say to Stubby, "Really. It's not porno. But there are these women who are totally into this nude dancing performance art thing."

"*Only* women," Stubby says with even more enthusiasm in his voice.

"Hold it down, will you? Yes, but it's not porno."

"You mean to tell me that a bunch of nude chicks piling on to music didn't get you hot?"

"Well, yeah, it did..."

"That's porno."

132

"You're hopeless, Stubby. Anyway, I was hired as a studio tech to clean the place up, and help out with the studio."

"That's cool. Good bread?"

"Nah. Two bucks an hour."

"Now that's obscene. Why so little?"

"You can't find jobs like these."

"Well, I guess, but shit, they should have the decency to throw you a few bucks, and maybe let you jump into one of them lesbo pile ons."

"Yeah, we'll see."

"Hey, I got a cousin who's into that shit."

"Porno? Why am I not surprised?"

"No. Video. My cousin Victor."

"I thought Victor was a tow truck driver?"

"He is, but he's into this video shit, too."

"He's a tow truck driver, and he's into video?"

"Yeah, he drives around during the graveyard shift and shoots accidents and homicides and shit."

"As a hobby? What is he a fuckin' ghoul or something?"

"No, he's a buff."

"A buff?"

"Yeah, ya know. A fire freak. And he gets paid by some guy that sells it to a TV station."

"Are you sure?"

"I'm going to see him tomorrow night. I'm working the overnight over in Woodlawn and I'm gonna hook up with him. Hey, get it? Hook up with a tow truck driver?"

"Hey everybody, Stubby made a funny!" I scream at the top of my lungs, shocking the hell out of everyone, because it's actually a cue for everyone to sing a song to the tune of "Camptown Races": *Stubby is a piece of shit, doo dah, doo dah. Stubby is a piece of shit, all the doo dah, day. All the doo dah day, all the doo dah day, Stubby is a piece of shit, all the doo dah day.* Which everyone sings in fine masculine voices, much to the delight of every patron who has had more than a couple of drinks.

"Stubby, when you talk to him, ask him what kind of camera he's using, alright?"

"You got it. Hey, Noel, Sambucca for everybody!" Stubby says, waving to the entire bar.

"See, when you got a real job, you can afford to do shit like this."

"Yeah, well someday I might get lucky," I tell Stubby, secretly praying that I never have to get a real job. "Oh, and another thing. I think I'm 'in like.'"

"With one of the lesbo orgy freaks?"

"Nah, I don't know if you remember, but on New Year's Eve...never mind, you wouldn't remember...but there was this extremely not from this neighborhood piece of exotic love..."

"Here? You must've been more fucked up than I thought..."

"No, it's confirmed. Turns out she works in the same library I do, and we already had the let's get it out of the way dinner, and I think she may be into, dare I say, having a sexually charged relationship."

"Then *she* must be fucked up."

"Go ahead, mock me, oh great masturbator, but this could be a keeper. Oh shit, I forgot to tell you! While Berta and I..."

"Berta? What is she an old Jewish washer woman?"

"It's actually Berta, without the "h", fuckface. She's Cuban. Anyway, just as we're standing there playing kissy face on the street corner waiting for her cab, who pulls up in a fuckin' pimpmobile but Mary Markowski looking like a high-priced call girl."

"Get outta here."

"I swear. She stopped the limo to say hi. She wanted me to see her. You know I used to go out with her."

"I know, I know, you went out with her the summer after high school, and didn't even get your finger wet, who cares? But do you really think she was hooking?"

"Well, the guy next to her looked like a bald and fat pork belly salesman from Idaho."

"That's freaky. She could've had any guy she wanted around here, and don't get a swelled head putz, but she could've had any guy, including mister I'm not even from the neighborhood, famous soap star actor Dickface Dillon. Did you know that asshole was in *Soap Digest* and said he was from the suburbs of Boston? What a schmuck."

"Even more disturbing is, what are you doing reading *Soap Digest*?"

"It was in the dentist's office."

"You haven't been to the dentist since the tooth fairy stiffed you."

"Hey, I wonder if Donnelly is her pimp, or if he's in the dark like everybody else around here?"

"That's a scary thought. But I still want to know why she'd stop a limo to say hi to me if she was hooking?"

"Maybe she needed to be seen."

"That's even scarier."

Merrill suddenly pulls both of us by the shoulders towards him. "You guys better keep it down. Look who just walked in," Merrill says, tipping his head in the direction of the cigarette machine next to the front door.

It's Ronnie Donnelly. Wearing a jean jacket with a tee shirt on a night when it's cold enough to keep rats in their holes. He probably knows everybody in the bar, but he's pretending to be invisible. And a few of the guys, like stupid Terry, are regular customers of his. But Ronnie doesn't say a word as he drops the exact coinage into the slot and pulls the rod connected to the Kools. I can hear him muttering something, like "motherfucker" and walking to the bar just next to where Terry is staring blankly at the TV screen watching Kojak interrogate some black soul brother in a feathered pimp hat. Noel is at the other end of the bar, talking to Mikey and Patty.

135

"'Scuse me, can I get some matches here?" Donnelly shouts to Noel. Up close you can see that his teeth are almost grey, and he's got more pimples than a high school freshman. His cheeks are sunken, and he keeps touching his nose and snorting like a prizefighter. It's hard to believe that this is the same guy who was the best basketball player in the park up until just a couple of years ago. And just as dumbfounding is why Mary Markowski would sit in a cold hallway on New Year's eve and cry her eyes out over him. Terry, in a sudden burst of lucidity, notices Ronnie standing right next to him.

"Hey, Ronnie, what's happening, man? Got any good shit?" Terry says thinking that no one else could hear him.

Ronnie picks up the matches that Noel practically threw at him from the other end of the bar and lights a Kool dangling from his lip, doing his best to totally ignore Terry.

"Thanks," Ronnie mumbles towards Noel, and looking at Terry completes his thought with "asshole" and walks out into the bitter winter night.

"I guess he didn't hear me," Terry says, turning back to watch the black pimp break down in tears and confess all to Kojak.

Merrill taps me on the shoulder and whispers, "Maybe Donnelly didn't hear Terry."

"He heard him," I tell Merrill coldly. "Pricks like Donnelly hear everything. I'm heading out."

"Wait, I'm ordering another round of shots. Noel, shots for the bar," Stubby yells down to Noel in deep conversation at the other end of the bar. "Stick around for a while, Jerry. Things could get interesting. You know, people on nights are just getting off from the job."

It seems there's always something just around the corner that could happen. If it's around five, people are getting off work. If it's around eight people are coming out after dinner. If it's ten people are stopping in after going to a movie. If it's midnight, people are getting off from the night shift, and just about every couple of hours there's another reason why a sudden rush of extremely interesting people may burst into the Base. Yeah, right.

"Are you staying, Merrill?" I ask Merrill, who is already digging his nose deep into *I and Thou,* by Martin Buber.

"Ah, yes. I am staying. My father is bombing the roaches this evening. First he closes all the windows for three hours while the bomb is going off. Then at precisely three hours and one minute, he opens every window in the apartment. So if the Raid doesn't kill them, the bitter cold will. And me, too, so I'm staying. I'll have a shot of Schnapps, please."

"Alright. I'll stay for one more round."

Which turns into two and three, and suddenly it's four in the morning again. And a long crooked walk home on the coldest night of the year.

Much to my surprise, the apartment isn't quite freezing, and the radiators are steaming up a storm. It's almost comfortable.

Charlie is in his cage with a towel over it. Birds, even pigeons, are quite sensitive to temperatures. I peek in to see him sleeping peacefully. His wing is almost better, but I don't think I'm going to release him back to the wilds of the Bronx until there's a taste of spring in the air. And I'm not going to just let him fly out the window either. I'm going up north into Westchester or maybe even Rockland County where it's nice so that he doesn't have to live on the top of an el pillar. I want him to be somewhere where he can actually sit on a tree branch and not have some ten year old throw a beer bottle at him. Somewhere where there's quiet when the sun goes down. Where the sidewalks aren't covered with frozen dogshit. And you don't have to look over your shoulder and into every dark doorway as you walk down the street. Somewhere where older guys like Mr. Boyle don't get there faces stepped on, leaving footprints on their foreheads.

But I've got to get up in the morning and work two jobs. I'll just drop here and get some rest.

(pause for sleep)

BBRRRIIIINNNGGGGGGG
BRRRRIIIINNNGGGGGGG
BRRRRIIIIINNNGGGGGG

Shit. Who the hell is calling me at seven in the morning while I've got severe membrane outrage?

"Hello?"

"Hi, Jerry. Hello, Jerry, boy"

"Oh, hi Mom, hi, Dad. It's early."

"Aren't you working today?" Dad says sternly.

"Yeah."

"Then it's not early. How's everything going?" Dad says a with a little bit of friendliness seeping into his voice.

"Fine, fine, fine."

"Are you eating?" Mom asks obviously worried.

"Oh, yeah, like a pig."

"Listen, Jerry," Dad says, "We'll need the car two weeks from today. We feel we'll be settled in. Is that OK with you?"

"Two weeks? Gee, Dad..."

"...now what's the problem," he jumps in.

"Well, I've got two jobs I'm working, and I have a good shot at going staff at the library."

"Staff? That's great! That's full-time civil service, right?"

"Yeah. So I don't want to screw anything up."

"Well, we know you can work it out, Jerry. Listen, we're using Vito's phone, so we don't want to run his bill up. Call us when you make the arrangements. So long."

"Bye."

Shit. Two weeks. I guess I could drive straight down on a weekend if I had somebody to go with me. But I'd have to find somebody to drive down who would be willing to spend the money to fly back. Or somebody willing to go one-way.

It's still colder than a slaughterhouse freezer on the train. If

138

there aren't any delays on the local and I catch the express at 96th Street I could make it to the library on time. Otherwise, I'm already looking bad as Mr. Healy processes my paperwork to go staff. Strange... but I swear I can hear... accordion music over the shake, rattle and roll of the subway car. It stops momentarily, and the car door at the other end of the train jerks open revealing a tiny shadow of a woman with deeply sunken eyes, a knit cap, and a massive accordion that seems to block three-quarters of her body. She is wrestling with the giant musical instrument as she balances it on her tiny emaciated frame. A home made redtipped cane is hanging from her right arm, and there is a tin baker's measuring cup bolted to the front of the red accordion.

"Goddamn it," she snarls, obviously having trouble getting the squeeze box into a comfortable position. Just about everyone in the car pulls their eyes from their Spanish novellas and *NY Posts* and *New York Daily News* and Bibles and whatever else they use to escape from subway world into someplace, anyplace else. But the sight of this sightless woman bursting and cussing onto the scene forces everyone to check in to the here and now of the moment.

She doesn't wear dark glasses to hide the deformity of her mutated eyes set far back into a face too thin. It's easy to imagine what her skull would look like. Once she has the large instrument in a workable position, she begins pressing a few keys which, after about three notes I recognize as the introduction to *When You're Smiling*. Like a locomotive slowly picking up steam from a dead start, she picks up her rhythm and plays the thing... well... alright. There's no doubt about it! It's *When You're Smiling*. As she sings and plays, she begins to walk ever so slowly, doing an excellent job of demonstrating her subway legs as she gives every passenger an ample opportunity to dig into their pockets and purses to come up with whatever they can. Since she's obviously so totally blind, it would be easy for riders to ignore her performance and not risk any embarrassment of being noticed. We all do it every day. There are pathetic excrement-soaked beggars, articulate black militants, whacked out junkies, Korean Moonies, well dressed Jehovah Witnesses, people posing as priests and nuns, and the occasional opera singer, but I've never seen so many people opening handbags, wallets, and change purses and actually watching this ghost of a woman sing *When You're Smiling*.

Perhaps it's precisely because she is blind that people don't mind staring at her. Normally, making eye contact with someone on the subway is the kiss of death. An invitation for the solicitor to hit on you even harder. But with this sightless wonder, there's no need to worry. As she approaches my end of the car, I can see that I'm not the only one who is getting teary eyed. How trusting she must be of the human race to walk totally blind in this no man's land of violence and danger. Everyone knows she has cash on her, and that accordion would be worth a few bucks to any pawnbroker. But she bravely pushes forward singing her happy song through her strained toothless grin with the tightly knitted brow made even more intense as she reaches for the high notes.

What a sight. Suddenly, the scene strikes me in a totally different way. What a documentary this would make! You can't make this stuff up. Radical Video has a video documentary festival coming up, and I can have access to the equipment. This has all the elements of a winner. A poor woman beggar singing her bittersweet songs juxtaposed against the working class masses and the cold dark oppression of the subway. Considering that Amy herself is doing a documentary on the street people of The Bowery, I'm sure she'd be thrilled with this. Oh, this is so good!

I follow her to the next car. And in a rare moment of courage, I begin speaking just before she is ready to hit up the next train full of listeners.

"Excuse me, but I'm a... film student... and I was wondering if you'd be interested in being in a, ah, film?"

"What?"

"I'm a film student, and I was wondering if you'd like to be in a film?"

"Who are you?"

"A film student."

Knowing this is going to be too difficult, I take out a piece of paper and begin writing.

"Here's my name and phone number. Call me. And here's..."

I reach into my pocket and grab all the change in my pocket, which is probably about two bucks.

"And here's a little something," I say dropping the loot into her tin cup.

She doesn't say thanks, but shoves the scrap of paper in her coat pocket and begins playing her instrumental intro to *When You're Smiling* as she begins her walk through this car, and probably every car on the whole train.

Hey! There's the express! Perfect. What a morning!

Catching the express got me to work a couple of minutes early. Here's my chance to finally hook up with Berta at work. It's been a few days since our big first date that ended on a bizarre note, thanks to that bizarre encounter with Mary Markowski.

She looks as beautiful at 8:52a.m. as she does anytime during the day. She has the kind of face that doesn't need makeup. But applying the slightest shading on her cheekbones, a subtle dark line around her eyes, and a touch of lipstick only a shade redder than her natural lip color puts her in the category of: "Thank you, God! I can't believe she sees anything in me."

"Is this a bad time?" I ask Berta after approaching her desk with total stealth.

"Oh, you frightened me," she says, dropping several of the dreaded Library of Congress cards.

"Unfortunately, I've been told before that I have that effect on women."

"You've got a couple of minutes. Mrs. Roberts will be right back," Berta says, getting back to her filing duties. "You know you're not easy to get ahold of. Aren't you ever home?"

"I've been quite busy."

"At midnight?"

"You called me at midnight?"

"Twice and nobody answered."

"Darn, I'm going to have to fire that butler of mine!"

"Well, where have you been?"

"Well, besides working two jobs and trying to figure out how I'm going to make a trip to Florida over a weekend, just hanging out with the guys."

"Are you sure about that?" Berta says looking up from her cards and giving me that smile she seems to only give when there's some kind of relationship question buzzing through her head.

"About what?"

"About the guys?" She coyly asks.

This can't be happening. Is she serious? We've had one date and she's asking *me* about hanging out with the guys. That's the most obvious, nothing to hide way to not so subtly drop a three ton hint that she's concerned about me seeing other women.

"Yeah, you're welcome to join us sometime. You've already seen them naked."

"Oh, *those* guys," she says resuming her alphabetizing. "I didn't realize you liked guys who danced around naked in public places."

"Oh, just on major holidays. Those guys are my best friends."

"You better be going now. Mrs. Roberts will be here any second."

"Oh, by the way, I want to tell you about this woman I met on the train. She's going to be the subject of my first documentary."

"You meet women everywhere, don't you? Are you really going to do your own documentary on her?" Berta asks with renewed curiosity.

"Maybe. If it works out and I can get it into the video documentary festival at Radical Video."

"That's marvelous! Will you call me later?" She eagerly

asks.

"Yeah," I say as I back away. "She's a musician! Wait until you meet her! Bye-bye"

Berta just looks at me with her head slightly tilted in a bewildered stare. For a woman of such mysterious beauty, she's tipping her hand a little bit too much. In my limited experience of dealing with potential girlfriends, things never seem to be what they appear to be. My guess is that if she's acting so concerned that I'm seeing other women, that may be the last thing on her mind.

"Look who's on time again," Greg exclaims as he begins unwrapping a hot breakfast sandwich of some kind. "Douglas wants to see you in his studio."

"Thanks. Hey, that smells good. What is it?"

"Provolone on a Twinkie," Greg says sarcastically.

Douglas' sitting at his workbench, dutifully editing more of what I suppose is the damaged audiotape of *Der Rosenklavier*.

"Hi, Douglas."

Douglas turns to me with a big, friendly, smile across his face.

"I'm just about done! It turned out much better than I thought it ever could. I'll just do this one last edit..." Douglas says as he swiftly slices the tape set across the aluminum block with the speed and grace of a Japanese chef and splices it to a reel. "Listen." He rewinds the tape and presses play and an absolutely seamless version of *Der Rosenklavier* floats through the studio speakers. "Well?"

"It's flawless!"

"It is, isn't it? And I understand congratulations are in order!"

"Oh, you heard about my possible staff job?"

"Indeed. I'm reluctant to offer too much encouragement, but I'm happy for you if that's what you want."

"That's very kind of you.'

"And I'd like to take you, er, let me rephrase that, how

would you like to go out for dinner this evening, as a congratulatory celebration?"

"Gee, Douglas, that's very nice. I do have to work at my other job until at least eight-thirty..."

"I was going to suggest nine."

"Well, yeah. That's great. Can we do it downtown?"

"Where do you work again?"

"SoHo"

"OK, fine. I know a couple of great places not far from there in the West Village."

"Great. Let's talk later."

"Splendid."

"See ya," I say as I exit, closing the door behind me.

I've never been asked out to dinner by a gay man before. I know I shouldn't have the slightest bit of apprehension about going out with him, I mean *going to dinner* with him. Shit. How stupid. Douglas' a great guy. A brilliant guy. And he's my boss! What a homophobic moron I am to give it a second thought. And it's totally paranoid of me to think it's anything other than a gracious gesture. I hope.

EIGHT

I can't believe what a pigsty they've let RadicalVideo become. You'd think that with students coming in here for classes and the occasional representative from some arts foundation stopping by, they'd try and maintain the place. Not to mention the fact that sweaty nude women roll around on a floor that hasn't been properly cleaned since this place was filled with Italian immigrants making corsets with pedal powered sewing machines.

"Sandra, would you mind if I rented some cleaning equipment for the floors?" I ask Sandra, who is currently sitting in front of a Sony reel to reel video player, transcribing an interview with an alcoholic street person who is drooling and swilling rotgut wine between sentences.

"Hold on," she says, intensely concentrating on her penmanship.

"Sandra, may I make a suggestion?"

She reaches to the large knob on the player and snaps it off. "What?" she says tersely.

"Isn't that the original tape you're looking at?"

"Yes, it is. Now may I continue?"

"Stopping and starting like that is really going to stretch that tape."

"I have to transcribe it."

"Well, what you should do for the interviews is just let it play through one time, and tape it onto an audio cassette recorder, and transcribe it from that."

"Hmmmm. I guess you're right. And go ahead and rent whatever you need to clean this place up. I'm allergic to dust, and working here is the worst."

"Can I ask you something personal?"

"Shoot."

"Do you like working here?"

"Liking it here isn't an issue. This is one of the few

places in the country that is exploring small format video. Can you keep something to yourself?"

"Scout's honor."

"Well, Amy is in negotiations to shoot a documentary for PBS. Network. It will be the first TV documentary to show a man having a sex change operation on national television. It's for May sweeps."

"Anyone I know?"

"Amy's uncle."

"Oh. That sounds...er, groundbreaking."

"It is. But to answer your original question, it's not a matter of liking it here, there's nowhere else I could get this kind of video production experience."

"I was just wondering. You've been looking kind of stressed."

"Thanks for noticing. I've got to get back to transcribing. By the way, do you know what something called the 'horrors' are?"

"You mean like in terms of alcoholism?"

"Yes."

"Well, the horrors are when someone who is an alcoholic wakes up screaming several times during the night and has no memory of it the next morning. It's a real pain for the guy sleeping in the next bed, believe me."

"That's exactly what this guy in the interview just said."

"Oh," I meekly respond knowing full well that Sandra now knows a little too much about my personal life. "Do you know when Amy is going to be around?"

"Well she's supposed to come by to pick up the transcriptions between seven and seven-thirty. Why?"

"I'd just like to discuss something with her?"

"Can I help you?" Sandra says, revealing the fact that she's not too keen on me having a private chat with Amy. I'm definitely sensing a little territorial marking going on.

"I need to talk to Amy, but I can tell you that it's about

an idea I have for a documentary."

"Don't bother. They've got a full plate for the next year or so."

"OK, well, I'll just run it by her."

"Don't say I didn't warn you."

"Uh, thanks. See ya."

As I walked through the bitterly cold alley, taking a short-cut to Canal Street, dodging derelicts picking through overflowing dumpsters, I thought to myself.... so this is show biz!

Douglas and I decided to meet at a restaurant in the West Village called The Eagle's Nest. It's right on Christopher Street which, of course, is the bull's-eye of the gayest area in New York City, and maybe the whole country. I don't usually walk down Christopher Street much since nearly all the establishments are strictly gay oriented. But it's one of the nicest parts of the city with it's well-kept brownstones, tree-lined narrow streets, and active street life. And occasionally I do find myself walking across Christopher to get from The White Horse Tavern on Hudson (where Dylan Thomas and Jack Kerouac are known to have tipped a tumbler or two) to Bleecker Street, which is the heart of the Village music scene. One time Stubby and I were walking along Christopher Street to go see the band, Elephants Memory at Mill's Tavern because we thought John Lennon might show up, and just at the moment Stubby commented to me that the place was teeming with physically fit handsome gay guys who were staring at us, a car with Jersey plates slowly passed us and called *us* faggot motherfuckers. Lennon never showed, but David Peel did. And that was certainly the highlight of the evening. Just when Peel went into the opening line of *Up Against The Wall Motherfuckers,* the owner tore ass onto the stage in a rage and started yanking everybody's cords out of the amps.

Even on a cold night like tonight, with a threat of snow in the air, Christopher Street is a hotbed of activity. There are even lines outside of storefronts that don't even have signs. From the outside of The Eagle's Nest I can see through the front window that it may be the absolute darkest restaurant I've ever seen. There doesn't seem to be any light source other than a single candle on each table. As I enter, I recognize music from the Broadway show *Most Happy Fella* being played softly by a man at a piano. A woman wearing a flowing tie-dyed dress with a matching turban of some kind approaches me.

"May I help you?" She asks with a charming smile.

"Yes, I'm a little late, and I'm supposed to meet a friend, Douglas Wagner."

"Yes, he asked for me to keep an eye out for a cute, small, wiry guy. Please come this way."

Uh-oh. The small, wiry part I'm used to. But cute?

Douglas is sitting at the table sipping from a glass of wine, and from what I can tell, he's already finished half a bottle. He's wearing one of his brightly colored hippie ties and a wool jacket, complete with suede elbow patches.

"Jerry. You've made it!" Douglas says, standing and warmly shaking my hand with both his hands.

"Sorry I'm late, but I had to freshen up a bit. I didn't have time to really change clothes but hopefully I'm presentable."

"Don't even think about it," Douglas says, pouring me a glass of red wine. "Oh, I didn't ask. You do drink wine, don't you?"

"Oh, yeah. Although the kind I drink usually has a screw off top."

"Well now that you're becoming a civil servant, you'll be swigging from corked wine bottles. Cheers."

"Cheers," I say clinking my glass with Douglas'. "Is it definite?"

"Well, let's just say that with the evaluation I gave you, and from what I saw of Mr. Healy's recommendation, you, my friend, are in like flint."

"Thanks, Douglas. This means a lot to me."

"I certainly hope so," Douglas says, intoning a certain amount of intrepidation in his voice.

"You hope so, what?"

"Mr. Healy and I went a little bit out on a limb to add a staff position to the department. It could have ramifications."

"Like what?"

"Not *like* what, *such as* what," Douglas says, correcting me. "Well, other departments have been told no new positions may be added, and it could even mean longer between raises for the rest of us."

"I see what you mean."

"But let's not dwell on that! Let's choose our food," Douglas says, handing me a menu. He moves his glass, his silverware, and his bread dish so that he can open the menu flat on the table. He then pulls out his tiny memo pad and short bowling alley type pencil, and three pennies, and begins his I-Ching ritual of shaking the three coins in his clasped hands and writing down the results. After about a half dozen times, he pulls out an I-Ching book, opens to a dog-eared page, and begins writing down more information.

"Have you tried just throwing darts?" I ask, immediately thinking I may have insulted him.

"Only on pictures of ex-boyfriends," Douglas says smiling. He catches the waiter's attention. "Excuse me, but another bottle of Cabernet. I'm sorry. Is that OK with you, Jerry?"

"Cabaret it is! I love Liza Minnelli just as much as the next guy in this place."

"Jerry, that's Cabernet as in Cabernet Sauvignon."

"Don't mind me. I think the last time I had wine was when we stole half a bottle out of the sanctuary when we were altar boys."

The waiter doesn't seem too keen on hearing anymore of my anecdotes and tilts his head down, looking directly at Douglas. "Will you be ordering now?"

"Not just yet, thank you," Douglas politely replies.

The waiter pivots and quickly walks away. Douglas shakes

his head. "They can be very prissy in this place."

"That can be annoying."

Douglas empties what was left in the wine bottle into his glass and dumps it down his gullet like it's water.

"Do you find Greg and me annoying?"

"No, not at all. But Greg can be a little prissy once in a while."

"He can be a total bitch. We've been through a lot together. He's a very dear person to me," Douglas says, barely above a whisper.

My mind began to race. I just hope Douglas doesn't lay some heavy "we used to be lovers" trip on me and drag me into the middle of it. It's hard enough getting dragged into that with a guy and a girl in the bar, never mind two men who you just may wind up working with until retirement.

"I think I understand Greg."

"I thought I did," Douglas says coldly.

The waiter appears at the table with a fresh bottle of wine. "Here's your Cabaret, old chum," he sings as he pirouettes away from us.

"That was rude," Douglas says, I think trying to gauge whether or not I'm pissed off.

"Are you kidding? If this was the bar I hang out in, he would've dragged the entire kitchen out to sing what a piece of shit I am to the tune of *Camptown Races*."

Douglas seemed to perk up. "Really? Would they do that?"

"At the drop of a hat."

"That's hilarious. I love that. What's the name of the bar?"

"Third Base."

"Let's see, I remember this. First base is a kiss. Second base is a feel. And third base is...."

"....you are way off base. Third Base, subtitle: last stop before home."

"Oooh, I love that," Douglas chortles as he pours himself a

full glass of wine, and also fills mine. "What makes it so perfect is that it's so true. To many people it isn't just the last stop before home, it is home."

"Tell me about it."

"Is it a typical Bronx saloon?"

"What might that be?"

"Oh, let's see.... a friendly Irish bartender. One or two colorful alcoholics who rarely leave their stools, a regular group of people who stop in to discuss sports and their sexual escapades. And hardly any women," Douglas says while swirling the wine around in his already half empty glass. "Which sounds exactly like any one of the bars on Christopher Street."

"I never thought of that. Here's to something else that we have in common besides our jobs: our hangouts!" I say holding my glass up for a toast.

We both down our glasses, and I'm beginning to notice that I'm getting well beyond buzzed. And by the way, Douglas appears to be having trouble focusing on the menu. I think he is, too.

The waiter took our orders. Douglas ordered another bottle of wine, which was a huge mistake, and by the time that was half gone, our food was served. The meal was perfection from top to bottom. But it seemed every forkful was followed by another sip of wine. Then it dawned on me. Despite the large salad, pasta primavera, several loaves of bread, lemon sorbet, and two cups of coffee, I am crocked.

"I think we should be going, Jerry," Douglas says in that way that drunk people who don't want to appear drunk talk and overcompensate by over-enunciating every syllable. "Do you need a lift?"

"Do you think you should be driving, Douglas?"

"How else would I get back to Jersey?"

"Well, as long as you think you're OK. I'm just need to get to the number one train."

151

"I'll give you a lift. I'm just around the corner."

As we walked out of the restaurant and down the street, I felt a little uncomfortable realizing that everyone probably thinks he is an older man out with his young boyfriend. But then again...who gives a fuck what other people think. We approached Douglas' VW Beetle, he opened the passenger side door for me, and I got in.

Douglas immediately started the engine and began revving it.

"It takes forever for this thing to warm up. But it has never failed me once."

There was a long, awkward silence as Douglas pumped the gas pedal.

"Jerry, I really like you."

I thought to myself, I'm fucked This is it. This is the moment I've heard about from girls in the bar. The moment the boss comes on to you.

Douglas is staring straight ahead. "I'm a gay man. And you're a good looking guy."

I don't know what I might do. I am a little drunk. I know I shouldn't punch my boss out, but I just don't know what's going to go on in my brain if he keeps climbing up this tree.

He turns to look at me with a crooked smile on his face. "But what's really neat is that even though I like you a great deal, and you are a cute guy, I'm not at all sexually attracted to you. It's weird."

"Douglas, I am so glad you feel weird about this."

We looked at each other with silly smirks and he threw that bug into gear. I'm only going a few blocks to the subway station, but narrowly missing a shopping bag lady and running a yellow light that was a nano second from dead-red, had me anxious to jump out of the car and into the relative safety of the subway. Compared to driving with Douglas, that is.

"Douglas, are you sure you should be driving?"

"I think I'll take your advice and maybe drop in one of my usual haunts over on St. Marks."

I know there's a gay bathhouse over there that I've heard Douglas and Greg talk about. I usually disappear when the conversation gets a little too explicit for my heterosexual ears. But what goes on there!

"Don't do anything I wouldn't do," I jokingly warn Douglas.

"Are you kidding? The things you wouldn't do cost extra," Douglas says as he waves, peeling out and swerving down the nearly empty, thank God, street.

The subway ride home was uneventful and quick. I thought better of stopping off at The Base in light of my present situation of still buzzing from way too much *Cabaret* and headed home. As I headed up the outside stairs in the courtyard of my building, I thought I heard something on an upper floor fire escape. It was pitch black and difficult to see anything six stories up, especially through the dark fire escape railings. Just then I heard what sounded like metal hitting metal, followed by a stage whisper going *"ssshhhhhh"* in the darkness above.

I began to panic. Fire escape windows are the most popular point of entry for scumbag junkie burglars, and Stubby's windows are just about where the sounds seem to be coming from. I rushed into my apartment and called the cops, only to be met with a reply that unless I saw someone actually entering an apartment there was nothing they could do, and to call back if I do, but it's not exactly a priority.

I ran up to Stubby's apartment and banged on the door loud enough for him to hear me even if he was asleep. Nothing. It's almost a sure thing that he's still at The Base. I ran back downstairs to call him there.

"Hi, Noel, is Stubby there? This is Jerry."

"No, he hasn't stopped in yet. He could be working overtime tonight. Can I give him a message?"

153

"No, thanks. I'll talk to him tomorrow."

I grabbed a flashlight and a butcher knife, pushing it up the sleeve of my winter jacket with the pointy end at my wrist, and ran up the stairs to the top floor. The six flights had me exhausted, and combined with the red wine still sloshing around my innards, has me feeling slightly nauseous.

I went up the stairs that lead to a door that goes out onto the roof of my building. Going on the roof of my building isn't a pleasant proposition in the daytime, never mind in the middle of the night. There are no lights up there, and needless to say, it's a long way down if you run into trouble.

I noticed that it was slightly propped open with a beer can, so that the door wouldn't accidentally lock. I knew that meant that there probably was someone already out there. Most likely the ones on the fire escape.

I turned on my flashlight, pulled out the butcher knife, and quietly pushed open the door. Fifteen years or so ago, I wouldn't have had to do this. Mr. McHugh, God rest his soul, the crusty old drunken Irishman who could kick anyone's ass well into his sixties, wouldn't have let this get this far. Whoever is out there would have met the wrath of crazy Mr. McHugh with his sawed-off black base-ball bat, and who knows what else. But now it's just me.

It was much windier on the roof than it was on the streets six stories below. And quieter. I could hear the coarse tar paper crunch with each step I took closer to the wall where the fire escapes in the courtyard are. Just a couple of steps from the low restraining wall, I could hear voices. But they sounded like girls' voices. I turned off my flashlight and peeked over the side to see two kids on the sixth floor fire escape just above Stubby's apartment. They couldn't be more than fifteen years old and my guess would be that they're closer to thirteen.

"Hey you kids!" I shout, trying to startle them. They look up towards me, but I'm sure they can't see me very well in the darkness. "What the fuck are you doing down there?"

"Uh, we're looking for a ball we lost."

"Get the fuck out of there now or I'll lock the two of yous up. Go down now you little prick motherfuckers," I yell, trying to sound as cop-like as possible. And I could hear them scurrying down the iron steps of the fire escape like their lives depended on it. I watched as they reached the bottom floor, jumped the ten feet to the ground, and tore ass out of the courtyard.

Little bastards. When I was that age I was afraid I'd get caught with cigarettes and *Playboy Magazines* and those little fuckers are already busting into apartments.

"Hold it right there! Don't move! Police!"

Great.

"I'm not moving officer. My name is Jerry Pellicano. I live on the first floor. There were kids on the fire escape."

"Drop your weapons."

"I don't have..."

"Drop 'em asshole!"

I drop my butcher knife and my black Mag Lite flashlite on the tar papered roof.

"Put your hands on your head and slowly turn around."

I follow their instructions as a bright light shines in my eyes, blinding me.

"Now get down on your knees."

I can't believe this. The two officers come up behind me and forcefully grab my arms and slap handcuffs on me.

"You guys got to be kidding me. I live on the first floor of this building. I was chasing these little punks off the fire escape."

"Just shut your mouth, don't be an asshole and come with us."

They drag me down to the fourth floor where there is a cop in front of Mrs. O'Sullivan's apartment. He's talking to someone with the door slightly ajar. He looks at the two cops holding me at the end of the hallway, winks, and then the cop at the door walks inside the apartment and the door closes. The two cops walk me right up to Mrs. O'Sullivan's apartment and have me stand

155

exactly in front of the peephole of her door.

Suddenly the door swings open, revealing the cop and Mrs. O'Sullivan in her robe.

"It's not him," the cop says.

"Jesus Christ, what are you doing with Jeremiah Pellicano in handcuffs," Mrs. O'Sullivan scolds the cops with an Irish brogue. "I told you the little bastards were twelve years old if they were a day. Are you alright Jeremiah?"

"Yes, Mrs. O'Sullivan, I'm fine" I say as the cop unlocks my handcuffs.

"We found him on the roof with a knife, lady," one of the cops, who I think was one of the morons who busted Mr. Lynch on New Year's Eve, says.

"Probably doing your jobs for you," Mrs. O'Sullivan says directly at the police officers.

"I chased the kids away. They were two little white kids is all I can tell you. I yelled at them and they took off."

"Can I get you a cup of tea, Jeremiah?"

"No thanks, Mrs. O'Sullivan. I'll just be going to bed now."

"Good night then. Thank you officers, anyway," Mrs. O'Sullivan says to the three cops.

As the three head off to the elevator, one of them turns and says to me, "Kid, you just happen to be in the wrong place at the wrong time."

So now that I'm totally rattled out of my cage, I can't face the sight of my empty refrigerated bachelor pad. The Base it is.

Thankfully, it's not one of those extreme weeknights at the bar; either a couple of comatose alcoholics or packed with full moonitis crazies complete with chicks hanging off the chandeliers with their tits hanging out, as Uncle Eugene likes to refer to them. It's just a cold winter's night with a moderate number of people seeking refuge from their own prewar apartment building woes.

"Good evening, Noel, and how are you this fine evening?"

"Greetings to you, Jerry," Noel replies, holding up a small nip bottle of beer.

"Nah. I need a stiffener tonight. Double J.D. straight up with a water chaser."

"Oh, and on a school night, Jerry! Everything OK at chez Pellicano?" Noel asks, already filling a tumbler with more than a double of the sour mash whiskey.

"Fine. Except for the fact that I caught two little pricks on a fire escape probably getting ready to bust into Stubby's window, and then almost got shot and arrested for my worthy deed."

"Now that's a story you'll be telling for a while. Stubby called in and said he'd be stopping by soon. I'll wait for the gory details."

Against my better judgement I dumped the smoky brown liquid down my neck and felt it warming my cells as it traveled to my stomach and spread its magic throughout my nervous system. There wasn't anyone else I felt like sharing my story with at the moment. Mikey and Patty were at the end of the bar a few sheets to the wind deeply engrossed in a Kojak rerun with the sound turned down while WCBS-FM played some doo-wop on the bar radio. I figured I'd tell my story once Stubby arrived since he was directly involved in the plot. Just then there was the sound of someone tapping a coin against the bar front window. I looked over to see a grotesque face with its lips and nose pushed hard against the glass. Stubby.

"A round for the bar on the city. I got paid four hours of overtime for sleeping in an underground rat infested storage room," Stubby says as he enters and starts peeling off his gritty work clothes.

"What'll ya have, Stub? And has Jerry got a story for you. He saved your worldly possessions from a certain pilfering."

"Nip for me. What story?" Stubby says with deep concern.

"Oh, it was nothing. Except I caught two little fuckers on a fire escape getting ready to break into your apartment, chased them away, got cuffed by a couple of cops, and dragged to the scene of a crime in my own fucking building, that's all."

"Did the cops catch the kids?"

"Nah, I don't think they actually got a chance to break in anywhere, but I was standing on the roof with a butcher knife when the man showed up with guns drawn. One wrong move and I would've wound up like Mal Evans."

"Mal who?" Stubby asks.

"Mal Evans was the Beatles' road manager from day one in Liverpool and a couple of years ago he flipped out on an LA rooftop and was blown away by a couple of cops."

"What crime scene are you talking about?"

"Well, I guess Mrs. O'Sullivan called the cops about the kids, and when they found me on the roof, they dragged me in cuffs to be ID'd by Mrs. O'Sullivan."

"No shit," Stubby says through hearty laughter. "I can just hear her.... 'Oh Jesus, Mary, and Joseph, praise their Holy Names, little Jeremiah Pellicano is the leader of a crime ring. Oh, I knew it was all downhill when they let eye-talians into the building after the war!'" Stubby says in his best Irish brogue, which caught the attention of Noel and even Mikey and Patty at the end of the bar, who joined in the laughter.

"She was very sweet and pretty much tore the cops a new one for cuffing me and dragging me through the halls."

Noel steps in front of me with another tall glass of bourbon. "This is on me. You deserve it for that sorry escapade with the law."

"Hey," Stubby chimes in, "speaking of criminal activities, I talked to my cousin Victor about his video job."

"Yeah, what about it?"

"He says this tow truck driver in Brooklyn started this company where he sends tow truck drivers out with professional video gear to shoot stuff on the overnight shift because the local TV stations don't have anybody on that shift, and he sells the footage to them."

"That is brilliant. Who know how to get to an accident scene before anybody else better than tow truck drivers? Shit, that's great! Did you ask if it was OK for me to call him about it?"

"Yeah, it's my fucking cousin Victor. Of course. Here's his number. And shots for everyone. And a double for fuckin' Columbo junior over here!" Stubby says, holding my arm up like the heavyweight champion of the world.

It didn't take too many shots to make me realize I better get my ass into bed if I wanted to get through my Friday working two jobs. So Stubby and I walked to our building with heads down, hands deep in jacket pockets, and the rhythm of our march-like steps the only sound we heard.

Upon ascending the five steps to the outer lobby, we both were utterly disgusted at the sight of the biggest spray painted "Latin Eagles" yet.

"Who the fuck are these Latin Eagle assholes, anyway?" Stubby asks through clenched teeth.

"You never see anybody hanging out in the halls. You'd think you'd see a group of Puerto Rican kids somewhere. But the only Puerto Rican kids in this building go to Visitation and are no more likely to be gangbangers than the little Irish Catholic delinquents who go there," I say, adding to the mystery.

"I'd just love to catch them doing this just once. Just once!" Stubby angrily announces.

"I tell you. All this shit started the month Donnelly moved into this building, Stubby."

"Yeah, so what do we do? Call the cops? And say what? You know as well as I do that unless you've got a line of junkies going down the hall and down the stairway shooting at each other, they ain't gonna do shit. You know just as many cops as I do. They can't do shit until the shooting starts," Stubby says referring to the line all the local cops use describing when they actually get involved in a situation. The reason you can walk down the street in New York smoking a joint, drinking a fifth a whiskey, and pissing down the middle of a sidewalk on 5th Avenue is the cops are told by the higher ups to only bring in serious offenders, i.e. people who are shooting at each other. They can't be bothered with "petty" crime. Oh yeah, that strategy's working real good!

Stubby stares at me and sticks his index finger into my chest. "We'll get that fuck Donnelly one day. We'll just wait for him to fuck up. We'll get him."

Stubby's not one to bullshit, so I know that this is no idle threat.

"Are you with me, Jerry?"

"I'm with you Stubby."

"No fucking around?"

"No fucking around."

"Fuckin'-ay. Let's crash, I'm too fucked up to do anything tonight."

"OK, Stubby."

We both walked into the lobby, and I started opening the five locks on my front door as Stubby pressed the button on the elevator. There's no light on the ancient button or a system to tell where the elevator is, so Stubby puts his ear to the elevator door and listens. "Fucking piece of shit elevator is busted again," he laments as he shuffles over to the stairs and begins his long trek to the fifth floor. "If you don't hear from me by morning, call a search party."

BBBBRRRRIIINNNNNNNGGGG
BBBBRRRRIIINNNNNNNGGGG

Who else is going to call at seven-thirty in the a.m.?

"Hello, Dad," I say answering the phone.

"Jerry! How'd you know?"

"I must be psychic."

"Did you make your plans for bringing the Olds down?"

"Not yet, Dad."

160

"Jerry, we're counting on you."

"Dad, I'll figure it out this weekend, I promise."

"OK, Jerry."

"Where's Mom?"

"Oh, she's out jogging."

"No, really."

"Seriously, Jerry. She is. Every morning. I go every other day."

"When did this start?"

"Right after we got here. So Jerry, call us this weekend, OK? Don't screw up alright?"

"Alright, Dad. Bye."

"Bye."

I can't believe my parents are in better shape than I am. I used to think retirement was the time when you got your life in order to go die someplace. Make out a will, buy a plot, tell the kids where the life insurance polices are and where you hid the extra cash. But I feel like my parents are beginning to live their lives and I'm the one getting ready to die. I mean after the way I've been working, drinking, and getting no sleep, I probably look like death. So I just hope there's enough hot water to get my juices flowing in the shower. I've got to look presentable this morning at the library. Today is the day I ask Berta to spend the night.

NINE

I'm glad Berta finally agreed to meet me for lunch. She never takes a real lunch. She just nibbles on some rabbit food in the vending machine lounge or at the work station away from the public's view. O'Neill's Baloon is just across the street from Lincoln Center. It's a very unusual name for a restaurant or bar, especially since "baloon" is spelled with only one "L." I heard that the owner wanted to call it O'Neill's Saloon and after he had the elaborate neon sign made, he found out that due to some obscure law, bars in New York City are not allowed to be called "saloons." So rather than order an entirely new sign, he just modified it by changing the saloon to baloon. I'm always amazed at the strange way New York City enforces its laws. For instance, fireworks are illegal. But if you come out of the Holland Tunnel anytime after about April 1st, there are scores of young men selling everything from ladyfingers to quarter sticks of dynamite in the open.... "Hey you lookin' for sumtin' good? Put one a dese under a car and fuhgedaboudit!" Drugs are illegal, but every neighborhood in the city has a storefront or apartment that sells drugs right out in the open. I'm surprised they don't have neon signs hanging out front. New York has the strictest gun control laws in the country, yet I know I could buy a machine gun in less than four hours from now if I had cash in my pocket. And gambling? You can walk into any bar in any of the five boroughs and bet on a horse race anywhere in the country. I mean, why even bother having laws?

I got to O'Neill's early. I know Berta, and she's going to keep this midday rendezvous to a minimum. I grabbed a table near the door so I could quickly nab her as soon as she arrived.

"Berta!"

"Oh good, you got a table! I've only got a half-hour, so we should order ASAP."

"You are the model of efficiency. What drives you anyway?"

"Promise not to tell?" She says slowly unfolding her white linen napkin and placing it daintily on her lap.

"I promise."

"A little birdie told me Mrs. Roberts is retiring. And all things being equal, I may get her position."

"Isn't that a director's position?"

"Well, she was promoted to a director, but that job can also be a manager's position, which I'm certainly qualified for."

"That's great! Congrats!"

"Don't jinx me! I'm only cautiously optimistic at this point, but I've got my fingers crossed. This would be a dream come true for me."

"See? All that dedication and hard work is paying off for you."

"I hope so. Dear God, I hope so. Maybe you're good luck," she says switching gears from worried to flirtatious. "How is the TV studio doing? I think it's so exciting that you're really working in television. That's a marvelous career. So, so, *creative*."

"It's a lot of dirty work right now, but I wanted to tell you about this woman I want to do a documentary on."

"Yes! That sounds so exciting! Is she like a rising star? Is she playing in the Village or something?"

"No no no. She's kind of, well, like a bag lady. Who's blind. And walks through the subway playing the accordion."

Berta's face went from one of eager anticipation to stunned silence.

"I gave her my telephone number last week, and she called me, and all I have to do is get the equipment from Radical Video and shoot if for the video doc fest."

"That sounds terrible. She's blind? And she's like a bag lady? How old is she?"

"Well, she looks maybe eighty but she could be sixty-five or seventy."

"That's awful. Why would you even think about doing that?

The poor woman," Berta says, just about scolding me. No. She is scolding me.

"It's interesting. It's real life. It's not pretty but..."

"...but but but. But it's not nice. The poor woman. It's wrong."

"Not if she cooperates. If this turns out good, and it gets noticed at the video documentary festival, she could get famous or something and maybe make some money off it."

"Oh, right. Or maybe *you* could," Berta says as she crumples her napkin, tossing it on my bread plate. Next thing I know, I'm watching her cross Broadway towards the library.

"May I take your order?" A waitress asks.

"Yeah, ah, two tuna fish sandwiches. But make them to go, please."

I'll try to explain to her. She's got her opportunity knocking. I've got mine. When opportunity knocks, you can't complain about the noise.

From my vantage point at her empty desk, I could just see Berta munching on something in the back. There's a tap bell on her desk, so what the heck.

DING

Berta appears around the corner and as soon as she sees it's me, a sad puppy dog smile comes across her face.

"Jerry, I'm sorry I got a little upset. But I'm going through something at home right now with a senile grand-mother..."

"...no need to explain. I brought you a sandwich."

"Thanks," Berta says as she takes the sandwich from me, and gently touches my hand with her left hand.

"I know you don't like to talk here, but do you think you'd like to get together Saturday night?"

"That's tomorrow," she says with that look that just screams she already has plans. "OK. Tomorrow night. Call

164

me later, here comes Mrs. Roberts. Bye."

Being careful not to bump into Mrs. Roberts, I cut through the stacks to take the other staircase. This just might work out. I'll pick her up in my father's car. I mean I hate taking it out of the garage only because I'm so paranoid that I might get a door ding, but I have no other choice. Getting Berta to my groovy bachelor pad is priority one, even if it means risking driving on the pothole capital of the world, the BQE.

Done. Just before I left the library, I set up my romantic interlude with Berta. But now it's time to hustle down to Radical Video for my second payday of the week, and my big pitch. If I play my cards right, I'll finally be doing my own video documentary on the lady accordion player in the subway.

This place isn't just clean and organized. It looks professional. And it's only because of my years of experience getting yelled at nonstop by my Mom: "pick up after yourself" and "a place for everything and everything in its place" or "what you lack is organization" and other admonitions that come into my mind every time I see a dirty shelf, a tangled cable, or a pile of tapes.

Sandra doesn't even notice that I've entered, or maybe she just ignores me while she types away on the electric typewriter.

"Is Amy in today?" I ask Sandra, realizing that, yes, she has been ignoring me.

"She's on her way over," she manages to mumble while still typing with a pencil in her mouth.

I head over to my latest project, the control booth. With a few screw hooks, freshly cut shelves, and a little ingenuity, the booth now looks like a TV control booth and not the inside of a electronic junk store. Monitors are clean. Cables are dressed and labeled. Alcohol and head cleaning swabs are standing by.

"By the way, the toilet is stopped up," Sandra shouts from

the office, with the pencil no longer clenched in her teeth since she had something really important to tell me.

This is exactly the type of assignment that separates the working class from the aristocracy. Some people have gone through life without ever having cleaned out a stopped up toilet. They are the same people who never saw a black person until they made a class trip from the suburbs to a Broadway show. Never worked a day in their lives until Daddy got them a job upon graduating from an ivy league university. And wouldn't survive a day in the real world if they didn't have Mummy and Daddy to fall back on.

I grab a bucket and a plunger and head off to tame the porcelain beast. Aha! This will be a snap. I plunge my plunger into the liquid mess that could have been way worse, and with a few hearty thrusts, the monster is once again tamed! Behave! You are frightening the women! But secretly I enjoy our battles. I get to be the hero and slay a dragon for the damsels in distress.

"The bathroom is in full operation," I announce to Sandra and Amy, who has just arrived.

"You are a prince," Amy says walking towards me, reaching to shake my hand.

"Stop right there, young lady," I warn her, holding up the plunger. "Not sterile, just yet." I walk back to the washroom to clean up and can hear Amy talking to Sandra as I wash my hands.

"How did we get along without him, Sandra?"

"Oh, we managed."

I clear my throat just before I enter the office again allowing Amy and Sandra to stop talking about me. "Amy, I was wondering if I could have a minute of your time?"

"Sure, come into my office"

Amy is wearing a black button-down dress shirt with one button too many left undone to qualify as being modest. Her blond hair looks like it has been ironed. It's hard to tell if it's just greasy or has some kind of hair product in it. She's the kind of person who looks like she has dirty bra straps.

166

"What can I do for you, Jerry? You're not quitting are you?"

"No, not at all. I want to pitch an idea I have for a documentary I'd like to do."

"Really? Hmm. Shoot."

"Do you ever ride the number one line?"

"What is that?"

"You know, the west side local."

Silence.

"The subway."

"Oh, yes! I've been on it. It's fun."

"Right. Picture this..." I say as I rise from my chair and begin using the Italian side of my brain to emphasize my story with my arms and hands. "It's morning rush hour on the subway. You're barely awake. Cheap perfume and cologne hangs in the air. Every person in the jammed car pretends there's no one else there. Each person is buried in some newspaper, or moronic world puzzle book, or simply has their eyes closed. When suddenly..." I pause. Amy is buying this hook, line, and sinker. "....suddenly the door slides open revealing a tiny wisp of a woman barely alive. She looks like a skeleton with skin draped over it. Her secondhand overcoat and knit cap are clean, but tattered and worn. She's not wearing glasses, but there's something about her eyes. Yes, now I see. She only has one. And the other one is just a blob of an eyeball, obviously useless. But even more unbelievable is what she's carrying...." Amy looks like she's going to jump out of her chair. "She's carrying a huge ACCORDION!"

Amy jumps up. "I love it I love it I love it I love it!!! And, yes, she shuffles forward, and plays some terribly ironic, symbolic piece... like..."

"... 'When You're Smiling.'" I say feeding into her frenzy.

"Perfect!"

"For real. That's what she plays."

"Are you shitting me?"

"No. And she has a tin cup attached to the front of it."

"It's beautiful," Amy whispers, painting an imaginary picture in the air. "And in her ghastly face, we see the pain and suffering of not just her own self...but the pain and suffering of all people. In fact, there's so much pain, she has to be blind. No one person could look at all that suffering. Yet, somehow...she plays...her...what is it again?"

"Her accordion."

"She plays her accordion and sings the bittersweet, tragically sad song of life. Oh, this is good. Good good good good. Do you have her locked in?"

"She called me and said she's in," I tell Amy, even though the woman told me on the phone that she might do it if I could promise to get her on the Johnny Carson show.

"Get for it."

"You mean I've got the approval."

"Yes. Here are the terms. Radical Video will give you the gear, the tape, the editing, whatever you need to pull it off. We'll run it in the documentary video fest; we get executive producer credit, you get associate producer." She stops short and studies my face as if she's counting my eyelashes.

Here it is. My show biz moment. I can nod my head and smile and walk out of here with the knowledge that I'm getting screwed or I suck it up and fight her on this associate producer bullshit.

"Ah, OK, that's fine," I say surrendering, and head for the door. "Wait!"

I could feel the cord that ties the back of my throat to my sphincter tighten. That is if there was such a thing, which I know there isn't. But I could swear that's what's happening.

"No. It's not fine."

"Excuse me?"

"I brought you this idea. I'm going to do all the work..."

Amy pulls an unlit cigarette out of her mouth and holds it between two fingers, slowly moving it away from her face as she stares at me with a neutral expression, studying me.

"...associate producer is not acceptable."

"What do you want?" Amy says, with the cigarette an entire arm's length away from her mouth in a grand pose.

"I want...producer slash director."

"You've got it," she says, quickly putting the cigarette back in her mouth and extending her hand for me to shake on it. "I wanted to see your reaction to the associate producer offer. I would've been worried if you accepted it that easily. A producer has to be aggressive..." She pauses as she lights her cigarette, inhales deeply, and opens her mouth releasing the smoke, which engulfs her face in an eerie fog. "...and on occasion, ruthless. Set everything up with Sandra and give me daily updates on your progress."

"Thanks, Amy This is fantastic.."

"Jerry..." She says moving uncomfortably close to me. I can smell the tobacco on her breath as she gets just inches from me and blurts out, "Don't fuck up."

"I'll try not to," I say as I turn to exit. Not wanting to look back to see the expression on her face.

I'm elated and terrified at what lies ahead. The prospect of having my own documentary shown at a video festival coupled with the fact that I could fuck up royally.

"Sandra, I need to set up some logistics for a production," I blurt out, interrupting her typing.

"Come again?"

"I'm doing a video, and Amy says you'll help me with some pre-production."

"Let me get this straight. *You're* doing a documentary? *Your* documentary?"

"Uh, yes. I am."

"Will you please excuse me for a moment," she says with mock sincerity plastered across her face as she heads over to Amy's closed office door. She gently knocks twice.

"Come in," Amy says, unaware what's in store for her.

Sandra shoots me a distorted sarcastic smile as she closes the only nice door in the studio behind her.

It's easy to hear what's going on behind the closed door.

"I work here for two fucking years and never get my own fucking video and you give this penis carrier his own video after being here for a cup of coffee..."

I could stand here and hear the rest of this tirade. But it just doesn't feel right. I grab my coat, sign out for the day and let my weekend begin.

The temperature must have dropped twenty degrees. Not only is the dog crap frozen on the sidewalks, but little frozen ponds of dog pee must be skipped over. I just hope it doesn't snow tomorrow. I have to pick up Berta in my Dad's car, and there's no way I'm risking anything driving in the snow. Then I thought about standing on Houston Street after that first dinner together and how she sucked hard on my tongue during our first passionate kiss. How she pulled me tightly towards her so I could feel her soft breasts pushing against me despite her heavy winter coat. It will take the storm of the century to keep me away tomorrow night.

Friday night is generally the wildest night of the week at Third Base. Most reserve Saturday nights for their "real" dates. Friday is when folks let loose after another horrible week on the job. Many people don't even bother going home after work. Patty and Mikey look like two grade school kids sitting at the end of the bar in their work clothes, which for them are cheap Alexander's suits and skinny ties that probably are left over from their days tormenting nuns. Patty is in an uncharacteristically good mood. He's got a huge smile across his face, revealing an overcrowded mouth of grey teeth as he listens to Mikey obviously relating a humorous story in his own charming Irish poet way. Only Mikey could weave a tail filled with obscenities and blasphemy and make it sound like Joycean prose. I take a neutral position in the middle of the bar and open up a copy of *The Daily News* that was laying there.

Noel holds up a small nip bottle for my approval as he listens in on Patty and Mikey's conversation.

"Yeah, Noel, thanks." Noel pops off the top with one hand and slides it perfectly to me without missing a word.

It's early yet. Guys who work the seven-to-three shift are already settled in with their boilermakers. The nine-to-fivers are just arriving, anxiously tearing off work clothes and playing catch up at the bar ordering doubles. The Christmas bulbs haven't been taken down, and the twinkling lights provide an unusually festive atmosphere for a bitterly cold dark Friday afternoon in the Bronx.

"It's started. Gonna be a fuckin' blizzard. A killer snowstorm. I just know it," Uncle Eugene says brushing a few snowflakes off his knit hat as he enters.

"Oh, what a glorious ray of sunshine from the cold, dark, gloom of winter you are, Uncle Eugene," Mikey says sweetly across the room.

"Bite me," Uncle Eugene says as he takes a stool at the opposite end of the bar next to Mr. Boyle with his dog King by his side. "Oh, can I say that, next to King, Al?"

"Sure. Just don't say 'you-know-what,' Al says with a fat, wet, unlit cigar in his teeth, referring to the dreaded "gas man" invocation.

As the early evening progressed, the floor grew wetter and wetter from new arrivals brushing freshly fallen snow from their shoulders and hats. And before long, people began stomping their feet as soon as they stepped inside the bar to shake the snow off their boots.

"Noel, want me to get the rubber mats out?" Uncle Eugene asks.

"That would be greatly appreciated, Uncle Eugene, if it's not too much trouble," Noel answers.

Uncle Eugene walks into the back storage room, that used to be a kitchen, and drags out a rolled up rubber mat, which he unrolls in front of the doorway.

"I told you this was going to be a fucking killer storm," Uncle Eugene says softly.

I've finished three small bottles of beer, the *NY Daily News* from cover to cover, and even did the Jumble. And just when I thought I may have to join forces with Patty and Mikey, here comes the snow-covered brigade of Stubby, Terry, and Stubby's cousin, Victor, who I haven't seen in years. I always liked Victor. He would ride his Sting Ray over from Allerton Avenue, (the bicycle NOT the sports car) to hang out with us once in awhile. He could fix anybody's bike in a flash, and even talked about taking apart a car engine when he was thirteen. I don't know why kids from Allerton Avenue somehow always seem to be motorheads, almost like they were from the Island or something. But Victor was a serious kid. Not a total goofball like his older cousin, Stubby, who would do anything for laugh. From what I can remember, Victor took shop at Evander Child's High School, worked in the Citgo Station on Gun Hill, and then was driving a tow truck. Sometimes I think cousins look and behave more alike than siblings, as is the case with Stubby and Victor.

"Oh Jesus, hide the women, it's Stubby and his band of bandits," Noel cries in mock terror. "What'll you be having, boys?"

"Hey, Noel, it's fucking payday. Shots for everybody," Stubby shoots back.

A roar of approval comes from all corners of the bar.

Stubby takes Victor by the shoulder and drags him over to where Uncle Eugene and Mr. Boyle are nursing their tumblers. Stubby points to King, quietly resting, and says, "And Victor, whatever you do, don't ever utter the words..."

"Don't be an asshole, Stubby!" Uncle Eugene yells stopping Stubby in mid-sentence.

"Just kidding." Stubby says, trying to calm Uncle Eugene down.

"Hey, Jerry! When was the last time you saw my cousin Victor?"

"I don't know, four or five years. How's it going, Victor?"

172

"Hey, great, Jerry! Sheesh. You still look like a kid!" Victor says, shaking my hand almost to the point of pain with his heavily calloused hand.

Victor doesn't look anything like a kid. He probably added fifty pounds to his five-foot six-inch large-boned frame and has a beard that hasn't been trimmed, oh, maybe since he started growing it in fifth grade. His hair is thick, long, and completely wild. If you told me he was an outlaw biker from Alabama, I'd believe you, but he's got a Bronx accent stronger than Bugs Bunny. He's wearing a black leather jacket that can barely close around his beer belly, a large silver chain hangs from his garrison belt holding a black leather billfold in his back pocket. In his other back pocket looks to be a walkie-talkie. And in his left hand he's holding something that also looks like a walkie-talkie but has a bunch of small red lights going on and off each time there's a soft crackle or beeping sound.

"Great to see you, Victor! Stubby tells me you're doing well."

"Yeah, I got my own tow truck business now. Here's my card."

"Hey! 'Victor's Towing.' Good name. What's that thing in your hand?"

"That's my scanner. It monitors whatever emergency frequencies you program in. You know, for car wrecks, fires, disasters and stuff. I use it for the TV stuff I'm doing too."

"I wanted to ask you about that. What kind of gear are you using?"

"I use an Ikegami camera and a Sony three-quarter inch deck."

"Are you kidding me? That's what the TV stations use. That camera's like fifty grand."

"I don't own it. The guy I work for leases 'em. I just shoot 'em."

"How many guys work for this guy?"

"We got two crews out a night, and we rotate, so there's

173

about six guys."

"And you get paid?"

"Shit yeah. Every time we get something good, he sells it to just about every TV station in New York and sometimes other cities. He's a tow truck dispatcher in Brooklyn and he's getting ready to quit to do it full-time. He might be looking for more people. Ever drive a tow truck?"

"No. Never. Is that a requirement?"

"Right now it is."

"I drove a cab for a little while."

"That might be OK. I'll ask the boss."

"What's his name?"

"Rocco Barbieri. You may have seen him on TV. He's as big as a two-family house with a fenced yard."

"Shit! I think I did see him. Did channel five do a story on him?"

"Yeah, that's him. He's getting a big head to go with the rest of him. I'll let you know what I find out. Hey, how's your folks?"

"Good. They moved to Florida just this month."

"Hey, so did my folks. Where?"

"'Lauderdale."

"My folks are in Hollywood. I don't get it. How could they ever leave New York?"

"Yeah, go figure," I say as another person stomps the snow from their boots.

Just then the door pushes open revealing Kelly McGillicuddy. And I'll bet you dollars to donuts, that's not his real name. Kelly is six-foot two-inch Black man about fifty-five years old, totally decked out in bright kelly green, including green flashing glasses, green stocking cap, and bright green pants. He's carrying two large shopping bags just brimming with Irish-themed toys, games, and the latest junk from Taiwan. This month it's clackers: those two stupid balls on a string that you clack back and forth. I heard that on other days, Kelly goes by the name of Speedy Gonzalez, and hits all the

174

Bronx and Inwood Puerto Rican bars selling PR-themed stuff. And I wouldn't be surprised if on some days, he's Guido Scambini selling Italian junk over in the bars on Arthur Avenue in Little Italy. And he's probably got a mansion in Riverdale, knowing how the drunks in this place shell out cash for anything with a shamrock on it.

"Kelly McGillicuddy," Stubby yells at the sight of the itinerant salesman. "How the fuck are ya, ya fuckin' black leprechaun ya!"

"Stubby, my main man. The only person I know named after his own dick! Long time no pee, so excuse me while I do," Kelly says, giving it right back to Stubby, cracking up everyone within earshot as he heads off for the head.

Victor pulls Stubby aside, but I can hear him say, "You let that nigger talk like that to you?"

Stubby shakes his head. "First of all, he ain't a nigger. Second of all, if I hear you talk that shit in here, I'm gonna kick your fat half-breed ass from here to fucking Woodlawn Cemetery, OK, asswipe?"

"OK, OK, sheesh, everybody's fuckin' sensitive these days," Victor says, backing off.

Kelly emerges from the bathroom waving his hand in front of his nose. "Man, you Irish need to stop eating so much cabbage and shit! Anybody need any authentic Irish mementos. How 'bout this?" He says as he pulls a little rubber thing shaped like an octopus out of his bag, throwing it across the bar onto the large back mirror. The octopus sticks, and then slowly the rubber tentacles come loose as the creature seems to walk down the length of the mirror. "I got 'em in all colors including green. Two bucks each. Three for five dollars."

Kelly was shoving fives and tens in his pocket as fast as he could hand out the sticky little rubber gizmos. What a genius! Everybody in this place is probably lucky to take home a hundred bucks a week, and Kelly probably pulled in fifty bucks in less than ten minutes.

Grizzled middle-aged and older men, who probably haven't even seen their own kids in days, are giggling like fifth graders as they throw their rubber octopi against anything glass and madly bang their clackers dangerously close to innocent bystanders. Even the usually dour Mikey is tossing a rubber toy against the glass front of the cigarette machine. Kelly moves to the middle of the bar and takes a seat right next to me.

"Not a bad take for one bar, huh?" I say to Kelly, who pulls out a small change purse, removing some coins and laying three dimes, three nickels, and five pennies on the bar as he motions to Noel and holds up one finger.

"Yeah, not bad. Not bad at all. But hard work, son. Hard work dealing with drinkers."

"Can I ask you something...personal, Kelly?"

"That depends. I don't like getting too personal when I'm working."

"Well, is it true that when you hit different ethnic bars, you have a different name, and sell different stuff, according to the nationalities in the bar."

"Let's just say, when in Rome.... Cheers." Kelly says, holding up his glass of coke. "There's an old saying that if God were to appear in physical form in front of a starving man, he'd appear as a loaf of bread. Well, to me he appears as a shopping bag filled with trinkets. The good Lord provides. I just make the most out of what's around me, that's all. You a college boy?"

"I just graduated."

"What are you gonna do now?"

"I got a job at the Geroge M. Cohan Library by Lincoln Center."

"That sounds safe. But you wouldn't catch me working nine-to-five. No, sir. I'd rather hustle on my own. Make the most out of what you got and what's around you," Kelly says, holding up his half-empty glass of soda, and then finishes it off in one gulp. "Just make the most of it. You grow up around here, kid?"

"My whole life right on this block."

176

"You hear about the Chinaman in the laundry?"

"Uh, yeah. I heard it was a suicide."

"Suicide my ass. I stopped in to talk to him a few days before they found him. He was making all kinds of plans about what he was going to do after he retired. Had a damn nest egg for him and his birds. Shit. Suicide my ass. Mr. Wang gave me the idea for my business on Chinese New Year. Told me I could sell stuff in Chinatown, hooked me up with a novelty wholesaler, and boom, I was in business. May God rest his gentle soul. And may the fucker that did him in burn in hell."

Kelly pushes back from the bar and takes a five dollar bill out of his change purse. He places his Coke glass on it and catches Noel's attention, giving him a nod and a wink. Noel returns the gesture as Kelly picks up his shopping bags and walks to the door.

"Man, this is gonna be a killer storm. Killer," he says as he pulls the kelly green stocking hat over his ears and exits.

I walk over to the window and watch Kelly go halfway down the block and get into a late model Oldsmobile as long as a small yacht. But more striking is the fact that the streets and sidewalk are covered with at least a couple inches of fresh snow. If this keeps up through the night, I'll never be able to pick up Berta in my Dad's car tomorrow. Not in this kind of snowstorm.

SMASH

Holy shit! The mirror behind the bar was just smashed, followed by a ghostly silence. I look the length of the bar and see Mikey sitting there with a clacker string dangling in his hand and only one ball on the end.

"I guess the ball came off." Mikey says, looking like a two-year old who had his balloon pop for the first time.

Stubby stands on his barstool and begins:

"Mikey is a piece shit, doo dah doo dah," as the entire bar joins in as they crowd around Mikey, pounding him on the back and on top of his head.

"Mikey is a piece of shit, all the doo dah day. All the doo dah day. All the doo dah day. Mikey is a piece of shit, all

177

the doo dah day."

"I'll just be adding that to your tab, OK Mikey?" Noel says as he delivers another shot glass in front of him.

"No problem, and shots for the bar."

A roar goes up from the gang, as they sing another full chorus of "Mikey is a piece of shit".

Yup, it's Friday, we're probably getting snowed in, and it's not even midnight yet.

"Hey, Stubby, where'd Terry go?"

"I don't know. He's been disappearing a lot lately. Even at work. Was Merrill in here earlier?"

"Nope. I wonder where he is. Maybe Terry's up in his apartment. You know, I could use some fresh air. Stubby, I'm going to go up to Merrill's and see if Terry's up there."

Since Merrill's building is right next to the bar, I don't even bother to put my jacket on, as I run into his building. My building is a prewar dump, but compared to Merrill's, it's the Waldorf. At least we have an elevator and a garbage chute. Merrill lives with his Dad in the same apartment he grew up in since the fifth grade. That's the reason he feels slightly ostracized from some of the guys in the neighborhood; he's only been around since the fifth grade. You've got to be here from the first to really fit in, I guess. Merrill's Mom passed away a few years ago, and his two sisters have long since moved out of the neighborhood. But Merrill's Dad won't move, even though he's been retired from Sanitation for three years.

Knowing that Merrill's Dad is more than likely home, I try listening at the door. Nothing. I knock three times. I hear shuffling on the linoleum.

"Who's there?"

It's Merrill.

"It's me, Jerry."

The door opens and Merrill comes to the door in a CCNY sweatshirt and sweatpants and half his Afro smooshed like he's been lying down.

"Come on in. My Dad's already asleep. We can sit in the

178

kitchen," Merrill says, leading me into the kitchen, which is right next to the front door. There's barely enough room in there for a table that's pushed up against a wall with two kitchen chairs that probably were manufactured and sold on Fordham Road when Benny Goodman was still packing them in at the Glenn Island Casino. "Would you like some tea, Jerry? I was just going to brew some."

"No thanks. Are you sure we won't be bothering your Dad?"

"Are you kidding? His hearing aid is out. He wouldn't hear a nuclear bomb if it went off in here. He may *feel* something..."

"I just needed a breather from the bar. I guess Terry isn't with you."

"I haven't seen him in days. Or anyone."

"What have you been doing?"

"Oh, lots of thinking. And praying."

I didn't want to sound too obvious and blurt out "PRAYING?" I let that one just float through the air to see where it might land.

"You know, I think I will have some tea, Merrill."

"Good. This is great tea. I got it in Chinatown. It's supposed to calm one's nerves. It's got something called St. John's Wort in it."

"St. John's wart? I don't know about that!"

Merrill is trying to stifle his laughter, which scrunches his eyes into two narrow slits.

"Not wart. Wort."

"You know if it was St. John's wart, it would be a first degree relic," I say to Merrill as he sprinkles the loose tea into my cracked Chinese teacup.

"How's that?"

"St. John's wart would be a first degree relic. Did you know that every Catholic altar has to have a first degree relic of a martyr in it?"

"Are you serious?"

"Totally. A martyr. Not just an ordinary saint. A bonafide, authentic martyr."

"What exactly is a first degree relic?"

"It's an actual body part of a saint. Like a bone, fingernail clipping, yes, even a wart."

"Are you certain?" Merrill asks, halting his careful pouring of the boiling water from a kettle that may have been a wedding present to his parents in the late thirties.

"Positive. They'd cremate saints and distribute the remains for inclusion in altars, which is mandatory, and for miracles. I remember when I was kid, my Mom would bring us to the chapel at Mother Cabrini High School in Washington Heights, and they had Mother Cabrini herself entombed by the altar on display for all to see. Except for one thing."

"Which was?"

"Her head. That's on display in Italy."

Merrill froze. "You're bullshitting me."

"I bullshit you not. It freaked the shit out of me. I had nightmares for months. I think I still do."

"Remember in Visitation they handed out those medals that had a little glass circle in the middle with a tiny square piece of white cloth underneath. What was that?"

"That was probably a second or third degree relic. I remember that was a medal for Elizabeth Seton, who founded the Sisters of Charity, our nuns. A second degree relic is something the person owned. Like a blouse."

"Or a bra?"

"Or a bra. And a third degree relic, I think is something that the saint merely touched."

"Like a bowling bowl."

"Yes, like a bowling ball, Merrill."

"You mean to tell me that every altar has a chunk of a martyr?"

"Every Roman Catholic Church."

"That is too bizarre," Merrill says, finally filling our cups with the no longer boiling, but very warm water.

"In fact, if you sell or distribute a false relic, it's automatic excommunication. And you know what that means?"

"HEEEEEEELLLLLLLLL!" Merrill screams maniacally.

"You'll wake your Dad!"

"He's dead to the world," Merrill says, realizing his over enthusiasm.

"So if those medals the nuns handed out in fifth grade weren't the real deal, they'll be sharing cell space with the little bastards they spent so much time beating the shit out of in class who went on to a life of crime."

Merrill sits down and picks up his teacup with both hands, holding it under his nose so he can smell its aroma before taking a delicate sip. Seeing Merrill in these austere surroundings seems very bohemian. Like the room filled with Allen Ginsberg and the rest of the beats in that movie "Pull My Daisy." I can see Merrill isn't thinking of another satiric relic joke. He appears pensive. Brooding. Like he's cooking something up in that huge eastern European skull of his.

"Jerry, this discussion really rattles my cage."

"You're not stoned, are you?"

"Not at all. But remember I told you I've been thinking and praying..."

Aha. Here's where it landed, I thought to myself.

"...I'm leaving."

"Leaving?"

"Leaving? As in leaving? For good?"

"Yup. For good is exactly right. Have you heard of 'The Source'?"

"Isn't that one of those new religions like Scientology or Est or something?"

"I'm glad you said 'new religions' and not 'cult,' Jerry. You're right. It's a religion. I've been reading about it for months, and I've met someone who is deeply involved and

181

I'm going to North Carolina to, well, join with them. You think I'm insane, right?"

"Do they keep dead martyr's toe nails inside their altars?"

"No."

"I guess they're not too insane then. But why do you have to go to North Carolina? I mean, can't you just go to their church or something?"

"I'm joining The Source to become a clergyman. An ordained 'brother' in the church."

"Holy shit. Sorry, I didn't mean that."

"That's OK, Jerry. I know what you mean. You're shocked, as is my father. But that's OK. It will all be right. For good."

"Who's the person you've become close with?"

"A woman I met at a service in Harlem. That's where the New York City services are held. It's right next to the Apollo on a hundred twenty fifth street. Her name is Ebony. She's black," Merrill says quietly, and studies me carefully to see how I react.

"Merrill, I don't know what to say. Except good luck."

"That's OK. We're taught that the most important things in life are impossible to talk about. The second most important things are always misunderstood. And the third most important things are what we can talk about."

"Listen, don't go away without telling me, alright?

"I won't. In fact, Jerry...oh, never mind."

"What, go ahead...."

"I was going to ask you if you could drop me off in North Carolina when you bring your father's car to Florida."

"Merrill, that's the answer to my prayers. That would be great. I'll call you."

"Thanks for being a friend, Jerry."

I walked out and couldn't believe what I had just heard. Merrill has joined a fucking cult.

182

It's amazing what can happen in a bar if you're gone for an hour or so. It's time to put Uncle Eugene's theory to a test; the one about anything that happens after ten p.m. is bullshit even if there are chicks hanging off the chandeliers with their tits hanging out. There aren't any chandeliers, but two women, stripped down to their bras are standing on the bar gyrating their slightly overweight bodies to the sounds of the Stones' *Satisfaction* with every male in the steamy smoke-filled bar hooting and hollering like a Bronx rodeo as they encourage them with rhythmic clapping and awkward dance steps of their own. I have no idea who these two exhibitionists are, but judging by the way Stubby and Victor are deep in conversation as they point out the attributes of the hefty hoofers, they must know them.

I push past Mikey and Patty, thankfully still wearing their clothes, and tug on Stubby's arm.

"Who's the entertainment."

"One of them works for Victor and the other is her friend," Stubby shouts over the deafening sounds.

I cup my hand and shout into Stubby's ear. "Isn't it nice that we live in a society where employees and their bosses can socialize without any stigmas attached."

"What?"

"Never mind."

The song ends and the two out-of-breath, chunky dancers hop off their "stage" and begin putting on their blouses, much to the disappointment of their crazed fans. Nope. No satisfaction here. Suddenly, in a renewed burst of energy, the chunkier of the two jumps back up on the bar and begins, "One, two, tie your shoe!" Now the other girl, with a little help from Mikey and Patty pushing her back onto the bar by her ass, joins in "Three, four, shut the door. Five, six, pick up sticks! Seven, eight, lay them straight." And with each number they both strike a provocative pose by sticking out or grabbing a particular body part. "Nine, ten, a big fat hen! Eleven, twelve, who will delve?"

There goes Mikey's shirt... 'I'll delve! I'll delve!'

"Thirteen, fourteen, girls a-courtin'. Fifteen, sixteen..."

The two females stop dead in their tracks and share a look of total wonderment, surprise, and glee.

"...girls a-kissin'" Yup. They start making out. As crazed as the drunken patrons of the bar were during the go-go routine, it pales in comparison to the rise they're now getting out of the sex-starved boys.

"Seventeen, eighteen, girls a-waitin'. Nineteen, twenty, my stomach's empty!"

"They don't look empty!" Mikey yells.

They take in the applause, cheers, and banging of stools with style, grace, and panache as they hold hands and bow from the waist as if they are making a Broadway show curtain call. The crowd begs for more, but they only throw kisses to the crowd, as they are helped, once again, down from the bar.

I look over and see Uncle Eugene sitting in his usual spot under the TV next to the ladies room. He looks as though he's next in line to have a root canal. I push my way past the stars for the evening and pause next to Uncle Eugene.

"What did you think, Uncle Eugene?"

"It don't mean shit."

"But you have to admit it was fun, wasn't it?"

"Don't mean shit."

"That's what I love about you, Uncle Eugene. You're consistent."

I can see the two talented ladies have joined forces with Stubby and Victor. I make my way over and soon realize I'm a fifth wheel. It appears Stubby and Victor have first dibs on the energetic pair. OK, they're not perfect, but they definitely have winning personalities. Enthusiasm such as that is hard to come by in this neighborhood.

"Hey, Stubby, I think I'm heading home. You guys hanging

out here for a while?" I ask Stubby, who's got his mind on one thing. Well, make that two things...as I see him fondling her breasts and they begin a very sloppy session of kissy face.

"I guess I'll just head out," I say to no one in particular.

Just as I turn to leave, I bump into Uncle Eugene who is also leaving. He turns to me as he pulls down his black knit cap. "Told you. It don't mean shit."

As I push on the outside door, it sticks for a moment from the newly fallen snow that has risen considerably in the last hour or so. It must be six inches. There's nothing more beautiful than a city blanketed with a fresh coat of pure white snow. Everything is hidden beneath the pure virgin wedding dress whiteness without exception. Garbage, dogshit, junk heap abandoned cars, garbage cans, vomit, broken bottle strewn empty lots, even the private house that the Howards used to live in and has sat empty for the past eighteen months which is now a graffiti covered symbol of the neighborhood's advancing urban blight, has a charming Courrier and Ives holiday charm about it. The only things that aren't covered with snow are the sewer manhole covers. The horrid heat and stench wafting through the holes of the cover are even too much for mother nature's cleansing of crispy white snowflakes which melt, upon contact.

"You're out late tonight, Uncle Eugene. It's after ten o'clock."

Uncle Eugene doesn't look at me but keeps his head slumped between hunched shoulders, hands deep in his short suede jacket pocket.

"You know how long it's been since I seen tits in a bar?"

"Aha, so you admit it was worth staying out for?"

"Tits don't mean shit either. You know what I'm going to do tonight? I'm going to put on a pot of tea. Feed my birds. And finish 'Finnegans Wake.' You ever read 'Finnegans Wake'?"

"No. Not for lack of trying though."

"This is my third time reading it. You know I'm an alco-

185

holic?"

"Not really. No," I lie poorly.

"Well I am. I've been drinking since I'm thirteen years old. We drank in the park, under the bridge, at the lake, by the river, the boathouse, in forts, on rooftops, stoops, alleys, even in the church sacristy for chrissakes. Back in 1957, half the mother's club danced naked in the bar they were so snockered on Saint Patrick's Day. You kids think you invented it."

A long period of silence ensued. The only sounds were the super dry snowflakes crunching under our feet, and an occasional car, barely audible, as it rolled over the fluffy snow. I could hear phlegm in Uncle Eugene's throat rattle around as his breath became short. He'd cough, and then hack up a huge green loogie that he'd spit into the snow, creating a bizarre gooey green blob on the pure white stuff. I tried not to look, but I couldn't help it.

Uncle Eugene lived a few blocks farther down the street than I did. He lives in the same apartment that he grew up in. And he's the youngest of four brothers. Guessing he's about sixty, his family must have control of that apartment for at least seventy years. He's probably paying fifty dollars a month rent for a three-bedroom apartment. Why would he move?

"Here's where I get off," I say to Uncle Eugene as I stop in front of my building. Surprisingly, Eugene stops and looks at me. His eyes are watery from the bitter cold. But if I didn't know any better, I could almost say that he looks teary eyed.

"Mr. Wang was a good man," Eugene says very slowly, barely able to get his words past his cold lips. "A fuckin' dog doesn't deserve to go like that."

"Like what?" I ask wanting to know his exact meaning.

"Wang committed suicide like I'm a fuckin' astronaut. You know somebody pretty good when you see them nearly every day for 30 years or so. He was a good man. Did things in a quiet way. Like Noel did what he did."

"Did he do something for Charlie, I mean Mr. Wang?"

"Know what happens when a loner dies and nobody claims

186

the body and he ain't got nothing or nobody?" Eugene says, tightening his lips the way Humphrey Bogart used to do when he was disturbed.

"No. What happens?"

"Potter's Field. Hart Island. A nameless hole in the ground with bodies piled on top of each other three deep on a godforsaken island in the Long Island Sound near City Island right here in the merry old Bronx. The last stop for the human flotsam and jetsam of New York City. They say if you dig down too deep when you dig those graves, the water starts to seep up, and it's warm from the heat from hell. Well, Noel made sure Mr. Wang had a proper burial. A nice little grave by some trees in Woodlawn Cemetery. In fact, it's next to a little pine grove near where Duke Ellington is buried. Lots of birds around there in Woodlawn."

"That must've been expensive."

"Nah, it's just a simple little marker and a few of us chipped in," Eugene paused as he pulled his cap a little further over his ears for warmth. "You seem like a bright kid. Don't wind up like me. Get the fuck out of here," Eugene says with his head still hunched over, but turning to me. His eyes are still watery from the cold, and there's spittle that appears to be starting to freeze at the corners of his cracked lips. "You see anybody hanging around here my age? No. They're all dead. I'm the one who made it. I'm the lucky one. Happy New Year."

Uncle Eugene salutes me with two fingers tapped against his black watch cap and continues on, crunching his way down the block towards his home; a railroad flat, fifth story walk-up that he's lived in his entire life.

Suddenly all I could see was myself walking those few blocks alone and cold on a dark winter night thirty-five years in the future. The same snow covered street, the same short suede jacket, the same black watch cap, the same lonely story to tell some other alcoholic kid in the making.

My building is still. There's a numbness to my face, my hands, even the air. It's beautiful in its early 20th century, post-industrial revolution architecture. The once majestic main court-yard entrance has a hint of its once grand stature. The snow sticks to the little nooks and crannies of the architectural brick along the side of the building. Buildings today don't have the little nuances and subtle details that were commonplace when this and all the prewar buildings that sprang up here shortly after the number one train began operating here in the early 1910s. I heard from old man Cotter, who used to live with his wife behind the stairs for many years before they both passed away within weeks of each other a couple of years ago, that all the bricks that were used in the construction of this building were actually ballast in the great cargo ships at the turn of the century. When we shipped the bounty of our industrial revolution from New York City to the port cities of Europe, what came back in return in those very same ships was human cargo. Countless numbers of poor immigrants hoping to break away from the class systems and poverty of the Old World to make a better world for themselves and their children in the New one. But human cargo doesn't weigh as much as freight, so the ships were loaded with Belgian bricks to help steady them. So not only were the ships delivering the new inhabitants from the other side, they were also delivering the bricks that would become the walls that would hold them captive for generations to come.

THWAP

I don't know what I've been hit with, but my face feels like it has been smashed with a frozen baseball. I slump to the ground with millions of tiny black and white asterisks rushing through my brain on in front of my eyeballs. I'm on my knees in the cold snow and just as the asterisks begin to dissipate and my eyes can focus on the ground below my slumping head I see dark red streaks. And drips of....bright red blood against the pure white snow as it melts its way through, looking like the remnants of a cherry snow cone someone dropped.

"Fuuuuccccckkkkkkk!" I scream at the top of my lungs, not giving a rat's ass that I'm probably waking up everybody who lives in the front of the building.

FUUUUMMMPPPHHH

Another iceball lands just a few inches from me. I look up and barely see a brown haired head jerking back from the precipice of the roof.

"You motherfuckers! If I catch you, I'll fucking..."

Hmmm. What will I do? Shit, I am hurt.

"....tear your fucking heads off and shit down your neck you little prick motherfuckers!"

...wait....I....think...I'm...blacking...out.....

"Are you alright, Jeremiah?"

"Mrs. O'Sullivan? Shit! My face!"

"Oh, Jesus, Mary, and Joseph, praise their holy names! Jeremiah, you're bleeding rather badly. Come with me."

Mrs. O'Sullivan struggles to help me get up off my now wet knees. I briefly slip, almost pulling both of us down, but she's strong as an ox for a woman who probably weighs ninety-five pounds soaking wet. I'll bet she had to lift a drunk and wounded Mr. O'Sullivan many nights from this exact same spot over the years.

"Thank you, Mrs. O'Sullivan. How do I look?"

"Like you went ten rounds with Cassius Clay, that's how you look."

I needed Mrs. O'Sullivan to keep me balanced up the courtyard steps and into my apartment, which was more convenient than her's a few flights up. We entered the apartment and began making our way through the foyer to the bathroom, which is at the rear of the apartment.

"Oh, your parents kept this place lovely, Jeremiah. My oh my, they must have painted and wallpapered every two years! Your mother is so lucky to have such a handy husband, Jeremiah. If the goddammed landlord didn't pay for it, we didn't do it, was my Seamus' philosophy. So nothing was ever done. You sit here on the toilet. Do you have any peroxide and small towels, Jeremiah?"

"Yeah, under the sink. And in the medicine chest."

As she swung the medicine chest door open, the mirrored door swung into perfect position so that I could see what a mess the left side of my face was. There was a deep red welt that felt as though it was growing with every pounding heartbeat. And less than an inch from my eye, a deep red gash. An ugly one. And the entire left side of my face looks like raw prime rib.

"This may sting," Mrs. O'Sullivan warns me as she pours the hydrogen peroxide onto a towel. "Hold steady."

"Yowsuh!" I scream through clenched teeth.

"This may need a stitch or two. Especially since it's on your face. You don't want to go through life with an ugly scar on your face. I mean you still have to find a wife and all. Do you know anyone who could drive you?"

"To find a wife? Now?"

"Are you delirious, Jerry? No, to the hospital."

"Well Stubby and his cousin are at Third Base."

"Stubby doesn't drive now, does he? That would be a tragedy in the making."

"No, his cousin does."

"I'll call the bar and ask for them."

"No, that's OK, Mrs. O'Sullivan, you've done enough. I don't know what I would have done without you."

"Believe me, Jeremiah, I'm sorry to say, I picked my Seamus up many a time from that same spot, God rest his soul. Are you sure you'll be OK? Make sure you keep ice or cold water pressed against that wound."

"Yes, mam."

"And you are going to call Stubby?"

"Yes, I'll do it right now."

"Well, I'll be leaving you then. Do you want me to call the police?"

"Nah. It's just a snowball."

"Yeah, just a snowball. Probably with a bolt inside. Alright, Jeremiah. Good night now."

"Thanks."

I walked Mrs. O'Sullivan to the door and watched her get into the elevator. Looking in the medicine chest door mirror, I could see that the gash next to my eye was indeed rather deep. And it most likely would develop into a nasty scar if I didn't get medical attention. Stubby and Victor are going to love this.

"Hello, Noel. It's Jerry Pellicano. Is Stubby there? Could you get him, it's sort of important...I'll wait. Stubby! Listen I need a ride to the hospital. I got whacked with an iceball. I need a stitch or two..... OK. OK. OK. Great."

I hung up the phone and waited for two drunk guys to take me to Montefiore Hospital in a the worst snowstorm in years. This *is* a tragedy in the making.

Thinking the guys will show up any minute, I soak a dish rag in cold water since I don't have any ice in the freezer, press it against my face, and head out front to wait for them. The silence of the snow seems more eerie now than it did before my face exploded. I might as well pick up some snow to wrap my towel around. As I scoop up a handful of snow next to the red-stained snow where my blood spilled, something solid comes up along with the snow. Mrs. O'Sullivan wasn't far off. It looks like a broken-off piece of pottery or porcelain or something. Dollars to donuts, it was strategically placed inside my iceball for a little extra pop. I'll say. It could've killed me.

"Whoooooohhhhhhhhh!"

Holy shit. I look in the direction of the screams to behold a sight for the record books. An early sixties, electric blue, beat up Lincoln Continental is doing 360s down the snow covered hill as if it was on an upside down car hood. But it wasn't a car hood. It was a car. Yup. Stubby, two girls, and Victor at the wheel all squealing in delight as the car spins around uncontrollably in the soft snow. Thank God there's not a vehicle or a soul on the street, or it would be an unmitigated disaster. Somehow, the spinning auto comes to a stop right in front of my front stoop, not more than two feet from the curb, albeit facing the wrong way, but a

191

perfect landing.

"Fuckin' ay," Stubby yells from the backseat sitting between the two women who are laughing so hard and loud I'm afraid Mrs. O'Sullivan may come back out again. "That was a trip! Let's do it again!"

"Woooohhhhh," the two females hoot in support.

"Shit! Jerry, let's see that," Stubby says crawling over one of his playmates. He pulls the lever on the "suicide" door, which means it's one of those old Lincolns where both the front and back doors open from the middle, and tumbles into the street. This brings the laughter in the car to a new decibel level.

Stubby gets up, brushes off the snow, and tries to act sober.

"Let's see that," Stubby says as he lifts the towel from my face to inspect the damage. "Ow. That's a nasty one. That's from a snowball?"

I hold up the broken piece of pottery. "Yeah. Cosmic debris."

"Fuck. That's cruel and unusual. Even for this neighborhood," Stubby says, shaking his head in disgust.

"Stubby, are you sure Victor's OK to drive? I mean I'd rather have a little scar on my face than wind up on a cold slab in the morgue."

"Nah. Victor's not even drunk. He's just screwing around. Hey, Victor, are you fucked up?"

"I swear I'm not."

"That's what you say," one of the female passengers chimes in.

"Seriously," Victor says in a sudden flash of sobriety. "I'm not fucked up at all. I got to work later tonight."

"Awwwww," the female chorus replies.

Stubby places his hand on my shoulder. "No fucking around, Jerry. He's really not drunk. He'll take it easy. I swear to God. Or I'll kick his pimply fat ass."

For some unknown reason, I believe Stubby, and go around

to sit in the front with Victor as Stubby gets in the back with the two fun girls. Victor slowly turns the car around, righting it, and begins driving quickly, but not too fast, and totally under control towards Montefiore Hospital. Under the dashboard are mounted two large scanner radios with red lights flashing sequentially, as soft crackling voices and beeps sporadically come over the speakers.

"You have to work tonight, Victor?"

"Yeah."

"Towing or shooting video?"

"Actually both."

"Both?"

"Yeah, I pick up my partner and try to judge what would make more money as we go along. Shooting a disaster or towing one."

"Is that hard to do?"

"You get the hang of it after a while."

Out of the corner of my eye, I can see Stubby making out with one of the girls so violently, he might get whiplash. Out of the other corner of my eye, the second girl is fast asleep leaning against Stubby's back as she gets a bucking bronco ride.

A crackling voice comes over a speaker.

"Base to Victor."

Victor reaches under the dash and gets a microphone. He holds it up to his mouth and pushes a button on the side.

"Victor here. Base come in."

"What's your ten-twenty?"

"Headed east on Gun Hill near Jerome, bringing a victim to the ER."

"What, are you doing EMS tonight, too?"

"Nah. A friend in need."

"OK. Once you're there, give me a land line. Got tonight's business to discuss. Base out."

"Ten-four," Victor says, putting the microphone back.

"What's a land line?" I ask Victor as he puts the mike back.

"You know, a phone call."

"Oh. Why would you do that if you have a radio?"

"Radios are monitored by all kinds of people. Some of those people aren't nice. Some of those people are bad. That's why we don't want them to hear certain things. Or they might do bad things to us. Like steal our fucking livelihoods if they get the drop on a good call by spying, if you know what I mean."

"Not really. But here we are. Great job, Victor. I really appreciate the ride."

"Want me to come in with you? I think my other passengers can keep themselves occupied," Victor says pointing to the backseat with Stubby and the two girls sleeping in a messy heap.

"OK, sure."

"Stubs," Victor says, pulling on Stubby's shoulder. "I'll leave the engine running and the heater on, alright?"

Stubby grunts his acknowledgment.

"They'll be fine," Victor says, cracking the window open a little bit before he closes the car door.

The Emergency Room reception area is busy with people in need of varying degrees of medical treatment. There's a two year old Puerto Rican boy holding his ear, wrapped in a Big Bird blanket, screaming like his finger is caught in a mousetrap while his mother rocks him back and forth on her lap. Right next to them is an elderly woman, and probably her husband, both barely visible in their pile of winter clothing with not even one button undone, except for the fact that the woman has one glove off with her middle finger wrapped in bloodstained gauze sticking straight up in a surreal "fuck you" gesture. On the other side is a middle aged black man, dressed to the nines, including a silk scarf sticking out of a cashmere overcoat with his eyes closed and his brow tightly knit as if he was trying to make some awful pain go away by sheer willpower. And just a seat away from him are two Irish looking teenagers, each one nursing a hand wrapped in a dirty, bloody towel.

"You sign in first," Victor instructs me, pointing to a middle

194

aged black woman sitting behind a bulletproof wall of glass. There's a microphone and speaker set up, just like at the bulletproof token booths in the subway.

"Can I help you?" The woman states without any hint of emotion.

"Yes, I, ah, got hit with a snowball, or something, and I have a nasty cut on my face, and I'd like to have a specialist look at it."

"Let's have a look," the woman calmly states.

I pull the towel off my wound and watch her eyes carefully for any hint of a reaction from her. Nothing.

"Not too bad. Have a seat, fill these out, and as soon as you're done bring them back to me, alright?" She says with a trace of a pleasant smile.

"Thanks," I say as I pick up the several pages of questions and look around for a seat. Victor already has two scoped out and waves me over.

"I wonder when they'll actually get to me?" I ask Victor. "It looks pretty busy."

"Busy? This ain't nothing for a Friday night. At about four, this place will be rocking."

"Come here often?" I ask Victor wondering how he would be so up on the situation.

"I'm usually around an ER two, three times a week. If I'm lucky."

"Lucky?"

"Yeah. Getting good news footage. They love it when you're at an accident, *and* you got ER footage to boot."

"They let you do that?"

"Sure. We got full press credentials. Look," Victor says as he pulls a chain from under his shirt holding three different picture IDs. "This one's from The Amalgamated Press, this one's from Channel 11, and this one...this is the real deal here. It's a Working Press pass issued by the New York City Police Department. This is pretty much your ticket to murder, mayhem, and other newsworthy situations. Cops and firemen see that, and you've pretty much got whatever you want."

"No matter what?"

"Well, if one of their own is down, they don't like it. But anything else pretty much goes. It's a great fucking feeling."

"What is?"

"Being able to go where nobody else can go and look at that stuff up close. It's unbelievable. I thought driving a tow truck was cool until I started shooting news."

"Excuse me, I better get these filled out."

To the background noise of screams, grunts, groans, and arguments, I managed to fill out all the information in less than a half-hour. By the time I was finished, half the room had already been in to see someone behind the bulletproof glass, and a few other weekend casualties had taken their places in the waiting room.

I handed my forms through a little slit to the nurse behind the security glass.

"It should only be a few minutes. Are you OK?" She asked looking concerned

"Yes, I'm fine."

"OK, good. Someone will be right with you."

I sat back down, and watched the new batch of walking wounded fill out their forms.

"Pellicano?" A voice announces.

I look up to see a man who appears to be about my age with blond hair past his shoulders wearing a white lab jacket, compete with a stethoscope around his neck.

"Here."

"Come with me, please."

I follow the hippie past the curtains where the various screaming kids, Irish teenagers, and others are now being treated in small rooms.

"Let's have a look at that." The dude says as he pulls the towel away. "You were smart to come in here. If you left that, it would leave nasty scar tissue."

"Are you the doctor?"

"Yup," he says as he whips around and starts pulling things out of drawers and cabinets and lining them up on the table next to where I'm sitting. "You're lucky. I'm a plastic surgeon. There's not always one on duty. This'll be a piece of cake. I'll give you a local anesthetic, and you'll be good to go in no time. Look away."

I follow his orders and feel a sharp pinch on my cheek.

"Now we'll just wait a few minutes. I'll be right back," he says as he exits the room.

I can feel the side of my face getting warm, as the drug pulsates in my tissue. I reach up to feel my cheek, and it's numbing effect is already working just fine.

The doctor comes back in and immediately gets to business, putting on gloves, laying stuff out.

"Look away," he says. I do. I can feel something going on, but before I can formulate a few smartass questions to ask... "That's it."

"You're finished?"

"Done. You'll be as good as new in no time. By the way, what happened?"

"I got hit with a frozen iceball with a delicious porcelain center."

"If I were you, I'd take that as a sign. Good luck," the doctor says as he quickly exits.

"Thanks, doc."

There's a mirror next to the door and I can't resist getting a peek at my mug. The bandage over my cut is medium sized. About double the size of an ordinary Band-Aid. I carefully pull up one side of the bandage and see the doctor's handiwork. It's ugly, but sewn up tighter than a baseball. I can see 2 tight stitches. Not bad."

I look around the reception room and there's no sign of

Victor. I don't blame him for not sticking around. I take a gander out the door, and his Continental is nowhere to be seen either. Well, I guess I'll just call a taxicab. But just to make sure, I'll stop by the receptionist.

"Excuse me. I'm Jerry Pellicano, and I was here with a friend..."

"Yes, he left a note for you," she says, not put out at all and pulls it out from her desk top drawer.

"Thank you very much. You know I expected this to be a nightmare, but you and the doc were really nice."

"Oh, it's just my philosophy in life."

"May I ask what that is?"

"Oh, an old fashioned thing called 'do unto others.'"

"I've heard of it. Thanks."

Man! Victor's handwriting is worse than a doctor's. Let's see if I can decipher this: "Meeting partner at end of Woodlawn line. Big job. Come by if you can. -Victor."

Big job? Meeting his partner? Shit, it must be something worth towing and shooting and maybe even making another visit to the emergency room. It's only a few blocks away. What the heck.

Once walk around the corner on Jerome headed towards the end of the elevated train line, I can clearly see that this is indeed a big job. Flashing lights, sirens, fire trucks, cop cars pointed in every which direction, and the sound of a saw cutting through metal. I can even see sparks flying.

An ambulance with its siren blaring zips past me with it's chains clanking on the snow covered street. Dead ahead I can see the disaster that awaits me. But on the left side of the street is Van Cortlandt Park with its majestic pine trees layered in pure white snow. Snowdrifts push up against the high chain link fence along the perimeter of the golf course. The golf course itself is pristine in its beauty as the hills roll away and into the darkness far from the street lights of Jerome. I could just make a left into the park and imagine I was in Vermont surrounded by the quiet winter night. The air crisp and clean. I can feel my boots scrunch the dry, deep snow. Perhaps I can even see some of the night creatures that still inhabit this magnificent park; raccoons, rabbits, possums. But instead I'm drawn to what lies ahead. If I'm serious about hooking up with Victor and his boss doing this TV news thing, I better see what I'm getting myself into. How bad can it be?

Bad. Really bad. I thought seeing the blood from my cut looked awful in the snow. I'm still an el pillar away, and I can see a red stream working its way under a couple of emergency vehicles. It must be an early seventies Chevette. It's wrapped around the el pillar like a pretzel. There seems to be chaos leading up to the scene; but as I get closer, I can see that right at the point of impact there's a focussed team of firemen who seem to be communicating through mental telepathy as they operate the jaws of life and some kind of super saw. In fact, I'm amazed at how little noise there is except for the sounds of the machinery, the little bit of controlled conversation, and the sounds coming across the assorted two-way radios.

I'm not going a step farther. I'm about twenty-five feet away, and I think I can hear whimpering. Yes. It's whimpering. And moaning coming from the twisted wreckage.

And emerging behind a large vehicle marked "heavy rescue" is Victor. He's holding a TV camera on his shoulder with a small, intensely bright light mounted on top. There's also a long black stick protruding just above the lens that has to be a special microphone. Right behind Victor is a small skinny guy with slicked back greasy hair and aviator glasses, carrying a large video tape recorder, making him lean to one side under its weight. Another bag is dangling, on his other shoulder, which bulges with cables and other bulky pieces of equipment.

Victor isn't making a sound. He just slowly walks in a big circle around the scene illuminating whatever his camera is pointing at creating a kind of spotlight on the action. He rarely takes his eye off the camera's view finder, only looking down to see if he's going to trip on something. As he rounds the el pillar, he turns around and is walking backwards. As he does this, the other guy grabs him by the shoulder to guide him around the various obstacles in the street.

I have no desire to get any closer to witness what has to be a gruesome mess of tangled steel, broken glass, and twisted flesh and bone. Victor and his partner move as one, never interfering with the emergency workers. They even seem to occasionally nod and acknowledge each other's presence. After many sweeping circles of the sordid scene, Victor leads them past an ambulance to a side street. I make a big arc myself, avoiding getting too close to the action.

Next to Victor's Lincoln is a dumpy tow truck with the words "Victor's Towing" painted on the side. It's a converted pick-up truck that looks like it's been through a demolition derby. I peek into the Lincoln where Stubby and the two girls are sleeping like infants.

"Hey, Victor," I say from a few feet away, not wanting to get in the way as his partner frantically begins labeling tapes and putting things away.

"What's the matter? I saw you hiding over there," Victor says.

"I didn't want to get in the way."

"This is my partner, Bender."

"Hi, Bender."

Bender grunts his salutation.

"Will you be going to the ER next?"

"Nah. That chick ain't going to no ER. Next stop is the cooler for her."

"You don't think she's gonna make it?"

"No way. She's got a stick shift sticking through her skull. I always say drive automatic, don't I, Bender?"

Bender grunts as he concentrates on wrapping his cable neatly.

A wave a sadness came over me. The sounds I heard were the last gasps of life. I felt like I shouldn't be there.

"Did you get....anything good?" I ask Victor, hoping he

doesn't answer my question. In fact, I'm sorry I asked it.

"Nothing sellable. Just another traffic accident in the Bronx, that's all. But we got the towing job after they cut her out anyway."

"Why'd you even shoot it then?"

"You never know what you got when you shoot a disaster. Could've been a celebrity or something. Or maybe the car explodes and more people get hurt. You just cover your ass, you know what I mean?"

"Yeah."

"Hey, would you do me a favor, Jerry?"

"Sure."

"Take my car home with you, drop them off if they ever wake up, and I'll get it from you later tonight or tomorrow. I want to stick around with Bender and take care of some business, and I'm working anyway."

"Sure. No problem."

"It's already running but take these keys, too," Victor says as he whips a key ring full of keys right at my face. Luckily I catch them before they smash me in my newly sewn cheek.

"Just checking to see how sober you are."

"Thanks."

This I can't believe. Stubby and his two playmates are still fast asleep in the backseat of the Lincoln. The heater has been blasting in here for probably the past hour and it's like an oven. It doesn't smell exactly like fresh roses either. Whew! I've never even been in a car like this, never mind drive one. It's got a couple of dents and some unpainted Bondo on the outside, but everything seems to work, including the power everything. And needless to say, by the sound of the engine, it probably has one of those four-fifty engines, overhead cam and double barreled whatchamacallits. I'm definitely not a motorhead. We leave that to the guidos in the east Bronx.

I open the windows a crack with the neato electric window button and pull out of the parking space. I'm under the Woodlawn el heading back to the neighborhood. This neigh-

201

borhood and the el itself (The Woodlawn line) are named for the nearby Woodlawn cemetery. It's one of the great cemeteries of old New York. Some of the original wheelers and dealers that set up this gotham of greed are planted there. F. W. Woolworth, Henry Westinghouse, Joseph Pulitzer, and other giants of industry found their final resting place next to the el in the Bronx. Oh, sweet irony. But according to Eugene, this is also the final resting place of Charlie the Chinaman. With my passengers blissfully asleep, I decide to take a stroll in the cemetery.

A high cast iron fence surrounds the cemetery, but there are a couple of bars spread enough apart for a beer-toting teenager, or a skinny young man such as myself to slip through. I remember Eugene telling me it was by a grove near Duke Ellington's memorial. Although there are no lights in the cemetery itself, the pure white snow is reflecting enough light from the streetlights and the half moon to illuminate the eerie landscape dotted with massive statues of angels and crucifixes. I have no idea where I'm going but up ahead, there is a pine grove off to one side of a large group of impressive gravestones. Suddenly a train comes to a screeching halt at the end of the elevated line just a few hundred yards away, sending bright lightening like flashes across the landscape before me. It's the end of the number four train, but Duke's "Take The A Train" naturally pops into my mind. Before me are fourteen beautiful plots. And each one is marked "Ellington" including one for Edward Kennedy "Duke" Ellington. On just on the other side of the pine trees I can see several grave markers barely rising above the snow. I walk through the virgin snow under the pines and stop in front of the first of the row. I begin to slowly wipe the snow from the marker, revealing the engraved words, "YING LONG WANG" and below that, "HE LIVED IN PEACE. MAY HE REST IN PEACE." And below that was a very simple engraving of a small bird. Not an exotic bird, but a simple sparrow on a bare twig. And as I pushed more snow away I discovered something else; two other names on the tombstone. Just below the bird were "LIEN WANG, BELOVED WIFE AND MOTHER" and "MICHAEL

WANG, BELOVED SON."

I instinctively knelt in the snow and made the sign of the cross. This wasn't any cheap grave site. Noel, Eugene and whoever else was involved spent some real dough to put Charlie to rest in such a beautiful place with his family, just a few paces from the Ellington family plots. And they probably had to conduct extensive research to merely locate it.

I closed my eyes and began reciting "Hail Marys." I started counting them on my fingers, and when I got to ten, I recited the "Our Father." It often amazes me how in times of deepest sorrow and greatest joy, it's always the first prayers I ever learned that bring me the greatest, most profound comfort. And as I silently prayed, I visualized poor Charlie, feeding those little birds with eye droppers and wearing that silly paper hat. But as I let the silence of the moment fill my soul, somewhere high above I began to hear the unlikely sound of a small bird chirping a simple song. God rest your soul, Mr. Wang. I hope I can become half the man you were.

Back in the car I could see in my rearview mirror that the emergency crews were finally pulling someone, or maybe now, some-*thing,* out of the mangled mess of steel and glass. Victor's light illuminates them as they place her into a black body bag and begin zipping it up.

"Shit, it's fucking freezing in here! Who turned on the air conditioner?" Stubby screams as he begins to come back among the living.

"I had to get some of the stench out of here. What have you guys been eating? Hard boiled eggs and pigs feet? Marrone!"

"Where are we?" The girl who is intertwined around Stubby asks. "Wake up, Peggy," she says, shaking her friend who is attached to her backside.

"Oh, shit," Maria says with a look of surprise on her face. "I'm gonna throw up!"

"Pull over! Open the windows! Unlock the doors," Stubby yells into my ears while hitting on both shoulders with his fists.

Unfortunately, never having had a power everything car, I'm pushing the wrong buttons frantically at precisely the wrong moment as I try to pull over to the curb and open her window and unlock the door all at the same...

BLAAAHHHPPPHHHHTTTT.

HUMMMBLAATTTHCH.

Oops. Right in the car.

"Open the fucking door," Stubby says as he reaches over his new girlfriend and tries to open her door before she dumps another serving of her innards on him. He pushes the right button, the door opens, and he shoves Maria's ass out onto the snowy curb.

BLAAAAHHPPPHHHHTTTT

I've seen some interesting colors in the snow this evening. Blood... radiator fluid... green loogies... and now this technicolor masterpiece.

"Are you alright Maria," Peggy says as she holds her forehead gently.

"Yeah, yeah. I feel much better now," Maria says regaining her composure.

"You didn't have to push her out of the car, Stubby," Stubby's date says, chastising him.

"Yeah, what am I supposed to do, Peggy? Sit there and watch her blast the inside of Victor's car again? I was thinking on my feet."

"I'll do the thinnin' around here, Babalooey," I say in my best Quick Draw McGraw voice, trying to lighten things up.

"Oh, it's alright. I don't mind. He had to do something," Maria says, calming Peggy down.

"I better start cleaning this mess up," I say, getting out of the driver's seat to look for some rags in the trunk.

"It's got to be one of these keys," I say, fumbling a bit and inserting a key into the trunk lock.

"Bingo!"

The trunk is loaded with tools, every kind of car fluid

imaginable, an unopened still wrapped Christmas present, a spare tire, and some rags. I reach towards the furthest corner of the trunk, which is about as big as my bathroom, for the pile of old rags and as I pull something tumbles out.... a gun. I've lived in New York City my whole life, and I've never actually touched a gun. Even though I know cops, they always hide them, and the smart ones don't even take them into the bar with them. I decide not to mention it to Stubby and put it back from whence it came.

I take an old towel, rub it in some clean snow, and begin to do the best I can under the circumstances to clean up the putrid mess.

"I'm sorry, Jerry," Maria says, obviously humiliated.

"Oh, that's OK, I'm used to wiping up vomit. I do it all the time. Right, Stubby?"

"Jerry was vomit valedictorian in high school. He's the sidewalk pizza Sinatra of the Bronx. The throw up king of Kingsbridge."

"That's enough, Stubby," Peggy yells.

"This is cleaning up fine," I say, trying not to gag as I do my dirty work.

"Victor won't even notice. Believe me, he's had worse smells in this heap."

"All done. Let's go."

We all pile into the not-so-continental Lincoln and head back to the block.

I pull up in front of our building and park right in front.

"Goodnight, Stub. I'll call you in the morning," I say to the crowd as I attempt to sneak off into my apartment.

"Wait a minute, Jer," Stubby says chasing after me, leaving Peggy and Maria behind. He grabs my arm and walks me a couple of steps up. "Hey, come on! What's the rush? Come on into my place for a nightcap. You know what I'm talking about."

I can see by Stubby's face that he wants me to overlook

Maria's recent gastronomic disaster and take her off his hands for a night.

"Sorry, Stubby. I'm not hooking up with her tonight. I'm sure she's a very sweet person, and I'm glad I got a bird's eye view of her boobs when she did the watusi in the bar, but the thought of swapping bodily fluids with her on this night of all nights is not my idea of a romantic interlude. See ya."

"But Jerry! She likes you!" Stubby whispers with eyes bugging out.

"What is this, third grade? Tell her I'll meet her by the flagpole in the school yard tomorrow if she's still interested."

"Don't pull an attitude, Jerry. I don't want her hanging around. Please?"

"Not tonight, Stub."

"That's alright, Jerry. I understand. But do me a favor?"

"Yeah?"

Stubby sticks his hand right under my nose. "Does my hand smell like vomit?"

"Fuck you, Stubby. Good night."

"Good night."

As I walk up the steps to the door, I can hear Stubby and his two friends in heated conversation about something. What? All I know is I heard my name being mentioned more than once, and I don't even want to know the rest.

It seems like a week ago that I was ready to call it a night and try to have sweet dreams about Berta finally spending the night right here. Yes, here. I haven't tried to actually have sex with a girl within these hallowed walls since three or four birthdays ago. My parents were away somewhere for the weekend and after months of blue balls, I finally convinced Lucille Bartolli to abandon our usual spot on the center field grass in the park, or next to the side entrance at her parent's house by the garbage cans, and see what happens if we stopped by my place for a cup of tea. Lucille was three years behind me at Visitation grade school, and was one of those girls who you didn't even notice until the last month of eighth grade, when all of a sudden they go from a training bra to wearing huge XXL mens' sweatshirts to hide their newly sprouted breasts. She rarely dated guys from the neighborhood throughout high school or college, but I know of several local guys with broken hearts and empty wallets who couldn't even get past first base. And we're talking about a woman in her early twenties! The word was that Lucille had sex one time, and one time only, and that was on one of those vacations where a pack of girls run amuck in 'Lauderdale or the Bahamas and manage to extend their infliction of blue balls not only on guys from New York, but from all over the western hemisphere. She ran into some Cuban stud from Miami who must've had something that nobody in the Bronx has discovered yet, because she pined over this guy for a good year before she realized she had been taken for a ride.

So after Lucille uncharacteristically had more than a couple of cocktails, she reluctantly agreed to stop by my apartment for a cup of green tea. Well, whatever got into Lucille I'll never know, but she pretty much attacked me on the living room couch and we rolled onto the rug, pawing one another in the dark, like two blind people trying to apply suntan lotion on each other. Much to my delight, things started getting unzipped, grabbed, and shall I say handled in a most pleasurable manner. Wow! Lucille must be ready! With my sneakers still on and my jeans around my ankles, my knees already are experiencing a nasty case of rug burn. She frantically began wiggling and gyrating trying to push her skintight jeans down into an accounts receivable position while I kept myself busy enjoying her other ample assets laid out before me. The supreme moment of truth was at hand, or should I say, *in* her hand, as she guided me towards her portal of pleasure. Here goes... attempt #1... (pause) attempt #2... (pause) attempt #3... (ouch) attempt #4... (ouch again)

"Stop! Get off!" She said in no uncertain terms.

"What'd I do? What's the matter?"

"Just stop right now."

"OK. Alright. What's wrong?"

"If you ever tried having a log shoved up your butt, you'd know."

Pants were pulled up. Buttons closed. Shirts tucked back in. The moment was gone, and so was Lucille. Never again would we even so much as shake hands. The embarrassment was too much for her. And for me, too.

Shit. More graffiti. Yet another "Latin Eagles" written in large black letters between the elevator and my front door. What a way to cap off the evening; get the turpentine out and spend the next half hour scrubbing the wall. Oh well. I've got nothing else to do. I can't have Berta seeing "Latin Eagles" scrawled next to my front door. I won't even get her as far as I got Lucille. And let's just hope it doesn't have a similar ending.

208

A winter wonderland morning it's not. I can see the Major Deegan Expressway out my bedroom window, and traffic is flowing as usual, despite the fact that mere hours ago it was a silent white road with hardly a vehicle to be seen. Now the shoulders are piled high with black piles of wet stuff that used to be called snow. Cars and trucks are crunching through the salt that was spread by the ton. Have you ever driven past one of those salt spreaders? They whip out little rocks of salt in a fifteen foot radius and your car is pelted by it. The noise scares the hell out of you and it leaves little micro dents in your paint.

Ow. Oh yeah. My face. It's more of a dull throbbing pain now. I look like I just lost a fight with a dashboard in a car wreck. The area surrounding the wound has transformed into a large black-and-blue shiner that reaches right into my eye. As I carefully lift the bandage to see how the hippie-dippy doctor sewed up my skin, I'm disturbed by the redness and pus that has oozed onto the gauze. Hmmm. Not so bad. The skin around the wound looks alive and healthy, and he has created a nice straight line of skin. I'll wait until it's all the way healed before I start sending fruit baskets to the emergency room. Oh, shit. Victor's car! Any car parked on Bronx Street is somewhat of a target for theft, but particularly one with several radios mounted under the dash. I put on the clothes I threw on the floor immediately before retiring and head out into the hall barefoot, knowing I can get a good glimpse from the lobby window.

No. No. No. It's gone. In the spot where Victor's car was sits a gypsy cab waiting for a fare.

I rush back into my house. Should I call Stubby first? No. I'll call Victor. Where's that card? Here. I dial as fast as I can. One ring... two rings... three rings... four rings...

"Hello, Victor? Yeah, hey, ah, is everything OK with your car?..... Oh, I mean, it started OK and everything when you picked it up early this morning, right? You didn't pick it up? Then I guess it's stolen. I'm very sorry, Victor. You don't have to call me names, Victor. No, I didn't call the police. I'll call them now. Victor I'm sorry. I'M SORRY.... Oh. You've had it for hours and everything's fine. Very funny, Victor. OK. What? Yeah, I'd love to. Thanks! No, thanks! Yeah! Great! You'll pick me up in an hour. See ya!"

Victor is a Bronx ballbuster supreme. He goes from tearing my heart out by making me think somebody stole his car while I had it, to inviting me to meet his boss who's going to be looking for a few new guys in the near future. Usually good-cop, bad-cop is *two* people.

Victor was five minutes early. I was running a couple of minutes late.

"Let's go! I'm double parked!" Victor's voice echoes through the lobby as he bangs on my door.

"Be right there," I answer, looking one more time at my multicolored face in the bathroom mirror.

"I'll be outside."

"Be right out." I'm not sure what the reaction to my bandaged mug will be. If I was going to an interview with Chase Manhattan Bank, I guess I'd be a little concerned. But a guy who hires only tow truck drivers I would think may have a different opinion of seeing somebody with a battle scar or two.

"Alright, alright, alright!" Victor is screaming greatly agitated because someone can't get out of his parking space because Victor has blocked it with his tow truck. He reluctantly pulls up the five feet that the guy needed to get out. I hop in the passenger side door, not a second too soon.

"Everybody's a fuckin' wiseass," Victor says, referring to the guy pulling away who flips him the finger without even turning his head. "Normally I'd chase that pencil-necked geek off the fuckin' road. But I'm in a good mood this morning. Whoa!" He exclaims, doing a double take on me. "Shit. You look like Jerry Quarry after

210

a title match."

"Yeah, it looks kind of bad. But it feels a lot better."

"I hope so. If it felt like it looks, I'd have to put you out of your misery."

"Will your boss be freaked out by it?"

"Nah. He's used to guys coming in lookin' like they were riding in the back of a cement mixer. One of our guys got stabbed once at a crime scene."

"He got there when the perp was still hanging around?"

"Nah. He got stabbed by another cameraman. It gets nasty out there. You ever been stuck or shot or anything?"

"Not exactly. Does getting hit in the face with an iceball count?"

"Don't tell Barbieri that. Tell him you were in a fight. A bar fight. He'll like that."

"Really?"

"Oh, yeah. He loves that shit."

"Sounds like an interesting character."

"Yeah. So was fuckin' Manson. Watch this."

Just before the entrance to the FDR Drive in Inwood, a group of Black and Puerto Rican kids were slowly jaywalking across the street in front of us. It's obvious that if Victor maintained his speed, he would safely cruise past the group missing them easily by the width of a car. Instead he presses his giant black steel-tipped work boot against his custom chrome accelerator pedal in the shape of a bare foot to the floor. The engine explodes with speed and the roar echoes against the giant twenty-five story projects amplifying the rumble of the giant V-8 engine even more. I can see the faces of the boys and girls looking in shock and horror as they come to the realization that a tow truck is speeding right towards them. He splits the group in half as some decide to cut back to the sidewalk while the rest dart the rest of the way across the street. Victor's face is beaming with glee as he slices through the crowd. I turn around and see the stunned group giving us the finger and calling us motherfuckers, cocksuckers, assholes, mixed in with assorted death threats.

"Victor! What did you do that for? You could've killed somebody!"

"Nah. That's why I got such loud pipes. They heard me coming in plenty of time. You never heard that saying?"

"What's that?"

"Loud pipes save lives."

"Yeah, but you're not supposed to be saving them from your own homicidal attack."

"Aw, I wasn't going to hit them. This thing stops on a dime. Besides, I gave them something to talk about. They'll be talking about that for the rest of their lives. Y'know, real life thrills and chills. That's what you always remember in life."

"Never mind, Victor. Just do me a favor and save the thrills and chills for Coney Island, huh?"

"OK, let me ask you something, Jerry?"

"What?"

"What do you remember about growing up? The boring stupid shit? All the times you sat on your fuckin' front stoop bored out of your mind with your thumb up your ass wonderin' what was for dinner that night? No. You remember what? You don't even have to tell me. I'll tell you. You remember sticking an M-80 in somebody's tailpipe? You remember the time you almost got caught by the cops after you busted some prick's window with a rock? You remember the first time the class whoo-ah let you stick your hand up her plaid skirt during recess while the nuns were standing on the other side of the school yard? You remember pushing an old jalopy off a cliff into the Hudson River and watching it slowly sink...?"

"...alright, alright already! If you tell me what else I did in my childhood, I may just turn myself in at the next police station."

"Am I right? Ain't that the shit you remember growing up? Ain't that what you talk about when you get together with the boys from the block?"

"You got me, Victor. You're right."

212

"So who says all that shit has to end. Now the thrills get bigger, and if you're lucky, you get paid for getting them."

"Like shooting video of disasters."

"Exactly. See? You're making the connection, right?"

"Right."

As we bounce down the FDR Drive hitting every pot-hole from Harlem to the U.N. and hanging six inches off of every bumper we're behind, Victor has a smirk plastered across his face like he just taught his little brother how to tie his shoes for the first time. Oh, he's pleased with himself. And for God knows what reason, I'm going along for the ride.

We exit the FDR at 23rd Street and head west. He pulls up in front of a "luxury" apartment building just past Second Avenue. In New York, a building that wasn't built before the war, has an elevator and a garbage chute, and doesn't have windows busted out or graffiti scrawled on the outside is a "luxury" building. Every "luxury" apartment in that same building, however, is rampant with cockroaches, and the basement is crawling with mice and rats. I don't care if you're living in a ten million dollar penthouse on Park Avenue, you've got roaches in the kitchen and rats in the basement. It's just one of those things that make New Yorkers bond so beautifully.

"Are we picking somebody up here?" I ask Victor as he hops out of the truck.

"Nah. This is where the office is."

"In an apartment building?"

"It's a converted basement apartment. He's the super, too."

"Wait a minute. Barbieri's a tow truck dispatcher, he's got a video news company, *and* he's the super of the building?"

"You got it."

"I can't wait to meet this guy."

"Yeah, and I can't wait to see the look on your face when you do."

Victor leaves the truck in the "loading and unloading

only" zone in front of the building and we enter the lobby. As in most "luxury" buildings, there's a front desk with a twenty-four hour attendant on duty. A man about sixty years old with the map of Ireland plastered across his mug, wearing a uniform that looks like a high school marching band reject from the 1940s, sits behind the counter watching a tiny black and white TV that has a bent coat hanger coated with aluminum foil as an antenna.

"Hey, Sean," Victor says, without stopping as he flings a set of keys onto the counter. "We'll be about a half-hour."

"Gotcha," says the man swimming in his ridiculously ill-fitting maroon uniform, with a gravelly voice belying his slight, bony frame.

"Sean takes care of us," Victor says, pulling open a stair-well door leading down to the basement.

Next to an empty laundry room is a steel door with a small peephole and a nondescript sign reminiscent of the kind you'd see on somebody's desk in an office with someone's name on it that reads: "Video News Services." Victor pushes the button on a small intercom box. An annoyed voice quickly responds.

"Who is it?"

"Victor."

The door buzzes and Victor pushes through. We enter. I could see that what was once a small living room, has been converted into a reception area. There's an industrial steel desk in front of a large, very professionally made red and white plastic sign that reads "Video News Services." There are several large framed photographs of black and white photos blown up to poster size, each one depicting the same hugely obese cameraman in a frenzied situation.

"Don't tell me," I ask Victor quietly, " Barbieri?"

"Himself."

On the wall to the left of the "Video News Services" sign there is a framed photograph with a blurry image in the foreground of a man about thirty with a large nose, a receding hairline, and bushy dark hair being escorted through an angry mob. In clear focus just behind the fuzzy image of the suspect is Barbieri with his video camera pointing directly at the action.

"Know who this is?" Victor asks me in a hushed tone, pointing at the fuzzy man in the foreground who is obviously the object of the mob's attention. "'The Subway Slasher.' And this over here," he says crossing to the photo on the other side of the sign with Barbieri again prominent in the frame as he shoots a line of looters, calmly and in an orderly fashion, exiting an electronics store with boxes of assorted electronic devices. "This was in Bed-Stuy during the blackout riots of seventy-seven. It was in almost every newspaper and magazine in the fucking world. And this one over here," Victor says, pointing to a photo with Yankee first baseman Chris Chambliss knocking a fan into full flight as he runs from home plate to the dugout in fear of his life as a crazed crowd surrounds him. "See Barbieri there," Victor says pointing to Barbieri aiming a small movie camera at the action, "that's Chambliss' homer that clinched the pennant in seventy-six. He's shooting with a fucking Filmo."

From behind a closed door just to the right of the photo a voice screams, "Victor, get your ass in here!"

"I guess that's Barbieri, huh?" I nervously ask Victor.

Victor just scrunches his face into a contorted laugh and nods in the affirmative.

Victor reaches for the doorknob. "It's locked."

A couple of bolts are turned on the other side of the secured door and it swings open. The first thing that struck me was the sound of ten, maybe twenty different scanner radios, several television sets all tuned to different channels, creating a cacophony of electronic noise. All kinds of buzzes and bleeps and tones and dull voices announcing unintelligible code words and commands over the radios.

"Hi, Rocco, this is a buddy of mine from my cousin's block, Jerry Pellicano," Victor says as the huge Barbieri returns to his oversized leather chair behind his massive oak desk. "He just graduated college and he's doing some hippie video shit in SoHo."

215

Barbieri plops down into the leather chair and the air hisses out like a deflating balloon. He looks at me and immediately his face contorts into a perplexed expression.

"What the fuck happened to you?" He asks me.

"Oh, this?" I say, instinctively pointing to my bandage.

"No. I mean you're fucking Italian nose. Yeah, what the fuck happened to you?"

"Oh, ah, I got into a ah, little, er, mix up in a bar," I stutter.

"I hope the other fucker looks worse. So, Victor, I'm watching your shit from the four alarm fire last week in Chelsea and I nearly fucking threw up. How many fucking times do I have to tell you to fucking set up your focus before the fucking tape is rolling. In and out in and out with the fucking zoom, trying to focus when you're in, when you're out, when you're in. Jesus H. Fucking Christ, you zoom in, get focused and that's it. Roll fucking tape."

"I think the back focus was out on that shoot," Victor says timidly.

"Well you're supposed to fucking check that out before you're out in the field, aren't you?"

"I know, but I was in a hurry."

"Don't give me that shit, we're always in a fucking hurry here. That's why we're in fucking business. We're in a hurry, and everybody else is not in a hurry, and we get the job done before anybody else and sell it. That's the whole fucking point. Get it?"

"Alright, I fucked up, I'm sorry," Victor says assertively.

"OK. Now what can I do for your buddy here?"

"Well, I heard you and St. John might be looking for some college guys for the new contract you've been talking about."

"St. John, come in here," Barbieri screams into an intercom on his desk.

"I want you to talk to St. John, what's your name again?"

"Jerry Pellicano."

"Hey a fucking paisan' too. OK. Good."

216

I wasn't about to add that I was half Irish.

The door opens and a blonde haired blue eyed guy about twenty-five enters with perfectly coiffed short blonde hair, a yellow alligator golf shirt, and designer blue jeans with a crease down the front.

"Jerry Pellicano, this is my partner, Schuyler St. John."

Schuyler reaches out and gives me one of those dead fish handshakes and a phony half-hearted smile.

"Where'd you go to school?" Schuyler asks.

"You mean, college?" I stupidly ask.

"Yes. College," he replies with an air of superiority oozing out.

"Manhattan City College."

"That's a city school, right?"

"Yeah. I guess you're not from the city, huh?"

"I've been here over five years..."

"St. John's from D.C. and don't fuck with him or his father'll hang ya from the closest yardarm."

"What's your father, a cop or something?"

"Not exactly. He's a judge," Schuyler says smugly.

"A fucking federal judge appointed by the president," Barbieri proudly announces, leaning forward in his chair as it creaks under his immense weight.

"You went to school, I mean college in the city?" I ask St. John as he steps away from me to sit on the edge of the desk near Barbieri.

"Yeah, Princeton."

"Princeton? That's Jersey!" I say, probably with an air of my own brand of superiority.

"I told you St. John! Don't fuckin' refer to Princeton as if it's New York. It ain't fuckin' New York. It's in a fucking huge smelly, stinking swamp called New Jersey," Barbieri says, riding Schuyler, who is obviously trying to pretend that he's not bothered by it.

"You fucking know what I mean!" St. John mimics back to

Barbieri in a weak imitation of a pissed off New Yorker. "It's in the New York metropolitan area. I spent every weekend in MAN-hattan..."

"We know, we know. You know MAN-hattan like the tip of your dick," Barbieri says, emphasizing the common mispronunciation of the borough by tourists. "OK, OK, you're a fucking New Yorker," He says, trying to calm St. John down, who at this time, is having a hard time hiding his flushed red face. "Pellicano, what do you want to do?" Barbieri says, putting the focus back on me.

"Work in television."

"Doing what? I hate when people say that. That's like saying I want to work for the city. You want to be a camera-man, an editor, a sound man, a fucking make-up artist, what, what, what?" Barbieri rattles off at me, waving his hands like a butcher on Mott Street arguing with a cheap old lady.

"I want to be an editor."

"There we go. Schuyler, we're going to need a couple of editors soon, right?"

"Yeah. If everything goes according to our second quarter proposal," Schuyler says, finally back to his normal color: pale white. "Can you show us some tape?"

"Like a demo reel?"

"Not *like* a demo reel. A fucking real demo reel," Barbieri says, shaking his head.

"Yeah, I can put one together this week at work."

"Where's work?" St. John inquisitively asks.

"I work at Radical Video in SoHo."

"You work with Amy Gold?" St. John says, charged with even more curiosity.

"Yeah."

"Cool. We've studied her work in college. Did you do production, or were you a gofer?" St. John asks, reverting back to his arrogant self.

"Well, if by production work, you mean have I directed a series of Amy Gold's nude dance pieces, the answer would have to be yes."

"Hold on there! You directed nude dance pieces?" Barbieri asks practically leaping out of his chair, which is nearly a physical impossibility. "Nude chicks or guys?"

"Nude females only."

"Now that's a fucking demo reel. You bring that in next week as your fucking demo reel and we'll fucking talk. I'm sick of looking at the same fucking boring shit on demo reels. Fires and car wrecks and body bags, I want to see some fucking artsy fartsy shit with a little tits and ass. Next week, OK? Anything else, St. John?"

"Nope."

"Anything else, Victor?"

"Nope."

"Next week. Demo reel. Bye."

"Thanks, Rocco; thanks, Schuyler. Nice to meet you guys," I say as we exit the office.

"Man, you are one lucky dude," Victor says as we walk through the reception area and head out the door.

"Are you serious?"

"They are asking you to come back next week. You know how many demo reels they've got in boxes. Tons. Piles of 'em. In fact, whenever we're low on videotape stock, we just put an ad in a magazine for demo reels, and we get truckloads of free tapes."

"And does Barbieri talk to everybody like that?"

"No. Usually he's much worse. I could tell he liked you."

"Man, I'd hate to get on his bad side."

"He's got a saying I'm sure he'll spring on you some time: 'Treat me good and I'll treat you better. Treat me bad, and I'll treat you worse.'"

"Thanks for the warning."

As we pass the counter in the lobby, Sean the attendant hops up to give Victor his keys. "I had to plead with two meter maids not to ticket your truck there, Victor," Sean says in a voice that has been shaped by decades of Irish whiskey and Old Gold cigarettes.

"Yeah, yeah, here you go, thanks, Sean," Victor says as he shoves a couple of dollar bills into Sean's hand, which he discreetly holds, palm facing the rear, right next to his front pants pocket.

"You really directed a video with a bunch of nude chicks?" Victor asks as we hop into his truck.

"Yeah. It was my very first assignment."

"Well, why the fuck do you want to work for Barbieri then?"

"Hey, his stuff's on real TV."

"What's the difference?"

"Hmmm. Good question," and just as I finish, Victor slams his foot on his chrome accelerator, peeling out and making a right on Second Avenue with tires squealing.

"I need an egg cream." Victor says, as he heads south.

"Don't tell me. Gem Spa."

"Fucking-ay!"

Second Avenue should be renamed The Second Avenue Speedway. It's always curb to curb with cabbies and commercial traffic avoiding the traffic on the FDR. I don't think there's another street in New York where the traffic lights are set any better. If you go fifty miles an hour, you're pretty much assured of getting six to ten green lights in a row. You couldn't go farther on the Jersey Turnpike in better time. If you're not used to it, it's a harrowing near-death experience. It's a cross between bumper cars and demolition derby. The only vehicles that dare to compete in the downtown death ride are Checker cabs, beat up delivery vans, and gypsy cabs. Throw into the mix bicycle riding kamikaze messengers, lost tourists, potholes that could swallow a small elephant, bums pushing their shopping cart caravans, and little old ladies jaywalking, and you've got a thrill ride better than Palisades Amusement Park ever had.

"You like Gem Spa better than Dave's Luncheonette?" I ask Victor.

"Definitely. Creamier head at Gem Spa."

I have great respect for an egg cream connoisseur. Not many people will make the effort to find the perfect egg cream. Used to be there was a place on every block that served up a good egg cream; a Coke glass wider at the top than at the bottom, a quality brand of chocolate syrup like "Diamond" or "Fox's U-Bet", chilled, fresh, whole milk, a soda fountain seltzer dispenser, and the correct wrist action while holding a teaspoon to spritz the seltzer properly creating a perfect "egg white" head. Of course there aren't any eggs in an egg cream, but by the look of the head a true egg cream artist creates, you'd swear it was egg white on top.

But now, you're lucky to find one place in an entire neighborhood that carries on the true egg cream tradition. Candy stores are tearing out their soda fountains and replacing them with shelf space for everything from disposable diapers to lottery machines.

"You know the secret to a really great head?" I ask Victor, trying to determine the depth of his egg cream knowledge.

"The wrist action... the seltzer... the syrup..."

"...Yes," I say interrupting him, "but the real secret, the one not easily viewed by the casual observer, is the fact that the really good places keep the milk in the freezer."

"Huh?"

"Yup. In the freezer. But only a place that makes lots of egg creams per hour can do that. Otherwise, the milk will actually freeze and be ruined. But a place that has high egg cream turnaround and can keep the milk in the freezer making it as cold as possible, but never allowing it to freeze, will have the best egg cream head."

"What are you, a fucking egg cream guru?"

"Just a purist."

"What about Dave's? Freezer?"

"Nope. In fact, you'll see that at Dave's, during busy periods, they'll even keep the milk on the counter. Worst thing you can do."

I glance down at the speedometer and see we're going

over fifty miles and hour, and rattletrap Checker cabs are still passing us. Suddenly a Checker cab speeding just ahead of us swerves sharply right in front of us trying to avoid a pothole.

"Shit!" Victor screams as he yanks his wheel to the right barely missing the nearly out of control yellow cab. But just as the Checker starts to straighten out, he nicks the left front fender on Victor's tow truck.

"Motherfucker!" Victor yells at the top of his lungs. The cab has stopped, leaving it kissing Victor's front end.

"Motherfucking moron," Victor howls as he jumps out of the truck in a rage. He runs over to the driver side of the cab and pounds on the driver's window. I also get out, and get myself into a better position to properly observe the situation in case I have to make a police report.

"Open the fucking window. Open the fucking window," Victor wails as he continues to punch the glass. I can see a small turbaned man sitting in the driver's seat with both hands clutching the steering wheel. In the backseat is a terrified middle-aged couple that looks like they just came from a Broadway show. The cab driver carefully opens his window a crack.

"I'm sorry! I'm sorry! I'm sorry to hit you! No damage! No damage! No damage!" The panic-stricken Indian cabbie says.

I look over at the point of impact, and there is a slight indentation about the size of a half dollar, and some scratched off paint.

"Gimme fifty bucks you motherfucker! Fifty fucking bucks right now! Fifty bucks!" Victor wails.

"No cash. No cash. I just came out of garage. First fare. First fare," the cabbie explains.

"Bullfuckingshit! Gimme fifty dollars! Now motherfucker!"

Suddenly I see some activity in the front seat. If this guy's reaching for a gun and blows Victor away, there isn't a jury in the world that will convict him. Victor is behaving like a madman, and a crowd of potential witnesses has already gathered. A gun barrel does not come through the opening of the window, but two twenties do.

"It's all I have. Take it, please. Please take it," the cabbie pleads.

"Alright asshole. But you know that's at least seventy-five dollars worth of damage. You fucking know it." Victor says as he shoves the forty bucks into his front pocket and heads back to his truck.

The cab peels out, blowing right through a red light. I get back in with Victor.

"What the hell was that?" I ask.

"If I didn't do that, I would've fucking been burned. He does that shit all day long, bouncing into cars and shit. Fucking towel head motherfuckers," he says, and then sticks his head out the window, "Learn how to fucking drive you assholes! Whoa!"

Victor swerves the truck sharply to the right, forcing a cab to jam on its brakes, narrowly missing us.

"Almost missed Gem Spa," Victor sheepishly says.

The cab pulls alongside and the driver and two passengers are giving us the finger, screaming "You fucking asshole! Learn how to drive!" among other rude suggestions.

"Yeah, fuck you, too," Victor mumbles, unaffected by the display of outrage. "Let's get some egg creams!"

Gem Spa at the corner of St. Marks Place and Second Avenue is egg-cream junkie heaven. Not only do they have the best egg creams in the city, but on the counter they have the sweetest most exotic cheap candies individually wrapped for under a quarter each, and an extremely liberal magazine reading policy. The corner is in the bull's-eye of the East Village just a couple of blocks away from "alphabet city" (Avenues A, B, C and D), the junkie capital of the northeastern part of the United States. There aren't any stools available to sit on. The few stools at the rear of the counter are always loaded with bundles of magazines, newspapers, and other mainstays of candy store commerce, but that's just to keep anyone from hanging out there for too long.

Although they do cater to the East Village literati and Eastern European immigrants with an amazingly eclectic mix of periodicals and magazines, they somehow have managed to hold onto the basic tenets of the traditional New York candy store that even predates Louie in the "Bowery Boys"; a cantankerous, but funny, richly ethnic personality behind the counter, a soda fountain, an outside counter with a newsstand underneath, and a plastic see-through cylinder filled with pretzel rods.

"Don't buy nothing you don't need. What'll it be fellas?" A short, pudgy man in his sixties wearing a *New York Daily News* apron bellows. He has a face that looks like a partially deflated basketball with thick dark hairs sticking out of his ears and nose, and grey stubble that west of the Mississippi would be called whiskers. He's wearing one of those black vinyl hats that has fake black fur flaps that fall over the ears, with straps dangling, and a front fake fur flap that goes straight up pressing against the forehead and snaps into position with a single snap-button. There's also a black vinyl covered button on the top. It's the very hat that for decades has sent boys running in a panic out into the freezing winter, bareheaded, rather than allow concerned mothers to affix such a ridiculous lid on one's skull. A kid only had to unknowingly wear it once, to suffer the humiliation and violent bullying that accompany such lame articles of clothing. But this guy could give a shit. The street side window counter is open all day and night in this place, and it's freezing.

"I'll have a large egg cream," Victor says politely.

"Me, too."

First thing he does is reach below the soda fountain and opens a door. He pulls out a quart size carton of milk.

"It's so fucking cold in here, I don't even have to put the milk in the freezer."

I elbow Victor in the side as the rumpled man creates the exquisite beverage with panache, just as he has done thousands of times before. There's a comforting feeling even in the preparation of the drink. The splosh of the syrup into the

224

bottom of the Coke glass, the dabble of ice cold milk that for a moment doesn't mix with the chocolate but just sits on top creating a perfect yin-yang of black and white. The first spritz of seltzer onto the spoon that begins the mixing of the two substances, and the sound of the spoon clanking against the glass, at first high pitched and manic, but quickly becoming only a rich thud as the thick faux egg white head takes shape, creating a dome of white that rises slightly above the rim of the glass.

"Two bucks," the counter man says as he wipes the bottom of each glass with his apron just before placing them in front of us on the counter.

"Hey, this is on me, sport," I insist as I pull a fiver out of my pocket.

"Hey happy fucking New Year to you, too," the egg cream man says in mock jubilation as he pulls two dollar bills out of his apron.

Victor picks up his glass and in one complete movement, not pausing even for a second to admire the chocolate concoction, dumps the entire glass down his gullet in one gulp, followed by a single "aaaah."

"That's no way to drink an egg cream, Victor."

"Huh?"

"You didn't even taste that."

"What're you talking about?"

"You didn't savor the richness, the subtlety of the fizzing flavor bubbles, the slight bitterness of the chocolate, the color at the bottom of the glass as you finish tilting it upside down to get the very last drop."

"Are you fucking nuts? I'll have another large, please, and two pretzels," Victor says, shaking his head in disgust as though I was telling him how to breathe.

"You drink your egg cream the way you like, and I'll drink mine the way I like. This is America you know."

"Damn right this is America," egg cream man butts in. "My old man came over here from Russia in 1919. He was lucky to get

225

out. Came over on a boat, landed on Ellis Island, moved to Canal Street, worked fourteen hours a day six days a week his whole life right on these streets around here. I don't think he ever went above 34th Street his whole life. Some day I'm getting out of New York. Can't take it anymore. Too many goddamned foreigners. You want another one too, kid?"

"Nah. I'm savoring this one. Hey Victor, could you do me a favor?"

"Depends. Shoot."

"Could you give me a lift down to my job in SoHo?"

"The place where you did the nudie videos?"

"I prefer you don't put it that way, but yeah."

"Yeah, I'll give you a lift, if you let me check the place out," Victor says with his mouth stuffed with the second pretzel rod.

"If you mean, can you come up and look around for a minute, sure. But don't say anything about the nudie video, OK?"

"Me? Nah. Waddyuh think I am, a jerk or something? I'll be cool. Let's roll."

The ride to Spring Street was a quick one, especially since Victor made every green light along the way, and only narrowly missing one major accident.

"Let me go up first," I suggest to Victor, thinking I can make sure that there are no potentially embarrassing situations awaiting. All I really have to do today is inspect the control room and make sure everything is in good shape for the following week of classes that are going to start. Hopefully, there's no one else up there.

Since the front door is double locked, and also the main entrance upstairs, I assume the place is empty. I step inside, and it certainly appears that way.

"Hello? Anyone here?"

"In here!"

Shit. That's Amy. Just what I need.

"I'm in the control booth."

Well, I guess I'll have to just feel this out whether or not I should have Victor come up.

Despite the hand drawn sign I made prohibiting smoking, the booth is filled with cigarette smoke. Amy is slouched in her chair with her feet propped up on the console. She's wearing a black leather jacket, skintight black corduroy pants, and a black beret. On the large black and white monitor, one of Amy's nude dance videos is playing back as she stares, eyes wide open, cigarette in mouth, her hands slowly keeping in time with the music as though she's conducting an orchestra.

"Is everything working alright?" I ask just as Amy herself leaps into the frame and squirms her nude body into the gyrating bare assed group.

"Yes, yes, sshh," she admonishes me as she holds up both palms straight out, like a traffic cop stopping oncoming traffic. "Yes, everything's fine, Jerry. Are you working to-day?"

"Only if you need me."

"No, not at all. Enjoy your weekend. We've got a big month ahead."

"OK, I'll be here Monday afternoon. Bye."

On the way down the stairs, I couldn't help but imagine what Victor's reaction to that situation might have been. Maybe he wouldn't have had any reaction. Or maybe he would've said something so embarrassingly rude, it may have gotten me fired. I'll never know.

"Sorry, Victor. Not a good time for a visit."

"Why not?"

"The boss is up there and she's busy."

"Busy doing what?"

"What's the difference, she's busy."

"Yeah, well I gotta hit the head."

"Oh bullshit."

227

"I do. I gotta take a leak. Can't I go up there?"

"Aw, Victor, use the bar on the corner."

"Hey, fuck you, I fucking bring you in to where I work to meet my boss and you're fucking...."

"...alright, alright, come on up."

Victor locks the truck as I open the locks to the office door.

"Man, this is pretty shitty in here," Victor says as we make our way up the stairs in the turn of the century industrial building.

"All these buildings are like this down here. These used to be manufacturing plants."

"Shit, I'm glad I never had to work somewhere like this."

I pause in front of the door to Radical Video.

"Victor, do me a favor. If we go inside, and you see that nude video playing, don't say anything, er, impolite, OK? Just pretend it's the same as a cooking show or something. No funny comments, alright?"

"Hey, what am I, a fucking moron? I didn't give you instructions...."

"....OK, OK, let's go."

I open the door once again, and it's easy to hear that Amy is still screening the video.

"I'm back, Amy."

"Come in here a minute," she says over the loud music playing at what I remember to be the climax of the piece.

"Hi, Amy, this..."

"Sshhh," Amy says with her finger positioned directly above the all stop button on the playback machine. She then pushes the button forcefully. "Right there! Can you fade to black right there, Jerry?" Amy says as she turns her head toward us. "Oh, you have a guest."

"This is a friend of mine. Victor this is my boss, Amy..."

"...please don't call me that. Amy Gold, nice to meet you," Amy says, reaching past me to shake hands with Victor.

"Victor shoots TV news."

228

"Really? You work for a television station?"

"Nah. I'm a stringer."

"A stringer? What's a stringer?"

"We shoot stuff, and then sell it to whoever wants to buy?"

"Oh. Like what?"

"Accidents. Homicides. You know, blood and guts."

The look on Amy's face has gone from polite friendliness to one of disfiguring shock and disbelief. Her face is twitching and her nostrils are pulsating as though she just got a whiff of something awful. The sides of her mouth are trying to form some kind of new expression, but just kind of quiver instead.

"Blood and guts, as in that's what you look for?"

"Victor, didn't you have to use the men's room, it's straight back on the left."

"Oh, yeah, thanks," Victor says as he shuffles away.

Amy is quietly staring at me. I don't know if I'm going to get fired or spat on.

"Jerry, this is fantastic. He's a friend of yours?"

"Ah, yeah."

"This would be a fantastic video verite' documentary! Think of it!"

"You think?"

"Of course! This is something new. Exciting. This is the kind of thing PBS dies for; portraying the mainstream media as the bloodthirsty whores we all know they are. The new video ambulance chasers, searching the bowels of New York for the grisliest sights imaginable. Feeding the insatiable bloodlust of the masses. It's extraordinary! I'll want a proposal by Monday. Use Sandra if you need to. This is great," she says excitedly, pulling me with both hands and giving me a big wet kiss on the lips just as Victor returns.

"The toilet's stopped up," Victor says. "I didn't do it. It's just stopped up."

Amy looks at me and makes a pleading gesture. "Could you fix it before you leave, Jerry? Oh, what happened to your face?"

"Oh, ah, I walked into a door. Sure. Come on Victor, you can help."

As we walk towards the toilet, much to my horror and dismay, I can already smell the disaster that awaits me.

Victor looks at me, shaking his head like a little puppy dog. "I didn't over paper, I swear. It just.... backed up."

"I thought you just had to take a leak?"

"So what? I'm supposed to announce to you I gotta take a dump? Sheesh, what a pain in the ass you are."

"Yeah, well who's the pain in the ass now?"

"Alright, alright. I'll help you," Victor reluctantly agrees.

"Victor, something tells me this is the beginning of a wonderful professional relationship," I say as I hand him a mop and a bucket.

"Next time use the bar on the corner," I urge Victor as I put the finishing touches on the tools of the trade in the slop sink.

"In *this* neighborhood? I'd rather use the subway toilet than drop my drawers in one of these fag bars."

"Yeah, right, Victor. The sight of your fat butt heading for the john in a fern bar is going to cause a real commotion. Only not to get into the bathroom, but to clear the fuck out! Don't flatter yourself."

"What do you know about gay bars?"

"I know that most of them are cleaner than the Bronx hell holes we hang out in."

"So you've been in gay bars?"

"Victor, you know what you are? You're a homophobe."

"Fuck you, I ain't no homo!"

"Not a homo. A homo-phobe. Someone who has an

undue fear of homosexuality."

"And what do you call someone with an undue *liking* of homosexuality?"

"I don't know. What?"

"A fucking homo. Case closed."

"Look, I got a date tonight and thanks to your gastrointestinal distress I've got to go home to take several baths and burn my clothes. Let's go back to the block, alright?"

Victor was silent all the way down the stairs, into the truck, and up to the 138th Street bridge which connects Manhattan with The Bronx.

"You ain't got a date with a guy, do you?"

"What?"

"Just answer the question."

"Are you out of..."

"Just answer the question!" Victor says through clenched teeth, gripping the wheel at ten and two.

"No, I don't have date with a guy. I have a date with probably the most beautiful female that anyone's ever seen this side of the 225th Street bridge. Are you satisfied?"

"OK, OK. Case closed. By the way, what did your boss say when I was walking to the bathroom? Was she cool?"

"Yeah, she was cool. She didn't say anything really. Just asked what kind of work you did?"

"Yeah? Cool? Is she a lesbo?"

"You are a homophobe! I swear!"

"Oh, just can it, huh. Here's your stop," Victor says as he pulls up in front of my building. "Are you going to be near a phone later if I need some help tonight?"

"Help what?"

"Working? Remember that thing? My J.O.B.?"

"Yeah, call me here at home?"

"Oh, planning a hot date at home, huh?"

"Yeah, maybe. If my evil plan works."

"Don't leave the phone off the hook, you devil, you!"

Victor says with a maniacal grin on his face as he burns rubber peeling out.

This could be one interesting job.

"Hello, Mrs. O'Sullivan, let me get that for you," I say to Mrs. O'Sullivan pulling her loaded shopping cart up the hill. Not the kind that people steal from supermarkets, the folding kind that decent city people buy in hardware stores for ten bucks and hang on the back of the front door of their apartments. By the size and wear of the two squeaky wheels, I'm guessing Mrs. O'Sullivan's was probably made in the late forties. People have survived in this city for centuries without automobiles, but I'll bet even the Native American Indians that lived a few hundred yards from the Hudson River on the far west side of the Bronx had little carts they'd load with fishing gear, and kids, and snacks for a day of recreation or food gathering. I don't know, but I'll bet I'm the last person under thirty from the block who still uses one.

"Oh, bless you, Jerry. How's that nasty wound healing?"

"Oh, fine. Everything worked out just great. There was a plastic surgeon at Montefiore who patched me up."

"Oh, you're a lucky one, Jerry. Your parents are very proud of you. Not being a lazy good for nothing bum, like some of the characters around here who will go nameless. Have you secured gainful employment yet, Jerry?"

She must have bricks in this thing. As I pull it up the stairs, it makes an awful sounding crash with each step.

"Nothing's going to break in here is it, Mrs. O'Sullivan?"

"No, no. That's why I get the quart bottles of Rheingold, they're much stronger than the other brands," she confesses matter-of-factly.

"Actually, I have two jobs, and I'm considering a third."

"Well, that's wonderful, Jerry. God bless you," she beams just as I get the cart to the top of the landing.

"Why don't you take the cellar entrance? You wouldn't have to drag it up these stairs."

"Not on your life, Jerry. Ever since this bastard super took

232

over with his dogs running loose and burned out light bulbs, I wouldn't be caught dead in there. It's a disgrace, I tell you."

"OK, Mrs. O'Sullivan. Good-bye now."

"Jerry?"

"I know you're a college graduate and all, but may I offer you a bit of advice?"

"Sure."

"Even if you dine with kings and queens, don't ever forget what your subway stop is."

"Thanks, Mrs. O'Sullivan, I won't," I say as I hold the elevator door for her.

I open the four front locks on the door and enter my dark foyer. I should've left on a light, but now that I'm paying the bills, I only leave a light on when I really need it. That's another prediction from the old man that came true. And I just know that my kids will treat me as bad as I treated him.

"Damn!" I say, stepping on something small and hard that almost makes me twist my ankle. I reach up and pull the cord, turning it on. It's a freaking empty beer can. Shit! This place is a disaster. Wait a minute.... it really is a disaster! I rush through the small apartment.... drawers open.... closets open... things scattered everywhere... hamper knocked over... I've been robbed! Wait. No I haven't. This is how I left the place. What a mess! And tonight is my romantic rendezvous with Berta. And since the whole point was to get her to spend the night here, I better get my butt in gear. This is what a serial killer's apartment must look like.

A quick estimate of the task at hand: at least six pillowcases of laundry; a half foot over a sink load of dirty dishes; three piles of mail and magazines; a bathroom that's been neglected since my parents left me in control; and mini-messes everywhere consisting of plates, bottles, dirty coffee cups, newspapers, dirty towels, cupcake wrappers, and bed linens. My guess is, if I cut corners by shoving only slightly smelly stuff into closets, get giant garbage bags for mass arm loads of trash, find a nearly empty laundromat, and clean the dishes, I can be done in five hours of non-stop cleaning

233

activities. That would mean the earliest I could see Berta is nine p.m. Doable. Now to call Berta.

"Hello, may I speak with Berta, please? Jerry Pellicano. (pause) Hi, Berta.(pause) I know, I've been really busy. (pause) I'm sorry, I know. (pause) Yes, I realize that. (very long pause) Well, I was hoping we could still get together tonight. (really long pause) I'll pick you up at your house at nine and we'll take it from there. (pause) I'd like for you to stop by here, and see how, I've, er, fixed the place up. (pause) OK, nine. Bye."

As I slowly hang up the phone, I look over to the overflowing kitchen sink and see several cockroaches enjoying the hardened remains of a recent meal. And I'm certain that's only the tip of the iceberg. But I've been planning for this evening for days, so I must attack the filthy by-product of my slovenly ways and make my world presentable for Berta. If she saw this disaster, she wouldn't want to have anything to do with me. And neither would I.

So for the next several hours, I will do nothing but the job at hand until it looks somewhat sanitary for a visiting female who might possibly be A) Removing her clothes, B) Getting into bed and, C) Using the bathroom.

TWELVE

I am exhausted. But I must admit the place doesn't look half bad, as long as you don't open any of the closets. And I'm very excited to see how kitchen utensils sparkle if you clean them with Windex! The seven pillowcases of clean laundry will have to be folded and put away on another day, but out of sight out of mind. It was certainly an exercise in self-control to clean out the refrigerator. If I had inhaled another breath of putrid gaseous odors, my gags would have quickly turned to actual vomiting. I had a little guessing game going trying to determine what substances in crinkled tin foil originally was before it transformed into a noxious poison.

I believe I have met my deadline. It's eight p.m. and the place is as presentable as it has been since my parents moved out. I must say I feel pretty good about my future right now. Shit. What about the car? Will it start after sitting in an unheated garage for weeks? And now that I'm thinking about it, when the hell am I going to drive it to Florida? Next week? Never mind that. Tonight is the night I'm concerned with. As Mark Twain said, "Don't put off till tomorrow what can be put off till day-after-tomorrow just as well."

You have to be careful walking outside. There are hidden patches of ice on the sidewalks and the streets. I can't believe my Dad kept his car in a garage that's a 15 minute walk from the house for over ten years. No wonder he only drove the thing on week-ends.

The garage must be part of someone's little Ralph Kramden-type gold mine investment from the 1940s. Buy an empty lot next to the elevated train and build single car garages for the apartment dwellers in the neighborhood. These garages don't look like they've been painted since the forties either. Maybe that helps keep the crooks away. No one would think that a mint condition 1965 Buick Skylark was holed up in this dump. My Dad's garage is way in the back, next to a chain link fence that separates the garages from the Kingsbridge Fence Company, and their two killer watchdogs. The dogs are so vicious and loud once you turn that corner, they go berserk, which is an even greater deterrent to vandals and thieves. Being all the way back here probably is the least expensive garage for rent, but with these crazy dogs, it's probably the safest.

Opening the three padlocks against the corrugated metal doors makes a racket that brings the dogs barks to a fevered pitch. I remember being a little kid and being terrified to come back here because of them. But now as I look in their crazed faces, I feel only sympathy for them. They see people on the other side of the fence as mortal enemies who must be frightened away. Only the fiercest, most violent display of terror can keep strangers at bay. Typical Bronxites.

It's pitch black in here. I guess if these garages had electricity, people probably would be living in here. Oh damn. The car cover. This duck canvas has been getting water dripped on it for weeks, and with the temperature drop, the damn thing is practically frozen stiff. Rather than pull the entire thing off, I manage to pull up the driver's side, giving me enough room to open the car door and squeeze through. Bad sign. No interior light. I put the key in the ignition and turn. Nothing. Not even a little click. Shit! Dead. No way do I have time to deal with this, get grease under my fingernails, and pick up Berta on time.

As I walk away down the gravel driveway, the dogs' growls and barks get even louder, I'm sure they think that's why I'm leaving. I turn and wave in the dark cold night at them, and as I disappear around the corner, they immediately quiet down, knowing they've done their job well.

After running, not walking, back to my place, it's time for quick thinking. I'll call Victor.

"Towing," a voice on the phone says coldly.

"Is Victor available?"

"He's out right now, who's this?" The voice asks, his patience already tested.

"Jerry Pellicano."

"Hold on," the voice says as he drops the receiver. I can hear the sounds of police scanners and several televisions on in the background as the voice says, "Unit one come in."

"Unit one here. What's up?"

"Pellicano's on the phone."

"Ask him if he's home."

The receiver is picked up again as the voice asks, "Are you home?"

"Yeah."

"He says yeah."

"Tell him to wait there for me, I'm in the neighborhood."

"Wait there for him, he's in the neighborhood. Got that?"

"Got it."

"Bye," the voice says, hanging up the phone.

I don't want to call Berta yet, even though I'm going to be at least a half hour late. I better wait to see what Victor says. Who knows, maybe Victor can give me a lift in his car. We can go out in Queens and at least have a date, and I can take the subway home, or maybe she'll have an alternate suggestion.

BANG BANG BANG.

Wow, that was fast!

"Who's there?"

"Reggie fucking Jackson, who do you think it is?"

I open the four locks and Victor is standing there in his greasy work jump suit.

"I'm double-parked. For some unknown reason, Barbieri liked you. He called me and said you better get a reel to him fast. He's got some shit cooking and he may be able to hire you. But he's gotta make some quick decisions."

"That's great. I think."

"Are you fucking kidding? You know how many

237

asswipes he kicks out of his office looking for TV jobs every week.?"

"Victor, I have a more urgent matter. Can you give me a lift to Astoria?"

"This is your lucky day. I've got to go a job at LaGuardia, I'll drop you off. Meet me outside."

This is working out. Finally, everything is falling into place. Clean apartment, three jobs, a date with a gorgeous female I'm deeply in lust with.... oh yeah.... call her.

"Hello."

"Berta! I'll be there in a half hour."

"You're already fifteen minutes late, you could have called."

"I'm sorry, but my father's car wouldn't start, and I'm getting a lift."

"Getting a lift? What are we doing tonight? I'm not all dressed up to go out in Astoria."

"We'll think of something."

"OK. Bye."

As I head out the front of my building, I see Victor and some guy in his forties yelling at each other. "I said I'll move it, alright already! You don't have to have a fucking conniption!"

Victor pulls his truck up enough to let the guy pull out of the parking spot he was blocking and as the car drives away, a hand shoots straight up from the driver's side window with his middle finger extended.

"Nice fucking neighbors you got here," Victor says as I jump into the toasty warm truck.

"Probably a customer. Buying shit."

"You got a dealer in your building?"

"Yeah."

"Is he good?"

"Never mind. I'm trying to put the guy out of business."

"I'm just kidding. Relax. Where you going?"

"I've got a date in Astoria. 29th Avenue and Steinway."

238

"No problem. It's on the way. So what do you think of Barbieri and St. John?" Victor says, driving way too fast on the icy streets towards the Major Deegan.

"They're an interesting combination."

"St. John's got some big deal cooking and I think they're ready to get some big contract with something called, I don't know, National News Network or something like that. Real legit shit."

"Let me pay the toll," I say to Victor as I hold out a five dollar bill.

"Soitenly!" Victor says in his best Curly voice.

When you cross the Triboro Bridge from The Bronx to Queens, there's a killer turn in a tunnel that requires vehicles to slow down substantially. Victor doesn't seem to conform to such arbitrary rules.

"Aren't you taking this turn a little fast?" I say as I reach up to the ceiling of the cabin, hoping to stop my sliding into his lap.

"Ah, this ain't nothing," Victor says maniacally as he turns to me with a creepy grin on his face.

"Watch it!" I yell as we swerve dangerously close to the concrete wall of the tunnel. "Whoa!"

Dangerously close is no longer an apt description. The side of the truck is scraping against the wall of the tunnel, creating a loud noise that sounds like the side of the vehicle is being shredded to pieces. There are even sparks shooting up from the side view mirror, which is now bent back. Victor looks over at me and laughs a slow scary laugh, getting the utmost enjoyment out of what my face must look like.

"Are you out of your mind?"

"You should've seen the look on your face," Victor says as he casually straightens out the truck into the middle lane. "I do that all the time. The only thing that touches is the edge of the running boards and the mirror. No biggie. Here's our exit," he announces as he crosses four lanes of traffic, narrowly missing a speeding yellow cab. I could see the terrified expression on the faces of the tourists on the way to the airport as they swerved out of our path.

"Victor, do you get many tickets?"

"Nah. The cops are usually cool. They like us better than cabbies. They know we got radios and can save their ass someday. Plus, if I get a call and it's an off-duty cop, I might even give him a freebie if I work in his precinct."

"Her house is the one on the corner of the next block," I tell Victor, hinting that maybe he should slow down a bit.

"What are you going to tell her happened to your mug?"

"I'll tell her the truth. I guess. Why?"

"Aw, come on. What's the difference? Tell her something good, like you got hit with a sap coming to the rescue of some old lady that was getting her purse snatched on the Concourse or something."

"And what exactly would the purpose of that fantasy accomplish?"

"Come on, Jerry. Chicks love that shit."

"I'll have to remember that."

Suddenly, over the usual din of noise from the scanner radios, the voice cuts through. "Unit one come in."

Victor quickly grabs for the cigarette pack sized mike.

"Unit one, go ahead."

"Listen I just got a hot tip. Give me a land line ASAP. Urgent."

"Ten-four. Give me a minute. Out."

Victor looks at me with a gleam in his eye, that frankly has me a little bit nervous. It's close to the look he had on his face just before he almost ran those kids over and while he was scraping the wall of the tunnel a few minutes ago.

"Think your babe'll let me use her phone real quick."

"Ah, sure," I reluctantly say, knowing full well that this is not exactly a culture clash that I'm looking forward to. I don't think Berta's mother is too thrilled with me even calling her pre-

240

cious little princess on the phone. Just wait till she gets an eyeful of Victor clomping through the house in his grease monkey outfit. And Lord knows what the conversation with the home base is going to be like.

"This is urgent shit, Jerry," Victor says as he pulls into Berta's driveway with most of the truck blocking the sidewalk and some of the narrow Astoria street. "Let me go in with you."

"Just give me a minute to smooth things over with her."

"Go cat, go."

I jump out of the truck and ring the bell. Berta quickly appears through the white lace cloth hanging on the glass of the inside door. The home is one of those typical Bronx/Queens/Brooklyn attached brick row houses built in the late fifties and early sixties. This is where the upper middle class of the outer boroughs raised their families. Unlike my neighborhood where bus drivers, transit clerks, and garbage men raised their kids. These are the homes where the Sanitation Department and Transit Authority supervisors, detectives, and public school principals live. Neat little gardens next to narrow driveways. And aluminum awnings hanging over the entrance and windows.

"Hello, Berta..."

"What in God's name happened to your face?"

"Oh yeah. I forgot to mention that."

"Forgot to mention? My God it looks awful! You poor dear! What happened."

"Uh, I got hit with an iceball. Off the roof of my building."

"Your building? Did you call the cops? Oh my God, let me take a look at it in the light," Berta says as she tenderly strokes my cheek just below the wound.

"No, no. We've got to get going," I say throwing my head in the tow truck's direction which has Victor sitting there, waving his arms at us.

"What's going on here?" Berta asks, obviously referring to the rumbling tow truck idling in her driveway with a crazed person behind the steering wheel.

"Can my buddy, Victor, use your phone? It's kind of an emergency."

"Oh. Certainly. But my mother has her sister over, so be quiet."

I wave to Victor, and he hurries over. Berta is already up the stairs, I guess to warn her Mom and aunt about what is about to transpire.

Victor is one of those people who just doesn't seem comfortable indoors. I'm a couple of steps ahead of him as he slams the front door.

"Sorry," He apologizes.

He sounds like a bear as he clomps his way up the carpeted wooden stairs. My feet don't make a sound, but every step Victor takes seems to make a thunderous noise. His breathing becomes heavy as he pulls himself up with the aid of the bannister.

"Fuck," Victor whispers as he stops.

I look back to see Victor pulling the handrail several inches from the wall, with a screw dangling.

"This just came out. I hardly pulled on it. I swear."

"Just stick it back in, and let's go," I tell him, knowing that's just one more thing I probably have to apologize to Berta and her mother before this night is through.

Berta meets me at the top of the stairs with an aquamarine colored princess phone that has a long cord.

"Here's the phone for your friend. He won't mind using it here, will he? My mother isn't feeling well..."

"...no need to explain, this is fine! Victor, here's your phone."

"Oh, thanks! Hey nice phone! We used to have one of these when I was a kid! Watch," he says as he lifts the receiver and the rotary dial lights up. "Ain't that cool!"

"Victor, this is Berta. Berta, Victor," I say as Victor dials.

"What's up?" Victor says into the receiver. "What?! Holy fuck!"

Upon hearing that expletive, Berta shoots me a look that could kill. I just helplessly shake my head in disapproval.

"Just tell him to wait. Tell him to give us five minutes to get there and two minutes to set up. Never mind, just tell him that. Go. Bye."

"Jerry, you gotta come. Now. I got a job I have to do. Let's go," Victor says as he hands the phone to Berta and begins flying back down the stairs.

"Should I come?" I ask as I slowly follow him, half watching Berta who is holding the phone, looking on in disbelief, and half watching him trying to decide what to do.

Victor stops at the door. "I've got a scoop. A TV news scoop. It's huge. Let's go!"

I look up at Berta still holding the phone at the top of the stairs. "Can I come?" She surprisingly asks.

"Yes! Let's go! Now!"

Berta puts the phone down. "Bye Mom. I'll call you later!" She says as she rushes down the stairs, zipping up her powder blue ski jacket with white fur around the collar.

And here we are. The three of us in Victor's tow truck speeding off to something I'm sure I'll remember for a while. And I'm dying to know what it is.

When I think of a scoop, I think in terms of something with historical significance. Perhaps Jimmy Carter is having a nosh with Anwar Sadat and Menachem Begin in The Second Avenue Deli. Or the Shah of Iran is getting ready to make a speech at the U.N. agreeing with the Ayatollah. Or they found Jimmy Hoffa hiding out in a duck blind in the Adirondacks.

"Where are we going?" Berta asks as she grabs my hand, probably less as a sign of affection than the sheer terror of realizing that Victor drives like a madman.

"The bridge," Victor responds icily.

"The bridge? For what?" Berta asks excitedly.

"A jumper."

"A jumper? What's that?" Berta asks with a look on her face revealing the fact that she probably doesn't want to know the answer.

"Somebody's jumping off the middle of the Triboro, and if I can get there in time, I'm gonna be a hero."

"A hero to whom?" I ask Victor.

"To the guy who signs my check, that's who?"

"What's going on, Jerry?" Berta asks, beginning to demonstrate the characteristics of someone getting ready to have a fit. Her teeth are clenched, and those beautiful dark, Latin eyes are shooting daggers.

"What's going on Victor?" I demand.

"We got a tip that a guy's going to jump off the Triboro Bridge to protest the fact that he can't get his play produced on Broadway. He's a writer or something. But he wants to make sure that it's not in vain, so we're going to shoot him."

"Shoot him?" Berta yells. "What the hell is this? Your going to kill a man who's committing suicide?"

"Calm down, sister..." Victor calmly says to Berta.

"I'm not your damn sister!"

"Look, I'm in the TV news business. That's what I do for a living. I got a call that some wacko is going to jump off a bridge. If I get there in time, I can shoot the guy jumping off. If I do, I'm happy, he's happy. He's gonna jump anyway."

"This is sick!" Berta, now on the verge of sheer panic, screams.

"Berta, Victor's right. He's got nothing to do with the guy wanting to jump. He's just recording it so that he can make his point and people can see what a dysfunctional world we live in. If the cops are there, we'll record that. If they're not, that's not our fault. He's simply reporting a news event."

"Yeah, and selling footage of some guy committing suicide."

"There he is!" Victor whispers as we approach an early '70s Ford Pinto in the far right lane with the flashers on. This end of the Triboro has one of the best views of the Manhattan skyline possible. The lights in the buildings from Midtown down to the South Ferry just glisten like millions of stars in the cold, crisp winter

244

sky. At the far end of the bridge, I see red lights approaching. Emergency vehicles, I'm sure, rushing to the scene for the same reason we are. Well sort of.

"Fuck," Victor yells as he pulls over to the wall just past the jumper's Pinto. We're riding so high in the truck that you can't even see the short retaining wall that separates the traffic from plunging into the fierce river hundreds of feet below. "Jerry, get your ass in gear and do exactly what I tell you!"

"OK!"

Victor jumps out of the cab, and opens the side compartment on the truck. Inside is a very large, expensive looking case. He pulls it out onto the road and opens it, revealing a bright, large Ikegami very professional TV video camera within.

"Grab that other case, and pull out the deck," Victor says as he quickly shoves in batteries, connects cables, and sets up the gear.

"Hey there!" A small man yells as he gets out of his Pinto. "I'm going! You've got ninety seconds!"

"Hold on! We're not ready!" Victor pleads to the suicidal artist.

Victor shoves a battery into the large video recorder, then a battery, connects a large cord from the camera to it, and hands it to me. He then pushes a couple of buttons on the deck.

"You're in standby mode," Victor tells me with a look of ferocious intensity. He's no longer a reckless wise-ass, but all business. "When I tell you to, push this, and just let it roll until I tell you I'm done. Stay close, but don't get in my way."

I can see a fire truck quickly approaching.

"Hey, Shakespeare! We're ready!" Victor says as he steadies the large camera on his shoulder and switches on a bright spotlight affixed to the front of the camera. "Roll!" He says, watching me as I push the right button. "Is it rolling?"

"Yes."

"Shakespeare, whatever the fuck you're gonna do, just

do it."

The small man is wearing a bulky jacket and carrying what appears to be a manuscript in his arm. "Can you hear me?" The poor soul yells over to us.

"Yeah. We got a microphone on this thing." Victor shouts back.

"I'm doing this because I can't get any attention for my play, which is a work of genius. Broadway has been taken over by the illegitimate infidels. They drove me to this!"

Just then the fire truck pulls alongside where we are in the other lanes on the other side of the road divider. Two firemen with only their dark blue FDNY T-shirts and suspenders on hop over the short wall and stridently approach the crazed playwright.

"Wait! Hold on? Don't jump!" They yell. It's too late.

In a totally eerie silence, the man puts one foot on the retaining wall, then the other, and as if in a dream where everything is deadly silent and in slow motion, he leaps into the dark abyss. The silence is pierced by Berta, who screams at the top of her lungs and begins sobbing inside the truck.

I feel numb. I can't believe what I've just witnessed. I hear the sound of something hitting the water below.

Now a police car pulls up just behind us.

"What happened here?" One of the cops says to anyone who will listen.

A fireman looking over the side of the wall down into the river below says, "We got a call that some crazy playwright was going to jump off here to protest his play not getting produced."

"That's right officer. I got the same call," Victor says, still shooting his camera at the water below.

"You got credentials?" The cops asks Victor.

"Yes, officer," Victor says as he pulls his several dog tag press passes out of his shirt.

"OK, but be careful. We don't want anybody else going off the plank tonight, huh?"

"Hey, look!" I yell, spying a small outboard motorboat on the water below with a bright searchlight reflecting upon the water.

246

Victor aims his camera at the boat below and in the distance, I can see another light approaching over the river coming north. It's a helicopter. Then, a loud horn begins blaring. It's a large Coast Guard ship, also searching the water below.

"This is fucking great!" Victor says so only I can hear him.

Within seconds, a full-blown search and rescue mission is going on below us, and traffic on the bridge has come to a complete standstill.

A fireman comes over to us with a hand-held two-way radio in his hand and taps Victor on the shoulder. "They got him."

"You're shittin' me?" Victor says in disbelief.

"No, and he's alive."

"Holy jumpin' shit," Victor says. "Thanks, pal," he says to the fireman. "Stop tape, and let's blow."

Just then, I can see running between cars stuck on the bridge, two people carrying what appears to be TV equipment just like ours.

"Who's this?" I ask, nudging Victor.

"Those stupid fuckers. It's our fucking low-life competition, TNS. Television News Service. Some assholes that used to work for Barbieri but got fired." Victor explains as he quickly breaks down the gear.

Just as they get to where we are in our little oasis of space, the guy in the rear holding the video recorder trips and in a pratfall worthy of a Tex Avery cartoon, tumbles to the ground, pulling his partner, who is connected to him by the camera cable. The cops and firemen just stand and stare in disbelief. As the two begin to get back on their feet, a fireman says, "Have a nice trip?"

"You guys missed all the fun," Victor says as he jumps into the driver's seat of his truck. "If you want to see what went on, just watch the news tonight on every fucking channel."

I hop into the passenger seat. Berta scoots her butt over and stares straight ahead. Not a word.

I put my hand on her right hand, which is on her right thigh. She picks my hand up with her left hand and tosses aside. Still looking straight ahead, she announces to no one in particular, "Take me home, please."

Victor's engine roars at the turn of his ignition key. "Sorry, babe, we got hot footage here."

"Am I to understand that you are refusing?"

"You can jump out here or ride with me into Manhattan. Your choice."

Berta is steamed. She slowly turns her head towards me and with icy eyes dead ahead, stops just as her face points ninety degrees from the direction of the rest of her body.

"Berta, look, as soon as we get into the city, we'll do whatever you want. If you want to go home, I'll take you home in a cab; you want to get a bite, we'll get a bite. Anywhere you want. I swear," I say to Berta in my best smoothing-over voice. She is one fiery woman. I can tell that she is certainly accustomed to getting exactly what she wants, when she wants it. I'll bet she's knocked more than one guy upside his head.

"That sounds like a deal. I'd take him up on that one. Believe me, we'll be there in less than ten minutes," Victor says as he picks up the radio microphone.

"Base come in."

"Go mobile one. Did you get the goods?"

"The whole enchilada. Should be at h.q. in less than ten."

"I'll notify. K."

"K," Victor says as he joyfully replaces the mike. "Barbieri's going to love this."

Berta, who has gone back to her original position of staring straight ahead, just shakes her head slowly.

Victor's driving is even faster than usual. Once he gets off the bridge and makes his way over to the FDR going south, he's weaving in and out of traffic like he's driving a Ferrari. For all his usual reckless driving habits, he is revealing himself to be quite the skilled driver. He seems to anticipate what every car around him will do and reacts accordingly. Even Berta doesn't appear as nervous as she probably should be.

"OK, kiddies, we're here," Victor yells as he pulls his truck in front of Barbieri's building, kills the engine and leaps out, all in one graceful motion. "Watch the news tonight, Jerry. You helped make history," he says in as serious a tone of voice that I've heard since I've known him. "Gotta go," he says as he rushes into the lobby.

Berta stands under the awning that leads up to the lobby with both hands defiantly placed on her hips as she stares me down. "Well, thanks for date."

"I'm sorry, but this could be my big break."

"A break? That was the most horrible thing I've ever witnessed in my life, and you think it's your big break? Look at me! My hands are still shaking."

"I'm sorry. Look, let's go somewhere nice and get something to eat," I say taking a couple of steps towards her. She doesn't move away, but stands there, still fuming. I cautiously get right in front of her and grab both her hands, looking her straight in the eye. I can see a slight relaxing in the lines around them. Her lips start to soften. I squeeze her hands gently. She squeezes back.

"Alright. Let's forget about it for now. I need to get it out of my mind. It's just that I've never seen anything like that before."

"There are horrible things that happen every day in this city. We just insulate ourselves from them. And when we do see something, we just block it out. Let's forget about it and go somewhere..." I briefly paused, almost choking on the mere thought of the next word I was about to utter. It's a code word, a euphemism for expensive, "...nice."

Her eyes lit up, briefly forgetting the trauma I just put her through for the sake of trying to land a job. "Sure. Let's get a cab."

The White Dove is one of the trendiest restaurants on the upper west side. It's not just a restaurant that serves small portions of elaborately presented food; the front of the establishment is one of the hottest pick up bars in New York. The custom-made oak bar is three deep with the "beautiful people" of New York, of which nine out of ten couldn't even tell you what borough Coney Island is in. You're more than likely to hear someone say, "Y'all" than hear the usual "deese dems and dose" that pepper the conversation in a Blarney Stone. What I find so hard to comprehend is why the media are always proclaiming these glorified tourist attractions as the next big thing in the city. And the yokels from the hinterlands come by the Checker cab load. But what I really don't understand is why real New Yorkers come into these tricked out Holiday Inn lounges. I'll take a night out in Dominic's over by Arthur Avenue in the Bronx any day.

Ah, Dominic's. Now that's New York. Everyone sits at long, common tables and not only don't they have menus, after you're done with your meal, you don't even get a check. The over fifty-five Italian waiter who wears his folded-over kitchen apron around his waist, just looks you and your table mates over, gives a couple of head nods and magically announces, "fifteen bucks." He then looks over to the guy at the register by the door, points at your party and again announces over the din of the festival-like atmosphere, "15 bucks." Obviously, no credit cards or checks. And I wouldn't want to see what happens to somebody who tries to beat a tab.

"I've always wanted to have dinner here," Berta says, soaking in the hanging plastic ferns. "We've only come here for happy hour."

We stand at the hostess podium waiting our turn to be seated for dinner and a twenty-ish blonde girl with poofed up hair and way too much make-up scrunches her nose with a big toothy grin, "How y'all doing this evening? Two for dinner?"

I contain my disdain. "Yes, please."

"There's about a twenty minute wait," She says as she runs her finger up and down the list in front of her. "Feel free to wait at the bar, and just give your bill to your waiter. Name please?"

"Pellicano."

"Thank yeeeeewwww," she drawls as she scrunches her nose again.

We squeeze our way over to the crowded bar and stake out a tiny space where we can have a cocktail. At each end of the long bar, two televisions are tuned to the local news on channel 11. I'd say half the patrons are captivated by the story now airing about a double homicide in Harlem. They cut back to the chatty male and female news bimbos who suddenly have their serious news faces on as they make an unusual announcement. "We've just received some shocking news footage that may be too explicit for some viewers."

Boy, did that get the other half of the place's attention quick!

"We must caution you that the footage you are about to see may be too much for children or the very sensitive. Less than ninety minutes ago, a tragedy played out on the Triboro Bridge more dramatic than anything William Shakespeare himself could have envisioned. A struggling playwright from Queens..."

Berta and I jerked our necks to check each other out as they cut to the video footage we had just shot. I can't believe this. They're going to show everything! I can't imagine what the reaction of the bar will be. I can only assume it will be total shock and disgust. Berta is silent as she slowly turns toward the television screen. Even the three bartenders are pretending to be wiping wine glasses with their eyes glued to the scene unfolding on the television. The video is on the part where the small man gets out of his car and approaches the wall of the bridge.

"...despondent over the fact that his play has been rejected by agents and Broadway attempted to take his own life..."

As he put one foot up on the wall, a man at the end of the bar starts chanting, "Jump. Jump. Jump. Jump." Much to my amazement, much laughter followed. Suddenly the crowd was moving excitedly in place as they jockeyed for position to get a better look at one of the televisions. Hoots and hollers and assorted shouts were being hurled at the screen; "Don't forget to write!" and "Going down!" and "Watch that last, step it's a doozy!" were among the suggestions, and all were followed with great guf-

251

faws and loud applause.

"A television news crew happened to be on the bridge at the same time and caught the horrifying scene on tape."

Just then, even though I knew the tape was being played back at normal speed, it once again appeared that the pathetic man was moving in slow motion as the stepped onto the small retaining wall and in a wisp, disappeared off the bridge. A loud burst of applause went up in the crowd as though someone has just scored a touchdown in the Super Bowl.

A sickening sensation came over me. I looked over at Berta, who was watching the revelers in total disgust. I never would have guessed in a million years that the crowd would have reacted in such a despicable manner. Bloodlust was everywhere.

Berta slammed her glass down on the bar and although no one paid attention to her except me, shouted, "You people are sick!"

She turned and pushed her way through the crowd, not even checking to see if I was following her.

She stormed down Second Avenue, and I ran to catch up with her. There were no tears. Only outrage plastered across her face.

"I hope you're proud of yourself," she sternly says, looking only at her feet as they pounded the wet sidewalk.

"I have no control over those assholes."

"Think. Just think. You were the reason for that."

I grabbed at her shoulder from behind and she shrugged me off, continuing on her mad dash away from me and the mob. I tried again and this time she stopped dead in her tracks. Her head snapped into position, glaring at me with those intense, dark eyes as if to say "go ahead asshole, let's hear it."

"Go ahead. Let's hear it," she barked.

"He would have jumped whether or not we were there to cover it."

"Oh yeah, that's why he called to arrange the whole thing. I'm surprised you guys didn't yell 'action,' telling him when to jump."

"If it wasn't us, he would've called somebody else."

"And right now I'd be upset at somebody else, wouldn't I?" Berta says softly, without a trace of bitterness.

I don't understand hormones. Here I am, being bombarded with vitriol, and out of nowhere a sudden wave of sexual arousal comes over me. Berta's venom, which is totally justified, has unleashed in me a dizzying state of emotional confusion. I've lusted after Berta for weeks but for the first time, I see only Berta's eyes. Maybe it's not sexual arousal I'm feeling. Although I'm charged with a tingling sensation, which I usually associate with an imminent boner, there's something else going on. Something I'm not sure I've ever felt in quite this way. Berta's eyes are waiting. Blinking in slow motion. I'm drawn to her, moving closer. I want to disappear into her. We're beyond words. In my mind, I know that Berta has every right to pull away, but I slowly turn her towards me. Her expression hasn't changed. She's not seeking pity. She's not wounded or hurt. She's taken a stance and is sticking to it. She is accepting me.

My only desire is to hold Berta close to me. Perhaps something can ooze out of this thick skull of mine and translate into something that tells her that right now, in this moment, I want her to know how deeply I care for her. I do disappear into her. As I sink deeper into the space between her jacket collar and her bare neck, her fragrance becomes stronger and stronger. I breathe deeply with my eyes closed desperately trying to transmit some kind of psychic message that will let her know that I'm not really an exploitative asshole. I don't think I've ever felt closer to a woman than I do right here, right now, as I inhale her perfume, the fragrance from her hair, and the smell of her skin.

"Take me home, please," Berta says as a van speeds by, nearly splashing us with the slush that had been filling a nearby pothole.

"Home, as in back to your house?"

"Yes, please."

We held hands on the long, silent cab ride back to Queens. I didn't even get out of the cab to walk her upstairs, and she didn't turn back to wave once.

"Drop me off at the nearest subway station," I say to the cabbie, knowing full well that I may have just blown the best thing that ever happened to me.

As I sat on the train headed back into Manhattan to switch to a Bronx-bound line, I thought about what awaited me at home. A semi-clean empty apartment with closets about to explode. What the hell. I'll stop in at Barbieri's office. Nighttime is when the real action is, so there's bound to be people around.

"Can I help you?" The night shift desk guy asks taking a break from his sloppy sausage and hot pepper hero.

"I'm new. I, ah, work for Barbieri," I reply, probably not exuding enough confidence for the desk guy to believe me.

"Yeah, well, hold on a minute," he says, as he picks up the phone, pissed that he has to delay a bite into another sweet Italian sausage. "Mr. Barbieri, there's a...."

"Jerry Pellicano," I tell him.

"Jerry Pellicano here to see you. OK."

"Go ahead," the desk guy says with his mouth already a half-inch from the next tasty mouthful of hero.

I press the buzzer outside the office door, and it immediately whips open to find Barbieri himself standing there, complete with a goofy joyful glee plastered from ear to ear.

"Yo! What a fucking baptism by fire! First fucking day on the job, and you roll on the best fucking footage since The Subway Slasher! Hey, St. John, Pellicano's here," Barbieri says as he ushers me into the office that's buzzing with a loud cacophony of scanners, televisions, and all-news radio, patting me loudly on the back of my leather jacket.

The office, which seemed much too large this morning, suddenly seems small, cramped, alive with people and activities. A guy who looks like a scaled-down version of Barbieri is sitting at a large steel desk with four microphones on stands surrounded by piles and piles of radios, scanners of every shape and size, two-way radio base units, Radio Shack AM/FMs tuned to different all-news radio stations, a large Heathkit shortwave radio, and a single news teletype machine cranking away, adding a backbeat to the already surreal symphony of electronic sounds. It's hard to tell which sound is coming from where, but the guy sitting behind the desk, now swung around in his chair facing the teletype machine, is bending over, putting his face just inches from the paper roll constantly spitting out news.

"Shit! I can hardly read this! Do we have any ribbons?" The scaled-down version of Barbieri yells to no one in particular.

"Fucking Trotta! How many times do I have to tell you not to let the fucking ribbon get too worn? You're fucking lucky you caught it when you did," Barbieri yells, no longer slapping me on the back. "If that fucking ribbon was unreadable, we could get royally fucked. And you're supposed to know if we have any fucking ribbons, moron," Barbieri says as he noisily pulls open a file cabinet and tosses a box on the desk.

"I'm sorry, Rocco," Trotta says to Barbieri as his picks a ribbon package out of the box. "You're right. I'm wrong. Case closed."

"Thank you!" Barbieri proudly proclaims, obviously happy with the way he handled the situation.

Against the wall on the far side of the office where several three-quarter inch videotape machines with a monitor above each one displays spectacular fires, sits a wiry guy wearing a black leather motorcycle jacket and heavy black boots with buckles on the top. His head is darting back and forth as he writes notes on a yellow legal pad. I can see from his profile he's wearing gold aviator glasses being held up by a medium-sized hook nose, of either Jewish or Italian extraction, and he's wearing small headphones. It's hard to tell how old he is, but he appears to still have a little acne on his forehead. If somebody told me he was a speed freak, I'd believe them. But his hair is too styled, his boots too clean, and his jacket too expensive for him to be a degenerate.

"You getting all that, Birnbaum?" Barbieri says to the guy

viewing and taking notes like a demon.

Birnbaum doesn't turn around.

"Hey, fucking Birnbaum," Barbieri yells at the top of his lungs.

Still no reaction from Birnbaum. Barbieri walks over to him and lifts the left earphone a couple of inches from his ear.

"What the fuck are you listening to?"

Birnbaum hardly flinches, and keeps his breakneck pace of viewing and frantically keeping notes on the fiery disasters playing out on the monitors in front of him. "I'm listening to the Ramones. It's fucking great," Birnbaum shouts back loudly, not missing a beat, as Barbieri snaps the headphone back onto his ear.

"Pellicano, you got to be fucking nuts if you're going to fit in here," Barbieri says as I follow him to another office.

"I'll try."

Barbieri pushes open a door, and I can feel the heavy pulsating bass drum of disco.

"Hey, St. John, Pellicano's here," Barbieri screams over the pounding disco beat. From just outside the door, I can see that the office is actually an editing room, and on the monitor there's a white woman with a huge platinum blond Afro in a gold evening dress rubbing her breasts, which are barely being contained in the flimsy gown. The guy sitting at the editing controller says, "Rocco, watch this!" Just then the woman takes her left breast out of her dress, begins massaging it, and then holds it up to her mouth. She then begins to suck on her own nipple in time with the music.

"Owwwwww!" Barbieri screams in delight. "Play that fucking back!"

"I can't. I'm dubbing right now," the editor says in a low-key voice.

"You fucking guys get paid to do this shit," Barbieri says as he takes St. John out of the room and closes the door behind him.

"Jerry, great job tonight," St. John says as he holds his hand out for another fishy handshake.

"Thanks. We lucked out I guess."

"I'll say," Barbieri trumpets. "We actually sold more copies of that than The Subway Slasher. Not that it was better, but there are more people buying now than there were two years ago."

"Precisely," St. John says, nodding his head in approval to Barbieri. "That's the reason we want to talk to you, Jerry. This is a growth industry. Did you notice what was playing in the edit room?"

"Did he fucking notice?" Barbieri roars. "If he didn't fucking notice that I'd have his pulse checked, unless he's a fucking fag or something!"

"I noticed, I noticed."

"We're doing a tape for Studio De La Disco," St. John says reverently.

"Cool," I say, unable to think of anything else.

"Although we've made our mark in news, we're heading into entertainment now," St. John says, very impressed with himself as he strokes the peach fuzz on his weak chin.

"Hmmm," I lamely add as I adjust the bandage just below my eye.

"This tape is for the owners themselves, which they'll use as a marketing tool for investors. Small format video makes this type of presentation economically cost effective for businesses," St. John says as if he's reading off a cue card.

"Yeah," Trotta chimes in between bites of a meatball hero, "and we get to dub off all chicks with their tits hanging out for our gag reels."

"Can we step into your office, Rocco?" St. John asks Barbieri, obviously annoyed at Trotta's observation.

The three of us step into Barbieri's empty office. His desk is neat to the point of looking unused. I notice that just behind his chair, next to a closed closet door, is a shotgun propped up against the wall. Barbieri walks over to his chair and touches the top of the barrel.

"This is loaded. Don't ever fuck with it," Barbieri says totally devoid of his usual biting humor.

St. John pulls a chair over and sits on it backwards, with the back of the chair facing me. I take a seat in the chair immediately in front of Barbieri's desk.

"Jerry, have you heard of Corley Broadcasting?"

"Isn't he that guy with that cheesy TV station in Miami that he puts up on the satellite?"

"Yeah, well, that cheesy station is leading a whole new era of communications," St. John says, pissed at me like I just cast aspersions on his family. "Strom Corley is a bold broadcasting pioneer."

"I thought he mostly ran 'Hee Haw' and 'Gomer Pyle' reruns?"

"That's what I said," Barbieri says, pounding his metal desk, rattling the pens in his plastic pen holder, and me as well. "That fucking hickory head takes that home fried shit, puts it on a bird, and all of a sudden he's a fucking broadcast pioneer. I don't fucking get it!"

"Rocco, that's his targeted audience. He made his millions and now he's diversifying into news," St. John says, mildly perturbed at Barbieri, but certainly not enough to ruffle his feathers.

"Ahhhh!" Barbieri screams, as he throws a spiral notebook at St. John. "You're not supposed to fucking talk about that yet, asshole!"

"Everybody knows it. It's in all the trades," St. John responds defensively.

"I don't care. Wilkins said not to mention Corley News until he said so," Barbieri lectures.

"Well, the cat's out of the bag now," St. John meekly says.

"Yeah, and you're the pussy who did it," Barbieri adds.

"Anyway, now that you know, 'Corley Satellite News' will be the biggest thing to hit broadcasting since Lawrence Welk."

"Don't fucking use that analogy, please!" Barbieri busts in.

"It's true, Rocco. Welk was the first person to break the stranglehold of the networks and go around them using syndication."

"I know, but it sounds so fucking stupid," Barbieri says, shaking his head and looking towards me. I nod in agreement.

"Anyway, CSN will be huge, and we're going to be hiring people for when we help him to set up his national news headquarters in Miami."

"We've got to check you out first, Jerry," Barbieri says seriously. "But all that means is you'll work for us here in New York for a few months before we send you down there. Are you interested?"

"Uh, sure I'm interested," I say, trying to sound enthusiastic.

"When can you start?" Barbieri says, jumping right on me.

"Uh, well, next week sometime?"

"Call me tomorrow and decide if you're in. We need people who can think quick on their feet. And where's that reel?"

"You just asked for it this morning."

"Oh, yeah. Well, send it over before you start.

"You got it. Uh, when will we talk about...er, uh, money and stuff?" I ask Barbieri, revealing my timid nature in such matters.

"Do you want to work here or what?" Barbieri says, jumping all over me.

"Yeah."

"Good. Call me first thing Monday. Me and Schuyler have a lot to talk about. And one more thing. Not a word about this to anybody. Anybody. See ya," Barbieri says, giving me a halfhearted salute, waving Schuyler over to his desk in the same movement. "Just push the button on the side of the door so it locks, would you, Jerry?" He adds with a hint of friendliness in his voice.

"Sure," I say as I hit the lock button and let it close behind me.

Birnbaum is still viewing and writing away with his head bopping to The Ramones, Trotta is hunched over the teletype machine, his hands black from replacing the ribbon, and two new faces

259

are sitting on the other side of Trotta's desk. These guys must be Barbieri's other team of tow truck driving video renegades. They are both in their mid-twenties, and if they told me they just finished putting a rebuilt engine in a '65 Chevy, I'd believe them. One guy is wearing a puffy dark blue jacket streaked with grease and the name "Moe" in script over his heart. The other guy is wearing a thin windbreaker over his XXXL frame.

Trotta pops up from the rumbling machine and turns towards me, revealing more ribbon ink across his forehead. "Oh, Pellicano! This is mobile unit two, Moe and Joe."

"You must be Moe," I say to the guy with "Moe" on his jacket, and reach out to shake hands. His hand has that black gunk under his fingernails that car mechanics can never seem to wash off.

"You a friend of Victor's?" Moe asks as he squeezes my paw like a vice grip.

I pretend I don't notice. "Yeah."

"Well, that's your fucking problem," he says totally deadpan.

"I'm Joe," the other guy says. "Pleased to meet you."

"Likewise," I reply as I shake Joe's hand, which is hard and calloused.

"By the way, Pellicano," Trotta says, leaning across his desk, "what happened to you?" As he finishes the statement, he touches his check in about the location where my bandage would be on his face, smearing more black ribbon across his cheek.

"Oh, this? Ah, I ah, got hit in a, ah, little altercation in a gin mill." I respond, trying to remember what I already told Barbieri this afternoon.

"Oh great. Another bar brawler," Trotta says, shaking his head and sitting back in his chair.

"Are you a shooter?" Moe asks.

"No, it was just a bar fight."

"I mean are you a cameraman? Do you shoot video?"

"Not really. I've directed a little..."

"Directed?" Moe asks incredulously. "What, like a movie?"

260

"No, you know with a switcher in a small studio. And I've shot with a studio camera a little. But I'm mostly interested in editing."

"Good," Moe says firmly. "We've got too many fucking shooters around here already. Everybody wants to fucking shoot."

"Barbieri wants everybody to know how to shoot," Joe says after a long pause in the scintillating conversation.

It's easy to see that this has come up before between Moe and Joe, since Joe jumped up from his chair and stormed across the room to the editing room where the Studio De La Disco edit session is in progress.

Moe looks over at Trotta, shrugs his shoulders with his hands waving. "What? What'd I do?"

"You didn't do anything, Moe. Joe knows he's supposed to fucking train you. And if he's got a fucking problem with that, then he's got a problem with Barbieri, OK? Not with you. End of story. Case closed."

I stand there awkwardly, trying to avoid making contact with Moe or Trotta and pretend that I'm not hearing any of this. Which is what I would definitely prefer. I hear a faint sound of what is probably The Ramones, coming through a set of headphones, which Birnbaum has in fact just removed from his head. I decide to take my chances on that side of the room.

"How's it going?" I say trying to be friendly and nonthreatening.

"Great!," Birnbaum says as he quickly starts pushing buttons and turning dials on the video machines that he has been using. "You signing up or what?"

"Uh, I believe so..."

"Just cover your ass, and you'll be fine. You smoke?"

"Cigarettes?" I say looking around the room, wondering who might be watching and listening.

"Weed," Birnbaum says casually.

"Uh, well, ah..."

"I'm going out to smoke a joint in the back alley. If you

want to come, I'll be out there," he says, zipping up his motorcycle jacket and heading for the front door. "Trotta, if Debbie Harry calls, tell her I'm busy."

"Yeah, right," Trotta says without even looking up from his copy of *The New York Post*. "I'll have her come over and blow me instead."

I look over at Trotta as Birnbaum leaves. "He's kidding, right?"

"Tell him, Moe."

"Don't ever believe Birnbaum. It's just not in his nature," Moe says earnestly.

"I got to head out," I tell Trotta as I head for the door.

"I'll tell Barbieri you said 'bye."

"See ya."

I walk out the door and pause in the hall. I'm not sure if I'm ready for this.

"Yo!" A voice gets my attention from down the hall. It's Birnbaum sitting on some steps, smoking a cigarette.

"I was just leaving."

"OK, don't be sociable."

"I'm running a little late..."

"I'm just breaking your chops. Welcome aboard. It'll be nice to have somebody else around with an IQ over 75. How'd you really get the shiner?"

"My story wasn't convincing?"

"You don't look *that* dumb."

"I got hit by a snowball. Off a roof. I was walking into my building and got hit with a snowball with a rock-hard center.

"Well that sucks."

"Totally."

"What was in the center?"

I remember that I've been carrying around the piece of porcelain, or whatever it is, in my pocket, and pull it out. "This is it, right here," I say holding it up.

"Can I see it?"

I hand it to Birnbaum and he begins studying it, carefully.

"That's weird," Birnbaum says examining it like a jeweler. "It looks like it might be part of a statue, or something," he says, as he hands it back to me.

"Whatever it is, it hurt like hell. By the way, where's the weed you were talking about."

"Weed? Oh that. I just have an image to maintain with those grease monkeys in there. A little separation is crucial in a work environment. Those guys think smoking pot is like shooting heroin. But they'll drink beer in their barco loungers watching a Giant game until they're comatose. Schuyler smokes like a Deadhead."

"Really? Schuyler?"

"I went to school with him. Not that we really knew each other. He was a year ahead of me. But that's how we hooked up here. He's more connected than Ma Bell."

"How about Barbieri?"

"Barbieri hates the shit. It kind of separates the Barbieri-ites from the Schuyler-ites. So even though I don't really smoke much pot, I just like the Barbieri-ites to think I do," Birnbaum says, punctuated by a long draw on his Marlboro. "Where you from?"

"The Bronx."

"Me, too. What part?"

"Near Van Cortlandt Park."

"I went to Science."

"Yeah, that's not too far. So you've got a brain, too? Science, Princeton. Sheesh. Where are you from?"

"Right next to Co-Op City."

"Co-Op City? Man that's a schlep to Science!"

"Where'd you go to high school?"

"Cardinal Hayes."

"Yeah, well, that costs money. Science was free. And so was Princeton."

"You went to Princeton for free?"

"Yeah. I got lucky on my S.A.T.s. By the way, has any-body said anything to you about Miami?"

"Miami? Ah, no," I say, probably about as convincing a lie as the bar fight story.

"No, huh. Well, when you hear something, let me know. If they're cutting you in, you're in on the ground floor of something you'll never forget."

"I've been living on the ground floor my whole life. I was hoping for something with a good view this time."

"There's a view. And it's all good. I've got to get back to work. When are we going to see you again?"

"Hopefully, next week."

"Glad to have you," Birnbaum says with a smile. Not a phony ear to ear grin. A mouth closed, crooked smile with a slight nod that you can't fake.

"Thanks," I say, hoping he knows I mean it. "See ya next week."

I caught a local, an express, and another local with impec-cable timing. I was back to the neighborhood in under thirty-five minutes. I can't believe that it's barely eleven o'clock. I decide to take a little detour to peek in Third Base. Hmmm. Uncle Eugene, Patty, Mikey, and Noel at the bar. One of those nights when the stars aren't aligned, and just a few regulars getting ready to watch the news.

I take a stool at the middle of the bar, a couple away from Uncle Eugene.

"Good evening, Noel. Good evening, gentlemen," I an-nounce to my fellow patrons. A couple of perfunctory "Hey, Jerrys" can be heard. "I'll have a nip, please."

Noel whisks a small beer bottle in front of me, and steps on an empty beer case to turn up the sound on the TV news as it's just beginning.

"...I'm Paul Gordon, and these are top stories at eleven. Tragedy struck on the Triboro Bridge when a suicide plot played

264

out in a bizarre scenario was made even more bizarre due to the fact that a TV camera crew just happened to be stuck in the traffic that a distraught playwright had caused. We now go 'live' to Kathleen Meadows in front of Bellevue Hospital. What's the latest in this unbelievable story, Kathleen?"

I can't watch the screen. I can only watch the faces of the people in the bar. I can't even hear the television. There's a feeling before you throw up, when you can sense the muscles in your stomach pushing in waves, up higher into your esophagus and then into your throat. I feel something very similar, only I know it's not really starting in my stomach. It's emanating from somewhere in my gut. Somewhere near the heart where feelings come from. The place where butterflies are born. Where guts get wrenched. Where knots are tied.

Everyone is drawn to the television as the footage begins.

"I saw this on the news before," Patty says. "It's totally fucked. I can't watch it," he says as he turns and heads for the men's room.

The mad playwright steps onto the retaining wall, and swoosh, there he goes. No cheers here. Just a common gasp of air from everyone at the bar.

"Christ almighty!" Noel screams as he jumps up and pounds the TV switch with a thud, turning it off. "How in God's name can they show such a thing. Is there no fucking decency left in this world? I ask you. Jesus, Mary, and Joseph!" he says, removing his apron and throwing it on the floor. He jumps the bar and walks into the freezing, dark night without his jacket.

"I'll cover for you," Uncle Eugene yells after him. Eugene walks around the bar and places Noel's apron next to the cash register. He picks up a glass, pours out a handful of quarters, and places them on the bar. "Jerry. Go play some tunes in the juke box."

I pick up the quarters and walk over to the jukebox next to the front window. I look across the street, and I can see Noel holding his head, sobbing uncontrollably. I drop the quarters into the machine and blindly start pushing buttons, not even caring what I'm playing. "The Unicorn" begins. I better start paying attention.

I walk back to my coaster at the bar and nervously start peeling the label off the almost empty bottle. "Uncle Eugene, I'll have another nip."

Eugene roots around the ice in the sink, fumbles while he pops off the top, almost drops it, and places it in front of me.

"What's with Noel?" I ask Uncle Eugene softly.

"His sister committed suicide by jumping off a building."

"How old was she?"

"Twenty-three."

"I'm sorry."

"Yeah. So's he."

Uncle Eugene shuffled away to the other end of the bar to tend to Patty and Mikey. He looks like an impostor. Noel always looks so professional with his apron, rolled-up sleeves on his white shirt, and clip-on black tie. Although he makes everyone feel that their jokes are funny, their wives are good looking, and their tips adequate, you would never call Noel a phony. He just has the old school bartender manner about him. He's got charm, manners, dignity, and the respect of everyone who walks through that warped front door. Which, of course, is another reason why I feel like such a shit right now. But that's no reason to think I did anything other than perform the duties of my job. I mean Noel is a man of compassion, principles, and fortitude, yet he serves booze up and down this worn old bar to whoever plops a buck down. Many a good man has gone to his grave with the help of Noel's generously measured boilermakers. And I'm sure Noel would say the same thing. He's just doing his job. Making a living. Trying to pay the bills.

What else does anyone do for a living around here, but mine these streets for gold? If we lived in Vietnam, we'd work in the rice paddies. If we lived in Saudi Arabia, we'd be working the oil fields. If we lived in Colombia, we'd be out in the coffee fields or dealing cocaine. But this is New York City. Most of us just live off of the natural resources we see all around us. Crime is everywhere, so there are plenty of police and court-related jobs. Millions of people with no cars, so there's the transit authority. Ancient, poorly maintained buildings means thousands of fires and fire fighting jobs. Desperation is rampant, so the bars and dope pushers do a bang up business. And to fill the air time on TV, they need camera crews to cover all the disasters and human misery possible to make everyone feel a little better about their own misfortunes. Watching the local news is merely an exercise in saying to yourself, "Gee, there's a problem I don't have."

The door slowly pushes open, and Noel comes back into the bar, perfectly composed. He walks the length of the bar and stoops down to scoot under the end of it into position. Without a word being exchanged between them, Uncle Eugene waits for him to start putting his apron back on before he leaves his bartending position and goes back to being a patron. He walks over to the glass next to the register and pours out a few more quarters. He plops them on the bar and looks over at me. "Jerry, would you mind playing some jolly music for me?"

"Not at all."

I scoop up the quarters next to my beer bottle and dig into my jeans pocket for a few more. "And it's on me."

"Thank you, lad."

I tried to keep away from picking any Irish songs that I didn't actually recognize. An Irish song could have a happy sounding title and turn out to be some tearful minor key ballad sung by an old tenor that'll have the whole bar crying about something. So I basically stick to upbeat Sinatra, Tony Bennett, Beatles, and Kinks. Hmmm.... *Sunny Afternoon* is that a depressing song? Actually, it depends entirely on your frame of mind.

And just as the opening notes of *Sunny Afternoon* begin drifting through the air, Stubby pushes through the door. But it doesn't look like Stubby. He's not wearing his usual thrift store olive drab army surplus winter coat that goes down below his knees. He's wearing what we would call an overcoat. And he's not wearing his purple Converse All-Stars but actual black leather shoes.

He pauses for a moment, holding the door. Shit, I hope he's not coming from a funeral. Just then, in walks Peggy also neatly attired. Oh, my God! Stubby's on a real date.

"Stubby! How are you?"

"Oh, hi Jerry. Good to see you!"

Good to see me? I've only seen the guy like every day of my life.

Stubby doesn't walk to the bar but leads Peggy over to a table, helps her off with her coat, hangs it up, and pulls out her chair for her. He then hangs up his coat and walks over to the bar.

"Hi, Noel. Hey, guys," Stubby says, covering everyone within earshot. "Two white wine spritzers, please," he says, placing a twenty dollar bill on the bar.

Two white wine spritzers? Uh-oh. I wait for Stubby to get his drinks and take his seat across from Peggy.

"Hi Stubby, how are you?" I saw politely to the well mannered couple, who last time I saw were just short of having the vice squad bust the place. "Hi, Peggy."

"Hi, Jerry. How are ya? I hear ya might be working with Victor?"

"Yeah, it looks pretty good. Well, nice to see you again." I say uncomfortably as I take a few steps backward and find my bar stool.

I've known Stubby my entire life. He's the first person I ever met that I wasn't related to. He was the only person my parents ever let baby-sit for me. And I've never been in a room with him where we weren't hanging out together at least to some degree. Not that we had to be right next to each other the entire time, but there was always a connection between us. We could both be on opposite ends of an outdoor concert, and still somehow hook up to take the subway home together. I could see what was on his mind just with a quick glance. Unlike right now.

"I'll see you, Noel," I say, putting a few bucks on the bar. I give a wave and a nod in the direction of Uncle Eugene, and Patty and Mikey, and turn to Stubby and his date. They're staring at

268

each other with their noses just inches apart. He doesn't even notice that I'm leaving. Oh, well, no sense in bothering them.

Uncle Eugene gets up from his stool and begins putting on his jacket. "I'm going out for a smoke, Noel," Eugene says as he places his coaster on top of his glass signifying that he will be returning. "I'll wait for you outside, Jerry," Eugene says as he leaves.

Noel still looks shaken as he begins to methodically re-wash some glasses. He notices me staring at him, and winks at me with a slight smile. I approach him and extend my hand.

"I just wanted to say, Noel...er..." What did I want to say? "I think it was great that you and Eugene buried Mr. Wang."

Noel stopped rubbing the wine glass with the white terry cloth rag as he looked at me with a perplexed look on his face.

"Me and Eugene? Jerry, all I did was give Eugene a lift over to Woodlawn," Noel says softly, as though the news may hurt my feelings.

"You didn't pay for it?"

"Not a cent, lad. That was all Eugene. But don't say a word. He made me swear I'd keep it a secret."

"I won't. Promise. You're a good man, Noel," I said shaking his hand, just before leaving.

It's still bitterly cold outside. I shove my hands into my jacket pockets, but Uncle Eugene pauses as he lights up a Lucky. As he cups the match in front of his face, the light dances across the deep creases and crevices of his face. Decades of smoking have formed a harsh leathery mask for Eugene, which he wears well.

"You walking down the hill, Jerry?"

"Yeah."

We begin the long walk down the hill. It's a good five minutes of passing apartment buildings, an empty lot, and a few private houses. Bronx residential. We walk a good hundred yards before either of us says a word.

"What was with that suicide on TV?" Uncle Eugene asks without looking over at me.

"What do you mean?"

Eugene took a long drag on his Lucky, walked a couple of steps, then turned and looked dead into my eyes, slightly squinting and nodding, as if to say "Come on asshole. What am I? Stupid?"

"I was on that TV crew that shot that jumper."

"You weren't there by accident, were you?" Eugene says, not altering his pace or his rhythm as he smokes his cigarette.

"No. The guy called the office and waited for us. I feel terrible."

"For who? The guy or yourself?"

"I don't know."

"Fuck it. It's not like he was family. You didn't even know the jerk. You gotta make a living, right? Just remember, you're gut'll tell you when you're fucking up and when you're doing the right thing. Want to go to McNichol's for a quickie?"

"Sure." I say quickly. McNichol's is what is commonly referred to as a donkey bar. Even the first generation Irish guys call it that. The patrons in McNichol's are old "off-the-boat" Irishmen, with Irish brogues thicker than Irish stew. "You'll have to translate for me, Uncle Eugene."

"Sure. Hey, you know what Dulligan Stew is? It's like Mulligan Stew, but not as exciting," Eugene says deadpan.

McNichol's is as old as the elevated train line it sits under. It has been a bar for nearly seventy years, except for the few years during prohibition when it became an ice cream parlor, with beer available only through special order. Every inch of the bar is original. From the beveled glass mirrors behind the ancient mahogany bar, thick with shellac, to the still working pendulum clock encased in glass and wood. Irishmen, all hard drinkers, sit here from morning until closing with their porkpie hats and rough hands. There's only one beer on tap, Guinness Stout. And I'll bet they go through more Irish whiskey in one night than at a Dublin wedding. But despite what you've heard about the poetic, friendly nature of the Irish, in McNichol's, certain locals are not warmly welcomed. And strangers are simply not allowed. Going there with Uncle Eugene is akin to walking into a bar across from Yankee Stadium with Mickey Mantle.

Uncle Eugene is first generation Irish, and considered a local hero to many of the men in McNichol's and the area. He was instrumental in getting many Irish immigrants to settle in this part of the Bronx, to bring up their families. Eugene is a union man. And in New York, the unions run the construction business. Tin knockers, steam fitters, wire lathers, carpenters, even ditch diggers are all strictly union jobs. A controlled father and son union. That means you're not getting in unless your father, or maybe your uncle, is already in. Regardless of your legal status. If the union says you're in, you're in. And if they say you're out, you're out.

When the Irish arrived, the men either worked construction or in bars. And here in McNichol's the two worlds have been coming together for three-quarters of a century.

The air is thick with smoke. Filterless cigarettes, cheap cigars, and several sweet-smelling pipes. But it doesn't have that sickening stench that many post war bars have. That's because the floor in here is tile. Not vinyl flooring tiles, but real tiles like you see in an old bathroom. The small hexagonal white tiles with decorative borders. You can bet that the last thing every night someone has a big ugly bucket and mop filled with steaming hot water mixed with ammonia and gives every inch of this place the once over. The ceiling is pressed tin with intricate square designs, which is also free of grease and grime. Many fancy restaurants could learn a thing or two about how to keep up an establishment by looking around this place. There aren't any television sets in here, but a dark jukebox from the fifties sits next to a cigarette machine. The only sounds you hear are the spirited voices of men talking mixed with the noises of two busy bartenders. There's no pool table, but a dart board with one man practicing his toss.

As I listen to the din of conversation, I begin to be able to distinguish individual conversations. Deep, gruff whiskey voices mixed with lilting sing-song high pitched ones. Brogues so thick, I'd need subtitles, interwoven with more familiar Bronx accents.

271

There are a few women in the bar. Not young babes out looking for husbands, but handsome, middle-aged women engaged in lively conversations with groups of men, and matching them drink for drink and pack of Luckys for pack of Luckys.

There isn't a bar stool available, so we take a position by the more quiet end of the bar and stand behind two elderly gents engaged in quiet conversation.

"What'll you have, Jerry," Eugene asks as he signals to the barkeep.

"When in Rome...I'll have a Jameson's and a short Guinness."

"If you get falling down drunk, I ain't carrying you one inch."

"Don't worry. I won't."

As Eugene orders the drinks, I walk to the men's room. The urinal is magnificent. It's got to be polished marble, and it goes from the floor to nearly as high as my chin. A small child could fall in and have trouble getting out, it's so massive. And the bottom of it is filled with a giant mound of ice cubes that steams when you hit them. The flusher is shiny brass and works perfectly. One of the stall doors is open, and the toilet has an overhead tank with a pull chain. Amazingly, it doesn't smell in here either. There is one bit of scratched-in graffiti above the real towel contraption that produces a clean portion of a mile-long cotton towel with each tug, and it reads; "Long Live the I.R.A. Fuck The Queen." Although there are other obvious patches of fresh paint where graffiti has been covered over, this bit has not been tampered with for what I would guess to be years.

The two old Irish gentlemen are gone, and Eugene is now seated with the stool next to him vacant. My drinks are at the ready, and Uncle Eugene has an empty shot glass in front of him and a pint of pitch black Guinness next to it with a perfect half-inch tan head on top. Eugene is talking to a burly man in his early sixties. I've seen him around the neighborhood, but I don't know his name.

I sit down on the vacant stool and try not to interfere with the conversation that doesn't have the trivial tone of most loose bar room talk. It's clear that Eugene is patiently listening to the man's complaints. Uncle Eugene turns and gives me a look signifying he needs to be rescued.

"I forgot what that urinal looks like. Did somebody lift that from Buckingham Palace?" I ask Uncle Eugene, during a lull in his conversation, to hopefully change the subject.

"I'd piss on every fookin' 'ting in Buckingham Palace if given the opportunity," Eugene's red-faced friend announces with a tumbler of whiskey held high.

"Jerry, this is Brendan. Brendan, Jerry," Eugene says, introducing us. Brendan mumbles something and takes a sip of whiskey.

"And what might your last name be, Jerry?" Brendan boldly asks for an obvious reason.

"Why do you ask?"

"Just natural curiosity, son. No harm meant," Brendan says, back pedaling.

"Jerry's lived in this neighborhood his whole life, Brendan. Graduated Visitation, too."

"Hmmm. You look to be about my Maggie's age. Did you know Maggie Moran?"

"Yeah. She was in my class first through fourth grade," I say, trying to be polite. Poor Maggie. She got left back in fourth, and I think tried a little too hard to be accepted in the class behind us. Last I heard she got pregnant, got married, dropped out of high school, and moved to Keanesburg, New Jersey. Not exactly a garden spot of the "garden state."

"And how is Maggie? She was a very nice girl."

"She's no daughter of mine anymore," Brendan says as he finishes his drink. "Another round down here, Terry."

"Me and Brendan worked together for many years in construction," Eugene says good-naturedly.

"Eugene's a good man. Got jobs for all three of my sons and two sons-in-law." Brendan says with pride just as three more drinks are put down in front of us. "But times have changed, haven't they, Eugene?"

"You got that right, Brendan. Things have to change," Eugene says sternly.

I'm guessing it's relating back to the conversation they were having while I was admiring the bathroom fixtures.

"Christ man!" Brendan says above a polite level. "You can't be forcing your own loyal union brothers to sell their own futures away. You're daft, man." Brendan says as his face becomes redder, his neck thicker, and his chin bolder.

"Things have to change, Brendan," Eugene says calmly, trying not to be drawn into battle.

"It's our fookin' livelihoods you're talking about," Brendan says loud enough for a few patrons at the middle of the bar to look our way. "I'd rather quit than train a fookin' nigger how to do my job, and that's that."

I can see Uncle Eugene bristling as he slowly turns to me and then back around even slower towards Brendan. "Go ahead. Quit," he says with a quiet intensity.

"And you'd put a fookin' nigger before me and my family," Brendan screams, momentarily stopping all the talk from our end down to the middle of the bar.

Eugene sat there silently, not acknowledging Brendan's tirade.

"I've got to take a piss," Brendan says as he storms off towards the men's room.

Eugene pulls a cigarette out of his pack on the bar and lights it up.

"That's the mentality of what I have to deal with. This ain't the fifties anymore. That shit don't fly."

"Do you want to leave?"

"Nah. He's a blowhard. He'll be back like nothing happened. He's actually a decent guy. There's a couple of old colored guys on the job he's on now, and he'd kick anybody's ass that messed with them. Go figure."

The door squeaks as Brendan pushes it open and walks

with a slight limp back to his place at the bar.

"Excuse me, fellas. I'm going to chat at the end of the bar with a couple of mates," Brendan says in a lilting tone as if nothing happened.

"Sure, we'll watch your money," Eugene says reassuringly.

"Thanks, lads," Brendan says with appreciation in his voice as he hobbles away. He walks to the other end of the bar and joins a few friends in jolly conversation.

"Eugene, how the hell does somebody go from such an insufferable prick to an affable leprechaun in the time it takes to melt a pile of urinal ice?"

"Sometimes a guy's just gotta blow off some steam. Forget about it. He'll go from Jekyl to Hyde and back again three more times before last call."

"Don't you ever blow off steam, Eugene?"

"Oh, yeah. But only when there are no other options left."

I chewed on that for a while and washed it down with several long gulps from my Guinness. There are times in a bar when you feel like you don't have to make idle talk. If you don't have anything worth saying, you just don't say anything. Kind of like when you're in love.

Suddenly the din of bar chatter came to a screeching halt as the sound of a rich baritone voice fills the pub with the opening lines of *Too-Ra-Loo-Ra-Loo-Ral.* Yup, Brendan. Who would expect that angelic voice is coming from such a hateful bigot. I remember once hearing Bing Crosby say in an interview that he knows how lucky he is to be so successful because he's been to many a party or pub where somebody has a voice much better than his. Here's living proof. Is it but for the grace of God goes Bing and Brendan down their own paths? Or was it a fork in the road they decided to take?

As all eyes and ears are focused on Brendan, I feel a light tap on my shoulder. I turn to see Merrill arm in arm with an attractive, young Black woman. She has a short Afro and sharp angular features in perfect contrast to Merrill's round eastern European qualities.

"Hi, Jerry. I was hoping I'd find you here," Merrill says, beaming with glad tidings. "I want you to meet Ebony."

Ebony extends her hand with a wide and bright smile across her face. "Hello, Jerry, I've heard a lot about you. Nice to finally meet you."

"Nice to meet you, too."

"Jerry, I had to find you tonight. I wanted to say good-bye."

"Good-bye? Like *good-bye* good-bye?"

"Remember we talked about you dropping me off in North Carolina when you took your Dad's car to Florida...?"

"Shit!" I say aloud and immediately realize that Ebony didn't like hearing it. "I'm going to have to call my Dad and tell him I'm delayed again."

"Well, Ebony and I decided to go together. Now."

"Really? Isn't this kind of sudden?" I say, fumbling for a way to express my own confusion of the moment. "Are you sure, Merrill?"

Ebony hugs Merrill warmly, and Merrill lights up like the Christmas tree in Rockefeller Center.

"Oh, yeah. We're married."

"What?" Not much is clicking with me. Brendan, who uses the word "nigger" like I use "Italian," is just finishing up his song and probably getting ready to take a bow and milk the applause for the entire length of the bar as he comes back to take his position next to his money. "Are you serious? Married? When?"

"Today. We decided to go to North Carolina together as one to join the community. We wouldn't want it any other way," Merrill says as he gazes into Ebony's dark sparkling eyes.

Just as I had feared, Brendan is making his way back to our end of the bar to applause and pats on the back. He walks between Merrill, Ebony, and me in an almost, but not quite, rude manner. He takes a seat at the bar next to Eugene.

"Variety is the spice of life, I guess," Brendan says not loud enough to be absolutely interpreted as an insult. He's ignored by our little group.

"Well, Jerry," Merrill says as he grabs me by the shoulders and pulls me toward him for a tight hug, "I'll miss you. Thanks for everything. Your friendship has meant a lot to me."

I was at a total loss for words. I'm not good at hellos or good-byes. "Yeah, me too, Merrill."

"Isn't an introduction in order here, Jerry?" Brendan says boldly.

"Allow me," Merrill says with a big grin on his face. "I'm Merrill and this is my wife, Ebony," Merrill happily says with his hand outstretched.

Brendan has an incredulous look on his face. "Your *wife*? Never mind." Brendan says turning quickly away.

Now there's no doubt about it. That was an insult. Merrill stands there with his hand outstretched. Waiting.

"Let's go, Merrill," Ebony says softly as she tries to pull Merrill's arm down.

Merrill just stands there frozen. A blank look on his face. He has that look when the adrenaline is flowing and the body tries desperately to conceal it.

Brendan sits staring straight ahead, ignoring Merrill.

"Shake his hand," Eugene says directly to Brendan.

"I will not," Brendan retorts.

"You will shake his hand or you'll have a mighty mess right here and now, so help me God," Eugene says with a conviction that now has my adrenaline pumping as well.

Brendan looks at Eugene with utter contempt in his eyes. "Why are you such a fookin' nigger lover?"

As if an explosion went off in Eugene's brain, he grabs Brendan with both hands right on his throat. Brendan's already red face immediately begins to turn beet red as the veins in his neck and forehead are filling in like country roads on a road map. Brendan is gasping for air as he grabs at Eugene's arms.

Merrill and I both grab Eugene arms trying to force his release of Brendan's neck as the entire bar rushes over to join in the melee.

"You're nothing but a mean old donkey, Brendan Moran," Eugene says, letting go of his victim.

Brendan begins rubbing his neck and reaches for his pint, "Can't anyone take a bloody joke anymore?"

Merrill takes a step towards Brendan and again holds out his hand. "God bless you, brother."

Brendan looks at Merrill, blinks hard three times and wipes his eyes. "Bless you, son. My apologies."

"Accepted," Merrill says, shaking Brendan's hand.

"Well, good-bye, Jerry. We must be leaving."

"Good-bye, Merrill. Me too. Someday."

With that, Merrill and Ebony walk out of the bar holding hands, not looking back.

Merrill and I have been through so much together. It wasn't until I was through with silly kid games (the street variety such as curb ball, stick ball, and ring-o-leaveo, and the childish macho psychological games we played with each other) that I began to know him. I always saw him around and said hello, but we never hung out together. Not until later in high school when the kids we were hanging out with since grade school started to disappear into cliques they would never again emerge from. The sexually obsessed group of guys who couldn't wait to have intercourse with any willing partner, got pregnant and are now busy being rednecks in the outer reaches of Long Island and Rockland County. The kids who went to various suburban colleges, majored in business and became Wall Street robots in their Brooks Brothers' uniforms, mortgaged to the hilt in Scarsdale and the North Shore. Then there were the kids who started hanging out in bars at fifteen and moved in the social hierarchy from fake draft cards, to card carrying alcoholics betting their paychecks with small-time bookies. The kids who smoked pot between classes, sniffed glue after school, popped pills, and snorted anything that was available until they started shooting the same; those guys are like ghosts even when they still live in the neighborhood.

But Merrill, Stubby, Terry, me and a handful of other guys never got to deep into any one scene. A little of this and a little of that, but never enough to get totally screwed-up on sex, drugs, and rock and roll. Well, maybe just a little.

But with Merrill, there was always a special rapport. Even when we were having the most basic kind of fun, perhaps in the bar, or at a concert, or a bonfire on a cold winter's night in the park, Merrill and I could always have a private discussion that went beyond the immediate pleasure. There was always a conversation or word or a glance that meant we understood the moment. And it was Merrill who told me to read Jack Kerouac's *On The Road*, *The Dharma Bums*, and *Vanity of Duluoz*, in that order. Three books that opened my mind like no others.

If I didn't hurry, they could be gone. I jumped up and ran to the door. They were still warming up their car. I knocked on the passenger side window where Merrill was sitting.

"Merrill! Hold on."

Merrill rolled the window open about an eighth of an inch and strained to put his mouth right next to the opening. "If you think I'm letting the warm air out of this car after spending five minutes trying to get it this way, you're nuts! Hop in!"

The car looked like a late sixties Ford Falcon, but it had a little rusted chrome sign hanging by one screw that read "Futura." It was a faded red and from this side of the car, there was a dent or rust hole about every eighteen inches. I reached for the handle, but it didn't work. Merrill reached behind and began jiggling the inside handle until the door opened. I pushed a large army surplus duffle bag over and took a seat.

"Hey, Merrill, you've got a full seabag here, but your name ain't stenciled right," I say, referring to one of our euphemisms for someone being a little nuts.

"My seabag isn't even half full," Merrill says, giggling at my reference. "I'm glad you came out. I was going to go back in and say good-bye. I didn't want that to be our last memory to-gether."

"Come on, this isn't our last memory," I say, grabbing Merrill by his shoulders and shaking him violently.

"Save me, Ebony. Crazy Eddie's prices are insane!" Merrill says through hearty laughter.

I stopped shaking Merrill and he stopped laughing.

"Actually, Ebony has already saved me," Merrill says softly.

"No, that's not true," Ebony says lovingly as she touches Merrill's lips with her woolen gloved finger. "You saved me."

"OK, it's settled! I saved Ebony! I'm positive, I'm posi-tive, I'm positive, positive, positive!" Merrill begins, and I follow with him.

"We're posititve, we're positive, we're positive, positive, positive!"

"What are you guys doing?"

Merrill stops. "Oh, that's from Abbott and Costello."

Ebony has a confused look on her face and asks "Which movie?"

"No, not a movie. From their TV show. You know with Mike the Cop, Hillary Brooke, Bociacalupe, Stinky, and Sidney Fields," Merrill replies enthusiastically.

The Abbott and Costello TV show was a constant source of entertainment for Merrill and me. I don't think there was ever a funnier or more surreal program on television, possibly with the exception of the Joe Franklin Show.

"You guys go way back, huh?" Ebony says to me.

"Oh, yeah. Centuries, huh, Merrill?"

"It feels that way, Jerry. But if we're going to make Wash-ington, before morning we've got to get rolling."

Merrill reaches into his pocket and pulls out a dime store memo pad, tears out a small sheet, and begins writing. "You can write to us here at the community until we get settled in a place of our own."

"Don't be a stranger," I say holding out my hand. Merrill

swings around and gives me a strong bear hug.

"Never. We'll never be strangers."

"Good-bye, Ebony. And whatever you do, don't ever let Merrill see a mouse when he's in a boxing ring."

"Huh?" She says totally baffled.

Merrill and I both begin chanting, "Moe, Larry, cheese, Moe, Larry, cheese, Moe, Larry, Cheese."

"Aha! That I know! The Three Stooges!" Ebony proclaims proudly.

"I knew I found the woman of my dreams!" Merrill says as he gives her a short but tender kiss on the nose. "Jerry, keep dreaming. Bye."

I jiggled the handle and watched as they rumbled off and took a left under the Broadway el as a train roared above. I went back into the bar and sat on my still vacant stool.

"Can I buy you boys a shot?" Brendan asks Eugene and me.

"Sure," Eugene replies without a trace of animosity. "Make mine a double."

"You're a good man, *Uncle* Eugene," Brendan says jokingly. "There's not a man alive I'd take that from. But you've put plenty a potato on the table for three generations of Morans and that I'll never forget."

"I'll remember that," Eugene says lighting up another cigarette.

"And what's your line of work, Jerry?" Eugene asks with a Guinness mustache still on his upper lip.

"Me? Oh, I've got a few jobs right now."

"A few jobs? Still searching, hey, lad? You're lucky then. Options! That's what we immigrants set out for our children, options. What sort of jobs?"

"Well, I've got two part-time jobs working with video, you know, TV equipment, and I work at a library downtown..."

"The library?" Brendan says with a look of shock on his face accentuated with his putting his pint on the bar with a dull thud.

281

"For the city?"

"Yeah. The New York Public Library."

"You're working for the city? Why are you dicking around with two part-time jobs?

"Um, I might want to work in TV."

"Son, you've got a city job! Don't jeopardize that for chrissakes. Milk it for all it's worth and get out in twenty or twenty-five, or whatever the hell it is. Don't be a fool."

"Thanks for the advice."

"What's this TV 'ting you're doing on the side?"

"Well, er, one is for a kind of an artsy kind of hippie documentary maker, and the other is doing, er, news."

"News! What channel?"

"Well, most channels. It's a company that shoots TV news and then sells it to all the stations."

"Really? I like that channel seven. That Grimsby guy. He's a tough bastard. I like him. What big news event have you put on the TV?"

"Well, we, er, shot, er..."

I couldn't help but wonder whether or not I should be opening this can of worms. Oh, screw it.

"We shot that guy jumping off the Triboro that was on the news today."

"Go on!"

"Really."

"You were there?"

"Yeah."

"Did you pay him to do that?"

"What? No!"

"And the asshole lived to tell it. Playwright my bloody arse. Free publicity is all he wanted. Another round down here, please."

"Eugene, I think I'm heading home. I don't think I can stand any more surprises."

"Go ahead, kid. Get some sleep."

"OK, see ya."

"And listen to your gut," Eugene says with a wink and a nod.

I walked out into the empty dark Bronx night and headed home. Wonder what I'll be dreaming tonight, I thought to myself.

I walked up the outside stairs into the cold tiled hallway, and noticed that there was a small yellow slip sticking out of my mailbox. It's a notice that I had a registered piece of mail at the post office. From Florida. My parents. Oops.

THIRTEEN

"Jerry! You've been telling me the same story for weeks. What is going on up there? The phone rings off the hook, you don't answer the letters, I was about to have Mrs. O'Sullivan smell under the door to see if she could smell a dead body!"

I've been trying to avoid this phone call for a while, and especially don't want to deal with it at six o'clock in the morning. Especially when I didn't attain my r.e.m. until about five-thirty.

"Dad, I'm trying to arrange to bring the car down, but all of a sudden I've got three jobs I'm trying to juggle. You should be proud of me."

"Yeah, I should be proud you're out drinking until five in the a.m. and playing both sides against the middle. Make your mind up and bring me my car!"

"OK, OK. I'll leave next weekend. I promise."

"Here's your mother."

Despite my father's hand being placed over the mouthpiece, I could hear him yelling at my mother. "Don't coddle him. He's too old to be coddled. The damn kid has to learn to take responsibility."

"Hi, Jerry."

"Hi, Mom."

"Are you eating OK?"

I could hear my father screaming from across the room "Don't coddle!"

"Yes, I'm eating."

"What?"

"Food."

"Very funny. Always keep potatoes and lettuce around, OK?"

"OK. Bye, Mom. See you in a week or two."

"Be careful. Bye."

"Bye."

284

I just hope I can go back to sleep. I need my nightly eight. And I have to be in at the library at eight tomorrow, so I know that will mean less time in slumber land. The only good part about living in a tiny dark apartment where the living room windows face another wall of windows about twenty feet away is that it makes for easy sleeping in. You don't realize it's daylight outside until about noon. And if you close the curtains and the blinds, you'd think you were in six months of antarctic darkness.

BBBBRRRIIIINNNNNGGGGGGG

Should I answer it? It's probably my father again. Maybe he changed his mind. Maybe my Mom talked some sense into him and he's going to tell me to drive the car down whenever it's convenient for me.

"Hello."

"Jerry, get your ass out of bed. Do you have a passport?"

"What? Who the hell is this?"

"It's your fucking boss! Do you have a passport?"

"Oh, hi, Rocco," I weakly mumble, trying to figure out what's going on. "Uh, no, I don't have a passport."

"Schuyler! Are you sure he needs a passport to go to Canada?"

I can hear Schuyler across the room, "It's recommended but not essential."

"OK, fuck the passport," Barbieri barks. "Just jump in the shower, scrape off the funk, pack light for about five days, and be in front of your building in twenty minutes ready to go. Victor will be there to pick you up."

"Five days? What are you talking about?"

"You're going with Schuyler on a shoot with French television doing a story on Yankel Raviv, the new...President or some shit of Israel. They've only got film crews, and they need a video crew to go on a whirlwind tour of the U.S. and Canada starting this afternoon at the U.N. and taking off right afterwards. So get your ass down here!"

"Why me?"

"You're the only one with half a fucking brain I can spare right now. Get your bony white ass down here or you're fired!"

"I guess that means I'm hired."

"Yes, you're hired. Now hurry before you're fired. Out," Barbieri screams as he slams down the phone.

I've got two jobs I'm supposed to show up for tomorrow, and today, Sunday, I'm being whisked away with Yankel Raviv and French TV. Go figure. And shit, what about Charlie? I hate the fact that I've been out so much, how the hell am I going to go away? Mrs. O'Sullivan? Why not?

KNOCK KNOCK

"Oh, Jerry, so nice to see you! Come in!"

"It's not too early?"

"Are you kidding me? I'm up at four. I still go to the six o'clock mass every morning. Come in, come in," Mrs. O'Sullivan says as she waves me into her home. I'm immediately struck by the aroma of fresh-baked bread. Unlike our apartment, Mrs. O'Sullivan only has a kitchenette. She has a teapot on the counter covered with a hand-knitted green and white tea cozy. Next to the teapot is a fresh loaf of Irish Soda bread sitting on a wooden cutting board. "Would you like some bread and a cup of tea, Jerry?"

"I'd love to, but I'm in such a hurry. I got called into work and it looks like I have to go away for a few days. I was wondering if you could possibly look after my bird for a few days?"

"I didn't even know you had one. Is it a budgie?"

"Actually, it's a pigeon."

"A pigeon?"

"It's a long story, but it was Charlie The Chinaman's, and when he died, I wound up taking care of it."

"Oh, may God rest his soul, that poor man. I never took my laundry there, but he was always so nice, and kept the sidewalk so tidy. Of course I'll take care of him. What's his name?"

"Charlie. I'll go get him."

"Is there any more news on Charlie's death?"

"Not that I know of."

"I hope they find the bastards that killed him."

"How do you know he was killed?"

"Oh, I can just feel it in my bones whenever I walk by his store on the way to mass."

Just at that moment, the sound of glass breaking echoes through the courtyard out the window.

"What was that?" I ask Mrs. O'Sullivan, who seems unfazed by the crashing sound.

"That's nothing. That's those people in that bastard Donnelly's apartment. It's like that night and day. There's evil goings-on in there, Jerry."

"I know, Mrs. O'Sullivan. They'll get theirs someday."

"Well, go get the bird and don't worry. It'll be nice to have some company for a few days."

As I was leaving I noticed an ancient, faded photograph on the wall next to the front door. I stopped to look at it and was taken by the sheer beauty of the woman in her modest wedding dress and the stern look of proud groom. "Is this your wedding photo?"

"Yes. Me and my Seamus. Back in Ireland. He was a good man, Jerry. But, he drank himself to death. Watch the drinking, Jerry."

"I will. I'll be right back with Charlie."

What a relief. She's a wise, old woman.

Victor is sitting in his truck with the engine gunning. I expected him to be friendly after we were heroes together last night. But he hardly grunts a hello as he takes a huge bite of an egg sandwich on a hard roll and peels out.

"Good morning," I say, just in case he wants to change his mood.

Nothing.

He drove downtown in his usual reckless fashion, which I

didn't complain about even when he blew through a stop sign just after exiting the FDR, almost running into a guy pushing a hot dog cart.

He pulls in front of the office and sits silently.

"Are you coming in?" I ask, trying to remain neutral.

"For what? I'm just a fucking delivery boy," Victor says, obviously referring to the fact that I've got a cherry assignment.

"I've got nothing to do with this," I tell Victor, knowing it's not a good time for excuses.

"Yeah. Right. Have fun on the trip," Victor says reaching across me and opening the door. I step out of the cabin and as he is pulling the door shut, I can hear him say, "College boy."

The office was going nuts. Big equipment cases were piled everywhere. Barbieri was standing in the center of the room and all activity revolved around him as he barked orders, questions, and insults as he checked off things on his clipboard.

"Don't fucking tell me you're not sure! Find out! Call the fucker at home. What am I dealing with here? This is the big time! Zero tolerance for stupidity."

Schuyler is sitting at Trotta's desk with a pile of official looking papers. "OK, the manifest stuff; serial numbers on everything. Let's go, Trotta!"

Trotta is huffing and puffing as he removes pieces of electronic equipment out of storage cabinets and places them next to the large equipment cases laid out. "I can't see these fucking numbers! You need a magnifying glass for this shit."

No one seems to notice that I've entered the room. "Uh, can I help?"

Barbieri looks up from his clipboard. "Can you help? We're doing your fucking job for you! Put your shit down and start getting your gear together! You ain't shooting in the Bronx with Victor; you're gonna be with the fucking President or Prime Minister or what the fuck of....now I forgot again, is it Israel or Egypt?"

"Israel! And don't make that mistake when French TV is around," Schuyler says with a concerned look on his face.

"Oh fuck those frogs! If it wasn't for us bailing their ass out, they'd be talking fucking German right now, the pussies," Barbieri says as he inspects a microphone cable. "This fucking cable is broken! Trotta, you gotta look out for this shit!"

"Sorry Rocco, lemme see that," Trotta says crawling across the room to retrieve the suspect cable. "Goddam Victor never checks this gear properly."

The next two hours were a whirlwind of unpacking, packing, uncoiling, coiling, checking and double-checking every piece of cable, connector, battery, and serial number, until a pile of disconnected gear became a perfectly packed set of professional TV news equipment. And Barbieri just soaked in the neatness of it all. Beautifully dressed cables, neatly marked labels on everything, equipment contents listed inside and outside of every case, and every last bit of gear tagged with a bright blue piece of tape and a label attached.

Barbieri is walking slowly in a large circle around the pile of cases that Schuyler and I will be taking on our trip with Yankel Raviv. He proudly taps his pen on his clipboard and each case as he surveys the results of his strict orders.

"This is what a job done right is supposed to look like. If I'm not standing over you guys, this would look like the fucking Little Rascals did it. And Jerry, here's my advice for you on this trip, which is probably the most important job we've ever had for reasons I can't even tell you about," Barbieri says as he slowly moves his enormous body towards me. I can feel the floor dip slightly and hear it creak under his weight as he gets right in my face. "Don't. Fuck. Up. Got it?"

"Got it."

"Alright, let's move this shit out!" Barbieri yells excitedly as we all hop to it.

I jump to Schuyler's side awaiting his orders, hoping to God he doesn't see that I'm scared shitless.

"Jerry, come into my office for a minute," Barbieri says softly.

I follow his waddle into his private office and take a seat while he goes around his desk and sits in his oversized leather chair, which gives out a gasp of air as he sinks into it.

"I've got some credentials for you," he says, reaching into his drawer and pulling out several plastic cards with long chains attached. "This is for the U.N. This one says you work for me. This one says you're accredited by the NYPD. This one says you work for Amalgamated Press. This one says you work for French TV. And this one gives you full clearance to travel with the official Israeli government entourage. Are you part Arab by any chance?"

"No, Italian and Irish."

"That's good, except tough luck on the Irish part, but I hope you realize I'm taking a huge chance on you. But since you came through last night under fire, combined with the fact that the only guys I could possibly spare right now are as stupid as chimpanzees, and Schuyler's going with you, I'm giving you a shot. Capeesh?"

"Capeesh."

"Alright, go hook up with Schuyler and don't get more than five feet from him for the next week."

"Week?"

"Yeah, week. You got a problem with that?"

"Uh, why, er, no. I'll just have to make some calls tomorrow, I guess. Um, we never talked about money, Rocco."

"That's right. We'll talk when you get back. Know what I'm saying?"

"Yeah. Got it."

"Good luck," Barbieri says holding out his hand. But in his face I could see he's again telling me not to fuck up. Or else.

"Thanks."

Unfortunately, Schuyler's driving isn't all that much better than Victor's. It's nice to be in a new 1979 Dodge van, but the fear factor is about the same.

"Are we running late?" I ask Schuyler, who is zooming up

1st Avenue just barely making the timed traffic lights before they go from yellow to red.

"No. We're a little early. I hate being late. We're meeting a French TV producer and their top correspondent. Do you know any French?"

"Just the kiss."

"What does that mean?"

"You know, the French kiss."

"Oh," Schuyler says without a hint of a sense of humor.

We pull into the United Nations parking garage, and Schuyler whips out some paperwork for the guard to approve. He does, and we park the van.

"Let's first go and meet our contacts before we start unloading," Schuyler instructs me as we exit the van and he systematically checks that all the locks are secured.

We must've been stopped at five security checkpoints before we were outside the French TV office at the end of the hall by the men's room.

We entered, and the room was about as big as a stall in the men's room next door. Just a small desk facing out a window with a small woman looking out upon a gorgeous view of Queens across the East River. She should know better. Never sit in an office with your back to the door. Somebody can get the drop on you real easy.

As soon as she turned around, I knew it was trouble. About twenty-five years old, flat red hair cut blunt to her shoulders, a tiny nose with traces of freckles, and a low-cut blouse that would cause a near riot walking past a construction site on a hot July afternoon in the city.

"Schuyler, you're early," she says in a voice deep enough to be called sultry.

"Hi, Monique. This is my sound man, Jerry. He's coming with us on the trip."

She shoves her hand quickly in my direction. "Pleasure," she says so quickly that it's hardly a word at all but merely a phonetic sound. My hand gets one fast, hard jerk and an immediate release, kind of like when you're throwing a buck on a craps table. Suddenly, less than thirty seconds into our meeting, the "trouble" I originally imagined upon her first impression; all consuming infatuation and lust, has transformed into a different kind of "trouble." I think she's a ballbreaker supreme.

"Nice to meet you," I say, just as my hand is thrust towards the floor.

"You have all credentials, manifests, itineraries, schedules?" Monique says to Schuyler as she sits back down in her chair and begins lighting a Virginia Slims cigarette.

"We're good to go," Schuyler says, injecting a little extra authority into his delivery.

"If you don't mind me asking," Monique says looking at me, taking a long draw on her cigarette, and flicking an ash on the hardwood floor, "what happened to your eye?"

"Oh, a little, er..." Think quick! No, not the true story... not the bar brawl story... er... "A little hockey accident," I say, recalling my early years as a second line center for the Cardinal Hayes ice hockey team.

"Oh, just pucking around, huh?" Monique says drolly. "We should go meet Sherrard Keetabershare and see what he wants us to do before we go to the airport. I'll be right back," she says as she puts the cigarette out on the bottom of her shoe, letting the hot ashes fall as they may on the hardwood floor. She then pushes the window open a couple of inches and flicks the still smoldering butt out, probably onto some poor unsuspecting schmuck twenty stories below. She gets up, pushes her skirt down with both hands where it settles into a position about four inches above her knee, and leaves the room.

"Who's that Sherrard Keetabershare?" I ask Schuyler.

"He's French TV's number one correspondent. Here's a little background," he says, handing me a piece of paper from Monique's desk.

"This says his name is Gerard Kittleberger."

"That's in American. In French, it's pronounced Sher-rard Keetabershare."

"Silly me. Is Monique French?"

"Don't say anything, but her real name is Monica and she's from Flushing. But she went to Columbia and speaks French fluently. Or so I'm told. And I think she's banging Sherrard so be careful."

"Ah, love."

Schuyler and I stand awkwardly in the tiny office, waiting for Monique's return. On her desk are copies of *Vanity Fair, Vogue, Interview,* and *Jane's International Defense Review* which I can't help but be intrigued by. On the cover of *Jane's International Defense Review* is a picture of a US Navy battle group, i.e. an aircraft carrier, a destroyer, and a flotilla of smaller war ships.

"Who is *Jane* and why does she have a magazine with a battle group on the cover?"

"That's the number one armament and defense magazine in the world," Schuyler says condescendingly.

"Oh. And Jane is...."

"That's Jane as in last name. Like my last name is John."

"I thought your last name was Saint John."

"No, Saint is my middle name; my mother's maiden name."

"Oh."

There must be some secret global aristocratic society of people with first names as last names and last names as first names. Probably when someone applies for a university, or job, or loan, the first thing they do is scan down the list of applicants for people who fall into that privileged category. What a simple plan!

I begin flipping though *Jane's Defense* and page after page are full-page advertisements for radar, sonar, bulletproof vests, and even tanks and fighter jets.

"You're holding in your hand the magazine that makes the world go 'round," Schuyler preaches to me proudly. "All the bullshit that you hear from Carter, and the other knee-jerk liberals is just lip service. That magazine is like the free world's Sears catalogue.

It's what keeps the economy going. That's all government is about; selling."

"Gee, silly me. And I thought government had something to do with, er, let's see, oh yeah, The Constitution," I say, dripping with sarcasm.

Just then the door pushes open and Monique enters followed closely by a middle-aged man who could have been a stunt double for Dudley Moore in "Arthur." He's shorter than I, and also shorter than Monique in her high heels. He has a leather briefcase under his arm that looks like five pounds of baloney in a two pound bag. His dark suit looks expensive but also slightly rumpled. And as he places his bag on the desk right next to where I am standing, I believe he hasn't had it or his shirt to the laundry in quite a while.

"You remember Schuyler," Monique says to Gerard.

"Ah oui! Hello, Schuyler," Gerard says warmly in a thick French accent.

"And this is our sound man, Jerry," Monique says.

"Ah, like Jerry Lewis! Oui!" Gerard says with a big grin on his face. "What is the illness on your face?"

"The illness? Oh this!" I say, pointing to my gash on my mug. "Oh, it's a, ah, from an ice hockey accident."

"Ice hockey! Oh the Montreal Canadiens! Our first destination! Ah, oui!" Gerard says enthusiastically. "Many beautiful women in Montreal!" Gerard opens a bottom desk drawer, pulls out a bottle of wine and a corkscrew, and begins to open it. "Do we have enough glasses?" He asks Monique.

"Yes, in the other drawer."

Gerard grabs the additional three wine glasses and begins pouring. "We will not be shooting here today. Monique has your tickets and itineraries. We will meet at the airport. After the flight to Montreal, we will meet at the hotel. Unfortunately, Schuyler, we will not be away for a week, but only for a day. I hope this is not a problem."

"Not at all," Schuyler says, even though we have a week's worth of gear we'll have to schlep around.

294

"Good. We will have a bottle of wine and then go. Oui?"

Schuyler takes a tiny sip of wine from his glass and places it on the desk. "I think we better get going to the airport. We have a lot of things to prepare for the trip."

"OK Monique and I will just have to finish the wine ourselves, eh, Monique?" Gerard says in mock disappointment.

Monique nearly smiles as she quietly kicks off her shoes.

"So, we'll see you out there," Schuyler says as we exit the tiny room. We were perhaps three steps away, when I could hear at least two locks snap shut on the office door behind us and the sounds of classical music being turned up.

According to my itinerary, we got to JFK Airport about two hours early. Schuyler pulls into a parking garage and leaves the engine running. He turns his head towards me, and I notice his right eye twitching a little bit. "Uh, Jerry, do you mind if I smoke pot?"

"Not at all."

"Would you like some?"

"No, thanks. In fact, I think I'll go look for a men's room while you're doing it."

"OK. It's just that I hate flying, and I don't want to be carrying anything. I'll just leave it in the van."

"I'll be back in a little while," I say to Schuyler, who looks quite pleased that I'm taking my little walk and leaving him alone with his best friend.

Every case was opened, searched, and matched against our manifest, not only by a U.S. Customs agent, but by guys in ill-fitting, cheap black suits and conspicuous bulges under their jackets. Just like their U.S. counterparts, Israeli Secret Service agents have dark glasses, solemn expressions, and mean dispositions. The dark Ray-Bans preclude getting a good look at their eyeballs, but I'm certain that I'm getting the once-over by them.

The jumbo jet is apparently a charter flight. There are scores of press people, and as far as I can tell, just one other video crew besides us. Schuyler carries his camera and a small equipment bag on his shoulder, and I'm carrying the heavy video tape machine and a not so small equipment bag. I'll never admit it to Schuyler, but I can barely carry all the gear.

People are being escorted to their seats on the plane by Israeli Secret Servicemen. Monique and Gerard are whisked past us, and barely give us a glance.

Now it's our turn. A diminutive young man, probably no more than twenty-one with eyeglasses as thick as the bulletproof glass at a subway token booth, takes our tickets and passports, and gestures for us to follow him. As we enter the plane, I can see the front of it is almost empty but the rear is lost in a cloud of cigarette smoke, loud chatter, and the sound of glasses clanking together. I can see Monique and Gerard chatting with Don Samuels, the famous CBS Middle East correspondent.

Surprisingly, our escort does not take us to the rear of the plane but sits us all by ourselves in row two. For about fifteen minutes, we were the only ones for several rows until a whole new wave of men in bad suits began boarding. They also had long black coats on. And as one reached up to open an overhead bin, I could see an Uzi hanging under his arm. It sent a chill up my spine but Schuyler, who also saw it, turned and gave me the biggest smile I've seen on his face since we met.

The seats around us began to fill with these men sporting bad hair and worse suits. And suddenly, right down the aisle comes two Secret Service guys struggling as they carry a long wooden crate that barely fits through the aisle. Another crate is being carried down the aisle on the other side of the plane. The men drop these coffin-like boxes with wooden rope handles just a few feet past where Schuyler and I are sitting and they are left in the aisle with the two men sitting in the sides alongside them.

"What the hell is that, or do I really want to know?" I whisper to Schuyler.

"You could take over a small country with what they've got in those crates," Schuyler whispers back with a sense of pure delight in his voice.

Just then, there he is. Right between the two largest, darkest, meanest looking, jackets bulging, Israeli Secret Service thugs you could imagine; Yankel Raviv. The plane suddenly becomes quiet. Even in the press section in the rear. One of the agents points to the seat right in front of Schuyler and me and much to my shock, Yankel Raviv takes his seat immediately in front of us. I look at Schuyler in total disbelief.

Schuyler leans over to me and quietly says, "We're just another layer of meat."

"Waddyuh mean?"

"If anything, you know, goes wrong, and bullets start flying, we're the buffer between the terrorists and Raviv," Schuyler says with a deranged look in his eye.

"Oh, nice. A human shield. Just what I always wanted to be when I grew up."

Once Raviv sat down, had a glass of wine, and began having a lively conversation in Hebrew with the people sitting around, the chatter started up again in the back of the plane, the wine flowed, the laughter occasionally erupted, and the cigarette smoke filled the cabin. And before we knew it, we were flying at forty-thousand feet.

As I sat silently, Schuyler was busy reading some kind of yachting magazine he brought along.

"Yacht much?" I blurt out.

"Whenever I can."

"Where do you keep your yacht?"

"Actually, it's the family's. We keep it in Chesapeake Bay in the summer and Palm Beach in the winter."

"I prefer lakes myself."

"Oh, do you boat?"

"Well, we used to steal rowboats at the lake in Van Cortlandt Park and play 'Huck Finn' in the swamps, but that's about it."

Schuyler doesn't look amused and begins reading again.

"What was your major?" I ask, making an attempt to be civil with my new boss.

"Well, I started out in law but switched to communications. Actually, I went against my father's plan."

"What was that?"

"I was supposed to become a lawyer, then go in the Marines, then run for office."

"Run for office?"

"Yeah, you know, Congress. The trick is to get your law degree first, then go in the service."

"And what was the master plan?"

"Congress, then if you're successful, the Senate, then who knows?"

"Yeah, that's what I always say, who knows?"

"But I couldn't handle pre-law. Too much memorizing."

"I know. And it's all so counter-intuitive."

A quizzical wave spreads across Schuyler's face.

"So I got into communications. Mostly video."

"Yeah, me, too," I say enthusiastically. "I began doing some theatre but gravitated towards video. It's the future."

"Totally," Schuyler says, connecting with me for the first time. "It's a great growth area. My father believes in Barbieri."

"Oh, you mean, philosophically?"

"No, in his company. That's why we bought forty-nine percent. Barbieri keeps control though."

"My father has some great connections. He's a federal judge but got fucked when Carter took over."

"Yeah, my Dad had a similar problem when they voted Lindsay in as mayor of New York."

"Your Dad's in government?" Schuyler beams.

"Well, sort of. He's a "G- Man," I say, pausing to see the look on Schuyler's face for that instant, then add, "Garbageman. Sanitation. When Lindsay got in, he cut back on overtime, froze wages, and cancelled all promotions."

"Yeah," Schuyler says coldly as he focuses once again on

298

the yachts of the rich and famous.

"I'm going to stretch my legs a little," I say to Schuyler, who can barely muster a grunt to acknowledge me.

The rear of the jet is in stark contrast to the muddled Hebrew conversations I could hear from my death seat. Loud laughter, wine bottles gurgling as they fill plastic tumblers, and English being spoken with every accent imaginable. It appears that the press corps is divided into about a half-dozen groups; and as I casually stroll down the aisle, I notice the same thing in the center of each of these cliques; a woman. Whether the females are tall, short, fat, skinny, dressed to the nines, or in jeans, the men of the press are paying tribute to the women of the world's press and foreign services brigade with great enthusiasm. And I do believe that the largest and most raucous group is gathered around Monique and Gerard.

It's obvious that most of the press on this trip is of the print variety. Their faces are as worn and rumpled as their suits. I notice more empty wine bottles than I do notepads. And the cigarette smoke is thicker than at an A.A. meeting. There are only three really good looking people from what I can see; two American network correspondents, one female, one male, and Monique. The third network correspondent is the famous Mid-East expert, Don Samuels. He looks like he has spent his whole life living out of a valise, cuts what's left of his own hair with Swiss army knife scissors, and shaves with a steak knife. Even with an unlit cigar butt hanging off his lip, an empty plastic tumbler in his hand, and a half bottle of wine in the other, he's holding court with Monique and company by telling a joke... I can just hear the tail end of it.... "So he pulls out his dick and starts smashing the coconuts on the table into hundreds of pieces. The other old man looks at him and says, 'Incredible! Fifty years later and you still can do it! But why the coconuts?' The Great Bandini looks at him and says, 'The eyes are the first to go.'"

Uproarious laughter from the crowd, including Don himself. Monique reveals that she has a most unattractive laugh. High pitched and nasal. It reminds me of the sound a '64 Galaxy makes after sitting overnight in zero degree weather.

Monique stands and pushes her skirt down once again to four inches above the knee. "Excuse me, I think I just wet myself."

More uproarious laughter as she heads for the ladies room with Gerard in tow.

Don Samuels, still reeling from the laughter, holds up his now full drink and says, "Ah, isn't she incredible? Look at us. Like bees around honey."

And for some unknown reason, in less time than it takes to blink an eye or stop one's self from saying something you know you will regret for the rest of your life as it's leaving your tongue, I say loud enough for all to hear, "More like flies around shit."

If I could have opened one of those cabin windows, I would have jumped out head first. Don Samuels was staring at me with a look that could melt ice. There was a deathly silence that shot through my brain as an inner voice screamed "You fucking asshole! Why would you say such an awful thing in front of some of the most revered journalists in the world! Am I insane?" But I believe in reality, I am merely standing here, as dumfounded as everyone else is that I uttered such a disgustingly stupid comment.

I broke into a big phony smile and started chuckling nervously. "I'm just joking! Really. It was a joke, that's all."

"Not funny, junior," Don Samuels coldly says as he lowers his head and raises his shoulders like a middle linebacker on a first and goal attempt.

"Can I buy everyone a drink?" I lamely say.

"How 'bout just excusing yourself. Recess is over."

"Uh, yeah. See ya," I say as I slink away.

Schuyler is still reading his yacht magazine.

"Anything happening back there?"

"Nah. Just a lot of joking around."

"Did you talk to Monique and Gerard?"

"I just missed them. They were headed for the washroom."

Schuyler raised his head and started peering towards the

rear of the plane. "Maybe they're doing a mile high club."

"Well, I guess the crew that screws together...," I say, not bothering to complete an axiom that I couldn't think of a rhyme for. And in light of my most recent witty comeback line, I should probably just keep my mouth shut.

We were just beginning our descent into Montreal when Monique finally stopped by to discuss the day's activities. Even though we've only been in-flight for less than an hour, she looks slightly cockeyed. Lipstick just ever so slightly smeared, a flat part of hair at the back of her head, and her short skirt seems to have more horizontal wrinkles than I recall from earlier today. Oh well, at least somebody's getting some.

"Hi, guys," Monique says with at least a little bit of friendliness in her voice for the first time today. I'm guessing Don Samuels was decent enough not to repeat my crude remarks. "Do you want to go over anything on today's itinerary before we deplane?"

Schuyler pulls his sheet out and begins reading from it. "Get feed from pool at after dinner speech. Possible gangbang or catch-as-catch-can to follow."

Hmmm. I like the sound of the gangbang.... I can think of several smartass one-liners for that one... but I won't.

"From what I'm hearing from the rest of the corps, it looks like the gangbang is probably out, and it'll be catch-as-catch-can immediately afterwards." Monique leans way forward across me to get closer to Schuyler. Her cleavage is just inches from my nose, and a mixture of delicate perfume and wine on her breath has me forgetting what a ballbreaker she is. "I got some inside information that we can grab him for an exclusive. Just keep an eye on me," she says in a hushed tone, with her freckled breasts staring me in the face.

"Roger," Schuyler says as she straightens up and returns to her wine and cheese party.

"And you keep both eyes on me," Schuyler says in a Barbieri-like voice.

"Roger."

301

This is one of those rubber chicken dinner fund-raisers where the rich pay big bucks to rub shoulders, and set up secret deals, with important foreign and domestic government officials.

All Schuyler and I have to do is get an audio and video feed from the pool technicians at the back of the hall. To make it easier on everybody, the networks take turns shooting events like these and just provide lines "out" for whoever wants them. Fortunately, Schuyler knows what the hell he's doing because I sure don't. He's doing all the work; running cables, checking video and audio. I'm just sitting on a folding chair about six feet away watching his every move with my portable gear ready to go on his order.

"I've got the feed going. Just watch me. When I get a cue from Monique, we'll break, you take the tape out of the machine, put in a new tape, disconnect the pool cables, shove in the shotgun mike, and stay with me. I'll help you, but you've got to listen," Schuyler tells me as though I was a total moron. I hope I'm not....

Speech after speech from policy wonks, assistants to the under assistants, and secretaries of something or other, in French, Hebrew, and mostly broken English, have me daydreaming like the first day of summer school.

"Let's go!"

Shit. What? It's Schuyler looking like a man possessed.

"I said, let's go."

"Right," I say jumping up, knocking the equipment bag off my lap and spilling most of its contents onto the floor. People are standing on their feet applauding as Yankel Raviv is waving as he crosses to exit the stage.

I hastily gather what I can and join Schuyler as he disconnects from the pool feed.

"Here's the tape," he says as he whips it towards me. Like an idiot, I drop it along with my equipment bag again. Oops.

"Here's the deck," Schuyler says, handing me the heavy

videotape machine. "C'mon, move it! Put in the tape and hit it!"

I fumble with the pile of cables, mikes, and tapes as I jam them back into my bag. Schuyler raises his video camera to his shoulder and hands me the "sun gun," a small but very bright light I'm supposed to use with the hand that's not holding the shotgun microphone. I put that down on the floor, too, as I try to make sense of the spaghetti city that's developing around my feet.

"Fuck it. Let's go!" Schuyler says. I look up from my panic to see Monique and Gerard standing there, wondering why in the hell this idiot isn't doing his job.

I take a tape, shove it into the machine, slam it into record, switch on the light, hold up the shotgun mike and put the equipment bag under my chair. "I'm ready."

Gerard is walking quickly, no... running, towards an exit doorway near the stage with Monique close behind and Schuyler trying to keep up with them. Unfortunately, I'm barely able to walk let alone run. And Schuyler's fucking camera cable is too damn long. My headphones are falling off, and this video recorder weighs more than a nineteen inch TV set. Schuyler pushes the exit door, and there is a mob of reporters trying to get close to Prime Minister Raviv. Gerard and Monique are giving elbows, shoving people aside, and dragging Schuyler along through the crowd until the only ones in the center of the circle of people are Israeli officials and us. Gerard begins interviewing Raviv. This is it. An exclusive. Schuyler shoots a look at me. "Got audio?"

"Yes," I say, barely hearing Gerard through my lopsided headset hanging off my head. Then, whoops! I hear a snap and nothing. Fuck. My head becomes filled with a droning sound. Gerard and Raviv are in an animated discussion, but I can't hear a thing through my headsets. I look down and see the worst possible thing any videotape operator can see: the tape has run out. Nothing. I must have put the wrong tape in the machine. Probably the one that Schuyler handed me from the pool feed. Schuyler is busy shooting away. It looks like the interview is going along famously. They're laughing, looking concerned, angry, surprised, understanding...only NONE of this will ever be seen again by any-body. Ever.

I am screwed. But I pretend everything is just fine as I continue to point the light and my microphone at history in the making just a few feet away. As my professional life flashes before my eyes, I try not to think of what awaits me back in Barbieri's office. If Barbieri threatens dismemberment for a minor screw-up, I can't begin to imagine what the punishment will be for this.

Gerard looks thrilled as he shakes hands with Raviv and muscles his way through the crowd towards us.

"That is it! Beautiful," Gerard beams with Monique boldly holding his hand. "We go back to the hotel room, have dinner, and fly back to New York in the morning. That was all I needed for this report. See you back at the hotel, yes? Don't lose that tape!"

"No problem. We'll call as soon as we get back there, Gerard," Schuyler says, sweating slightly after battling the mob scene for the past ten minutes.

Schuyler takes the heavy camera off his shoulder and disconnects it from my video recorder. "Are you sure you had good audio?"

"Well, er, um, I'm actually not sure. My headphones slipped off, and er, I couldn't really tell," I say, just starting to drop a hint that there may be a slight problem.

"We'll check it out when we get back to the room."

I can see Gerard and Monique walking swiftly through the still thick post-dinner crowd, with Gerard waving to get my attention.

"Gerard wants something, Schuyler."

Gerard is breathless as he pushes his way past the last layer of people milling around. "Schuyler! I was just talking to Don Samuels of CBS, and he wants to make a copy of the interview. May I have the tape, please, to give to him. And in return, he has given me a copy of his interview."

"I don't really like to give original tapes, Gerard," St. John says, his voice full of nervous tension.

"Oh, I'm sure it's OK. They have an edit room at the hotel. I'll drop it off and get it back later."

"OK, but I don't like doing this," Schuyler says as he removes the tape from the recorder and hands it to Gerard.

"Hey, if they fuck it up," Gerard says, "then they owe us big time, right?"

My eyes zoom in on the tapes being exchanged, and I hope for a major catastrophe to save me. An earthquake, a terrorist attack, anything to prevent my screw-up from being discovered. But no such luck. The tapes are safely exchanged. Schuyler and I begin to slowly and silently pack our gear.

On the way back to the hotel, I was so stunned by the imminent disaster that lies ahead for me, I didn't even notice the streets of Montreal passing by. All I can see is the scene of Gerard, Monique, and Schuyler flipping out, quickly followed by an all out assault by Barbieri back at the home office. My head aches. My ears are buzzing. I can't even see straight.

I check into my room, which is right next to Schuyler's, turn off the lights, lie on the bed, wait for the shit to hit the fan in the dark, and somehow manage to doze off.

I hear voices through the walls. Loud, agitated voices. This is it. A loud banging on the door. I jump up in the dark, bang into an unknown piece of furniture, and go down. Fuck me! I hit my head on the corner of a table right on my cut. Pain screams through my brain, recreating the initial blow.

"Just a minute...," I manage to say while pulling myself up and turning on a lamp. I stumble into the bathroom to see that it's once again bleeding. Hmmmm. It's worth a try... I'll just leave some blood on my face and hope to throw myself on the mercy of the court.

I open the door to see Schuyler, Gerard, and Monique with expressions on their faces not unlike the townspeople outside Dr. Frankenstein's castle.

"What the fuck happened?" Schuyler yells as he pushes

305

his way into the room.

"Oh, my God! Your face, Jerry!" Gerard says with gentle compassion in his voice. This just might work.

"I got dizzy and fell, I don't know how long I was out," I boldly lie.

Gerard and Monique grab me by both arms and sit me down on the edge of the bed.

"Jerry, should we call a doctor?" Monique asks.

"No, no. I'm fine. I think." I say weakly.

"What the fuck happened to the interview, Jerry?" Schuyler says with slightly less aggression in his voice.

"The interview? Oh my God! Was something wrong with the interview," I say as I jump up and take a step toward Schuyler. But I make my legs go wobbly and nearly crumble to the floor. Gerard and Monique catch me and place me back on the bed, this time making me lean back all the way.

"Schuyler, I think we can discuss this later. Jerry needs some rest," Gerard whispers.

I begin twitching the eye next to my bleeding bump for effect.

"Are you sure you don't need a doctor, Jerry?" Monique asks as she tenderly strokes my hand.

"No, I'm fine. I just need some rest. And maybe some aspirin. And maybe a drink."

"I'm calling room service right now," Gerard says as he picks up the phone. What do you prefer?"

"Uh, Bayer, I guess."

"No, the drink."

"Jack Daniels. On the rocks. With a splash. A double."

"Room service, please bring some aspirin, and a bottle of Jack Daniels and some ice to 1310. And bill room 1302, please. Merci," Gerard says as he hangs up the phone. "Monique, you stay with Jerry until room service arrives. Schuyler and I will be in my room discussing the matter. Just come when you can, Monique," Gerard says as he and Schuyler head out the door. Schuyler just looks at me like he's trying to make my head explode. The door closes.

"Are you sure you don't need a doctor, Jerry?"

"No, Monique. Really. I'll be fine as soon as my medicine arrives. And the aspirin, too."

Monique manages a very slight chuckle. "So what happened?"

"Well I hit my head..."

"What happened to the interview?"

"Oh. Well, I guess I was feeling light-headed and didn't want to ..."

"Jerry, don't bullshit me. What the fuck happened?"

"I guess I fucked up. I must've grabbed the wrong tape when we broke from the stationary position and hastily jammed it into the deck."

"Well, you're one lucky bastard. The interview Gerard did with Raviv was just as much bullshit as your little acting exhibition. And, thank God, we got something from Don Samuels. If we had to use that interview of Gerard jerking off Raviv for ten minutes, we would've been screwed. Samuel's interview is fantastic. Concise. Controversial. Candid. And off-camera."

"What did Gerard interview him about?"

"His fucking wife knows Raviv's bodyguard's wife from some fucking yoga class someplace and that's practically all they discussed. Exclusive, huh? CBS felt so sorry for us, they gave us their interview to use uncredited."

"Hey, lucky us."

"Lucky you," Monique says as though she was cursing me out. "One time Napoleon was given a choice of two men to promote to general. As his underling tried to recommend one over the other because of his military record, Napoleon had one question to ask, 'Which one is luckier?' Luck counts."

There was a knock on the door. Monique gave me a look that certainly did not look like she wanted to curse me out. In fact, if I didn't know better, I could've sworn she was giving me the

307

eye. She stood up, straightened her skirt, and opened the door. Room service pushed a cart into the room, and she took a bill out of her purse and handed it to him. She held the door open for him as she left. She turns to me, seductively. "Take it easy. Maybe next time you'll really get lucky," Monique says, accentuated with a slow eye blink and head nod as she, too, heads out the door.

What luck. My head is throbbing with pain. I imagine getting fired is still a real possibility. In fact, I could get fired from all three of my jobs. If I'm lucky, I'll get Douglas on the phone at the library first thing in the morning, and hopefully he'll let me slide. The same goes for my afternoon gig at Radical Video, since I have equipment arriving for the documentary video festival and nobody knows anything about it except me. And Barbieri is probably going to fire me after a long humiliating tongue lashing in front of everybody at the office.

I take three aspirins and pour myself three fingers of J.D., which I down in two gulps. I almost gag on the smoky bourbon, but somehow I don't. I go into the bathroom to see just how awful a sight I was for my angry mob. No wonder! My face looks awful. Fresh blood seeped through my Band-Aid, and several tributaries of blood trickled down my face, onto my neck, and even stained my shirt. Fortunately, only the scab was broken, which is an old wrestling trick. Always keep a fresh scab handy; you never know when you may need to bleed a little for effect. By the time I finished cleaning myself up and put on a clean undershirt, the aspirin and J.D. were doing their job. It was time for a good night's sleep, and just pray that tomorrow isn't the second worst day of my career.

In the rush to the airport, I didn't have time to call the library or Radical Video. Well, maybe I could have made time, but I didn't have the nerve to ask for any special considerations from Schuyler, who is giving me the silent treatment. I pretended to be asleep the entire flight home, and Schuyler seemed quite happy that I did.

Not a word was spoken other than, "Does this go here?"

or "Do you want me to carry that?" until we pulled up in front of the office. Just before we got out of the van, Schuyler looked at me like I was a naughty child and says, "You don't know how lucky you are. Gerard and Monique are letting you off the hook. Barbieri may not be so accommodating."

The office is abuzz with scanners, all-news radio stations, televisions blaring, and loud disco music emanating from an edit room, but only Trotta is present, alone at his station, reading a copy of *Mad Magazine*. He jumps to his feet as soon as he sees us. "You guys are back already? Great!"

"Trotta, can you get the rest of our gear out in the hall and put it away," Schuyler says.

"No problem, buddy. How was the trip? Everything go alright?"

"Oh, yeah. Fucking perfect," Schuyler says, oozing with sarcasm.

"Sorry I asked," Trotta replies as he heads out into the hall.

Schuyler walks directly towards Barbieri's office, knocks softly twice, and pokes his head in. He turns to me. "Let's go."

To recall a situation similar to this, I believe I have to go back to first grade. I was playing in the alley next to my building and discovered a pack of cigarettes hidden behind a wall. There was even a pack of matches tucked in the cellophane wrapper. The kid I was hanging out with that day, was Billy from across the street. He was just in kindergarten. I thought it would be lots of fun for each of us to light up one of those smokes and have a few drags, which we did. But Mrs. Paccione from the first floor, who certainly knew who we were, stumbled upon us, and marched me upstairs with the cigarettes in hand. It was a Saturday, so both my parents were home. Needless to say, I received the most terrifying scolding of my brief life, and a spanking that wasn't really that hard, although administered with great dramatics.

Barbieri is sitting at his desk with a small portable tape recorder in front of him. He silently motions for me to sit down. He pushes a button on the machine. Obviously, the tape is a recording of a phone conversation.

Barbieri: Hello.

Gerard: Hello, Rocco. We need to discuss the problem.

Barbieri: I don't know what to say, Gerard. It's totally inexcusable. I'm deeply embarrassed and humiliated by the whole thing. It's a disgrace.

Gerard: Yes. All of that is true. Totally inexcusable. Of course, you know we can't pay you.

Barbieri: Gerard, you know you're my most reliable client. You tell me what you want to do, and we'll work something out. You name it.

Gerard: I think it should be no charge.

Barbieri: You know all of this is because of one employee, Gerard. He's already fired. So you just tell me what you want me to do, and it's done. But keep in mind, I've got a business here. I can't afford to lose money. We've always been fair.

Gerard: Have you fired him?

Barbieri: It's as good as done.

Gerard: I hate for that to be the case. Well, you did provide most of the service as promised, I guess. And mistakes do happen. And we did get more than we had hoped for. OK, just maybe, give us a few tapes, no charge. That's all.

Barbieri: Done. You want them delivered?

Gerard: No, just bring them next shoot.

Barbieri: Done.

Gerard: And, Rocco, give the boy another chance.

Barbieri: If you want me to.

Gerard: Oui.

Barbieri: For you, I'll do it. But if it was up to me, I'd fire his ass.

Gerard: Thank you, Rocco. Bye.

Barbieri: Bye.

Barbieri pushes a button on the tape recorder and stares at me. Schuyler isn't saying a word either. I've been squirming in my chair, wishing I was invisible for the past several minutes, and say, "Guess I fucked up."

Barbieri leaps out of his leather chair, pushing it straight backwards and crashing into the wall as he does. When he's pissed he certainly doesn't move like a man approaching four hundred and fifty pounds.

"You're fucking right you fucked up. Our fucking biggest client. The only reason we sent you on this job was it was idiot proof. Boy was I wrong. Weren't you keeping an eye on him, Schuyler?"

"Don't implicate me in this! It's his fault for putting the wrong tape in the machine, not mine!"

"I don't know who the fuck to blame! Pellicano, if it wasn't for Kittleberger, your fucking ass would be out the door for good, and you'd never work in news in this town for the rest of your fucking life, so help you God. And if you ever cost me money, not only will your ass be fired but you'll fucking make up for it too, no matter what I've got to do. Got me?"

"I got you. But what exactly does that mean?"

Schuyler looks at me like I just hit the teacher with a spitball.

"What does that mean? Do I have to spell it out for you?"

"I would appreciate it, yes."

"You are fucking walking on thin ice, Pellicano. Don't fucking get under my skin anymore than you already have. You're NOT fucking fired because a client stuck his neck out for you. So don't stick your own fucking neck out. And don't think I won't fire your ass at the drop of a hat either. You're an inch away. One more fuck-up and don't let the door hit you in the ass on the way out. Got it?"

"Got it."

"Good-bye."

"Good-bye," I say, surrendering.

311

It's just not worth it right now. I made a huge mistake, and it's but for the grace of God that things worked out for everyone involved. I definitely would've fired my ass.

As I exit the office, Trotta is pulling the last of the equipment cases from the hall. He looks at me and begins to laugh. "You are one lucky bastard, Pellicano. I've seen Barbieri pull his shotgun on people for doing less than you did."

"Yeah, well, you're right. I'm lucky. That's all. See ya."

If I hurry and take a cab, I can show up at the library only an hour and a half late. Maybe I'll pick my scab open just one more time...

The fine print will get you every time. I thought my position at the library was rock solid. I mean it's a city job. I didn't know they'd be counting every minute I was late, add it up, and use it to screw me out of my job. I didn't even realize there was a probation period of six months where they could change their mind. Douglas wouldn't even look at me. And Greg, forget about it. I should've known something was up when he told me to report to Mr. Healy's office and he had that smirk on his face. But immediate dismissal? Escorted out of the building by security? With everyone looking at me carrying my little cardboard box loaded with the meager accumulations of less than a year on the job; a Yankees' coffee mug, a clipboard, an 8X10 of Jack Benny wearing a top hat. I didn't even have the nerve to put up a fight.

I walk down to the 66th Street subway stop, where I witnessed that token booth guy flipping out on that skinny Black kid. I haven't seen him in a while. The old Asian guy is still there, but now there's a middle-aged Puerto Rican woman also on duty. If I catch the trains in time, I won't be late for Radical Video.

I'm only fifteen minutes late. They can't fire me for this. I rush around the corner, and see a large truck in front of the Radical Video building. Shit, that must be the equipment for the video documentary festival. They got here early. Damn. I wonder who took care of it? Wait. They're not taking equipment in... they're taking equipment out! Standing in front is a black guy wearing a long overcoat and a fedora. He's holding a clipboard and watching carefully as the workers wheel the equipment into the truck.

I approach him slowly, trying to overhear what I can before I say anything. Finally, he says to a worker wheeling cases of tapes, "Is that shit worth anything?"

"Probably not. It's labeled 'Nude Dance Project' though," the worker says with a smile on his face.

"Oh, we'll hold onto that lot then!" The Black guys says, laughing.

"Excuse me, sir. May I ask what's going on here?"

"And what business is it of yours?" The now officious Black guy says looking me over.

"I work here."

"You work here! Well, glory be! And where is your boss at?"

"Nobody's up there? Did you look across the street where they live?"

"What's your name?" He asks, much like a cop.

"And who are you?" I shoot back.

He pulls out a small black leather folder and opens it revealing a badge and an identification card. "Glenn Williams. Federal Marshal. What's your name, and how long have you been working here."

"Jerry Pellicano. A few weeks. What happened?"

"Well, I'll deny telling you this, but the people who run this joint ripped off many individuals, foundations, government agencies, and split town. Any idea where they might be?"

"Nope. I'm not even sure who they are. Is Amy Gold one of them."

"Nah. She's just an employee. No controlling interest. I'll need some identification and a phone number for you, just in case."

"Here's my license," I say, pulling it out form among my

plane ticket, boarding passes, and other obvious paperwork revealing that I was just on a trip.

"Been traveling?"

"Yeah. I was working for French TV in Canada."

"Were you up there on VideoVision business?"

"No, sir."

"And you have witnesses that you were in Cananda?"

"Boy, do I."

"Don't leave town without telling me. Here's my card."

"Those pricks at RadicalVideo owe me five hundred bucks."

"Yeah, well you're one of the lucky ones. Those pricks owe a ton of cash to a lot of suckers, including Uncle Sam. Let's go. We've got to get this stuff tagged and stored before nightfall," he says, ignoring me.

I gave him my name and phone number and then walked slowly down the block, turning to see boxes of equipment being loaded onto the truck. Maybe my luck is running out.

Parked in front of my building with the engine running and "Duke of Earl" blasting over the distorted speakers is Victor. I'm sure he knows all about my ill-fated trip to Canada with Schuyler and is ready to pile on with the rest of them. There's no way I can avoid him sitting there unless I sneak in the basement, but why bother?

"Hi, Victor. What's new?"

"Hey, Jerry, how are ya? I heard you fucked up in Canada," Victor says in an usually jovial manner.

"Yeah, the *royal* fuck-up in Montreal."

"I would've loved to have seen Barbieri's face when he was playing that tape for you," he says, squeezing in the words between chuckles.

"My face would've been worth the price of admission, too."

"I'm waiting for Stubby. Did you hear?"

"Hear what?"

"Stubby's moving out. He's moving in with his girlfriend.

314

They're getting married in June."

"Really?"

I look up to the roof where the snowball was launched just a few days ago and started this whole mad rush of life changes, just in case something else was about to come hurling down at me. Maybe a giant plaster statue of the Blessed Mother would come flying down, like the one that fell on Robert Damroe's head in fourth grade. "When?"

"Actually, he's already moved out. Terry's taking his apartment."

"Terry? I haven't even seen him lately."

"Yeah, he's out on some bullshit extended sick leave from the job. Stubby says he thinks he's getting strung out."

"Oh, that's great. Just what the building needs. Another strung out junkie. At least he doesn't have to go far to score. Just one flight up to Donnelly's."

"Hey, didn't you used to go out with his girlfriend?"

"Yeah, in high school."

"I just saw her going up there with Terry. She didn't look too good either. But she was dressed like a three hundred dollar an hour hooker. Unbelievable."

The front door of the building swings open and bangs loudly against the other one. Stubby emerges carrying a huge pile of boxes which he can barely see over. He tiptoes to the edge of the first step, feeling for it.

"If you fall and break your neck, I got first dibs on the record collection," Victor yells out the tow truck window.

"If I fall and break my neck, a pox on you and your truck," Stubby shouts as he carefully negotiates the stairs.

He walks around the back of the truck and places the boxes there.

"Jerry! Where the hell you been?"

"Oh, nowhere. Just Canada, getting fired from a city job, getting screwed out of five hundred bills from another job, and almost losing a third one."

"...because he fucked up," Victor happily interjects.

"Because I fucked up. What's this about Terry taking over your apartment?"

"Congratulations to you, too."

"Well, what's the story?"

"What the fuck business is it of yours who I give my apartment to?"

"I hear he's strung out again?"

"Who the fuck are you? Monsignor McNulty or some shit? He needs a pad. What am I supposed to do? He's a fucking friend, or did you forget what that means?"

"Alright, alright, girls, we're all white here," Victor says trying to smooth things over in his own inimitable way.

"I'm just stressed, Stubby. Congratulations on... everything," I say as I hold my hand out.

Stubby puts his boxes down, pushes my hand away, grabs me by the shoulders, quickly puts me into a headlock, and begins giving me noogies. "Don't forget who gave you your first hangout card on the block, OK?" Stubby says, accenting each word with a noogie. He releases me and gives me a strong bear hug. "We're brothers. Friends 'til the end," he says softly into my ear.

Somehow I knew that this was the last time that Stubby and I would be this close. You just know deep down in the dark subway tunnel of your soul when things like this play out in front of you. Despite the words, and reassurances, and kidding, you just know it's the end.

"Friends 'til the end," I say, knowing full well we're both lying.

"Come on, I'm going need a hanky over here," Victor moans. "Hey, Jerry, are you going to be around for a while?"

"Yeah, why?"

"Can I come back to hang around for a while until I got to go in later tonight?"

"Yeah, er, sure," I say as Stubby hops into the truck and changes the radio station from oldies to WNEW-FM just as "Psycho

Killer" comes on.

"Later," Victor yells as he peels out, spitting loose gravel and dirt from his tires.

"Ba Ba BAAA Ba Ba BAA BAA BAA," Stubby sings along, happily waving good-bye.

As I turn to go into the building, I see something unusual lying on the top of the dirty snow that's still piled along the wall of the courtyard. It's actually a dark object sticking out of the snow. Upon closer inspection, I can see that it's a little dead sparrow. Damn. Poor little thing. It's eyes are shut tight and its head is bent at a grotesque angle. I can't just leave it here. I find it ironic that if you looked straight up from where this poor little creature is, it lines up perfectly with Donnelly's window. Not wanting to touch it directly, I reach into my pocket for my handkerchief. It's one of those little habits I've kept since kindergarten when my Mom made sure I never left the house without one.

I guess that I can pick the bird up with the hanky, wrap it in it, and find a spot for a proper burial. As I pull the handkerchief out of my pocket, the piece of porcelain, or whatever the hell it is that was in that iceball, comes flying out along with it, plunking the dead bird right on its head. I keep forgetting that I've been carrying that thing around. I reach for it, and as I do, I see something on it I've never noticed before. One side of it is jagged, as though it was broken apart, but on one of the sides, there's a tiny bit of a smooth, contoured surface. I bring it close to my eyes with both hands to see what appears to be...a finger. Or perhaps, more specifically, a thumb. Shit. My mind rushes with the imagery. I reach up and put my finger on the bandage over my cut; jagged, hard, dark brown, tiny thumb...BUDDHA! That's it! The object inside the iceball was part of the broken Buddha. Charlie's Buddha. It came from Donnelly's window. That motherfucker. Who knows what else he has in there.

I shove the Buddha piece back into my pocket and wrap the tiny dead sparrow in my handkerchief. I walk around the back of my building where there's some weeds growing and use my boot to kick open a hole large enough to bury the poor creature. As I place him inside the grave and begin to cover him with dirt, I silently recite three Hail Marys. And as I say my last "Amen," an image of a smiling Buddha came into my mind. A Buddha with Charlie the Chinaman's smiling face.

Written across the elevator door right next to my front door is freshly applied graffiti reading "Latin Eagles." And there's some kind of dried gook on the floor just in front of my welcome mat about the size of pizza, and I don't even want to know what it is.

What the heck. I have Lieutenant Paolicelli's card. I'm going to call him and tell him my Buddha theory. I pick up the phone and dial his number. He'll probably just blow me off, like most cops....

"Lieutenant Paolicelli, please," I say to the curt officer who answered.

"Paolicelli here."

"Hello, Lieutenant. I'm Jerry Pellicano. We talked at the Chinese Laundry suicide scene."

"Yes, I remember. What can I do for you?"

"I have a piece of evidence you might be interested in."

"Evidence? Like what?"

"I have reason to believe that I was struck with an iceball that came from an apartment in my building and that inside the iceball was a piece of a Buddha statue that I gave to Charlie the Chinese laundry guy 20 years ago." As the words left my mouth, I knew how preposterous it must have sounded.

There was a long pause.

"Who's apartment?"

"Donnelly. On the sixth floor."

"Look, I'm real busy now. Just keep it in a safe place and if I need, I'll call you. Thanks."

"Yeah, thanks"

I guess I was right. He blew me off.

I used to hate it when my mother cleaned with ammonia.

318

You could smell it from the front courtyard when she was using it. We didn't have a bunch of different types of toxic cleaners under our kitchen sink. Basically there were three things that cleaned every imaginable stain, mess, or organic accident: Ivory soap, Clorox bleach, and ammonia. We didn't even use dishwashing liquid. We kept a bar of Ivory soap on the kitchen sink, which you soaped your dishrag with. Every other imaginable substance could be cleaned to the point of sterility with either bleach or ammonia. No Mr. Clean, Spic and Span, Easy Off, or any other solution. If ammonia or bleach couldn't get it out, it wasn't coming out anyway.

I grab a bottle of ammonia left behind, fill a bucket with hot water, get the mop, and prepare to tackle the disgusting dried crud that people have been walking over for the past few days. There was a time when we had a building janitor *and* a super. The janitor used to live in a tiny apartment in the cellar right next to where the elevator equipment and incinerator were. I remember one time going to the incinerator room with my Dad because the garbage wouldn't fit in the chute, and the janitor was working the fire in the incinerator. He had a long rod and huge gloves on, and a roaring immense inferno was blasting away as he poked and prodded the trash. Flames were actually leaping out of the superheated opening which scared the hell out of me. When the elderly black janitor, Mugsy, noticed us, he closed the door on the roaring fire and smiled at me. "You ever hear the story of Hansel and Gretl?" He asked me. "Well, this is where they stuffed that mean old witch," he said earnestly. Still feeling the intense heat of the room even with the incinerator door shut, I had a whole new sense of sympathy for that witch from that moment on. And as my Dad dropped off the items, I turned to see that Mugsy had left the door to his apartment open. I saw what must have been his living room, which had a concrete floor, just as drab, grey, and cold as the rest of the basement of our building. He had a throw rug with ragged edges in the middle and much to my shock, an old overstuffed chair that we threw out the year before as the centerpiece of his room. And if we threw something out, it truly was nothing more than garbage. It was old and close to falling apart when one of our relatives gave it to us second-hand years before. And the sight of that poor old pink upholstered chair in Mugsy's living room gave me the first glimpse of what it meant to be *really* poor.

As the bucket fills with hot water, I pour in a half bottle of ammonia, the vapors of which make me reflexively jerk backwards with a wallop. I immediately flash on my Mom wearing an old Woolworth's housedress, curlers in her hair, and rags in hand, pouring a homemade concoction of ammonia and water into an old Windex bottle, explaining how much money could be saved by using ammonia and water instead of Windex. But that smell!

Despite nearly fainting, I take my bucket and mop out into to hallway. Luckily, there isn't anyone around, and I begin to swab the deck. Like magic, the dried, crusty funk begins to melt away into a brown liquid, slowly disappearing and revealing the beauty of the pure white tiny square tiles underneath.

With each wet mop full of ammonia, the hall floor becomes whiter as the water gets darker.

"Do you do windows?" An unfamiliar voice echoes through the hall behind me. I turn and standing there with a bouquet of flowers with a black ribbon around them in one hand and a bottle of wine in the other, is Douglas, my former boss from the library.

"What the hell...?" is all I can muster at the touching display of sympathy.

"I feel terrible about this," Douglas says, taking a few steps to the edge of my clean white area.

Suddenly, the elevator bounces to a squeaky halt and the door opens revealing Mrs.O'Sullivan, who stops dead in her tracks at the strange sight in front of her.

"I was going to clean that, Jerry, but never got around to it," she says ignoring my boss and his bouquet. "That bastard super doesn't do crap around here," she says propping her shopping cart against the elevator door as she heads over to check her mailbox. "It wasn't like this when Mugsy was the janitor and Mr.

Jaeger was the superintendent! Bastards! You know, I've gotten attached to that pigeon, Charlie. He coos when he's happy. Let me know when you want me to bring him back to you. Good day, Jerry. And those are beautiful flowers, mister," she says, closing the elevator door.

"That was Mrs. O'Sullivan. Can you come inside?"

"I thought you'd never ask."

I pick up my cleaning gear and step back to admire the large oval white patch of pure cleanliness outside my door as well as the path of white that leads to my door.

"The place is a little messy right now. I just cleaned it, but it takes about an hour to get gross again," I say, leading Douglas into the apartment.

Sometimes you forget what something really looks like until someone else steps into the scene. I'm so used to this place ever so slowly becoming a bachelor pigsty that I don't even notice it anymore.

We stop off in the kitchen and just as I'm about to dump the disgusting bucket of water down my kitchen sink, Douglas butts in, "No! Not there!"

"No?"

"No. Dump it in the toilet."

"Yeah. You're right. I guess that would create a toxic waste site in my kitchen sink."

"Exactly."

I carry the bucket to the toilet and flush the frothy slop away as Douglas watches from the end of the hall.

"You can have a seat in the living room, Douglas. Just throw whatever's on the couch to the side."

"Do you have any clean glasses?"

"Yeah, I'll get them."

I find the last two glasses in the cabinet, rinse them off, open the bottle, and join Douglas in the living room.

"Do you have a vase?"

"Uh, no."

"I'll just leave them here for now," Douglas says, placing the flowers on top of a pile of mail and magazines on the coffee table. "I wish I could've prevented this, Jerry."

"Oh, I'm sure you do, Douglas. It's not your fault."

"But it is."

"What do you mean?"

Douglas begins shifting his weight on the bouncy overstuffed well-worn couch cushions and licks his lips like a third-grader about to recite the pledge of allegiance. "Actually..."

"Yes...."

"I had you fired."

It's moments like this that one discovers what one is truly made of. One doesn't normally have adrenaline rushing through the system when trying to react to a situation. Usually we just go through life saying, "hold the onions" or "I'll take the blue one instead" or "OK, I'll have another" with no emotional involvement. But when a situation arises where your mental faculties are influenced by raging emotions, hormones, and essential body fluids, it's hard to predict just what might transpire in the next, oh, five seconds or so.

Douglas picks up the bouquet and ever so slightly pushes them in my direction.

In that nanosecond just before launching into an all out attack, I stop myself. I take a deep breath. I reach up to wipe my brow, and my fingers run across the bandage over my wound. As I touch the bandage, I get a tingling sensation. Not exactly pain, but a hot, undulating pulsing feeling that's almost pleasant. For some reason, it calms me down. I push slightly on the exact point of my cut with my pinky, triggering a weird, dull sensorial kind of awareness. It lingers somewhere between pain and pleasure. I've heard a theory about dreams that says when one dreams complicated plots, like trekking across hundreds of miles of desert with no food or water for days and days, that the actual amount of time that the brain uses to transmit the experience is a split second. Intricate dream storylines with countless subtleties and character-driven choices take place in only an instant of actual time. That's what I feel right now. A multitude of emotions, and yes, messages have been zapped into my consciousness. I feel no hatred. No anger. I feel at peace.

"Are you OK?" Douglas asks with a deep look of concern.

"Yeah. I'm fine."

"I hope you understand, Jerry. I didn't want this to develop into some ugly situation that people just deny exists until it's too late, and things get out of control, and there's no turning..."

"Douglas. I totally understand. You were right to do it."

"I was?"

"Absolutely. You know it. You don't want me to wind up like...," I paused because I almost said *like you,* but instead said, "...like Greg."

"You're very wise, Jerry. We can have a drink in sympathy or in celebration," Douglas says, holding up his glass.

"In celebration. Salut!"

We both have a sip.

"There was a moment there," Douglas says, "when I thought you were going to kill me."

"Me, too."

"Oops."

"Yeah, oops."

"So what's next for you?"

"Well, since my three job bonanza has suddenly become one job hanging by a string, I'm not quite sure."

"I thought the library job was ranked a distant third on your list. In fact, that's one of the reasons I went along with the firing. I thought I'd be doing you a favor. Freeing you up, so to speak."

"Oh, I'm freed up alright. In fact, I'm close to being freer than a Times Square porno handbill."

"What happened to jobs number one and number two?"

"Well, job number one at Radical Video has gone bye-bye. Literally. The guy who was running it, whom I suspected all

323

along of being a small-time con man, proved me wrong. He turned out to be a world-class con man. He's on the lam, with the feds and probably a VW bus filled with performance artists trying to get the money he owes them. And job number two, well let's just say I've managed to piss off people on three different continents. I think I'll be fired if I so much as breathe crooked."

"And when did all this happen?"

"Oh, today."

"Ever think that maybe things are supposed to happen in carefully laid-out plans designed by some greater force, and that we'll never understand the reason why, and if you tried to explain to someone that you think you are part of such a thing, they will think you are going mad?"

"I didn't until now..."

KNOCK KNOCK KNOCK

That's got to be Victor. This is one of those moments of truth that I always fear. Bringing two people together who have absolutely nothing in common other than the fact that they both know me. I can't think of two more opposite people than Victor and Douglas. But right now, they are the two people on the planet I think I need most.

"That's probably my friend Victor from work. He's the one that got me hooked up with job number two."

I open the four locks on the door. Victor is standing there with his video camera, the tape deck, and a large equipment bag.

"What's with all the gear?"

"You think I'm leaving this shit in the truck around here? What are ya, nuts?"

"Come on in. Leave your stuff here. I've got a friend visiting," I say as I lead Victor through the hall to the tiny living room. "Victor, this is Douglas, my boss who just fired me. Douglas, this is Victor, who could get me fired in an instant, if he so desires."

"Hey. Nice to meet you," Victor says, I think already picking up on the fact that Douglas is not a typical "from the block" kind of

324

guy, with the flowers and wine and earring and well-groomed beard and all.

"Hello, Victor. You look familiar. You've never been to The Man Hole have you?"

Oh, boy. Douglas has picked up on the fact that a lot of the really macho gay biker types often try to capture the wild street look that comes so natural to guys like Victor. I just hope Victor doesn't pick up on the fact that Douglas is asking him if he hangs out in S&M gay bars.

"Nah. What's that, like a construction worker hangout?" Victor innocently asks.

"Not exactly," Douglas replies diplomatically.

"Want a glass of wine, Victor?" I ask.

"Actually, I want to go see if Terry's up in Stubby's yet. I'll be back in a few minutes, if that's cool."

"Sure, let me lock you out," I say, walking Victor to the door.

When we get to the door, Victor summons me closer and puts his index finger over his mouth signalling a whisper. "Listen. I've got a tip that there's some kind of shit going down in Donnelly's apartment tonight."

"What? Oh, no. Are you kidding me? What kind of shit?"

"Something. I'm not sure. But let's just say if we can get some video of it, we'll both be heroes, alright? Can I see Donnelly's windows from anywhere?"

"Yeah, on the roof, across the courtyard in the back."

"OK, take me there. I'll check it out. And I'll be back later for you and the gear."

"Hey, Douglas! I'll be right back," I shout from the hall.

"OK," Douglas says.

We leave the apartment, and I lead Victor to the other end of the lobby where there's a second elevator. "If we take the elevator by my door, Donnelly's door is too close to it. We'll take the elevator on the other side of the building and walk across the roof."

"Step lightly. The people can hear you below."

We walk across the tar-papered roof that in the summer we used to call "tar beach" as tenants escaped the heat and grit of the world below by sunbathing up here. I motion to Victor to stoop down as we approach the low wall directly opposite Donnelly's windows just below. There is actually an opening in the shape of a fortress turret that we used to point our toy rifles through when we played "army" up here. That was until Mr. McHugh chased us downstairs with a sawed-off black baseball bat. Victor points to the turret and says, "Perfect. I can shoot through this with the camera. I'll hang out here for a while and see if I can spot anything worthwhile," he says, pulling a tiny pair of folding binoculars from his pocket and placing a small earphone in his ear.

"What's the earpiece for?"

"It's connected to my scanner."

I just shake my head and go back to the apartment. I'm in no position to question Victor's tactics. Not if I want to keep my job and pay the rent this month.

As I approach my front door, I can hear a Kinks song called "Celluloid Heroes" playing. Douglas is sitting there, tossing his three I-ching pennies as the song's chorus plays.

"I hope you don't mind. I picked up the album, read the lyrics, and simply had to hear it. It's rather good. The lyrics anyway. The music is a little simplistic for my taste. But it's good in a music hall kind of tradition. Where did you go?"

"Oh, just a little job security errand. I'll have a refill."

"Hmmm, not much left I'm afraid," Douglas says, pouring just two fingers of red wine into my Flintstone's jelly jar glass. "Is there a liquor store around here?"

"Right around the corner."

"I'm off."

"Are you sure you, er, feel safe?"

"You're talking to a man who gets his thrills by putting his penis through a hole in the wall..."

"Enough already! Yes, Godspeed. Get wine. Around the

326

corner!"

"Any preferences?"

"Yes. No more glory hole anecdotes."

"Indeed. Good-bye," Douglas says, waving good-bye as he ventures out into the cold, dark Bronx streets.

The thought of Victor on my roof spying with binoculars into someone's window has me biting the cuticles on my fingers in a frenzy. Even though it is scumbag Donnelly, I mean Mary Markowski is in there. I just hope to God she's not caught up in some bad joojoo. Donnelly is a confirmed skell. If he wasn't from the block, he would have been driven away ages ago. Yeah, so Mary's caught up in some obvious bad shit. Really bad. That happens. She's got to want to get herself out of it. Who knows where her bottomed-out mark is. Some people don't hit bottom until they're lying in the gutter, soiled with blood and excrement and dragged off to jail. And for some people, that's just another day. And for yet others, bottoming-out is one thing: the last inch of the body bag zipping up.

KNOCK KNOCK KNOCK

I feel like one of those schmucks on "Let's Make Deal" wondering what's behind the door I just picked. Let's see... will it be a thirty-foot sailboat or a barn full of horse manure?

I look through the peep hole. ZONK!

Victor is motioning frantically for me to hurry, and pushes his way in as soon as locks are undone.

"This is it," he says excitedly as he begins dialing the phone.

"What is it?"

"I just heard the code on the scanner. It's me. How long? Got it," He says, as he hangs up the phone and immediately starts assembling the video gear.

"You've got to tell me what's going on. I live in this building you know. I've got neighbors."

"Yeah, nice fucking neighbors. You're nice neighbor Donnelly is getting raided. They've got enough shit on him to make the ten o'clock news on every channel."

"Like what?"

"Major fucking heroin dealing, prostitution, armed robbery, burglary, endangering minors, shall I go on?" Victor says as he slaps a tape in the video deck and puts the camera on his shoulder.

"You ready?"

"As ready as I'll ever be."

"Get the gear and let's roll."

We head across the lobby and wait for the elevator. The Puerto Rican guy who was involved in the New Year's Eve knife fight steps out of his apartment and looks at us like we're mad.

"How ya doing?" I awkwardly say. He ignores me as he lights a cigarette and heads out.

No one else spots us as we make our way to the roof. We crawl with our equipment the last few feet so we can't be seen over the wall.

"Here's my plan," Victor whispers. "The moron's got his blinds wide open. I've got a bird's-eye view of everything. By the way, you ex-girlfriend is built! Marrone! I'm going to shoot from here, right into the living room where they're hanging out."

"Aw shit. No. Mary's screwed then."

"Too bad. I'm shooting whatever goes on until the raid starts. When it does, we shoot a little from this angle, right as the cops bust in, then we head downstairs and get the rest from the hallway and in the apartment."

"I can't believe I'm doing this."

"Hey, you wanna go from goat to hero or what?"

I don't even bother answering him.

Victor takes the camera, places it in the opening between the walls, takes a black piece of velvet and covers it, leaving just enough for the lens to stick out slightly. He peeks a little next to the camera. "Oh, shit. He's fucking tieing her off. God. How does a gorgeous babe like that get hooked up with a puke like him?"

Mary Markowski. The girl every guy wanted. Every guy lusted for her from the time they got caught in that first twinkle in her eye. Even in third grade, guys got silly because they "liked" her. Sister Fidelis dug more valentines out of that shoebox for her than

328

for all the other girls combined. She was smart, too. The only girl in the class that made it into Bronx High School of Science. We didn't see too much of Mary once she got into Science. Oh, sure, I went out with her a little and played kissy face for a summer, but I could tell from the get go that I didn't give her a thrill the way she thrilled me and every other guy from the block.

"Now he's tieing himself off in a chair right next to her. This is sick. I love it!" Victor whispers with glee. "I'm just going to roll on this for a while."

I don't want to look ten seconds into the future. I can't comprehend what's about to unfold. Me and Victor busting in on Donnelly and Mary. Then the whole sordid scene playing in living rooms across the city with Mary and Donnelly nodding out. Then the cops busting in, and who knows what else?

"Fuck!"

"What?"

"Fucking asshole Terry."

"No! He's in there?"

"Yes, that fucking perv! He's fucking making out with Mary and feeling her up while she's out cold."

"You're bullshitting me!"

"I wish I was. That prick."

I'm beyond angry. I'm heartbroken. Mary Markowski. Mary fucking Markowski.

"Wait'll I get my hands on that fucker Terry," I say a little too loud.

"Sshhh. I hear something..."

I can barely hear a knock on the door. I peek over the wall slightly and see Terry starting to fidget wildly. He steps towards the door and says something. I can't hear what's being said on the other side of the door, but it must be the cops, because Terry is freaking.

Terry runs over to Donnelly and begins shaking him. Donnelly appears to be dead weight. "Ronnie Ronnie! Get up! Get the fuck up," I can barely hear Terry scream.

Terry is holding his ears with his elbows sticking straight out. He begins spinning around slowly like he thinks he may screw himself into the apartment below. I can hear somebody yelling from behind the apartment door louder and louder, screaming something like they're gong to bust in.

Victor grabs the camera. "Let's go!"

I grab the deck and follow him down the stairs. There are about six cops standing in front of the door with guns drawn, bullet proof vests, and a small battering ram.

"Who the fuck are you?" One of the cops says.

"We're with Barbieri," Victor says.

"Oh, OK." The cop says matter of factly.

"You've got three seconds," the lead cop yells motioning to get the battering ram into position.

Suddenly, the locks on the steel door begin to become undone. The door opens an inch, and the cops all push through with weapons extended and grab Terry, throwing him onto the floor. Victor and me are right behind them.

One of the cops grabs Mary's wrist and pushes open her eyes. "Get the paramedics up here. O.D."

As two cops cuff and frisk Terry, who is whimpering and still hasn't even realized he's being videotaped by us, another cop checks out Donnelly. "This guys whacked, too. Bad."

Three paramedics burst into the room with their gear. Two gurneys are parked outside the door in the hall. Victor is whipping his camera around getting everything. A cop turns Terry around to lead him off, and he sees us. I can see the rusty wheels spinning inside his brain as he is trying to make sense out of what he is seeing before him. It's probably pretty close to the look I have on my face. He cocks his head to the side and says, "Hey, Jerry," as if he was saying hello in Third Base.

I nod my head and smile. "Hey, Terry." And the cops take him away.

The paramedics are working on both Mary and Donnelly. Clothes are torn, oxygen masks flying, chests thumped. Much like the accident scene at the el pillar, I'm surprised at how quietly everyone works together. It's not like a TV show where everyone is dramatically yelling at each other, screaming their lungs out. The conversations are about as ordinary as a holiday family dinner. Instead of "pass the meatballs", you hear "I think this guys a goner."

To me, Donnelly already looked dead. Even before this. His skin had a kind of pasty grey pallor, and the acne he had didn't look like a teenager's where you could imagine hormones just bursting through the surface of the skin, but more like sores. He has a blank expression on his face, and his eyes are slightly crossed, the way you look when you've had about a half-dozen too many shots of tequila.

I'm keeping on eye on Victor, who's all business right now. I can tell he's remembering Rocco's warning about too many zooms and keeping a steady hand. The chunky red-faced paramedic begins thumping on Donnelly's chest and shouts towards Victor, "You guys better wait in the hall. This could get a little messy in here."

"Gottcha, chief," Victor says promptly and leads me into the hallway.

The gurneys are rolled out. Mary comes out first, and the guys working on her look frantic. The Donnelly cart isn't moving as quickly. Victor follows them as Mary is rolled into the elevator and we manage to squeeze in.

We get to the lobby where Douglas is standing with an old lady. An old lady who looks vaguely familiar.

"Jerry? What the hell is going on," Douglas asks, totally bewildered.

"Just working."

"Jerry. I met this woman. She's looking for you.

"Hello, Jerry."

Oh no.

"Mrs. Markowski?" I ask. Knowing it is in fact, Mary's mother. I haven't seen her since I dropped Mary off at home after the Beach Boys' concert in Gaelic Park.

"Have you seen my Mary, Jerry?" Mrs. Markowski says

with a look on her face that reveals she knows something awful is about to happen.

Suddenly, Mary is pushed out of the elevator with Victor shooting away right behind, and Mrs. Markowski grabs on to Douglas so as not to collapse to the floor.

"Mary! Mary! Oh, my God, Mary!" Mrs. Markowski screams, which echoes like a nightmare through the tiled lobby.

A cop approaches her. "Are you related to this young woman?"

"It's my daughter."

"Come along with us," the cop says as he escorts her away.

"Jerry, what is going on?" Douglas asks again.

"I'm working. We're shooting a raid."

"On Mrs. Markowski's daughter?"

"Let's go back up," Victor says, jerking the camera cord and leading me back onto the elevator for the ride up to get Donnelly. Douglas stands there in utter disbelief.

I close my eyes, and all I can see is Mrs. Markowski's sad, crying eyes and the still beauty of Mary Markowski being wheeled past my front door.

"This guy's fucked," one of the paramedics says to the other as they wheel him into the elevator back on the top floor.

We reach the first floor and Douglas is still standing there frozen.

We follow Donnelly's gurney out into the street where it is pushed into an awaiting ambulance. Victor shoots it as it drives down the hill away from us and disappears around the curve.

Then it all hit me at once. What am I doing? Why am I doing this? For whom? For me? For my career? For Victor? For Schuyler St. John? For fucking Barbieri? Is this what working in television is all about? Is this how you make a career? I just wish I was going to inherit a fucking lawn chair factory in North Carolina.

"Let's go. We got it. We got it," Victor yells joyously. He runs to the tow truck and begins to break down the gear for the ride downtown to the office. "You didn't run out of tape, did you?" Victor says with a big goofy grin.

"No."

As Victor carefully packs everything, I take my deck a few feet away and pop out the video we just shot. I take a blank tape out of my bag, and insert it in a box and mark it; Bronx Drug Bust. I place the tape containing the footage of the mad scene and place it under my jacket, hiding it beneath my armpit.

"Here's the tape, Victor," I say, handing the blank video to him. "Oh, and one other thing. Tell Barbieri I quit."

"What the...?" Victor gives me strange look. "Don't jerk my chain. I'll see you later."

He takes the tape from me, hops into his truck, and peels out.

I walk back into the lobby, and Douglas is still standing there. Only now he has the newly purchased bottle of wine opened and he's drinking from it.

"I was in the liquor store, and that old lady starts crying about her missing daughter," Douglas says excitedly. "Next thing I know, your building is mentioned and some guy named Donnelly and I mentioned you, and before I know it we're gabbing away and here we are."

"Douglas. Just go inside for a minute. I've got something I need to do," I tell Douglas as I let him into my apartment.

I close my door, noticing yet another smaller version of "Latin Eagles" written just next to the elevator door. Now I know what I need to do. Uncle Eugene said my gut would tell me. Well, my guts are singing like a bird.

The incinerator chute is just around the corner next to the elevator, and it's time for me to make a deposit. As I walk past the elevator door, a cop pushes it open, knocking the video onto the tiled floor, which makes a loud crashing sound.

"Sorry about, that pal," the cop says as I reach down to pick up the videotape.

"No problem," I say rising up, and immediately see that it's

Lieutenant Paolicelli, and he's got something under his arm as he holds the elevator door for me.

"Hey, Lieutenant. It's me, Jerry Pellicano, again," I say, holding out my hand for him to shake.

But as he reaches for my hand while still holding the elevator door for me, he drops the package under his arm, which silently falls to the ground. I instinctively reach down to pick it up for him, and stop dead cold. Time stands still with the realization of what is at the end of my fingertips. There it is. Untouched by time. Still wrapped in cellophane, with the yin-yang symbol showing through.

"Lieutenant. Do you know what you have here?" I say looking through mist in my eyes.

"You tell me."

"This is the happy coat we gave to Charlie the Chinaman, Christmas Eve, twenty years ago."

"Are you positive?"

I wanted to shout "I'm positive, positive, positive, positive...," but simply said, "Yes, sir."

He took it from me, and carefully slid the robe out of the now translucent cellophane wrapper of over twenty years. But as the robe emerged from its time capsule, the black and white yin-yang was as clean and bright as the day we bought it.

"Jerry, I've been working on busting this Donnelly bird for a while. But when you gave me that call today, about the Buddha, I pushed everything up into high gear. We decided we better move on it A.S.A.P. I think you better come upstairs and have a look around," the lieutenant said, reaching for the elevator door again.

The room was deathly quiet now. There were articles of torn clothing and wrappers from medical equipment and supplies strewn all over the floor. In the mad rush of the moment, I didn't notice what the apartment looked like while all hell was breaking loose. Now I could see the world that Ronnie Donnelly lived in. One wall was covered in tin foil. Another was painted a glossy black. The rug in the middle of the room was stained and smelly, with cigarette burns every three inches. I could smell the kitchen from here and see a huge pile of garbage next to the sink. And another wall had a huge indentation about the size of a head. I hated to even think that maybe it was Mary's.

"Just look around, and see if anything else joggles your memory," the lieutenant says softly.

On a folding snack table still littered with pot seeds, stems and a jagged broken mirror with traces of a white powder on it, there is a small scale. The kind you measure drugs with. These scales usually use a small metal weight on one side, but instead of a weight, there is a dark jagged object on it. It's an unusually shaped dark brown object.

"May I pick this up?"

"Go ahead."

I reach down and touch the strange object used as a balance weight, and my gut starts singing again. It's half a Buddha statue. And as I turn it over, I read an inscription on the base of it for the lieutenant to hear: "To Charlie: Wishing you the merriest Christmas ever! The Seventh Grade boys."

I just shake my head as the tears stream silently down my face. Fucking Donnelly. That low-life prick killed Charlie.

"What's that?"

"This was Charlie the Chinaman's. This is the one we gave that to him the very same night we gave him that robe."

"So Donnelly killed him. He probably heard about the money he had hidden in there."

"Yeah. Probably."

"Are you OK?"

"Yeah. I think I'll be fine. From now on," I mumble as my lips still slightly tremble like a little kid who scraped his knee.

"Better give me that bit of the statue you have. I'll need it. And a statement from you when you're ready."

I hand him the half statue, my broken part of it, and hold up the video in my hand. "No problem, I just need to make a deposit."

I walk out the door and make a left to take the long six

flights down instead of the elevator. And as I turn the corner, I see the incinerator door. I open the door and pull the chute open. I can see the orange glow of a fire burning reflecting off the ancient bricks. There's an inferno raging six stories down. This must be what the entrance to hell looks like. I hold the tape in my left hand as my right one holds the chute open. I place my hand all the way into the chute, so I cannot only hear the fire below but I can also feel it. I open my hand and the tape bounces off the walls as it plunges into the fiery pit.

"Burn in hell," I say loud enough to hear an echo through the hall, still watching the orange glow from the dancing flames below.

I flashed on a saying my Mom always used when somebody seemed to get away with something terrible. She'd nod her head and say, "He'll get his. If not in this life, then in the next one."

I enter my apartment and Douglas is holding the phone in one hand, his glass of wine in the other. He acknowledges my entrance and shakes his head back and forth with a wild mad clown grin on his face. "I'll tell him. Yes. Got it. Never again. Fair enough. Check. OK. Uh-huh. Ditto. Yes. Indeed. Most certainly. Ablsolutimundo. Oui. Si. Bye."

He hangs up the phone and begins talking faster than his wine-soaked brain can handle. "Well, that was job number three. Messrs. Barbieri and St. John relaying their wishes that you never darken their doors again. And someone named Victor, whom I do believe I had the pleasure of meeting earlier this evening suggests that you go fuck yourself, but he was laughing at the time."

"Really? Victor was laughing?"

"Yes. And he said to say hi to Mary for him."

"Hmmm. I better make a couple of calls."

I take the card the cop just gave me and call the fiftieth precinct. "Hi. I was um, uh, a witness at a crime scene and, ah, Lieutenant Paolicelli said I could call and check on the status of the people involved. Jerry Pellicano's my name. He is? She is! Oh, thank God! Thanks, officer."

I hang up the phone and close my eyes. The only prayer I'll never forget is "The Hail Mary." I silently recite it with my eyes closed, alternating between smiles from the Blessed Mother and Mary Markowski.

"Mary's going to survive. Donnelly's dead," is all I can say to Douglas, now reclining on the couch, who appears to be just a few breaths away from nodding out.

FIFTEEN

I don't know how, but I managed to sleep a deep, wonderful sleep. I feel rested and calm. I step into the bathroom and peek under my bandage. Much to my surprise, the wound is almost healed. Just a little redness. I take off the bandage and toss it into the toilet, flushing it away.

I hear groans from the living room. And then words begin to form; "Where the hell am I? I hope this isn't like that night last summer on Fire Island. I couldn't pee for days."

"Good morning, Douglas," I say to Douglas, still fully clothed on the couch.

"Did we make mad, passionate love last night, Jerry?"

"No, Douglas."

"Good. I've got enough problems."

BRRRRIIINNNNNNGGGGG

"Oh, my God," Douglas yells as he grabs two pillows to smother his ears, "stop that noise!"

I pick up the phone knowing who it is.

"Hi, Dad."

"Rise and shine! Tell me some good news."

"OK. I'm bringing the car down. Today."

Douglas drops the pillows and looks at me in shock.

"That's great, Jerry. Is everything OK?"

"Yeah, Dad. Everything's fine. I'll call you from the road, but I'm leaving today. See you in a few days. Bye."

"Are you leaving today, for real?" Douglas asks, straightening up to a sitting position. "Just like that?"

"Yup. I'm Florida bound. Got nothing going for me here."

"I envy you, Jerry," Douglas says, rising. He extends his hand and much to my amazement, gives me kiss on the cheek. "Good luck."

"Well, Douglas, that's the first kiss a man has planted there since my Uncle Anthony was over from Rome. Thanks."

"I've got to be going, Jerry. Don't be a stranger."

"And you? Stop having sex with strangers."

I walk Douglas to the front door and as he exits, he notices the marking between my door and the elevator that reads: LATIN EAGLES. He looks at it with great interest. He then takes a pen out of his pocket and begins to alter the letters of the graffiti. After a few moments he reveals his creation; with a few short strokes of his pen, *LATIN EAGLES* has been changed to *EATIN' BAGELS*.

"You make your own reality," Douglas says as he taps his forehead with his pen.

"Douglas, one more thing."

"Yes."

"Did you use the I-ching to decide whether or not to fire me?"

"For the first time in years, I just listened to my heart. Bye, Jerry."

And just like that, Douglas was gone.

I didn't pack much, but I could be away for a while. Amazingly Dad's car started right up with a jump from the guy who worked in the fence company next door. He even brought the guard dogs with him while he helped me out. And they were as sweet as could be.

I pull out of the garage and decide to stop by the fiftieth precinct before I go, which is literally just around the corner.

A cop is sitting at the front desk looking like his hemorrhoids are bothering him. "What do you want?" He asks, obviously hating his life.

"Is Lieutenant Paolicelli available?"

"Hold on." He turns around and points towards the vending machine room. "He's in there."

I walk in, and the lieutenant is sitting there drinking a cup of vending machine coffee out of a paper cup.

"Good morning," I say startling him.

"Oh, yeah. Jerry. Excuse me. I've been up all night working on the case. Looks like the girl's going to be OK."

"I heard."

"That skell Donnelly was one sick bastard. We've made him on Mr. Wang's murder. There were more prints of his at the murder scene than on a hooker's ass at a bachelor party. Too bad he's not going to rot in prison for it. D.O.A. If not in this life, then the next," the lieutenant says.

"I heard that from a very good source."

"I hope it's true," he says with sleepy, sad eyes. "By the way, I've got some good news for you. There was some unclaimed money from Mr. Wang that we found. And it looks like you're going to get it. Let's call it a reward."

"Really? How much?"

"Ten big ones."

"Ten thousand?"

"You got it."

"Wow. I don't know what to say. By the way, if Donnelly couldn't find the money, how did you guys?"

"A bird in hand," Paolicelli says with a smile.

"In the bird cage?"

"Yup. Come with me."

He takes me down the hall into his cramped office, piled high with orderly piles of papers, files, and photographs. He unlocks a bottom drawer and takes out a plain white envelope.

"There was a note inside," Paolicelli says, unfolding it and handing it to me.

It's written in a very childish handwriting and reads "To Whom It May Concern: If you have this money, please do something nice with it. And remember me when you do it."

"Nobody knows about this," the Lieutenant says softly. "You can do whatever the hell you want with it."

"Thanks. I know just what to do with it."

I had a hunch Uncle Eugene would be at Third Base. He

was sitting there reading "The Wall Street Journal" while Noel was at the end of the bar talking with the beer delivery guy.

"Hi, Eugene"

"Oh, hi, kid. How's it hanging?" Eugene says as he neatly folds his paper and places it on the bar next to his beer glass.

"I've got something for you," I say as I hand him the envelope filled with the cash.

Eugene's eyes narrow, and he tightens his lips like Humphrey Bogart.

"If this is a fucking summons I'll kill you," he jokes as he takes the envelope. He lifts the flap ever so slightly, peeking inside just enough to see its contents. "What, are you crazy? If you're looking for a bookie, I'll just make a call for you."

"I know that you paid for the Wang's burial plot. That had to cost thousands of dollars. Take this. It's the reward the cops gave me for helping to solve Charlie's, I mean Mr. Wang's, murder."

"How much is in there?"

"Ten grand."

"What am I going to do with ten grand? I don't have a car, a family, a house upstate, a mortgage or a mistress. I pay sixty-seven dollars a month for crissakes. All I have are a few parakeets and a tab at this watering hole. Between my pension, social security, and my investments, I got so much money socked away I don't know what to do with it. I don't read "The Wall Street Journal" for my health. That's real sweet of you kid, but you keep it. You deserve it. How'd you know I buried him?"

"A little birdie told me. That gravestone looked brand new. Were his wife and son always buried there?"

"Nah. They were at some dumpy bone-yard in Jersey. It's bad enough having to go to Jersey to get to Atlantic City. Imagine spending all eternity there? So I had them planted there with Mr. Wang." Uncle Eugene hung his head low and slowly shook it three times. He looked at me and stared deeply into my eyes as he said, "There's an old Irish wive's tale about a murder going unsolved.

341

The ghost of the dead man will roam the earth until the killer is brought to justice."

"Mr. Wang didn't have to go too far from the block."

"You helped Mr. Wang, Jerry. Do whatever you want with the money. But do me a favor."

"Anything."

"Do something nice for Mr. Wang."

Eugene blinked both eyes one time, real slow. And when they opened they were watering. He reached for his beer glass, held it high, and softly said, "Don't wind up like me, kid."

"I hope to God, I do, Eugene."

I shoved the envelope in my coat pocket, shook Eugene's rough hand and walked out without looking back.

The Bronx Zoo is one of the great zoos of the world. Kids in the Bronx start going there from the time their parents can't stand being cooped up in an apartment only a few weeks after a kid is born. They load up the stroller, hop on the bus, and roll the baby through the zoo.

I've never been in the administration building before. I didn't even know it existed. I step up to the receptionist. "Excuse me. I'd like to make a donation."

"Oh, how nice!" The elderly Black lady with neat beauty parlor hair sings. "Come with me"

She leads me to an office and knocks once.

"Come in," a female says.

I open the door to see a young woman in a drab green zoo keeper's uniform sitting behind a workbench. She's wearing rubber gloves and a surgical mask, and is feeding a baby bird with a tiny eyedropper. She finishes what she's doing, takes off her gear, and crosses the room to her desk. Up close I can see she has green eyes. Not those grey-green eyes, but kelly green almond-shaped eyes. She's not what would be considered drop-dead gorgeous, but she has a beauty that I can only describe as being...

342

simple. No makeup. Plain hair. No huge bulges at the front of her uniform. But there's something about her...

"How may I help you? I'm Rose Mallard."

"Hi, I'm Jerry Pellicano. I'd like to make a donation."

"Oh. Couldn't you just mail it in?"

"Uh, no. It's in cash."

"Cash? I have to ask you where you got it."

"It was, um, an inheritance. From a friend who passed away."

"I'm so sorry. Please, just fill this out," she says, handing me a form.

She patiently sits there as I fill it out. Her fragrance has finally come across the desk. She smells wonderful. Yet, there is still an earthy smell of wildlife in the air. I finish writing in the information and hand it to her.

"Ten thousand dollars?" She says joyfully. "Mr. Pellicano! That's wonderful!"

"Just, please, put up a plaque or something by the bird house. A nice one."

"Certainly." She looks down at the card and reads my dedication. "'Donated by Ying Long Wang -- A man who loved to heal all God's creatures, great and small.' That's very sweet," she says, looking deep into my eyes. "We can put an extension on the aviary with this. He must have been a very special person."

I can feel my eyes welling up. I'm not sure I can get the words out. I think of Yogi Berra nude again and manage to utter, "Let's just say, he managed to knock some sense into me."

Rose reaches across the desk to shake my hand, and as our hands touch, we both get a slight shock and pull our hands away. We look at each other in silence for longer than a moment.

"Static electricity," I say.

"Yeah," she whispers. "Don't you want your name someplace on the plaque."

"Please, no. Well, I've got to go."

"I hope you'll come back to see what we've done with the donation."

"You do?"

"I do."

"Hey, you don't have any jobs around here for somebody with some video experience do you?"

"Funny you should ask. We're starting an audio-visual department in the next few months. Would you be interested?"

"Well, maybe. If I'm still living in The Bronx, I'll call you."

"I hope you will."

"I've got to get going. My pigeon is waiting for me in my car."

"A pigeon?"

"Yeah, he's recovering."

"That's sweet," she says, with a dear, sweet smile. Good-bye, Mr. Pellicano."

"Call me... Jeremiah."

"Jeremiah."

I left the zoo and hopped on the Cross Bronx Expressway headed towards the George Washington Bridge. It was a beautiful day for driving. Clear, dry, sweet smelling air. I can use a few days on the road. Empty the head out. Start anew. Get away from the block. Charlie is sitting quietly in his cage right next to me on the front seat. He seems to be sleeping.

There's a little sign right in the middle of the bridge that reads NEW YORK--NEW JERSEY with a line between the words which separates the two states half-way across the majestic Hudson River. Just as we pass that sign, Charlie suddenly awakens, and frantically starts flapping his wings. His head is bobbing, and his eyes are darting around as if he's looking for something. At the end of the bridge, there's a beautiful park famous throughout the east coast for its view; Palisades Park. A magnificent series of bluffs, cliffs, and greenery directly across from New York.

Could it be that *this* is what Charlie wants? Now that he's recovered, he wants to fly free in the fabulous park lands of New

Jersey with a killer view of New York? There's only one way to find out. I take the first exit, and find my way back to the park. Charlie is still excitedly flapping his wings. The real name for a pigeon is rock dove. Maybe Charlie's instincts are telling him he needs to fly among the rocky cliffs of New Jersey.

As I reach to open Charlie's cage to set him free in the park, a sudden sadness comes over me. This is the end of line for me and Charlie. The end of a lot of things in my life. I know I have tears running down my face, but nobody but Charlie can see me. My eyes are filled with water and I can taste the salt from my tears in my mouth. What a fool I am. Standing here like a moron, bawling my eyes out. But as I shut my eyes and continue to sob silently, I feel calm. Mr. Wang was killed. And in an epiphany it hits me; because of his death, Mary Markowski lives.

Charlie is pushing at the door like he wants to out. Now! I pull myself together. This is the right thing to do. I'll miss him. But this is what Mr. Wang would want. I feel it in my gut. I open the door and Charlie zooms out. But he doesn't head for the fifty foot spruce tree just to our left... NO! He makes a bee-line, directly towards the cliffs, and heads straight across the river in what could only be described as heading right for the old neighborhood in the Bronx, "as the crow flies."

I stood there and watched as Charlie became a tiny black dot in the distance, still heading straight for the neighborhood. I guess some instincts run deeper than others.

I got back in the car and headed for the Jersey Turnpike-south. I need this trip. I think the first thing I'll do, if, and when I get back, is look for Charlie hanging out, like most pigeons do, under the el. That's his home. He knows it. He's a lucky bird. And I wonder if that job at the Bronx Zoo is a city job?

Also by the author:
"Sewer Balls"
a novel by
Steven Schindler
ISBN 0-9662408-6-3

"Schindler writes with a style that reflects the
best of Betty Smith's *A Tree Grows in Brooklyn*
and Philip Roth's *Portnoy's Complaint*.
[He] brings the '60s alive with images as
clear as if they were photographed...
[Sewer Balls] was probably the best novel
produced by the small presses in 1999."
-Small Press Review

Order it direct from
The Elevated Press
PO Box 65218
Los Angeles, CA 90065
(818) 550-1963

Or order from any bookstore or
on-line retailer
or visit:
www.theelevatedpress.com
for special discounts

ORDER FORM

Name_____

Address_____

_____

_____"From The Block" @ $12.95 ea.

_____"Sewer Balls" @ $11.95 ea.

Please add $3 per book S/H
CA residents add sales tax

_____Total Enclosed

nd check or money order to:
The Elevated Press
PO Box 65218
s Angeles, CA 90065

elevatedpress.com or call
63 for special discounts.